Before You

RECKLESS LOVE
BOOK TWO

LAUREA MATTHEWS

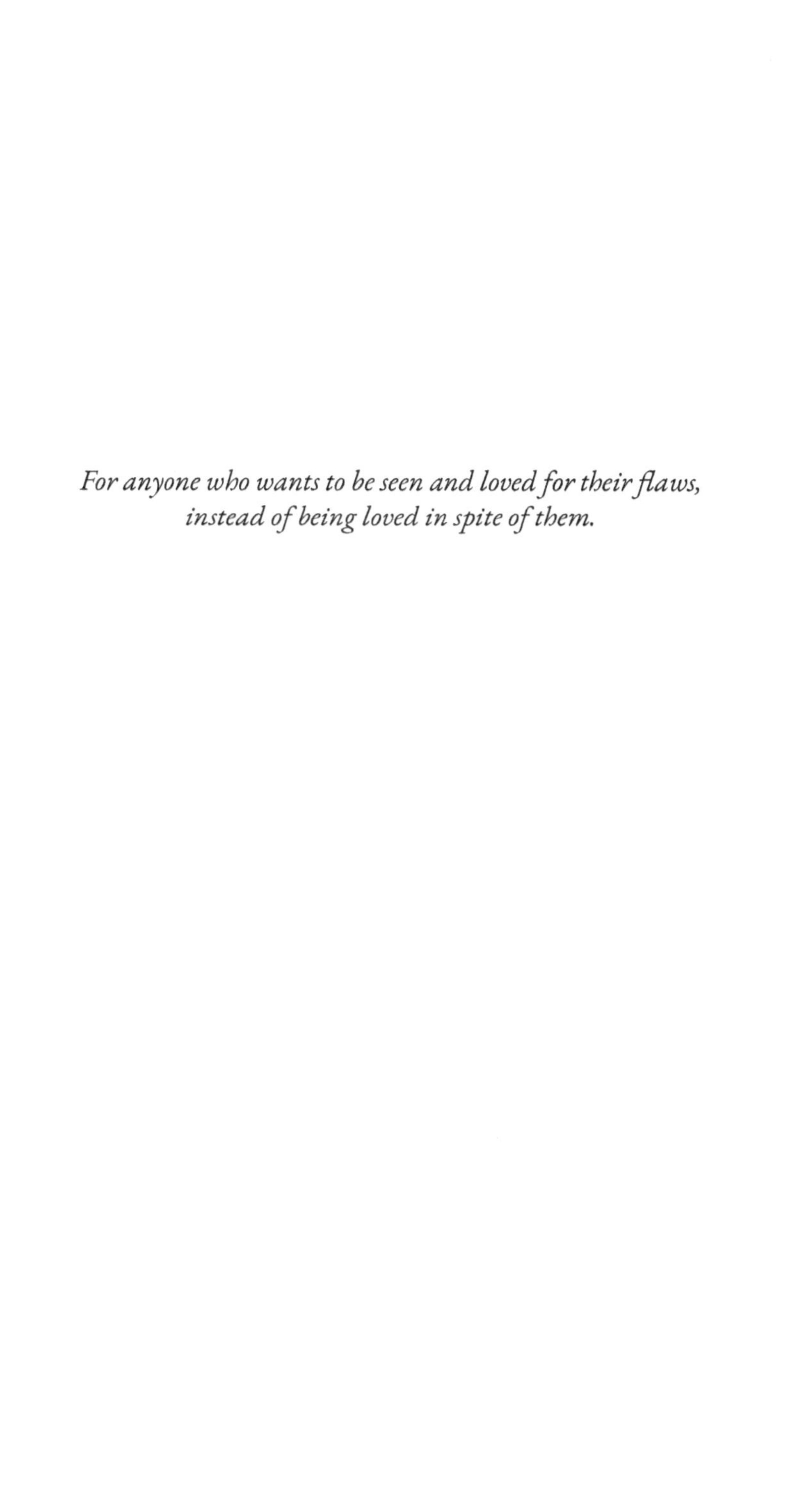

*For anyone who wants to be seen and loved for their flaws,
instead of being loved in spite of them.*

The Characters

The ages in this character list are accurate at the start of Before You, but please keep in mind while reading that birthdays do take place, and the ages will change throughout this book.

<u>THE WALKERS</u>
Sebastian Walker (51) & Thalia Lewis (49)
Mirabelle ~ 22
JJ ~ 21
Hunter ~ 19
Bailey ~19

<u>THE LEWISES</u>
Owen Lewis (51) & Blake Morgan (50)

<u>THE PRICES</u>
Chris Price (51) & Penelope Baudelaire (49)
Henry ~ 27
Kaitlyn ~ 19

FRIENDS AND ROOMMATES

Marley Benson ~ 21
Asher Locke ~ 22
Charlotte [Charlie] Locke ~ 18
Trent Hart ~ 22
Briar [Bria] Taylor ~ 20

If you do not wish to read through the content warnings listed in the author's note following this, you may skip to the first chapter of *Before You*.

I would like to start this off by saying if you or a loved one are struggling with drug abuse, please reach out to the *Substance Abuse and Mental Health Services Administrations* at their **24/7 Substance Abuse and Addiction hotline 1-844-289-0879** for help. There are resources to help support anyone on their path to recovery at any stage.

Before You was written from a place of hope with the intent of shining a light on a very real struggle that athletes can face when pursuing the dream of playing at a collegiate or professional level. I grew up playing competitive softball, and during my time on the field, I suffered countless injuries that probably would have healed differently (and better), and allowed me to continue playing past my freshman year of college had I taken the proper time to rest and rehabilitate them. While JJ's reality did not become mine, I know I was lucky because there are so many athletes that do struggle with returning to play earlier than they should, and abuse pain medication to play at the level they did prior to their injury.

Like JJ, athletes become well-versed in telling everyone *I'm fine*, because saying anything else means they won't play. I think we could all use with a little less *I'm fine* in our lives.

You and your feelings matter.

While this book is first and foremost a love story, it does deal with some heavy topics including:

- *Alcohol and drug (pills) use*
- *Addiction*
- *Mature language*
- *Sexual content*
- *Anxiety*
- *Panic attacks*
- *Non-main character cheating on FMC prior to MCs getting together*
- *Death*
- *Car accident*
- *Grief*

Prologue

JJ

Two truths and a lie.

I feel guilty for wishing my brother, Bailey, would call one of our other siblings instead of only me.

I'm addicted to pain killers.

I've been hopelessly in love with Marley since meeting her two years ago.

Actually—I guess that makes me a liar, because all of these are true.

Three truths and a liar.

JJ

"Fuck, it's freezing!" I swear, lowering myself further into the ice bath, my knee throbbing from the grueling practice I suffered through, the pink scars standing out against the rest of my tanned skin.

"Kind of the whole point, Walker," Asher says. I flip my best friend off as he exhales sharply, climbing into the tub next to mine.

"Don't be a bunch of pussies," Trent says, shaking his head at us as an athletic training assistant helps him stretch his shoulder.

"I'm not being a pussy," I mumble under my breath, sore as hell from all the running we did today in the dry California heat. It's crazy how different the climate is from North Carolina.

"What would you call it then?" Rose asks, pouring more ice into my tub as she flashes a smile. Rose is studying kinesiology and works as an aide with Billy, the head athletic trainer for the football team.

I jolt as the water rises higher on my body. "I think my

dick is trying to crawl up into my body for warmth because of how fucking cold the water is.”

“If that’s what you need to tell yourself to make up for your size,” Asher taunts, and I wink at him.

“You don’t seem to complain about my size at night.”

The room erupts into laughter, but Billy sends me a dry look as I smile apologetically at her. She only rolls her eyes, but I think she misses my humor after all the months I spent here rehabbing my knee last year.

I tune out the room, attempting to focus on my breathing so I have a shot of making it through the next eight minutes of hell.

I feel like I’m forgetting something I was supposed to do today, but the headache I can feel beginning to come on is jumbling my thoughts. I know I have to call Mirabelle to check in and ask if she has an update about Bailey from our parents’ private investigator. I already know she won’t have one, but I have faith he’ll turn up somewhere eventually.

It’s syllabus week, so I’m sure the team is planning on going out tonight, but I haven’t decided if I’m going yet. It’d probably be smarter to stay in and ensure I have all the textbooks I’ll need this semester since I actually give a shit about my grades, unlike half the guys on the team who are only here for the hope of going pro.

Was I supposed to go grocery shopping?

Asher taps my hand clenching the rim of the tub, pulling me from my thoughts.

“What?” I ask, my tone sharper than usual.

He ignores it, exhaling as he adjusts in the water. “Did you know Trent has a girlfriend?” he whispers, and if I had to guess, he’s trying not to draw our roommate’s attention. I raise my eyebrows in surprise, waiting to see where he’s going with this. “I guess she’s coming over tonight.”

“Interesting.”

Trent's decent looking and gets the job done on the field, but it's his pedigree that makes him a magnet with girls on campus. His family belongs to the New York elite, dollar signs attached to their last name to match. It's news to me that he has a girlfriend, though. I wonder how long they've been together, considering he had a girl over last weekend after a bonfire thrown by one of the frats on campus.

Trent, Asher, Luka, and I share one of the houses designated to upperclassmen on the football team. Luka and Trent are seniors, while Asher and I are juniors.

"She's a Benson," he continues, and it makes me miss my sister, Mirabelle. She'd know exactly who Asher is talking about, and my chest pangs with homesickness. I'm the one who chose to attend a college on the other side of the country, so I have no one to blame but myself.

"A who?" I ask, feeling my toes go numb. *I should have put on the damn swim socks.*

Asher looks at me like I'm stupid, and maybe I am. "A Benson—you know, like Benson Pharmaceuticals? Her father is the CEO, Hayes Benson, and her mother was a famous ballerina. She's the heiress set to inherit the golden crown, and Trent was bragging on the sidelines earlier about how she transferred from Columbia to be here with him."

"Someone ought to tell her to find a new boyfriend because I'm positive the chick he had over last weekend wasn't her," I point out, biting back a string of curses so filthy, I think Mom would smack me. I don't know how anyone can enjoy the misery that comes from the torturous hell ice baths bring.

"Tell her yourself. You won't catch me touching that mess with a ten-foot pole."

"Maybe I will," I reply. If some douchebag ever pulled that shit with Mirabelle, no one would be able to find the body. It's a good thing her boyfriend, Henry, is as obsessed with her as she is with him. I'm not sure why respect is such a hard concept for some people to understand.

Asher nudges me again. "When are you going to ask Rose out?" he asks, and I shake my head.

"Why?"

"Because she's into you? Why else?"

I glance over to where she is watching Billy, and Rose is pretty, but I don't feel anything when I look at her. I haven't felt anything toward another girl since Marley. "We're just friends," I say. In the nicest way, everything about Rose is wrong for me. Instead of the caramel tresses I once had my hands tangled in, Rose's hair is an inky black color, and her eyes are dark brown as opposed to the cerulean blue I find myself searching for in the ocean sometimes. No matter what way you spin it, even if she's here and available, Rose isn't Marley.

"You're not seriously still pining for your mystery girl, right?" he asks.

My body involuntarily shivers from how fucking cold I am. "What does it matter?" I ask through clenched teeth. The only reason Asher knows about Marley is because I was plastered at a party freshman year, and he was curious why I hadn't hooked up with any of the girls throwing themselves at me.

"You're never going to see her again, so maybe it's time you move on, JJ. There's plenty of girls who would jump at the chance to be with you."

My head is starting to throb behind my temples. "Leave it alone, Ash."

"Fine." Asher puts his hands up in self-defense. "Shit, it's cold in here."

"Kind of the whole point," I mimic, repeating his words. I crack a faint smile, trying to lighten the mood, because I know it seems dumb to him I'm holding out for a girl I met two years ago, but he doesn't understand she's *the* girl. She's worth waiting for. I just have to find her first.

"So the private investigator hasn't found anything new?" I ask, clicking through the syllabus for my number theory class this semester.

Mirabelle sighs on the other end of the phone, and I hate how defeated she sounds. "No. At this point, I'm wondering why I'm paying him when it's been seventeen months, and he hasn't found a single damn thing."

Our younger brother, Bailey, ran away the day after almost lighting our family's home on fire for a second time. He stole cash out of our parents' room, left anything we could use to track him on his bed, and our security cameras saw him leave with only a backpack. All of his social media accounts were cleared and locked out with no way for us to access them.

"I haven't heard from him in over two months, Mira. He usually calls by now," I say, rubbing my temples.

According to the last conversation Bailey had with Mirabelle and Henry, he called everyone a liar . . . except for me. The first time Bailey called me after he left, I dropped the phone out of shock. It was five weeks after he ran away, and he's never called anyone else.

Hunter's coping by throwing himself into football, and Mirabelle calls the private investigator every week, hoping for new information.

Mirabelle, Henry, and I are the only ones who know he was behind the fire at our home in Charlotte.

Our parents were already so upset about him leaving, we didn't know how to tell them the severity of the situation. They've been blaming themselves ever since for not taking him with them on their trip, and we agreed there was no reason to break their hearts even more than they already were.

I sleep with my ringer on every night in case Bailey calls, and the only time I don't have my phone within reach is during football. The last time I talked to him, he told me he was safe. He's careful to never slip up, but without knowing where he is, can he really be safe?

"Do you think Bailey will come home?" she asks the question I've been asking myself ever since he left.

"I hope so," I say, clearing my throat. "How was the flight?"

"It was good. Henry's unloading the car now, but I'm excited we were able to get away before the craziness of the season begins," Mirabelle says, laughing. "I'm really looking forward to having his full attention for a few days."

"Oh, I bet," I tease, and she laughs. What she doesn't know is Henry's proposing while they're there. He wants it to be a private moment, and ever since the pictures and recording of them hit the internet my freshman year, the cameras are never far behind. The only reprieve they get is when they're in France.

"Shut up. I meant not having to share Henry with all the sponsorship deals he's been at since returning from training camp. I feel like I've barely spent any time with him."

"I think it'll be good for you guys to get away."

"I think so too," she agrees, and Asher pokes his head in.

"Trent's girl is here, and she brought her roommate. I think I'm in love with her," he says, grinning, and I grab a pen off my desk, prepared to throw it at him.

"I'll be down in a minute. I'm talking to my sister," I say, regretting it immediately as his face lights up.

"Dude, can I talk to her?" Asher asks, and this time, I actually throw the pen. "Mira! If you can hear me, there's still time for you to leave Henry before I'm off the market."

"Get out." I groan as Mirabelle laughs again, and Asher wisely decides to exit, shutting my door behind him. One of his favorite things to do since we were roommates freshman year is hit on Mirabelle during our conversations. "I don't want to go down there to meet this poor girl dating Trent."

"Why not? I thought you liked Trent?" Mirabelle asks, and I close my laptop.

"I tolerate Trent. He's an egotistical ass who flaunts how rich his parents are. He's also cheating on his girlfriend, knowing she apparently transferred here from Columbia to be with him."

"If you tolerate him, then why are you living with him?"

"Because he's on the team," I say, because it explains everything there is to it.

"I hope you're planning on telling this girl her boyfriend is cheating on her, regardless of him being your roommate and teammate," Mirabelle says, and I feel bad I haven't decided what my plan is. It'd be awful of me to tell this girl I don't even know that her boyfriend is cheating on her, but I think she deserves to know.

"I'll let you know what happens. I gotta go, but have fun, and eat some pastries for me, okay?"

"I will, JJ. Good luck. I love you."

"I love you too," I say, hanging up to walk downstairs for some form of my own personal hell. *How am I going to get the girlfriend alone to tell her Trent's cheating on her?*

There's a girl I don't recognize on the couch, but since she's talking to Asher, I'm guessing she's the roommate.

"All done jerking off, JJ?" Luka teases, and I roll my eyes.

"I was talking to my sister, asshole," I retort, sitting in the recliner.

He laughs, shaking his head. "Whatever you say. Ash, stop flirting and introduce JJ to Bria."

The girl I'm assuming is Bria waves at me. "Hi."

I lift my hand in greeting. "Nice to meet you. I'm JJ."

"Bria. I'm Marley's roommate," she says, and I straighten at the name, but Asher steals her attention again by saying something to make her roll her eyes.

Is it . . . *No.* There's no way it could possibly be her.

"Is he finally done shooting his load?" Trent asks, walking back into the living room.

"Sure," I respond as Luka chuckles. *Do they really think I'm up there jerking off all the time?*

He turns to where I am, distracting my attention from the girl behind him. "Finally. This is Marley Benson, my girl-friend," he says, wrapping his arm around her shoulders to press a kiss to her cheek.

She laughs, the sound music to my ears as she pushes him away. "Trent, come on," she says, a soft lilt to her voice making my heart race. She turns, her smile faltering as we make eye contact.

I jolt to my feet, staring at the girl I've been dreaming of for so long. *It's her.*

Her hair is longer than when I met her, but it's the same rich color, falling over her shoulders in waves. Her eyes are the exact shade of blue I'll never forget, standing out against her golden complexion.

She's here.

"What's wrong with you?" Luka asks, but I refuse to tear my eyes from Marley. I've waited this long to find her, I'm not letting her out of my sight.

"Nothing." I clear my throat, wiping my palms on my pants, walking toward Marley as my heart flips and leaps in my chest. "It's nice to meet you, Marley," I say, offering her my hand to shake.

Her beautiful eyes are wide as she stares at me in disbelief. "JJ," Marley whispers, slipping her hand into mine. My name sounds like heaven coming from her lips, and I nearly drop to my knees as the same electric feeling jolts through me—the same one I felt all those months ago.

Trent clears his throat, and I look at him in surprise, remembering there's other people in the room. "Do you know each other?"

My heart drops, realizing what's happening.

Fuck.

Marley is Trent's girlfriend.

My Marley . . . except she's not mine.

CHAPTER TWO

Marley

"DO YOU THINK THIS IS FINE?" I ASK BRIA, MY BEST friend and roommate. We've grown up together our entire lives as her parents are best friends with mine.

She's lounging on my bed as I turn around to face her in our two-bedroom apartment. She's a sophomore, whereas I transferred for my junior and senior year here instead of Columbia. I liked Columbia, but everyone there knew me, and I wanted an opportunity to figure out who I am outside of New York City where paparazzi wouldn't follow me to class or offer to pay people in my dorms to get pictures of me rolling out of bed. Bria loved it here so much last year, so I filled out an application to transfer.

Bria looks up from her phone, her face scrunching up. "I thought we were just going to Trent's house to meet his room-mates? I'm literally wearing this," she says, motioning to her Beaumont Track & Field hoodie and athletic shorts.

Bria is the definition of a tomboy, and despises wearing any type of dressy clothing, not that it matters what she wears. She inherited her striking features from both her parents. Bria's stormy grey eyes stand out against her long dark hair and fair skin, and she has enough confidence to draw everyone's attention to her when she walks into a room. I guess it's to be expected with her mother being Tessa Kaplan, famed supermodel, and her father, Grayson Taylor, a hotshot corporate lawyer.

I look down at my blousy shirt and the denim shorts I thought helped dress it down. "I want to make a good impression on his roommates. Is it too much?" I ask, my nerves starting to get the better of me.

"They're boys, Mar. I don't think they're going to care what you're wearing."

I chew my nails nervously as I face the mirror again. My hair is in its natural waves, and I put on a little mascara to make my blue eyes I inherited from my father appear brighter. "So you think I should change?"

She tries to smile, but then nods. "I mean, you look nice, but I think you'd be better off ditching the top and wearing a T-shirt?" Bria suggests, and I sigh, deciding to grab my favorite shirt from one of the many boxes I haven't had the chance to unpack yet.

It's a Beaumont Lacrosse short sleeve from when my dad went here, except it's been washed enough times over the years the lettering has faded.

"Perfect, tuck it into your shorts, and you're golden," she says, and I realize she's right. *This is better.*

"So what exactly do you know about Trent's roommates?" Bria asks, slipping into her sneakers while I grab my keys.

Honestly, he hasn't told me much about them. "They're on the football team with him. I met Luka this summer, and he seemed nice."

"Awesome, a bunch of jocks," Bria muses, and I roll my eyes. Her logic is flawed and biased.

"Bria, you're a jock."

"No, I'm an athlete. They're a bunch of jocks."

"What's the difference?" I ask, walking down the stairs to the lot where my car is parked.

I deeply regret asking the question after Bria spends the entire five-minute car ride to Trent's explaining the complex difference. It sounds like the same thing to me, but what do I know?

I danced growing up because I loved it, but music is secretly my true passion. I love writing music, but playing my guitar is my favorite thing to do. It's my escape from reality when the world becomes too much.

Unfortunately, it's not something I could ever pursue as a career because my future has been set in stone my entire life: get a degree in biology or chemistry, and then my master's degree while working for the family company, and once my father retires, take his place.

I knock on the door as Bria finally concludes her rant, taking it upon herself to enter before anyone has a chance to answer. "Bria," I whisper, irritated because I have no choice but to follow after her. Is she seriously just walking into their house?

"What?" she whispers, looking at me over her shoulder. "He should have been waiting by the door for you to get here, and if they don't want anyone walking in, maybe they should have locked the door."

Yeah, or maybe we could have waited more than two seconds?

Trent appears in front of Bria, a smile forming on his face. She shrugs, looking up at him. "Your door was unlocked."

"Nice to see you too, Bria," he says, and she steps aside so he can get past her.

"Hi there," I greet, hoping he doesn't hold my best friend's rude behavior against me. Trent leans down, kissing me briefly on the lips. My heart swoons a little at his quintessential all-American football player looks from his short blond hair to his brown eyes and lean build. We met at a charity event both of our families were invited to in April, and he asked for my number. He took me out for drinks the next night, and we were dating by the time he was home for the summer.

"Hi yourself. I'm happy to see you," he says, kissing me one more time before grabbing my hand to pull me with him. "We got our asses handed to us at practice today."

"Yikes," I say, following him to the living room where two guys are sitting on the couch. I recognize Luka from a trip to Trent's family's house in the Hamptons this past summer, but aside from him playing with Trent, I don't know much about him.

The one I don't know laughs, shaking his head. "You can say that again," he says, smiling at me. "I'm Asher. It's nice to meet you."

"I'm Marley, and this is my best friend, Bria," I reply, motioning to Bria behind me, and his eyes instantly widen. *Perfect, I knew bringing her would be the perfect ruse to take attention off me.*

"Hey, Marley. Good to see you again," Luka says, and I wave back awkwardly. God, I'm making this way more diffi-cult than it needs to be. I'm awful around new people, never knowing the right thing to say.

"Do you guys want beers?" Trent asks, and Luka holds his up, shaking his head.

"I'm good," Asher says, still staring at Bria like she's the most beautiful person he's ever seen. *I'm tempted to wish him luck, because I have a feeling Bria will eat him alive.*

"My eyes are up here," she says, and Asher simply smiles at her. *Or maybe not . . .*

"I was reading the front of your shirt. You're on the track team?"

I didn't have this on my bingo card, but maybe I should

have. "She is," I confirm, and Bria throws a stormy glare in my direction.

"Ash, can you tell JJ to put some pants on so he can meet Marley?" Trent asks, and he nods, standing up from the couch.

"Sure."

"Want to come with, Bria? I can show you my room, so you know where to find it later," Asher says, and I'm thoroughly looking forward to how this will play out.

"Eat shit." She scoffs, and he laughs, heading up the stairs, but my brain finally processes what Trent asked.

"Do you guys normally walk around without pants?" I ask, and Luka shakes his head.

"No, it's just a series of running jokes we make when his door is shut because he doesn't ever bring anyone home."

Oh, well, okay then?

I don't have a chance to respond—nor do I really know how to—when Trent pulls me along with him to the kitchen. I lean against the counter as he grabs a beer from the fridge, setting it on the counter. "Your roommates seem nice," I say, relaxing a little.

"They're going to love you, but not as much as I love you," he says, moving to stand in front of me, confidence radiating from him. There's hope in his brown eyes as he looks down at me.

"That's sweet, Trent," I say, and I don't miss the hurt on his face because I don't say it back, but he hides it quickly.

He told me a couple weeks ago he loved me after only three months of dating, and I couldn't say it back. It didn't feel right—and it still doesn't—but I'd sound insane if I explained why.

I lean up, looping a hand behind his neck to pull his mouth to mine. Trent's eager to respond, teasing his tongue over my bottom lip to deepen the kiss, but I pull away at the sound of someone coming down the stairs.

"Later," I promise as more chatter comes from the living room.

He steals one more brief kiss, snagging his beer from the counter to head toward the living room. "Is he finally done shooting his load?" Trent asks, and I guess it is a little funny if everyone else is laughing.

"Sure," a deep voice responds, sounding unamused. *Why does that voice sound familiar?*

Trent distracts me by wrapping his arm around my shoulders, pulling me into him. "Finally. This is Marley Benson, my girlfriend," Trent says, pressing another kiss to my cheek. He's awfully affectionate today.

I giggle, pushing him off me because the last thing I need all of them thinking is they're going to see PDA all over their house if I'm here. "Trent, come on." I smile, turning to face the final roommate.

Oh my god. I'd recognize him anywhere.

My smile wavers, and I will it to stay in place as he stands immediately, looking at me the same way he did when we met the first time.

Fuck, somehow he looks better than I remembered. His roguishly handsome features are now . . . *devastating.* JJ's very presence threatens to shatter my common sense telling me why I can't run straight into his strong arms. His midnight hair is messy, and his eyes are the color of spring, but those lips . . . I remember vividly what it feels like to be kissed by them.

Based on his expression, I'd say he definitely remembers me.

I think someone says something, but I can't look away. I'm trying to process him being here. JJ's really here, and he's walking toward me.

How is he here?

"Nothing," JJ says, wiping his palms on his shorts. "It's nice to meet you, Marley." He extends his hand to mine, and when I slide my hand into his, I feel like I can breathe for the first time in years. Meeting JJ in France two years ago felt like lightning being injected directly into my veins, and I've been chasing it ever since.

"JJ," I whisper the name I've only said aloud to a select few —Bria being one of them.

He's taller than I remember, towering over me, and he's filled out more, radiating pure masculinity.

JJ's going to consume me, and I'd happily let him.

Trent clears his throat next to me. "Do you know each other?"

The question is laughable. *Do we know each other?* I'd argue JJ knows me better than anyone in the world. I open my mouth, but I'm at a loss for words. Thankfully, JJ notices, pulling his hand from mine, looking from me to Trent.

A short laugh escapes his mouth, and he smiles ruefully at my boyfriend. "No. I think I would remember if we'd met already because Marley would be dating me instead of you," he says, and Trent relaxes, laughing. *Oh my god, he thinks JJ's joking.*

He's being entirely serious, and one look at the clarity of his eyes says everything left to be said.

I wonder what Trent would think if he knew the reason I can't tell him I love him is because I already gave my heart away to his roommate?

"Hands off, Walker. She's all mine," Trent says, pulling me back into him, and I let him. I let him because I don't know what to do right now.

I look at Bria who looks as surprised as I feel. *"Sapevi che era qui?"*[1] she asks me in Italian.

---

1. Did you know he was here?

"Ovviamente no,"[2] I respond, and Trent looks at me confused.

"What language are you guys speaking?" he asks, moving us toward the loveseat closest to where Bria is sitting on the couch.

"Italian," JJ answers on his way back to the recliner.

My stomach twists. *"Pensavo parlassi solo Francese?"*[3] I ask him and his mouth lifts into a smile.

"Ho imparato l'italiano,"[4] he responds, his voice smooth as silk.

I told him I spoke Italian. Is it stupid a part of me hopes he learned for me? Is it possible to lov—*like* hearing someone's voice so much?

Bria shoots me an impressed look, no doubt coming to the same conclusion, and I switch to Portuguese. *"Senti sua falta?"*[5] I ask, looking for any inkling of understanding.

He laughs, the sound reminding me of music. "Sorry, you've got me there. I'm only fluent in Italian, French, and English."

"What language is that?" Trent asks, pulling my legs to rest over his lap, his hands running up the length of my legs.

"Portuguese," I say, feeling mildly uncomfortable.

"I didn't know you could speak Portuguese?"

I'm lucky languages come naturally to me, because it's the best thing I bring to the table as the future CEO of a billion-dollar company. "Yeah, I like to learn new languages. I speak French, Italian, Portuguese, Spanish, and I'm learning Mandarin," I say, growing self-conscious as his jaw drops.

---

2. Of course not.
3. I thought you only spoke French?
4. I learned Italian.
5. What about now?

"You're so sexy," he says loud enough for everyone in the room to hear, and my cheeks burn.

I can feel the weight of JJ's stare on us, and I want nothing more than to untangle myself from Trent. I feel so off-balance right now, and my mind is all over the place.

I don't know how I'm supposed to act when I'm stuck in the same room as the man I'm trying to love and the one who made me love him in less than a day.

~

He pulls me along the narrow street. "This is one of my favorite places to go when we're here. They have the best pastries, and if we're lucky, there might still be some of the good ones left for us," he says in fluent French, his accent perfect. I never would have guessed JJ wasn't from here if he hadn't told me.

His excitement makes my smile widen as I abandon all logic to wander around a foreign town with a stranger. I never do anything like this, especially with a guy pretty enough to make me forget my own name. "Good thing I love pastries."

"What a relief, I'm not sure this would work out if you didn't," JJ teases, winking at me over his shoulder.

"Oh really? And what is this?" I ask, curious to hear his answer. I've met a lot of people across the world, and I'm positive I've never met anyone like JJ.

"I'm not sure, but I'm hoping to find out. I know we only met an hour ago, but I have this feeling about you I can't shake," he says, and my heart sputters in my chest. "It feels like fate you were lost at the same time I was sitting in the café, and who am I to argue with fate?"

I stop in my tracks at the pure honesty in his words. Maybe it should freak me out, but I know exactly what JJ's getting at. It's the same reason I asked him to be my guide after he offered me directions.

"No. Not at all. Just the opposite, actually."

Maybe I can convince Trent to drive me back to the apartment, and we can hang out there tonight. I can't think straight knowing JJ's here, and I having to pretend like I don't know him.

There's a soft knock on the bathroom door, and I turn the faucet off, looking at my reflection in the mirror. I look as awful as I feel. My skin's leeched of color, making me appear clammy.

"Just a minute," I say, hearing my voice shake. I pinch my cheeks to bring color back in them before I open the door.

My heart skips a beat at the sight of JJ standing there. He looks over me intently, worry warping his strong features. "You don't look so good," he murmurs, pressing the back of his hand to my forehead before I can react.

"Gee, thanks," I say, and his green eyes soften.

"I didn't mean it that way. You're just as beautiful as I remember, but you look like you're going to be sick. You don't have a fever, but I can drive you home?" he offers, causing my head to spin.

"I should ask Trent."

I don't know if it's a good idea for me to be alone with JJ.

JJ takes a step back, giving me space, even if every fiber of my being wants to pull him closer to me. "He's on his fourth beer. Asher told me Trent started before you got here. He shouldn't drive."

I hesitate, but I also know what kind of person JJ is. He'd never put me in a position where I'd cross any boundaries.

"Marley, please, just let me take you home."

I look at him carefully, seeing nothing but sincerity.

Against my better judgement, I nod. "Thank you," I say as he motions for me to lead.

Trent is talking to Luka, and I can't tell if Bria is annoyed with Asher, but Asher is the first one to notice we've come back.

"Are you okay?" he asks, his gaze flitting between me and JJ.

"Babe, what's wrong?" Trent asks, looking in my direction.

"I'm not feeling very good. JJ offered to take me home since you've been drinking, but I can call you later?"

"I can take you," Bria interrupts, and I shake my head quickly.

"No, it's okay. You should stay. I'll leave my keys on the counter for you."

"Are you sure?" Bria asks, hesitating.

"I'm sure." I muster a pathetic smile, and Trent stands up from the couch, looking over my shoulder at JJ.

"Thanks, man. I appreciate you looking out for my girl."

"No problem," JJ says, smiling.

I press a hand to my stomach as the feeling of nausea returns. Trent leans down, pressing a kiss to my cheek. "Feel better soon. Love you," he says, and I look away before I can see the look of disappointment when I don't say it back.

"Thanks," I say, stopping in the kitchen to leave my keys on the counter for Bria as JJ waits patiently by the front door with his keys in hand.

JJ walks toward the souped-up Jeep Wrangler, opening the passenger door for me, but neither of us say a word until we're both in the car.

"You're here," JJ says softly, breaking the silence. "You're *really* here." He opens his mouth and then shuts it, shaking his head as he pulls out of the driveway. His hands clenching the steering wheel tightly tells me everything I need to know.

"JJ, I swear, I didn't know you were roommates with Trent," I say, resisting the urge to bite my nails.

"I was starting to think I'd imagined it all. There's so much I want to tell you . . . to ask you." JJ looks over at me again, ignoring the fact I brought up my boyfriend.

"You didn't imagine it. It all happened." *I've wondered the same thing more than a few times.*

I close my eyes to rest my head against the headrest, hoping it helps calm my stomach.

"Well, the sight of me has never made a girl want to vomit before," JJ tries to joke, but I don't have it in me to explain the confusion swirling around in my head right now.

"I think it's something I must have eaten today," I mumble.

"I hope you feel better," he says, glancing over as if he's checking in.

"Thanks for taking me home."

When JJ doesn't respond, I open my eyes to look over at him to see him silently laughing. "What?"

"Marley, I don't know where your home is. I'm just driving in circles."

Oh. Good point.

My cheeks flush, and despite everything, I can't help laughing.

"I live in the Poppy Apartments off Main Street. Do you know where they are?" I ask, trying to remember what street they're on, I only moved in yesterday.

He cracks a smile. "Yeah. I know where those are. It's only a couple of minutes away."

"Nice." I don't know what else I'm supposed to say.

JJ flips his radio on, and music begins playing quietly from the speakers. He still has a death grip on the steering wheel.

"Is there a reason you're choking the steering wheel?" I ask, and JJ's jaw clenches.

"Honestly?" I have a feeling whatever he's going to say isn't going to help make my brain any less confused, but I still want to hear it. JJ glances over at me, and I nod, telling him silently to continue. "I'm trying to respect you have a boyfriend by not touching you, and it's a lot harder than you would think."

"JJ—"

"Are you still playing guitar?" he asks, abruptly cutting me off.

I blink in surprise because I can't believe he remembered after so long. Maybe I shouldn't be, though. *JJ learned Italian.*

"Yeah, every day." I've also written a couple songs about him, but he doesn't need to know that.

"Have you worked up the nerve to play for a crowd yet?"

Another thing JJ's remembered: I have terrible anxiety about playing in front of others.

I smile at him, shaking my head. "Not yet."

"Will you let me know when you do? I need to be prepared if I'm going to be your number one fan with signs, flowers, and random shit for you to sign."

I laugh easily now, a snort escaping me, which only makes me laugh harder. "You sound like a stalker," I struggle to say through my laughter, which results in JJ laughing with me.

"I guess it does sound like something a stalker would say," he agrees, smiling widely enough his dimples are showing. "I promise I'm not a stalker."

"I didn't think so. If you are one, you're not a very good one," I say, noticing JJ pass my apartment building clearly labeled *Poppy Apartments*, instead of turning into the parking lot. "Um, JJ, you passed my building."

"Oh, sorry. Guess we'll have to go around the block again." See, I would have thought he accidentally missed the turn if it wasn't for the faint smirk JJ's trying—*and failing*—

to hide. "Are you in danger of puking?" he asks, looking over to check on me.

Should I tell him to turn around? *Absolutely*. But is it what comes out of my mouth? *Hell no.*

"No, it's settling."

It's settling because JJ is being himself, and it's calming my thoughts.

He smiles again and I greedily commit it to my memory. "Good. Have you seen this one part of campus?" JJ asks, and now I'm confused.

"What part are you asking about?"

"Whatever part you haven't seen."

It reminds me of how JJ was my tour guide in France. Except, unlike the little countryside town, there's no part of this campus I haven't seen. My dad usually makes it out here once a year for lacrosse and school fundraisers. He's brought me and my brother, Kaden, countless times. I think he shed a few tears when I said I was transferring here.

"The sculpture garden, I haven't seen the sculpture garden," I lie, instantly feeling horrible, but not horrible enough to tell him I've seen everything. JJ knows I have a boyfriend, and he's made it clear he isn't going to try anything.

"What a coincidence! There's a spot to turn around right next to the sculpture gardens," JJ says, going in the opposite direction of my apartment and toward the gardens.

"Can I ask you something?"

"You can ask me anything you want, Marley."

"How's your family? Did your sister ever tell that guy how she felt about him?" It's something I've wondered about in passing ever since. The way he spoke about his family is one of the reasons I fell for JJ. I could tell how much they meant to him.

"She did. They're on a trip, and Henry's actually going to propose while they're there," JJ says, but then his face falls for a moment, quickly masked with a smile. "My family is a longer story for another time. My brother, Bailey, ran away a year and a half ago. He calls me every couple months to check in, and it's just . . . *a lot.* No one here knows about it, except Asher."

I don't stop myself from reaching over to rest my hand on his, squeezing reassuringly. "I'm really sorry." I can feel how tense he is, and as his gaze slides to meet mine, I pull my hand back, trying to respect his personal space I invaded. "I'm sorry," I repeat for a completely different reason. "I shouldn't have done that."

"It's okay, Marley. I don't mind," he says. There's a long pause of silence before he clears his throat, his cheeks pinking. "Um, this might be a little awkward, but I'd like to clarify I wasn't in my room jerking off before I came downstairs. The guys like to bust my balls for not having a girlfriend, so it's a running joke. I was on the phone with my sister."

I laugh, because I'm not sure how to respond. "Good to know. Where are they going for their trip?"

"They're at my parents' house in France for a few days." His smile returns, however it's nowhere near as vibrant as before.

"I'm so jealous they get to be in the same town as those pastries. I've thought about them nearly as much as I've thought about you." The words fall from my mouth, and JJ's head snaps to look at me. *Oh shit. What is wrong with me?*

"I told her the same thing earlier, but if Henry's smart, he'll put the ring in the pastry and propose to her that way," JJ jokes to my relief and the mood lightens.

"So what else has happened since I last saw you?" I ask, not letting myself linger on how easily I slipped when normally, I'm careful with my words.

The conversation flows like a smooth legato, our words blending together harmoniously, and I slip into a peace I've only experienced with a select few.

I don't bother pointing out the extremely long route JJ is taking to my apartment, selfishly drinking in every second with him. Seconds I never thought I'd experience again, and as JJ pulls into the lot of my building, my stomach rolls for the first time since the beginning of the car ride, but this time because I'm not ready to pretend I don't know JJ.

I exhale nervously, spinning the ring on my thumb. "JJ, I know I'm dating Trent, but I'd really like if we could be friends?" I ask, terrified he'll say no. I wouldn't be able to blame JJ if he said no, but I'm hoping he says yes.

He taps his fingers absently on the steering wheel, and I hold my breath. "I don't know if I'm capable of just being your friend." My heart sinks as JJ looks at me, his expression torn as he tries to smile. "Don't look at me like that, Marley. I'm not done. I would never put you in a position to risk crossing any line, but I-I'm too fucking selfish to walk away from you again, so I'm willing to try being your friend if it means I get to have you in my life."

Logically, I know this is a bad idea, but for the second time in my life, I don't want to play it safe. JJ makes me want to be reckless.

"I'll see you soon then?" I ask, and he nods.

I slip out of the car, unable to say goodbye because it feels final, and nothing about us is finished yet.

I'm halfway to the stairs when I glance back, expecting JJ to already be gone, but he's still there, watching me. I wave, turning as the invisible string connecting my heart to JJ's pulls defiantly against every step I take away from him.

CHAPTER THREE

SHE'S HERE.

Marley is at Beaumont, but she's with *Trent.*

I look at where Trent is sitting, drinking his beer without a care in the world. It takes everything in me not to punch him in the face. He's cheating on her—multiple times as far as I know. The football team arrived two weeks ago, and in that time, I've seen him with at least three different girls.

I didn't think anything of it until Asher told me he had a girlfriend. My plan was to let the girl know he's cheating on her, but I didn't realize it would be Marley.

My Marley.

There was a part of me afraid I had put her on this pedestal she'd never be able to live up to if I did find her, but it couldn't have been further from the truth today. She's everything I remembered, and more.

My hands ball into fists in my lap, because I don't know what to do. Obviously, I know I should tell Marley. I almost did tell her when she asked if we could be friends, but I'm worried it's going to seem like I'm only doing it so she'll be with me.

I'm damned if I do, and damned if I don't.

Fuck, I need to get out of here.

I get up from the couch, making my way to my room without saying anything. What the hell would I say? *Sorry you're a piece of shit, Trent?* Well, I know what I'm not apologizing for—I'm not sorry for being in love with her.

I grab my prescription, popping a pill quickly to swallow it dry. My plan is to run as long as it takes for me to decide what the right thing to do is. My knee is still sore from practice, despite the fact I took my meds beforehand.

Slipping into my running shoes, I grab my headphones before jogging down the stairs.

"Didn't run enough at practice, Walker?" Luka asks, as I pass by the living room. His eyebrows are raised, looking at me like I'm insane for going running after the grueling practice we had in the heat earlier, where I did nothing but run routes the entire time.

"Guess not." I shrug, walking out without sparing a look at Trent.

I put my headphones in and turn my music up as loud as it will go before taking off down the street, losing myself to the music pulsing in my head, and the feeling of my feet striking the pavement.

I feel like a creeper, sitting in the café, watching this girl across the street.

She's been looking around for the last ten minutes, even spinning around a few times, but I can't tell if she's lost. What I do notice, even from a distance, is she's cute.

Fuck it. I'm going to help her.

I walk up rather easily as she stares at her phone, her

eyebrows scrunched in confusion while trying to decipher whatever's on her screen.

"Excuse me, are you lost?" I ask in French, trying to come across as non-threatening as possible. It's a little hard to do when I tower over most people at six four, and I'm built like a tank from training for football.

Her head snaps up, and I'm instantly ensnared by the color of her eyes. I don't think I've ever seen eyes this shade of blue before. Her nose is petite, her lips full, but it's her eyes that are truly captivating.

Cute is the wrong word to describe her. She's beautiful.

A flush of red crawls up her neck, and she laughs. "I think so? My mom's friend gave me the address to this artist's house, but I can't find the street. I must have gotten turned around somewhere," she stammers, and I wrack my brain trying to think of anyone in town she might be talking about.

"Are you talking about Madame Bellefleur?" I ask and she smiles brightly.

My.

Lungs.

Stop.

Breathing.

"Yes! Do you know her?" she asks, and I wish I could respond, but my brain isn't functioning. I think she might be the most beautiful girl I've ever met. Her eyes narrow, her smile fading as I gawk at her, deciding I'll do anything to earn another smile from her. "Hello?"

Fucking snap out of it, JJ. This isn't the first time you've talked to a girl.

I recover, flashing an apologetic smile. "Sorry, yes. I do know her. She's friends with my mom."

"Would you be able to point me in the right direction?" she asks, skepticism crystal clear on her face after I malfunctioned.

No. Wait—she can't leave yet. I don't know anything about her, and my gut is telling me I have to know more.

"I'll do you one better. I can take you there myself."

I have nothing better to do today anyway. Mom is out taking pictures in the mountains with Bailey, and Dad is with Hunter and Mirabelle on a run. I came into town out of pure boredom.

"No, it's okay. I really only need help finding the way," she says, and I take a step back in case I'm overwhelming her.

"It's really not a problem, but I understand. If you go down there"—I point toward the street to my right—"and then take a left at the flower shop, it's two doors down. The house covered with ivy."

Her shoulders relax, and I feel bad for making her feel uncomfortable. "Thank you, I really appreciate it."

Every fiber of my being is screaming at me to stay where I am, to stay by her, but I shove it down to walk away from her.

I don't even know her name.

"Wait!" she calls out after me, and I instantly turn to face her. "If you don't mind, maybe a guide would be better than instructions?" she asks, and I'm surprised, but I'm not going to blow this.

I can't help smiling. "On one condition."

"You're going to make a condition after you already offered to take me?"

"I guess I am," I say, laughing quietly. *I like her.*

"What's your condition?" she asks, crossing her arms, and I walk up to her.

"Your name."

"Marley . . ." She hesitates again. *What has her so nervous she won't tell me her name?* "Just Marley."

Okay. I can play this game too. I offer her my hand to shake. "I'm JJ. Just JJ," I say, winking at her, praying to God she'll smile again.

She does.

~

I shake my head.

It makes sense now why she didn't tell me her full name. I've replayed the moment we met in my head hundreds of times, wondering why I didn't press harder for her last name. I guess I was just satisfied with the fact she asked me to stay.

Marley's a *Benson*.

I don't care, though.

It's easy for me to say, because I know my future will always be comfortable, regardless of whether I'm drafted after college. Don't get me wrong, my family has more than enough money, but the Benson's are in a whole different tax bracket.

The money means nothing to me.

I only want her.

Seeing Marley today was more than I could have ever hoped for.

The only thing I would change is the word *friend* coming from her mouth. I absolutely hated it, but not as much as I hated seeing her look at Trent with her incredible smile. I don't know how to be *just* her friend, nor do I really want to. I've finally met the person I'm incapable of saying no to.

I simply cannot fathom a world where I'm not the one Marley is smiling at.

So I run.

~

The pain in my knee finally outweighs the pain in my chest as I stagger to a stop in the driveway. Practice is going to be hell tomorrow morning. My breathing is ragged, and my knee aches with every step I take, telling me I made a mistake not wearing my brace as I limp to the front door. Trent's car is gone, and I'm praying Asher and Luka went with him.

I'm not in the mood to talk to anyone right now.

Unfortunately, Asher is sitting in the living room, watching something on the television I could give two shits about. He does a double take after spotting me, immediately shaking his head.

"You're an idiot. You shouldn't have left without your brace on," he says, and I'm aware he's right. I forgot, and now I'm paying for it.

"I'm fine," I say, doing my best to walk normally to the stairs, so he can't see I'm hurting more than I'm letting on. Shit, and this is with pills in my system too. *I'm afraid of what it'll feel like tomorrow.*

"Can you even fucking walk? JJ, we have five a.m. weights tomorrow."

My knee barks in pain as I climb the stairs. "I know, Asher. Leave me alone."

I'm halfway up the steps, thinking he'll let it go, and things will return to normal tomorrow. Except Asher doesn't.

"It's her, isn't it? Marley is the girl you've been pining over."

My lack of response says everything.

Asher gawks at me from the bottom of the stairs. "She's our quarterback's girlfriend—you need to get over her. Maybe find a different way than running your knee into the ground, or you can kiss any shot at a pro career goodbye, regardless of who your father is and your last name."

I can't say anything to defend myself. What I did tonight was reckless and stupid.

I shower quickly before my knee has a chance to give out, pulling ice packs out of the mini fridge in my room. There's only one person who will understand how I feel right now.

Mirabelle answers after the line rings a couple times. "JJ? Is it Bailey?" she asks, her voice filled with panic.

Fuck, it's seven here, which means it's four in the morning in France.

I drag my hand over my face, swearing under my breath. "No, it's not Bailey. Fuck—I'm sorry, Mira. I forgot about the time difference."

"Hey, no, it's okay," she says, exhaling.

"*. . . Everything okay?*" Henry asks in the background, but Mirabelle whispers her response too quietly for me to hear.

An ugly feeling forms in my chest, and I hate being jealous of them. This might be a new low for me, especially when they deserve all the happiness in the world after everything they've been through.

"It's not okay. I'll call you in the morning—my morning. I'm sorry," I apologize, gritting my teeth as my knee throbs.

"No, it's fine. I'm awake, so tell me what's going on," she insists, and I feel my resolve start to crumble.

"How did you know Henry was the one for you?"

If she's confused why I'm asking, Mirabelle doesn't let it show as her answer is almost immediate. "Because he makes everything better. He's the one I've always pictured by my side. There was never another option for me."

I hum in response, not really having the words right now to explain what's going through my head.

"Not that I'm not happy to gush about how much I love my boyfriend, but I'm assuming there's a reason you're asking?" Mirabelle hedges, and I exhale a shuddering breath, adjusting the ice packs on my knee bringing little relief as I recline on my bed.

"I found Marley."

Mirabelle's excited gasp is pure joy. "No fucking way! How the hell did you pull that off? Was it a big romantic reunion? You at least got her full name this time so I can properly stalk her on social media to make sure she doesn't leave you hanging for another three years, right?"

"Two years and five months," I correct, as if knowing the specifics off the top of my head makes this any less pathetic than it already is. *How could I not know?* I've been writing Marley letters since the day I met her, but I never thought I'd have a chance . . . actually, that's a bad idea. I shouldn't give her those letters. They're the only place I've been honest.

"Whatever, get on with the story. I want to hear how you told her you've been looking for her for twenty-nine months. Did you kiss her? Please tell me you kissed her."

"She's with Trent."

Mirabelle falls silent, and then she laughs. "Oh, like she's his sister? For a second, I thought you meant they're like *together together*."

"Because they are." The words are acid in my mouth. "Marley is the girl he's cheating on."

I hate this, and not for myself. I hate it for Marley. She deserves so much fucking better than Trent, and I'm not saying it has to be me, but I'd give up everything for it to be me.

"JJ . . ."

"It fucking sucks," I admit, laughing bitterly, and there's a long pause between us.

"I'm so sorry. I know this has probably been on your mind since seeing her, but what are you going to do?" she asks.

"I don't know. She asked to be friends, so of course I said yes. I just feel like if I'm the one to tell her about Trent, Marley will think I'm only telling her so she'll be with me. It's not like I have any proof."

"You have a point there. What if I message her on social media, and tell her myself as a concerned third party? Then it's not you technically telling her. Hang on, I'm putting you on speaker," Mirabelle says. "What's her last name? I bet I can find her on social media."

"Benson. Her name is Marley Benson," I say. "Sorry for waking you guys up."

"It's fine, JJ. Happy to help," Henry grumbles, and I can hear the tapping on the screen from Mirabelle's fingernails.

"Are you sure that's her name? The only Marley Benson popping up is the daughter of this ballerina and billionaire, but that doesn't make sense?"

"Yeah, um . . . that's her," I clarify.

"Shut the fucking front door. The girl you're in love with is a Benson? Do you know how much fucking money they have?"

"Do you know how much fucking money the two of us have?" Henry asks, and I swallow back my laughter.

"No, Henry. You don't understand. Yes, we have a crap ton of money, but they have *billions* with a capital *B*. They're one of the richest families in the world," Mirabelle says, her voice filled with awe. "Damn, JJ. Her dad is hot. At least you know she'll age well."

Henry scoffs, clearly not amused. "In case you forgot, your very hot, and real boyfriend is right here. Tell JJ your all-knowing girl wisdom so we can go back to bed."

"I'm following her," Mirabelle says, and I sit up too fast, pulling my knee the wrong direction, a groan slipping through my clenched teeth. *Shit, goddamnit, motherfucker.*

"Don't," I croak out, my voice contorted with pain I can't hide.

"What just happened?"

"It's nothing. I pushed myself too hard today, and my knee isn't happy with me. I'll be fine," I insist, breathing through the pain slowly subsiding.

"*JJ*," she scolds immediately.

"What?" I ask, dragging a hand over my face.

"Were you wearing your brace?"

Do I try to lie? *No, she'd hear the truth through it.* "No," I admit. "I will tomorrow."

"JJ, seriously?" Mirabelle chides, sounding an awful lot like our mother.

"It slows me down," I complain. "I'll wear it tomorrow."

"Listen to your body if it's telling you to stop. You're only hurting yourself if you don't," she warns, and I know she's right, but I've already heard this lecture tonight. "As for the thing with Marley, I don't know what the right thing to do is. What do you think, Henry?"

"What do I think about what?" he asks, yawning.

"If I were dating Wilson, and he was cheating on me, would you tell me, or let me find out on my own?"

"Fuck that, you're not dating Wilson."

"Henry, it's a hypothetical question."

"No. There isn't a universe where we're not together, and I'd rather die than cheat on you, so I'm not even going to entertain the stupid hypothetical question," he says, and Mirabelle laughs.

Awesome, this has been so helpful.

"You're right, I'm sorry. JJ, he's getting grumpy, but we can try to figure this out tomorrow. Try to get some sleep, okay? I love you."

"I love you too," I say, hanging up. I double check the volume on my ringer in case tonight is the night Bailey calls, it's loud enough to pull me from even the deepest sleep.

I don't fall asleep for a long while, spending hours staring at the ceiling as I wait for the darkness to drag me under.

CHAPTER FOUR

Marley

I SLIDE INTO THE FRONT SEAT OF TRENT'S Corvette, trying to contain my excitement. The football team is having a party, and I'm actually planning to be social tonight.

I've made a couple of friends in my classes, but if I'm being honest, I struggle with trusting people, so I have a hard time making friends. My core circle I don't stray from often includes my little brother, Kaden, my mom's best friend's kid, Leo, and Bria. I learned the hard way when I was younger that people will stop at nothing to tear you down.

Too bad Kaden defaulted on his plan to attend Beaumont to attend the University of Milan with his boyfriend. I can't blame him, though. One of us being here can fly under the radar, but both of us attending Beaumont would be far more interesting. He's never shunned the spotlight from our last name, but he has zero interest in the family business.

Leaning over the center console, I kiss Trent hello before even shutting the door.

"To think it's only been a couple of hours since I've seen

you. Miss me?" he asks, smiling as I pull the door shut behind me.

"I did," I say, smiling. When I look at him again, Trent pulls me into another kiss, taking it deeper than the one I initiated. Despite seeing him earlier today for lunch, I haven't seen Trent much between classes starting and football practices in full swing.

"I'm glad because I missed you too."

Trent shifts the car into drive, and I lean back in my seat, fidgeting with the ring on my thumb, my nerves beginning to get the better of me. "So who is going to be at this party?"

"Probably most of the cheerleaders and the dance team, but the entire football team for sure. Actually, you have to know someone on the team to even get into the party," he explains, but logistically, it doesn't make sense to me. If it's a house party, then can't anyone just show up? How is everyone on the team supposed to know who should and shouldn't be there?

JJ will be there, my brain reminds me, and my heart involuntarily races in my chest. How am I supposed to be with Trent, when even the thought of being in the same house as JJ is enough to make my heart do cartwheels in my chest? I shove the thought to the back of my head, because I can't be sitting next to my boyfriend as I consider the idea of breaking up with him. This is so messed up, but my head hasn't stopped spinning since seeing JJ again, and I'm not sure how to feel about it.

"Oh, cool. Sounds very exclusive," I say, trying to sound interested, and Trent straightens in his seat.

"It is. Are you still planning on staying the night tonight?" he asks, glancing over at me.

"Yep," I reply, forcing my smile to remain bright when in all honesty, it only makes me feel guilty. I've avoided Trent's house the past few days because I don't want to make things awkward for JJ. He agreed to be my friend, but it doesn't mean I'm going to rub it in his face that I'm dating his roommate.

Trent rests his hand on my knee, pulling me back to reality. "You look great," he says, squeezing reassuringly. "I promise I didn't forget to tell you when you got in the car. You distracted me."

"Thanks," I say, resting my hand on top of his, squeezing it as he turns down a street. My nerves spike as the sound of a booming bass gets louder the closer we get to the end of the street, and it sounds like the football team knows how to party.

Trent parks the car, climbing out. I follow his lead, exhaling anxiously, second guessing my plan to be social now that I'm actually here.

"Are you going to be okay to drive us back to your place later, or should I hold onto the keys?" I ask, knowing I'm not going to drink, but Trent shakes his head.

"I'll only have two beers, and I'll be fine by the time we leave."

I'd prefer if he was staying completely sober before driving, but I guess if he doesn't stick to two beers, I can always take the keys later.

"Are you drinking tonight?" he asks, wrapping an arm over my shoulders, and I'm caught off guard by the question. Trent knows damn well where I stand when it comes to me and drinking.

"No, I'm not. You know I don't drink," I say, my tone stronger than I intend, but I'm not going to apologize.

I don't mind being around others while they're drinking, but it's personally not something I choose to partake in.

My parents have always been honest with me and Kaden about our mother's struggles with addiction. Her sobriety is something she works hard to keep, and I know the hereditary risk. They gave us all the information and told us it was our choice to decide what we were comfortable with, and I made mine. I decided I wouldn't touch alcohol or pills because I've seen firsthand how they can destroy someone. Maybe I'm being overly cautious, but it's not a risk I'm willing to take.

I guess that's what finding your mom unconscious on the bathroom floor after overdosing on pills will do to a kid.

"I'm sorry. You're absolutely right, I do know. I guess I wasn't sure if you would change your mind after coming here."

What does transferring colleges have to do with deciding whether to drink or not?

"It's not something I'm going to change my mind about. You're welcome to do whatever you want, but it doesn't mean I'm going to do it with you," I say, sliding out from under his arm. I feel like I'm not wrong for being hurt about this. *Am I overreacting?*

He puts his hands up in defense, genuinely seeming taken aback by my reaction to his question. "I'm sorry, babe. I didn't mean anything by it."

I need to chill. I think I'm letting my nerves about all the people inside get to me, and I'm getting more upset than I should about this. "It's okay, Trent. Let's just go inside. I want to see what all the hype is about," I say, forcing a smile and his shoulders visibly relax.

He seems relieved I still want to go inside, pulling me with him before I do something like change my mind.

It's funny how I get stage fright about playing my guitar in front of others when I'm putting on the best damn show tonight, smiling at all the people Trent introduces me to. No one gives me a second look because right now, I'm not known by the zeros in my bank account. It's a refreshing feeling, even if I'm being paraded around this party like a show pony, tugged in whatever direction Trent pulls my lead.

Everyone I see has a drink in their hand, including my boyfriend, who by now I'm certain has had more than the two he said he'd have.

I scan over the crowd from where I sit, perched on Trent's lap as he talks to a couple of his friends. I'm not even sure what I'm looking for until my attention catches JJ leaning against a wall, talking to a pretty blonde girl. *Who is she?*

I flinch, realizing I shouldn't be worried about JJ talking to anyone. Trent's hand rests on my hip, and my cheeks burn with embarrassment. "You okay?" he asks, whispering into my ear, and I nod, forcing myself to look away from JJ.

"Sorry, just jumpy, I guess." I stumble over my words, feeling like an idiot. *What am I doing here?*

"Marley, it's okay to relax. I'm sorry about earlier. If you don't want to drink, then I don't want you to feel like you have to. It's okay." He presses a kiss to my shoulder, and I wish I felt like I did a month ago, before seeing JJ created pure chaos inside my head.

A month ago, I probably would have melted against him to keep the peace, but tonight, I'm swallowing back a sarcastic response on the tip of my tongue. I don't need Trent to tell me it's okay, because I *know* it's okay. I don't need his permission.

"I'm going to get some water," I say instead, deciding it's the safest option I have right now.

"Will you bring me back another drink?" he asks, not seeing anything wrong with what he just said, flashing me a smile I'd normally cave to. I realize one of his teammates is watching me, but I ignore it.

"If you give me your keys, then sure," I say, standing up.

His handsome face twists in confusion, blinking at me in surprise. "Babe, I've barely had anything. It's fine."

I surprise both of us when I turn, walking away from him.

I find my way to the backyard, which still has people in it, but there are significantly less than inside the house. The temperature drops nearly ten degrees, and I greedily breathe in the cooler air, hoping it can soothe my frustration. There are coolers against the side of the house, but all I see after opening the lids, is hard seltzers and beer. *Of course, there's no water. It's a college party, and I'm the abnormality.*

A throat clears behind me, and I look over my shoulder to find JJ standing there. Something I didn't notice before was the shirt he's wearing, bringing out the green in his eyes.

"I thought you might want this?" he asks, offering me the water bottle in his hand.

I consider telling him no, but it's so damn stuffy inside the house, and I'm not finding any others out here. "Thanks, JJ," I say, accepting it.

He smiles, shrugging as if it's not a big deal when my boyfriend couldn't be bothered to save one for me. "No biggie. They're hard to find at these, so I snagged one earlier before they were gone."

The irony of this isn't lost on me, and I should go back inside, but I don't want to.

"Why are you out here? The party's inside." I motion toward the house, my head spinning with the emotional whiplash I'm feeling.

"I know," he says, chuckling. "I needed a break from all the noise. Why are you out here?"

"Because I..." I trail off, knowing how unfair it would be for me to say I'm mad at Trent for not giving me his keys, but I also can't say I'm jealous JJ was flirting with a girl. "I needed a breather."

"Are you okay?" he asks, moving closer to me as concern bleeds into his smooth voice.

"I'm fine. You should go back inside, I bet you're missed." *I probably shouldn't have said that.*

"Missed by who?" he asks, and I shrug, opening the water

to take a sip. *I shouldn't be out here, but especially not with JJ.* "Marley?"

"I should go find Trent. Thanks for the water," I say, avoiding looking at him as I hold tightly to my drink to escape into the mass of people. *I would have thought with this party being exclusive, there'd be less people, but I guess not.*

Trent is not where I left him by the time I find my way back, and everyone from the group we were sitting with have dispersed into different corners of the party.

I pull my phone out of my pocket, beginning to text Trent to ask where he is, before deciding to call him. I can barely hear the phone over the music, but it goes straight to voicemail. Looking around, I'm not sure I recognize anyone here, but I've met so many people in the last week, all the faces are blending together.

Where the hell did Trent go?

Combing my fingers through my hair, I pull it back into a ponytail to get it off my neck. I can't tell if I'm hot because it's a thousand degrees or because my social anxiety is climbing. I wander the party some more, scanning over faces to find one I recognize, but I'm not sure how long it is before I spot JJ again, this time talking to Asher in a corner.

Is it fair for me to go up to JJ, knowing I ran away outside after being a jerk to him? I absolutely owe him an apology, because he's not the one I'm upset with. I'm upset with myself for caring he was talking to another girl. I'm upset with Trent because . . . JJ and I are friends.

I walk up, wiping my sweaty palms on my denim shorts as they notice me. "Hey, guys. Um, do you know where Trent is? I've been looking all over, and I can't find him."

Asher looks at JJ before turning to muster a smile at me. "Haven't seen him, but I'm sure he's around here somewhere?"

I look at JJ, who's staring intensely at me, and my stomach

sinks. I fucked up. He was only trying to be nice to me, and I was rude.

"Yeah, I'm sure you're right. Sorry for bothering you," I say, twisting my thumb ring. That's not what I should be apologizing for, but some apology is better than no apology. They were in the middle of a conversation before I interrupted, after all.

"You're not bothering us," JJ says, finally speaking, to my relief.

"Je suis désolée pour tout à l'heure,"[1] I say, not wanting Asher to hear me apologize for something having nothing to do with him.

"Ne t'en fais pas,"[2] he replies, giving me a reassuring smile helping to ease some of my guilt.

"I have a feeling this is going to get old fast, so how about we just speak English for those who aren't trilingual, and whatever Marley is," Asher jokes.

"Don't be a sore loser because you can't speak a different language," JJ says.

"I'm not being a sore loser, but I do feel out of the loop thank you very much."

I laugh, smiling genuinely for what might be the first time since walking into this party. "Sorry, Asher. It won't happen again."

Actually, I can't promise that, because I like hearing JJ speak in different languages. I'm aware I shouldn't, so maybe it's a promise I should plan on keeping.

"I knew I liked you. You're a lot nicer than JJ," Asher says, nudging me.

"Some best friend you are." JJ snorts, leaning against the wall behind him.

---

1. I'm sorry about earlier.
2. Don't worry about it.

"I'll let you guys get back to whatever you were doing before I interrupted. I'm going to try again to find Trent. Will you let me know if you see him?"

"If you still can't find him, I can give you a ride home," JJ says, but there's still a tenseness to him I can't place my finger on.

I push the thought out of my head, smiling appreciatively before taking another lap around the party to look for Trent. *Seriously, where could he have disappeared to?*

I'm ready to give up and ask JJ for a ride when I turn around, finally spotting Trent as he's coming out of the bathroom. He's zipping up his pants as he shuts the door behind him quickly. "Trent!" I call out over the music, taking a couple steps toward him.

He looks startled, his eyes widening before he relaxes into a smile. "Marley, where have you been?" he asks, wrapping an arm around my back to pull me with him in the opposite direction.

"Looking for you? Where have you been? I got my water, and when I came back, you were gone."

Trent smiles softly at me, pressing a short kiss to my forehead. I'm irritated, but it's overpowered by the relief I feel from finding him. "I was looking for you too. I had to take a leak, but if you're ready to go now, we can leave. You were right, I had too much to drink. Here's my keys," he says, pulling them out of his pocket to hand them to me.

My jaw nearly hits the damn floor. *At least I don't have to ask for the keys and whether we can leave.*

"Thank you," I say, smiling at him, doing my best to push everything else from my head.

CHAPTER FIVE

I CALLED IT QUITS EARLY TODAY, DESPITE everything in my head screaming at me to continue running. I've been pushing myself harder than I should, yet somehow, I still have endless amounts of energy to burn.

It's a little after six, and with the way Trent was drinking at the party last night, I'm not expecting him to be awake for a while. Asher takes full advantage of our days off by sleeping in, and Luka didn't come home last night, so I should have the house to myself for a couple of hours before everyone's up. With all of us being upperclassmen, none of us have particularly early classes in our schedules.

Coach gave us the day off, which is probably why Trent went so hard last night, but we have a camp this weekend with high schoolers. That alone is enough to make me wish for practice instead. On the bright side, I should hear from Mirabelle any minute since Henry texted me yesterday to tell me he was proposing today.

The front door shuts softly behind me as I slip out of my running shoes and move toward the kitchen to mix a protein shake together while I make my breakfast.

We're technically on a meal plan, but my cooking abilities don't go past scrambled eggs and sandwiches.

I set my phone on the counter, whisking eggs in a bowl as the pan heats up on the stovetop. I take a drink of my shake when I hear someone coming down the stairs. I'm taken aback when Marley's head pops around the corner. Her mouth falls open when she sees me, immediately tugging down what I'm assuming is Trent's shirt. "Shit. I'm sorry, I didn't think anyone would be awake. I came down for a glass of water," she explains, a red flush climbing up her neck to her face.

I didn't know she stayed here last night. I can't decide if that's better or worse than Trent bringing another girl home, but after what he pulled at the party, I think I'd prefer if it weren't Marley.

"Glasses are in the upper cabinet next to the fridge," I say, tilting my head before turning away to give Marley privacy to get her water without leering at her like a creep. As much as I'd love to take a longer look, it'd be wrong.

Just like it was wrong of Trent to hook up with a freshman on the cheer squad in the bathroom as Marley looked for him.

I knew exactly where he was when she found us, and I didn't agree with Ash choosing to say he hadn't seen Trent around when we both saw him go into the bathroom with a cheerleader. By staying silent, it's technically a lie of omission, but I think a part of me hoped she'd catch him cheating on her. It'd selfishly save me the agony of deciding what to do.

She almost did when she saw him coming out of the bathroom, but he steered Marley in the opposite direction before she could see the girl come out after him.

Fucking asshole.

"Do you want breakfast?" I offer, pouring the eggs in the pan after Marley turns off the faucet.

"Sure, um . . . let me go put pants on. I'll be back down in a minute," she squeaks out, hurried footsteps telling me she's left the room.

Maybe Asher is right. Maybe it's time I move on. However, the argument could also be made that it seems like Marley's attracted to me, despite her status with Trent. I saw the way her face changed when I offered her a water, and I'm more than a little curious who Marley saw me talking to last night and why she thought I'd be missed. If I didn't know better, I'd think she was jealous, and if that's the case, then Marley has no idea I spent the entire night keeping tabs on her to make sure she was okay.

Marley was playing the part of the perfect girlfriend, but she looked like she wanted to be anywhere else. It's why I followed her outside to check on her before she ran away to go find Trent.

Fuck moving on. I'll wait forever for her to fall for me a second time.

"Earth to JJ?" Marley waves her hand in front of my face, and I snap out of my thoughts, causing her to giggle. "You're going to burn the eggs if you don't turn them."

I look down at the pan to find she's right. "I'm not going to burn them," I say, flashing her a quick smile as I grab the spatula to move them around in the pan.

"Do you always get up this early to make breakfast?" Marley asks, sitting on a barstool.

"Kind of. I'm from a family of insomniacs," I say, pulling two plates out of the cupboard. I leave out how I haven't slept for more than three hours consecutively since Bailey called me sixteen months ago. "Are you a morning person?" I ask, turning the heat on the stove down.

"I usually sleep in if I don't have somewhere to be, but I couldn't fall back asleep this morning. I didn't want to wake Trent up with all my tossing and turning so I thought a glass of water would help," she explains.

I steal a glance at Marley to find her already staring at me, and I feel my breath catch as our eyes meet. It still feels unreal she's in front of me after all this time. Marley's spinning the ring on her thumb, and her long brown hair is falling in tangled waves over her shoulders and down the length of her back with mascara smudged under her eyes, but she looks beautiful.

"If you want to go back to bed, it won't hurt my feelings," I say, despite every word feeling like I'm walking barefoot across glass.

"I'm where I want to be," she says, the corners of her mouth pulling up.

I turn away to hide how wide my smile is.

Take that, Trent.

"You're welcome to take however many eggs you want. I'll eat whatever you don't," I say, changing the topic because I'm certainly not going to convince Marley to go back upstairs if she doesn't want to.

Marley walks around the island to serve herself, and when she's done, I dump the rest on my plate before sitting next to her.

"JJ, that's so much food," she says, gaping at my plate.

I shove a forkful in my mouth, shrugging. "I'm a growing boy."

She covers her mouth, smothering her quiet laugh. "I'm sorry, I didn't catch that?"

"I'm a growing boy. We need a lot of food," I repeat after swallowing the food in my mouth.

"Oh, believe me, I know. My brother eats so much food it's insane, but your plate makes his look small." Marley shakes her head at me, spearing scrambled eggs with her fork.

"What can I say? It takes a lot of protein to keep these muscles," I joke, flexing with the hope Marley will laugh again. Everything about her is musical, but especially her laughter.

She rolls her eyes, but her cheeks flush as she takes a drink of her water. "You know, speaking of siblings, I think your sister followed me on social media."

I'm going to kill Mirabelle.

"I'm sorry, she can be . . . *weird*." There's no way around Marley knowing I've talked to my sister about her.

"She's really pretty. I think I recognize her from somewhere, but I can't think of where," Marley says, and I'm hoping it's not from the naked pictures taken of her and Henry a couple years ago. They've worked really hard to put the violation of their privacy behind them and move forward from it. I'll never forget my friends in class turning to look at me after the article dropped my freshman year.

"She was in the Summer Olympics in Paris six years ago, and Mira and Henry have been in the media quite a bit with their careers," I answer, trying to keep it vague. They're so much more than one moment in their history.

"That must be it. They're a really cute couple."

My phone starts ringing as if we summoned the devil herself. I smile widely, but Marley looks confused. "Why is your sister calling you this early in the morning?"

"Because it's the afternoon in France, and she just got engaged."

I answer the phone, putting it on speaker because I want Marley to experience this moment with me.

"JJ, holy fucking shit! You won't believe what just fucking happened!"

I stifle my laughter. "What happened?"

"Henry fucking Price just proposed to me! Like down on one knee, with a ring and everything!"

It's the pure happiness in her voice that makes my smile somehow wider. She deserves this more than anyone I know. "And?"

"Well, of course I said yes! I'm not an idiot," Mirabelle

exclaims, and I hear Henry laughing in the background. *"Je suis si heureuse que je crois que je pourrais en mourir."*[1]

"Non, mon cœur. Nous ne mourons pas. On va se marier,"[2] Henry says and Mirabelle squeals with excitement.

"Je t'aime,"[3] she says, and I know it's not directed to me.

"Congratulations, but you're so sickeningly sweet, I think I'm going to go throw up now," I say, and Marley hits my arm, gaping at me.

"Gross, JJ, be happy for me. You're the first one I called to tell my childhood dreams of becoming Mrs. Price are finally coming true."

"Mirabelle, we can't cross it off the list unless I take your last name," Henry says, and I have no doubt he would. I've never seen someone as in love as Henry is with my sister.

"You actually want to?" Mirabelle asks, and this is starting to sound like a conversation they should have without us listening.

I clear my throat, interrupting them. "Thanks for calling me first. I hope you know how happy I am for you guys. I love you both, but if you don't call Mom and Dad next, it's going to be the end of the fucking world."

"I will, I promise. We love you too, JJ."

Marley sniffles next to me as I hang up. "Are you crying?" I ask, surprised.

She sniffles, wiping at her face quickly. *"No."*

Right, because Marley has the ability to produce fake tears. She's totally not crying.

"It looks like you're crying," I continue, trying not to laugh.

"Shut up, JJ." Marley sniffles again, casting a feigned look

---

1. I'm so happy I think I might die.
2. No, my heart. We're not dying. We're getting married.
3. I love you.

of annoyance in my direction. "They just sound so in love. I mean, he literally calls her *my heart*. How freaking romantic, and he wants to take her last name?"

All I can think is one day, that will be us too. I'm willing to wait.

"They deserve to be happy," I say, simply because I don't trust myself to not cross the friend boundary she set by blurting something else out.

"Thank you for letting me listen. It really was something special," she says, her eyes growing misty again. A stray tear escapes, and my thumb is wiping it away before I realize what I'm doing.

Marley inhales sharply, and I brush my thumb tenderly over her cheek, doing my best to commit the feeling to memory before pulling away. I focus on my plate like nothing happened, but my heart is thundering in my chest from an innocent touch. *She's not mine to touch.*

"Where does your brother go to school?" I ask, stabbing the eggs with my fork, trying to keep the conversation moving forward.

Marley takes a moment to reply. "University of Milan. He's studying Italian and art history."

"Nice, sounds cool."

"Don't tell Bria. Her mom is an art collector, and my brother caught the bug when he was little," she says, laughing quietly.

"You're studying music therapy, right? I mean, if I remember correctly, that's what you said you wanted to study," I say, tripping over my words as I glance at her.

Her posture stiffens, and she sets her fork down on her plate. *Oh shit, Marley thinks it's weird I remember everything she told me.*

"I-I'm majoring in chemistry with a minor in business. I'm taking over my family's company in a couple of years so my dad can retire," she says, each word sounding like she has to force it out. If anything, it sounds like the last thing she wants to be doing.

"What? Marley, is that really what you want to do? What about your brother?"

She picks at her nails absently, forcing a smile feeling similar to a punch to the gut. "Yep. My dad has worked his entire life, and he deserves to live a little. I want him to be happy, so if taking over the company does that, then yes, it's what I want. Kaden's never had an interest in it. Art is his true calling."

"That's really admirable," I say, and she gives me a puzzled look.

"I thought you were going to say it's dumb, and I should be studying music therapy."

If I thought it'd help, yeah, I would say she should switch instead. On the flip side, I know better than anyone what it's like to sacrifice your own happiness for others, so who am I to judge her?

I shrug as if it's not a big deal. "You should do whatever makes you happy. What I think doesn't matter, as long as you can live with the choices you make."

"Do you regret any choices you've made?" Marley asks, and my mind jumps immediately to Bailey.

"Yeah, I do. Do you?" I turn the question around on her as I inhale the last of my eggs.

"I think so, but I also want to believe second chances exist for a reason."

I slide off the stool to take the dishes to the sink, unable to let myself look at her. It's probably unreasonable for me to hope there's an underlying meaning to Marley's theory on second chances.

"*JJ*," Marley says softly, pulling at my heartstrings like she owns them. My name sounds like a prayer and a sin coming from her lips, but I regret nothing as I turn around to face her. Marley hesitates, and I hold my breath instinctively. "Do you still think people are meant to be together?"

There's a vulnerability in her face as she waits for my answer to one of the last things I said to her in France before we parted. I wonder what she would say if she knew about the box of letters addressed to her just upstairs in my room?

"Yes, I do," I say, as my brain screams at me to go for another run.

Marley smiles at me, and I commit every single one of her features to memory. "I hope you're right," she whispers, reading my mind.

My entire body is trembling, fighting the urge to close the distance between us that feels more like the Grand Canyon than a small kitchen, to feel her soft lips on mine. I won't make her a cheater, knowing it'll break her heart more than it's probably already going to when she finds out Trent's cheating on her—even if it means further breaking my heart in the process to stand in the background watching.

"Me too."

CHAPTER SIX

Marley

MY FINGERS STRUM OVER THE GUITAR STRINGS AS I play the same melody again, trying to put words to it in my head.

I shake my head, glaring at the notebook open on the bed beside me. The page is blank and has been for a couple of weeks now. All I have for this new song is the melody.

A knock on my door startles me, and Bria pokes her head in. "Mar, you know I love you, but if I hear you play the same thing one more time, I might kill you."

"Sorry, I'm stuck," I say, not even caring if she can hear me play—that's how frustrated I am. Before moving in, I would have been embarrassed if she could hear me playing, but now I'm using it as exposure therapy to take baby steps toward playing in front of others.

Bria falters, opening the door further to step in. "Is everything okay?" she asks, sitting next to me on the bed.

"Yeah, I guess." I shrug and set my guitar down next to me. "Have you heard from Asher?" I ask, trying to sound upbeat, and she rolls her eyes.

"Of course, I heard from him," she says, but she doesn't hide the smile tugging at her lips very well.

"And?" I hug my knees to my chest, hoping to hear her say she's giving Asher a chance.

"And what?"

Of course she's going to be difficult about this. "Has Asher heard from you?" I ask, rephrasing my question to the one I should have asked.

"I haven't decided if I'm going to respond," Bria says, but I'm not sure if I believe her. She tilts her head to the side, watching me. "What's on your mind?"

Everything. Nothing. JJ. Trent. *JJ.* Home.

"I honestly don't even know. It's probably why I'm struggling to put lyrics to the music. Sorry, I'm not trying to make you crazy." I'm definitely making myself crazy, though.

"We both know I'm already crazy, but maybe talking about whatever it is might help you figure it out?" she suggests, but I feel like if I say it out loud then it becomes real. Bria sees right through my hesitation, immediately calling me on my bullshit. "It's JJ, isn't it? He's what you don't know."

"We're friends," I protest. *I'm awful.*

"Is that what you want?"

"I'm with Trent."

Bria shrugs, her dark hair slipping over her shoulder. "So? People break up all the time. Do you want to be with Trent?"

"Yes. I like him a lot." *Liar.*

"I've heard you talk more about JJ since seeing him again than I've heard you talk about Trent the entire time you've been together. I'm honestly a little shocked you're still dating after the way you looked at JJ when you realized Trent's roommate was him," she says.

"I was surprised," I protest, but I don't think she buys it for a moment.

"You were starstruck."

"How else was I supposed to look after finally accepting I'd never see him again? I've moved on, Bria."

"Have you, though? Because you fell in love with JJ after spending a day with him, and you've been with Trent for four months, and still can't tell him you love him."

It hurts to hear because I don't want to hurt Trent. I might not love him, but I do care for him. I swallow my guilt, thinking about how his mother's already dropping hints for our hypothetical future wedding. "I'm not going to say I love him if I don't," I say, twisting my hair up into a bun to get it off my neck. I feel like the walls are closing in, and the claustrophobia is getting to me.

"JJ still loves you," she says, and I involuntarily shiver, thinking of how he looked like it caused him physical pain not to be next to me. How tender his touch was when he brushed his thumb over my cheek before pulling away. I didn't want him to, but I know how unfair it is for me to even think it.

"Bria, I'm with Trent," I repeat, swallowing the lump forming in my throat.

"So you keep saying."

"I thought you liked Trent? It feels like you're telling me to break up with him."

Bria shakes her head. "No, I'm not telling you to do anything. I tolerate Trent because you like him, but right now, it feels like you're trying to convince yourself you still like him." She exhales, softening her voice. "It's okay if you changed your mind."

"That's not . . ." I trail off, scoffing. *It's exactly what I'm doing.* "Bria, just say whatever you're hinting at."

"I think JJ would make you happier, but I don't think you're ready to hear and believe it, so I'll be ready to tell you again when I think you'll listen to me. For now, you need to know it's okay to not be with Trent. You deserve to be happy."

I'm entirely taken aback, and I know she means well, but Bria's right. I'm not ready to hear it.

"I'll keep it down," I say softly, unable to form a different response.

"Mar, I'm not trying to hurt your feelings. I've listened to you talk about JJ for almost three years, and I don't want you to miss out on something great with him, because you're settling for something mediocre with Trent," she continues, reading me as I grab my guitar to hide how my hands are trembling.

"It's okay, Bria. Don't worry about it."

"I'm going to take a nap, but if you need anything, wake me up, okay?"

"Thanks." I muster a short smile, but my mind is racing.

After Bria shuts the door behind her, I strum the melody again quietly, the words pouring from me, unlocked by something she said.

Trent grips my hand tightly as we walk around campus, enjoying the fresh air. He radiates this confidence I wish I had. He seems so sure about everything: football, school, us. I don't know how he does it.

I've been doing my best to push what Bria said yesterday out of my head.

"What are you humming?" Trent asks, pulling me out of my thoughts.

"I'm humming?" I ask, looking up at him, shielding my eyes with my other hand. He was smart, grabbing sunglasses, but I left mine in my car.

He smiles, swinging our hands gently between us. "Yeah. The same tune over and over again. It's cute."

"Just something I heard on the radio," I say, my cheeks warming. "How was football this morning?"

"I think we have a shot this season to make the playoffs. Everyone's working really hard, but goddamn, Walker has had a stick up his ass lately. He needs to get laid, but I don't think I've ever seen him even kiss a girl, let alone bring one home," Trent says, but now I'm lost. Who are we even talking about?

"Walker?"

Trent chuckles, his dimples popping. "Sorry, JJ. Walker is his last name, and what we all call him."

Of course we're talking about JJ, who is the one person I shouldn't be talking about.

"Oh," I say, my head spinning. "I thought I saw him talking to a girl at the party last week?" I ask, despite knowing I shouldn't touch this topic with a ten-foot pole.

"I'm not sure what his deal is. Sometimes I think he could be gay, but I've never seen him show any interest in anyone, and it's not like he hasn't had plenty of opportunities. Usually, he has a good sense of humor, but he's been keeping to himself, snapping at things that wouldn't have bothered him a month ago."

That doesn't sound at all like JJ. "I wonder what changed," I say, as someone waves at Trent. I should be changing the topic again, but now all I can think about is that morning in the kitchen with JJ. *He seemed fine to me. I wonder if something happened with his brother since then?*

"What if we set up JJ and Bria?" Trent asks, and my foot catches on a crack on the sidewalk, sending me pitching forward. Trent reacts quickly, catching me before I can fall flat on my face. "Woah, are you good?" he asks, his brown eyes scanning over me quickly with concern.

I laugh nervously, forcing a smile. "I wasn't looking at the ground, so thanks for catching me."

There is absolutely no way Trent thinks it's a good idea to set Bria and JJ up. Aside from JJ being . . . JJ, Asher made it pretty clear he's *very* interested in Bria.

"Always," Trent says, smiling warmly at me. I lean up on my tiptoes, kissing him, catching him by surprise. I should have butterflies exploding in my chest . . . but perhaps the butterflies are as confused as I am. "What was that for?" he asks, brushing my hair out of my face.

"Am I not allowed to kiss you?"

He wraps an arm around my shoulder, pulling me closer. "You can kiss me anytime you'd like, babe."

"Good to know," I tease, trying to recover.

Trent kisses the side of my head, and I can feel myself relax a little, the sun shining warmly on us.

"So what do you think?"

I tense, looking up at him. "Think about what?"

"JJ and Bria."

"I don't think it's a good idea," I say slowly, my stomach twisting.

"Why not? They're both single, and I'm sure he'd play even better than he is now if he's getting laid."

Is he serious? I untangle myself from underneath his arm, my stomach twisting in disgust. "Why do you have to keep saying it like that? It's gross, Trent," I say, and I can tell by his expression he wasn't expecting me to have a reaction. "Bria's my best friend, and she can decide for herself who she wants to hook up with, just like JJ. Maybe you could talk to him instead of assuming he needs to get laid to relax."

This isn't at all how the Trent I met this summer acted and spoke. It's like coming here has brought out different versions of us, and I'm not sure I recognize either of us anymore.

"Okay, you're right. I'm sorry," Trent apologizes, looking around almost like he's nervous. *What is he looking for?*

"I'm sorry, I don't know what's wrong with me," I say, dragging my hands over my face.

"Babe, there's nothing wrong with you. I shouldn't have said any of it."

I'm self-sabotaging this, and I shouldn't be. Trent still fits the mold of our relationship, but I'm not even trying to fit when I should be. I exhale, taking a second to collect myself, slipping back into the calmer, more rational version of myself. "It's fine," I say, reaching for his hand to squeeze it briefly. "Do you remember the day we went to the Hamptons?" I ask, staring up at Trent's kind features, seeing my reflection in his dark lenses. Everything was easier in the summer, or maybe it still could be, and I'm the one making things difficult.

"Which time? We spent more than a couple of weekends there," he says, and I wish I could read Trent's mind to know what's going through his head.

"The day we went to the little ice cream shop by the marina."

"Of course I remember. You got a mint chocolate chip cone. What about it?" he asks, and I thread our fingers together.

"It was just a really good day," I say, remembering how easy everything was with him. We walked along the beach, and Trent pushed my ice cream cone up when I went to take a bite. Some of it went up my nose, and we laughed so hard, he snorted, getting really embarrassed after. It was cute to see Trent get flustered compared to his usual confidence.

"It was a really good day, wasn't it? We should do something like it soon," he says, and I actually really like the idea of us going on a date. I think it'll help things feel more normal than whatever's going on with me right now.

"What about sometime this week?" I ask, my chest filling with hope, but I know when his smile dims we won't be going this week.

"I'm sorry. We're busy with the pep rally and the first game," Trent says, dragging a hand through his usually styled short blond hair. Everything about him is curated, fitting into a perfect, pretty picture.

I try not to deflate, but really? I know football is important, but he doesn't have any time to go get ice cream? "You don't have an hour to spare? It doesn't have to be for long, but I think it'd be fun." I don't care what we're doing, but quality time matters to me.

"I wish I could. I don't want to make any promises I can't keep," he says, shrugging.

"I'm not asking you to keep a promise, I'm asking you to go on a date with me?"

Trent tilts his head in confusion, but I don't know what there is to be confused about? "I have football. You're not seriously upset with me about this, are you?"

I drop his hand and take a step back. This has backfired majorly. "Trent, I'm not upset. I just want to spend time with you, but you're telling me you can't promise to see me for an hour this week to get ice cream?"

"Well, you're obviously welcome to stay the night any time you want. I love you, Marley, but I don't have time this week," Trent says, and I don't know if it's the combination of him telling me he loves me but doesn't have time this week, or him telling me I can stay the night any time that hurts more. Maybe it's not fair for me to compare this to my parents' relationship, but my dad as a CEO always made a point to be home for dinner. He might've had to return to the office after or work from his home office, but he made time, even when he had none to spare. How could my father do all of that, but Trent can't get ice cream this week?

"I think I'll just stay at my apartment this week," I say quietly, once again avoiding Trent telling me he loves me.

His jaw drops as an irritated scoff escapes his mouth.

"Why are you acting like this?" Trent asks, an edge to his voice, putting a bad taste in my mouth. So he didn't seem to care about not being able to see me all week, but me reaffirming I wouldn't be staying the night with him is upsetting?

"You really don't see anything wrong with what you said? I'm asking you to carve out a small fraction of your week to go get ice cream with me, and your response was I can stay the night. I'm your girlfriend, not some means to 'getting laid' as you like to put it," I say, standing up for myself, and he reels back as if I've struck him.

"I've *never* said you were a means to getting laid." Trent's entire demeanor has changed, but if it walks like a duck, and it talks like a duck . . . the dots weren't hard to connect with what his implication was for saying I can stay the night.

I cross my arms defiantly over my chest, and Trent shakes his head at me.

"I think we need to take a breather and talk about this later before one of us says something we regret," he says, and as much as I don't want to take a breather right now, he's probably right.

"Fine," I agree, and Trent steps closer to press a kiss to my cheek.

"I'll call you later."

I say nothing as Trent shoves his hands in his pockets, walking away, and my head is spinning. Seriously, what the fuck just happened?

Moving to sit on the bench a few feet away, I pull my phone out, my hands shaking. I should call Bria or Kaden, but for some awful reason, I press JJ's number.

He answers immediately. "Your knight in shining armor, how may I be of service?" his deep voice asks, and the absurdity of it causes laughter to bubble from me, my frustration subsiding.

"Please tell me that's not how you answer the phone."

JJ chuckles. "No, who do you think I am? What's up?"

Shit, I shouldn't have called JJ. I know better—especially because he's Trent's roommate—but I think he's also the only person who could make me smile right now. There's nothing wrong with it because we're just friends.

"Are you busy?" I ask before I can talk myself out of it.

"Never too busy for you," he says, and if only he knew what a shot to the heart that is.

I look around, gauging how far I am from the nearest parking lot. Beaumont is not friendly for students who commute, most of the buildings on campus are only accessible by walking, but it's not too far. "Any chance you could come pick me up? I'm by the lion fountain."

"I'm leaving now. Am I rescuing you from an evil dragon?" he teases, and I wonder if JJ knows the weight he's taking off my shoulders right now.

"You're so weird, but yes, in a way you are rescuing me." He'll be rescuing me from myself because I'm the evil dragon, not Trent.

"Anyone I need to beat up? You know my muscles are huge from how much food I eat, so I think I could take anyone."

"I do know how much you eat, but I'm not sure I can confirm the size of your muscles without inflating your ego," I retort, shaking my head as I stand up to head toward the lot. "You don't need to beat anyone up. I could just use a friend right now," I say quietly, hoping he doesn't think I'm selfish for calling him.

"One friend coming right up," JJ says without missing a beat.

"Great. I guess I'll see you in a few then." I smile in relief, because maybe JJ and I can successfully be friends.

"Wait, Marley," he says, and I keep the phone up to my ear.

"Yeah?"

"Thanks for calling me."

A smile forms on my face. "Thanks for making time for me."

CHAPTER SEVEN

JJ

I DIDN'T KNOW WHAT TO EXPECT WHEN MARLEY called me, but I'm glad she did. I haven't asked again what happened, and I'm not sure I want to know. I don't trust what will come out of my mouth, and I'm not sure I'd be doing it for the right reasons.

Marley's smile is wide as she throws her arms out and spins in the fountain. This is our fifth stop on our fountain jumping spree. It's tradition here, and while it's something usually only freshman and graduating seniors partake in, it's worth it to see her face light up.

I splash her as a couple other people jump in, wanting momentary relief from the California heat.

"JJ! You're getting my clothes wet," she pretends to complain, frowning at her maroon shirt, speckled with wet spots from the fountains. Her denim shorts and sneakers were a lost cause after the first fountain.

"Sweetheart, your clothes were already wet. Me splashing you isn't going to make a damn difference," I say, shaking my head at Marley. I falter, realizing I just called her sweetheart, but Marley smiles, thankfully not commenting on my slip, before splashing me in return.

"Where are your manners? It's not polite to splash others."

"Oh, but you can splash me?"

"You splashed me first, making it fair game."

I lean down, sending a large spray her way as she shrieks with joy. *I think that might be my new favorite sound.*

"I'm going to get you," she says, trying—and failing—to sound threatening.

"I'd like to see you try." I grin at her, feeling lighter than I have in weeks. I think I needed this as much as she did.

This is one of the larger fountains on campus, so the water goes up to my knees and she has a little room to back away from me. Marley must trip on something, because the next thing I know, she's falling backward into the water, a small yelp escaping her mouth on her way down. The people on the other side of the fountain turn to see what the loud splash was, and Marley sits up, her wet hair covering her face.

"Shit, are you okay?" I ask, moving closer, looking to see what she tripped on, but it looks like it was only a pipe.

She moves the hair out of her face, creating a tangled mess, but I'm shocked when she starts laughing. "I fell," she says, pointing out the obvious.

I choke back my laughter, offering her my hand. "You did, but are you okay?"

The smile forming on her face is radiant, pulling me further in. "I'm great, but now my clothes are drenched. Good thing you suggested I leave my phone in your car."

I would have left mine too, but I couldn't risk the anxiety of not knowing whether Bailey would call, so mine is sitting next to my keys and water on the ground next to the fountain. The ringer is on full volume, so I'm not worried about missing a call.

"Well, I didn't think you were going to fall in the water,

but I'm glad I suggested it," I say, and Marley takes my hand, letting me pull her upright. I let go once she's steady, despite how much I don't want to.

"Is it okay if we hit the rest of the fountains another day? I feel really gross now, and I'd love to change into something else," she says, adjusting her denim shorts before wringing out the ends of her hair. I look away, trying not to stare at the sight of Marley's wet shirt clinging to her curves in a way that'll haunt me in my dreams. I'd love to get Marley out of those clothes too, but the last thing I want to do is scare her off by popping a boner.

"Sure, I'll drive us back," I say, stepping out of the fountain, snagging my things.

We walk in silence toward the car, our shoes leaving wet footprints in our wake. I tried to tell Marley she should take her shoes off before the first fountain, but she hopped in with hers on before I could say anything, and it only made sense to follow Marley's lead.

"Thanks for doing this with me. I had a lot of fun," she says, and it feels selfish to be glad she called me. I've been trying to leave the ball in her court, because if it were up to me, I'd spend as much time with Marley as I can, but I'm trying to respect her relationship, even if Trent isn't.

"I did too. I haven't done this since my first week freshman year," I say, spotting my Jeep parked on the side of the road where we left it.

"I bet football keeps you plenty busy," she says, and I notice the smile on her face fading.

I gently nudge her with my elbow. "I mean, it does, but it's all about finding a healthy balance. You make time for the things you want."

She kicks a small pebble on the sidewalk, sending it skittering across the concrete. Her shoulders sink a little as she sighs. "My dad has always been really busy with his job, but he made a point to be home every night for dinner—even if my mom was cooking, and she's a really horrible cook. She's successfully burned water before, and if I hadn't seen it with my own eyes, I wouldn't have believed it happened. He's never missed a birthday, or a school event, and if he can do it . . . then why can't other people do the same?" she asks, and years of being my older sister's best friend has trained me for this moment.

"Do you want me to think of an answer, or just listen?" I ask, opening the passenger door for her. I know what Marley's implying, and I hate Trent for making her head spin like this.

Marley's cheeks flush and she shakes her head. "Sorry, I'm just thinking out loud. Don't mind me."

"It's okay. I like hearing what you have to say," I say, shutting the door behind her, walking around to the other side.

I flip the air conditioning off so Marley doesn't get cold, but there's not much I can do about the hard top being off. She gasps as I turn the car on, contorting herself into an awkward position so she's not sitting directly on the seat. "I'm getting your seat wet. Fuck, I'm so sorry," she apologizes, and I pull her back down into the seat.

"I don't care. Do you have any idea how many times these seats have been rained on because I forgot to put the top on? They'll be fine," I reassure Marley.

I tap my fingers restlessly against the steering wheel, sniffling as my nose runs. *How long has it been since I've taken a pill?* I can feel my knee start to ache, and it's only a matter of time before the ache turns into a sharp throb I can't ignore. After I've parked in her building's lot, I reach into my center console for the small bottle I keep for emergencies. Marley climbs out of the car first, and I grab a pill, swallowing it back with a swig of my water.

"What are you doing?" she asks, peering at me.

"I can feel a headache coming on so I took some meds to

help," I explain, flashing her an easy smile as my heart pounds in my chest.

"Oh, well I had some Tylenol inside I could have given you."

"No worries. I usually keep some stuff in my car, but thanks. You should head inside so you can change," I suggest, hoping she doesn't ask more questions because I don't have answers for her.

Marley laughs, looking down at her clothes, before cocking her head as she looks at me. "Are you not coming in? I'll be quick, I promise."

The only thing I have waiting for me at home is statistics, and I'd much rather hang out with Marley. "Are you sure it's fine?" I ask, scratching the back of my neck.

"Considering it's my apartment, and I'm inviting you in, yeah. I think it's fine," she says, and I follow along after her up the stairs. "I don't think Bria's here. She said something this morning about going out with some of her teammates after practice."

"Damn, I was actually only here to see her," I tease, trying not to let Marley know how fucking nervous I am right now.

Marley shakes her head, pulling a key out of her pocket to unlock the door. "Shut up, JJ," she says, motioning to the couch. "I'm going to change quick. You're welcome to sit anywhere, but the couch is super comfy."

Unlike Marley, I was able to keep my clothes fairly dry, except for when she started splashing me, and the breeze combined with the heat outside was enough to finish drying them on the way here. I sit down on the couch watching her disappear through a door in the back of the apartment.

"Your place is nice," I say, loudly enough for Marley to hear through her shut door. The decor fits her personality: simple, but tasteful.

"Thanks. My mom and Bria's had a blast picking every-thing out," she calls back.

I hear the opening of a door, and I turn to see Marley poking her head around the door. "Okay, I'm so sorry, but I have an odd question?"

"What's up?" I ask, leaning forward onto my knees.

"Do you mind if I take a quick shower to rinse off? I'm so sorry, I just feel gross, but if it makes you uncomfortable, I don't have to," she says quickly, and I can feel my heartbeat quicken in my chest. I should leave because this is a bad idea.

Is it what comes out of my mouth? *Nope.* I finally under-stand why it took Mirabelle so damn long to tell Henry how she felt about him. This is fucking terrifying, but I'm willing to take the pieces I can of Marley.

"Not a problem. It makes sense—you did take an unex-pected swim."

"Thanks, I'll be out in a minute! You can put a movie on if you want, and help yourself to anything in the kitchen." She smiles in relief, and I know I'm torturing myself. I nod, unable to form words, and I grab the remote to distract myself, but my thoughts are all over the place right now.

I hear the shower turn on, and all I can picture is Marley undressing, and what it would feel like to touch the soft curves of her body. My cock stiffens in my pants, and I know how wrong it is, but apparently my brain isn't getting the same memo.

I'd love to memorize every part of her body, treating Marley the way she deserves.

She's the best damn thing to ever happen to me. Trent deserves to rot in hell, because how dare he make her second guess herself? It doesn't take a genius to figure out Marley was talking about him earlier, and I'm a fucking coward for not telling her the truth. I can admit it's partially for my own selfish reasons because I think a part of me knows once she finds out, she'll want nothing to do with any of us.

The irony isn't lost on me the only reason Bailey calls and checks in with me is because I'm the only one who never lied to him. While everyone else kept things from him, I wasn't one of them.

How can I claim to love Marley when I'm not being honest with her?

If I ask him to, I know Asher would have my back, but I need to talk to him first before I do anything. I need proof if Marley doesn't believe me, and I'd rather not be scrambling for it when I tell her.

I pull out my phone, shooting her a quick text to let her know I had to run home quick, but I can come back later.

I feel like an asshole for letting Marley know I'm leaving in a text, but I have to do the right thing, even if it erases any hope of a future for us.

Driving back to my house feels like forever, but the anxiety in my stomach only grows when my phone buzzes with a text from Marley, asking if everything is okay. I shove the phone in my pocket, ignoring it as I walk by my roommates' cars. *Great, everyone is home.*

Luka is in the living room gaming with headphones on, and I find Asher in the kitchen working on his homework. "Hey," I say, and he groans, shoving the notebook away from him.

"Thank god you're back. I'm so tired of studying, but I need your help with stats. Don't these professors know it's only the third week of school? Why are they assigning so much," he complains, but Asher falters when he looks up at me. "What's wrong?"

"I was with Marley, and I need to tell her, Ash. I can't hide this from her."

"She's not here with you, right?" he asks, his words careful as Asher glances behind me.

My stomach turns to lead. "No, why?"

Asher drags a hand over his face, swearing under his breath. "Next year, we're getting a house with just us, okay? This drama is stressing me out, and I can't afford to have a breakout on my face right now. I'm trying to woo Bria, and she's stubborn as hell."

"He's up there with a girl, isn't he?" I connect the dots, laughing in disbelief. "Are you fucking kidding me?"

"This girl was with Trent when he came back, and they went straight up to his room," Asher says, only confirming I'm right to tell Marley the truth.

"This is fucking cruel. I should have told her that first day, and I'm not saying this because I . . ." I trail off, clearing my throat. "Marley deserves better than a boyfriend who can't keep his dick in his pants."

"Shit, you actually are in love with her," he says, staring at me.

"Yeah, I am, but this isn't about my feelings. This is about doing the right thing, and by saying nothing, we're enabling Trent," I say, just as a loud thump sounds from upstairs, perfectly on cue, proving my point for me.

"No, you're right. Keeping it from her is wrong," Asher agrees. "What do you need from me?"

I exhale in relief. "I just need you to confirm I'm telling the truth when I tell Marley, so it doesn't seem like I'm only telling her because I want her to be with me."

"Is that why you're doing it, or are you really doing it for her sake?" he asks, raising a dark eyebrow questioningly.

I'd be lying if I said it wasn't so she'd be with me, but that's not the *reason* I'm telling her. "I'm doing it for Marley. She deserves to know."

Asher stands up, shaking his head. "You know this will

start shit on the team, right? We have to live with Trent the rest of the school year," he says, stating the obvious as if I hadn't already considered it.

"He started this by cheating on Marley. I don't think he's going to care, because if he did, Trent would be with her right now, instead of some other chick." It's bullshit I haven't told her already, and I can only hope Marley will be able to forgive me for it.

"When are you going to tell her?"

"Now," I say, and Asher laughs.

"Goddamn, if I didn't know better, I'd think you have a death wish. Let me know if you need anything."

"Thanks, Ash. I appreciate it," I say, pulling my phone out to ask Marley if we can talk.

"Good luck!" my best friend calls after me, understanding I'm going to need all the luck I can get before this conversation.

Maybe Marley won't hate me. Actually, that's wishful thinking, but a guy can dream.

Jogging down the stairs quickly, my heart stops in my chest when I see Marley climbing out of her car parked on the side of the road. "Hey, I just sent you a text. I was about to drive back to your place," I say, forcing the words out.

Her long hair looks like she towel dried it, and her nose is tinged red with the beginnings of a sunburn. Marley smiles at me, and I wish she wouldn't. "I'm sorry, you just left in such a rush, I wanted to make sure everything was okay."

My insides twist with guilt, and I continue walking toward her. "Yeah, I'm sorry about that. Everything's fine, but Luka's inside gaming, so we should just go back to your place."

"Well, I kind of wanted to talk to Trent quick?" Marley reaches to play with her necklace as she looks at the house. *Oh fuck.*

"Actually, I'm pretty hungry. Do you want to get something to eat first? There's a smoothie place nearby," I ramble, trying to remain nonchalant as I step closer to my car.

"It won't take long, at least, I think it won't."

I hate this. I might have thought before it would be easier if Marley caught Trent in the act, but I don't want that for her. The last thing I want is for her to be hurt, and while I don't know the depth of their relationship, I think walking in on Trent with another girl would be worse than me telling her.

"Are you sure it can't wait until after smoothies?"

Marley looks at me with those blue eyes of hers making my knees weak, and I can tell she sees right through my bullshit. "Why don't you want me to go into the house, JJ?"

"Marley, we should go," I say softly, trying to be as gentle as possible. Her head looks back and forth between me and the house, and she shakes her head.

"No, I'm going inside."

Why didn't I tell her sooner? I catch her wrist loosely, stopping Marley as she turns. "Please, let's just go," I say, and Marley's right to look at me like I've betrayed her. *In a way, it's exactly what I've done.*

She slips from my grip, darting up the stairs to disappear into the house. "Oh fuck," I swear under my breath, following after her.

I'm through the door when Luka pokes his head in the hallway, his face twisted in confusion. "Why is Marley here?"

"Motherfucker," Asher swears, and I ignore both of them to follow after Marley as I hear her raise her voice for the first time since meeting her.

"You fucking asshole!"

CHAPTER EIGHT

Marley

I. THINK. WE. SHOULD. GO.

Each individual word echoes in my head, and I can't believe how stupid I've been. I didn't piece it together until JJ said a second time we should go, and then I saw the guilt lying in his features. Knowing JJ knew might hurt more than learning Trent's cheating on me.

I pause in front of Trent's closed door, and then I hear a moan from inside the room.

I.

Think.

We.

Should.

Go.

I push the door open, a hurricane of emotions swirling inside me at the sight of another girl riding my boyfriend.

"Oh yeah, just like that, baby." Trent groans, his hands tightly holding her hips, and my jaw hits the floor.

"You fucking asshole!"

Trent freezes, his head snapping in my direction, and the girl shrieks, covering her chest with her arms.

"Marley, babe, it's not what it looks like," Trent stammers, pushing her off him, and I see at least he had the decency to use a condom with her.

"Really? So you died, and she was trying to resuscitate you? Or was it the other way around?" I ask, laughing in disbelief as he grabs a pair of pants off the ground and she covers herself with a blanket. "Actually, last time I checked, CPR didn't involve getting naked and sticking your dick in another girl. Maybe I need to take the course again to find out."

"Who are you?" she asks.

"His *now* ex-girlfriend." *Judging by the look on her face, I guess he fooled us both.*

I actually felt bad driving over here because I was going to break up with Trent. I wanted to check on JJ too, but my main goal was to end my relationship.

I realized this afternoon when I was hanging out with JJ, I felt more like myself than I have in my entire relationship with Trent. Bria was right when she told me I shouldn't miss out on something great by settling for something mediocre.

I feel *way* less bad now.

"You have a girlfriend?" she snaps at him, and Trent ignores her, tugging the pants up over his hips to walk toward me.

"Babe, please, I made a mistake. She doesn't mean anything to me, I promise. *It's you, I love you.* I was upset and stressed about not being able to see you this week, and I'm so afraid I'm going to lose you. I've been so nervous you'll figure out I'm not good enough for you," Trent murmurs, speaking quickly as he reaches to cup my face.

Oh my god. Is he serious right now?

I shake my head, moving away from him before he can touch me. "No, Trent. Don't you dare try to twist this to make me feel bad for you. You don't get to say you love me when you were just having sex with another girl! I mean, did you even bother to change the sheets?"

"It's you and me. Don't do this to me. Think of what our parents will say? They are so excited about our relationship," Trent pleads, panicking because I'm not giving in. If anything, he should be fucking afraid of what my parents will say.

He tries reaching for me again, but I shove him away this time. Apparently, dodging his hands before wasn't clear enough of a message.

"Don't touch me," I say, my voice shaking from how angry I am. "You cheated on me."

He takes a step back as the girl finishes pulling her clothes on awkwardly. She walks wide to avoid Trent, her cheeks flaming red. "I'm so sorry. I had no idea he had a girlfriend, or I never would have come here. I got his number at a party a couple weeks ago, and Trent called me today," she says as I step aside to let her leave, and the weight of her words hit me square in the chest.

A. Couple. Weeks. Ago.

If Trent wasn't panicking before, he is now. "She's lying. She was all over me, Mar. I didn't do anything wrong. You have to believe me," he pleads.

"*Il ment. Trent t'a trompé. Je suis désolé. Je revenais pour te le dire,*"[1] JJ's soft voice says from behind me, and I flinch.

I can't look at him, or I'm going to burst into tears. Seeing Trent with another girl is awful, but not as awful as JJ knowing about it and not telling me immediately.

"JJ, you told her it's not true, right?" he asks, his voice full of distress, looking to the wrong person for help.

"How many?" I ask Trent, finally thinking logically. She got his number a few weeks ago, so I don't think I'm wrong to

---

1. He's lying. Trent has been cheating on you. I'm sorry. I was coming back to tell you.

ask if there's more. He has the nerve to feign confusion, attempting to reach for me again. "I don't want you to touch me so stop," I snap, and Trent freezes.

"What?"

I inhale a short breath, trying to reel my anger back in. "How many girls?" I clarify, and he falls silent, looking away. "Once? Twice?" I ask, and I think I'm going to be sick. "You're unbelievable. Do you even know how many times you've cheated on me?" I ask, laughter escaping me as Trent finally looks at me. He probably thinks I'm crazy.

"What was I supposed to do when you wouldn't say you love me back?" Trent asks, and I only laugh harder. *That's his excuse?*

"You're trying to defend yourself by bringing up how I didn't say I love you? I'm not going to say it if I don't mean it because it's not fair, and definitely not an excuse to fuck other girls, Trent!"

He doesn't even think he did anything wrong. What the actual fuck is wrong with him?

"Fuck you. Don't call me ever again," I say, whirling around, only to wind up face to face with JJ. He steps out of my way as Trent continues spouting lies behind me I don't care to listen to.

I'm distinctly aware JJ's following behind me, but I don't want to talk to him right now. I want to go back to my apartment where I probably should have stayed in the first place, eat ice cream, and punch a pillow I can pretend is Trent's face.

"Marley, I'm sorry," JJ says before I get to my car.

"Go away. I don't want to talk," I say, grabbing the door handle of my car. JJ's hand quickly falls on the frame, keeping it closed as I pull, effectively trapping me against the vehicle. "I want to leave," I say, seeing his reflection in the window.

"I know, and you can leave, but please let me drive you. I need to explain—"

I turn to face him, and he's standing so close to me, I can smell the salt from his sweat earlier. *Fuck, it's easy to forget how much taller he is than me, and I'm not short to begin with.* "Explain what? What can you possibly have to say to make me trust you again?" I whisper, half of me praying JJ has a magic trick up his sleeve.

His emerald gaze is filled with hopelessness, and I'm actually afraid of what he's about to say. "Marley," JJ falters on my name, and I don't think I want to hear this, but I'm frozen in place. "I didn't know what to do when I found out it was you. I was going to tell whoever Trent's girlfriend was that he was cheating, but then it was you standing there. It felt like a goddamn miracle, and I didn't know what to do. I'm sorry."

All of the anger whooshes out of me, and now . . . all I feel is devastation. This hurts more than everything inside a minute ago. "Wait—you've known since you first saw me?"

JJ's been lying to me this entire time.

"I swear, I was on my way to tell you. I didn't know if you'd believe me, so I needed to ask Asher if he'd back me up."

"You didn't think I'd believe you? JJ, I trust you more than I've ever trusted anyone. *Trusted*—I trusted you more than I've ever trusted anyone," I correct myself, willing my voice not to crack.

"Marley, I'm sorry I didn't tell you sooner, but you can trust me. I've always been on your side, rooting for you," he says, his shoulders sinking with defeat, but I think I've reached my capacity for the day.

"I want you to leave me alone," I say, tears filling my vision. I rest my hands on his chest, pushing him away, and this time, JJ doesn't fight me, or try to stop me when I climb into my car.

CHAPTER NINE

JJ

"I KNOW YOU ALREADY KNOW THIS, BUT STILL, HERE we are, JJ. What the hell are you thinking?" Billy asks, crossing her arms over her chest as the e-stim pulses on my throbbing knee underneath the heating pad.

"I'm cleared to practice and play like normal," I respond, and she scoffs.

"But you're not one hundred percent yet. It can take up to two years after surgery to play the way you used to."

I know.

I fucking know.

"How much have you been running?" Billy asks, narrowing her eyes. Considering she's working through her lunch to help me right now, I'm not really sure I want to piss her off. "Do I even want to ask if you're wearing your brace?"

I flash a charming smile at her, hoping she'll drop the lecture sooner than later. "I'll give you whatever answer helps you sleep better at night."

"JJ, do I look like I'm in the mood to laugh right now?" she asks as the machine beeps, the electrical stimulation machine turning off, and Billy takes off the heating pad, beginning to disconnect the pads. "Lay back," she instructs, and I sigh, following her directions.

Billy starts rotating my leg, testing to see my range of motion. I focus on my breathing, do my best not to let it show how it hurts when she starts massaging my iliotibial band on the side of my thigh, but fuck, the muscle there is wound tighter than I am. "You need to take it easier. If you don't, I'll be forced to tell your coaches how often you're in here for treatment," she warns, and I clench my jaw as she digs her fingers into a particularly tender spot.

Billy understands better than anyone what this injury did to me. She's been working with me since I returned to Beaumont after my surgery, angry at the world, and essentially, Billy told me to get my shit together.

"I'm fine, I promise," I say, but I'm not sure if I'm lying to her or myself.

This time, I can't hold back a hiss when she presses the heel of her hand down on the band. "Lay off the running, or you're going to spend this season the same way you spent the last."

I can't stop running. It's the only thing helping me breathe easier. The last two weeks have been rough without Marley. I've been trying to put pen to paper, but even knowing she won't get the letters, I still haven't been able to justify my actions. I ran into Bria a few days ago, and she's started joining me on my early morning runs when the rest of the world is still sleeping. It's nice having company, and we run at a brisk enough pace that there's little oxygen left over for us to talk about the elephant in the room.

I spent eight hundred and ninety-two days dreaming about Marley. I never expected I'd have to start counting again so soon after finding her.

I've heard my father explain the word *almost* a thousand times—it can be used to describe all the things you could have done or didn't do.

I think watching Marley leave me again is the perfect description of *almost*.

"I'll try," I mumble, dropping the facade. It's not like Billy doesn't already see right through it.

But if I can't run . . . then all the thoughts in my head are going to be rampaging constantly with no reprieve. My fists clench as I try to get through the temporary pain I'm in right now. This is nothing compared to the constant ache in my chest, though. The pain I feel on a daily basis is worse, threatening to pull me into the ground, swallowing me alive. I just need a break where I don't feel like I'm wading through quicksand, where everything isn't so fucking hard.

Running is where I find my quiet.

Without it, I don't know who I'll be.

"Is there anything you need to talk about?"

"Not unless you want to hear about my pathetic love life where I fucked things up with a girl I'm not even dating," I say, and the only hint of surprise is her eyebrows raising ever so slightly. I've never spoken to Billy about girls, but there's no one else in here, so I don't have to worry about someone hearing me admit to fucking over my teammate.

"First of all, language. Secondly, how?"

"By not telling her that her boyfriend was cheating on her," I grit out, feeling both my mental and physical pain spike.

"JJ."

I exhale sharply, closing my eyes as Billy continues torturing me. "I know. I messed up, but we kind of have history, and I was worried if I told her, she'd think I was making it up so they'd break up. I hadn't seen her in almost three years, and it caught me off guard seeing her again."

"So you said nothing," Billy interprets correctly, finally letting up on some of the pressure she's applying.

"Marley transferred schools to be here with him. I wanted to tell her, but selfishly, I was content to take what I could without crossing any lines, so I didn't tell her. In my defense, I was leaving to tell her when she showed up at the house while Trent had a girl over, and she walked in on them."

"You can sit up, we'll ice and then you're good," Billy says, and I sit up, leaning against the wall. "I'm sorry, you said Trent, as in Trent Hart, the quarterback?" she asks, bringing over the compression sleeve attached to an ice machine.

"Yep," I answer, helping her slide the sleeve into place, tightening the Velcro.

Billy's mahogany features soften as her dark gaze meets mine. "Sounds like a fucked-up situation to be in. How are you dealing with it?"

"Language," I mock, trying to lighten the mood, but Billy doesn't laugh. *Okay, then.* Turning my head to avoid her scrutiny, I opt to look at a chart on the wall explaining the different colors of urine and how hydrated it means you are. "I run," I admit quietly as she flips the machine on, feeling the relief immediately.

"Oh, so she's the reason you're killing your knee. Good to know," Billy says, letting my comment about her language slide. A little unfair Billy can curse, and I can't, but she makes the rules in here.

"I'm not killing my knee," I protest. "It's fine."

"Do both of us a favor and talk to her before you tear something again. I don't want to spend every day with you rehabbing this knee again."

I laugh, smiling at Billy. "You know you miss having me in here every day, but I'm not going to tear anything."

Billy shakes her head, but it's the smile she's fighting that tells a different story. "Whatever you say, JJ."

"Hey, Dad," I answer, trying to catch my breath after stopping my run to answer his call.

"Hey, buddy. Sorry I missed your call earlier," Dad says, and at the sound of his familiar voice, I feel a pang of home-sickness. "What's up?"

I walk to keep my muscles from cramping as my lungs thank me for the break. "Nothing much, just out on a run."

"That's my boy," Dad says. "How's your knee holding up?"

"It's practically perfect," I say, stretching it out in front of me, not a single twinge of pain. It could be on fire right now, but I wisely waited until my meds kicked in before taking off. I just can't forget to ice it after.

If he finds out it's bothering me at all, he'll make me go to the doctor. It's fine, but it needs time to get back to how it used to be.

"Great. I've been looking at Hunter's schedule and yours to see what games we'll be able to make it to."

"Don't forget Henry's games," I remind him, using the bottom of my shirt to wipe some of the sweat from my face.

"And to think I thought retiring would mean less time dedicated to football," he jokes, and I laugh quietly. "Has Hunter said anything about the transfer?"

I chuckle, recalling the cluster of texts I received the other day, explaining the situation with the new running back on the team, followed up with Hunter asking if I'd consider trans-ferring. "I've heard plenty about it. Hunt asked if I'd transfer, but I like it here."

"That's what I told him too when he asked me if I thought you'd go for it. He'll figure it out, but hopefully sooner than later. Hunter's always been the sensible one of you all."

"I would take offense, but you're not wrong." I've been in my fair share of scuffles on the field playing against guys who thought it was okay to make comments about Mirabelle to me. My temper runs lower than my siblings, but the one thing I can't stop from getting to me are comments about my family. Guys tend to go one of two ways when it comes to my family: they either think it's really cool my dad is Sebastian Walker, or they think I've been handed everything and I don't deserve to be on the field.

The game my knee was injured in last year is a prime example. The linebacker I was up against was spouting shit all game to get in my head, and I tried my best to ignore it, until he vividly described how he'd like to pass my sister around their locker room since she clearly likes being on display, and I lost it. I shoved him, telling him if he played half as well as he ran his mouth, they'd be winning instead of getting blown out—with a few more colorful words added in. It wasn't enough to attract anyone's attention because Asher pulled me away before it could escalate further. On the next play, he came out of nowhere as I was catching a pass from Trent, hitting me at the right angle with enough force to cause my knee to twist underneath me as we hit the ground, tearing the ligaments almost instantly.

The linebacker was ejected for targeting and unnecessary roughness, but I'm not sure if he was actually trying to hurt me or not. All I know is the hit wasn't an accident. I never told anyone what he said or how I think it wasn't an accident because I didn't want Mirabelle to feel guilty for something else out of her control.

"I'll let you know when we've figured out which ones we're coming to, but at least when I come to your games, I'm not committing a cardinal sin by rooting for the enemy," Dad continues, and I know it drives them nuts Hunter picked Duke's rival, Oceanside.

"You're ridiculous," I say, shaking my head. "Hunter's happy there."

"I know, but literally any other school would have been better," Dad complains.

Uncle Owen and Dad played for Duke with Henry's dad in college, but because of how much Dad donates to the program, they were nervous about putting the money at risk if things went sour with either Hunter or I on the team. It was different when Mirabelle went there because she was on the gymnastics team and a gold medalist, but I'm not mad about it. I wanted to make it on my own somewhere other than where I would always be known as a legacy—hence, ending up at Beaumont.

"It was his choice," I remind him, laughing under my breath. "I miss you guys. I'm sorry I haven't called much since getting back here."

"It's okay. You're in college and busy with your own life," Dad says, and I know he doesn't mean it the way it sounds, but I still feel guilty.

"How are you and Mom doing?" I ask, and it's when Dad hesitates before responding I know he's lying. I wonder what Bailey would say if he knew in the aftermath of him leaving, we've all become professional liars trying to take care of each other.

"We're doing alright. Don't worry about us, though. Your focus should be on football and school. Mom's happy about Mirabelle and Henry getting engaged because it gives her something new to put her energy into."

It's what he doesn't say that kills me. They haven't been doing well since Bailey ran away, and while it's affected us all differently, everyone blames themselves. My parents have never done anything but love us, and I don't know what it is Bailey thinks they lied about, but it breaks my fucking heart for them. If I weren't so damn relieved every time Bailey checks in,

I'd probably scream at him. *I'm terrified if I start screaming, I'll never stop.*

I pull at my shirt as if it can help assuage the pressure building in my chest, compressing my lungs to the point I'm struggling to take a breath. "I haven't heard from him," I say, guilt bleeding into my voice.

"JJ, you don't need to carry this weight. It's not your burden to bear," he says, but my stomach still churns with guilt. I need to keep running.

"He's my little brother, of course it is." Everything is getting too loud in my head, and I need it to stop. "Bailey should be calling any day to check in."

"Will . . ." Dad trails off, clearing his throat. "Will you please let us know when he does call?"

This is so fucking unfair. None of this should be happening.

"Of course, Dad," I say.

"Thanks, JJ. I really appreciate it."

My heart is pounding in my chest, and I can't fucking breathe. "Sorry, but I still have a couple of miles left to go. I'll call Mom when I'm done."

"I love you, son," Dad says, and I know he does. I only wish it were possible for us to have a phone call without being reminded I'm the one Bailey calls. I can't remember the last time we talked and he wasn't brought up.

"Love you too," I say, ending the call. Double checking the arm strap for my phone holder, I adjust my headphones before taking off at a fast jog, my knee momentarily protesting at the abruptness.

I need to run until I can't feel this anymore.

I don't want to feel like this anymore, but I don't know how to make it stop.

My pace finally slows when the only thing I can focus on is how my lungs are gasping for air while my knee throbs incessantly. I can feel the sweat dripping down my body, and I drop to the grass next to the sidewalk, trying to catch my breath. I'm not even sure I want to know how pathetic I look right now, but it can't be worse than I feel.

I drag my hands over my face, my hands shaking as I take out my headphones when I spot the small store on the other side of the road, tucked between two larger ones making it nearly invisible to see.

Hope's Flowers.

Maybe I could use a little bit of hope right now.

Despite the way my body protests any movement, I pull myself up, staggering across the street following the instinct tugging in my chest. After stepping in, I'm embarrassed by how ragged my breathing is as I look around at all the delicate flowers.

What the hell am I doing? Marley wants nothing to do with me now, and I'm a walking disaster.

I shouldn't be here.

"Are you okay?" an older man asks from behind the counter.

"I'm sorry, I just . . ." I trail off, unsure if I have it in me to tell another lie today. Eventually, I'm not sure I'll know what the truth is.

"It's okay. Let me grab you some water from the back," he says, standing up, and I stare in surprise as he uses a cane to move toward the door on the back of the store.

"You don't have to," I protest, and he waves me off.

"You need it more than I do. Besides, it's better for me if you don't die in my wife's shop. Hope might come back from the dead to take me with her if I let that happen," he jests, and I relax a little.

"I'd prefer not to die," I agree as he returns, water bottle in hand. "Thank you, I'm JJ," I say, accepting his kindness.

"Eddie," he replies. "So what brings you in? Young men

like you don't usually come in unless it's Valentine's Day," he says while I take a long drink of water, and it makes a world of difference.

"A family tradition," I answer, and for the first time in a long time, it feels like maybe there's a chance things will work out.

CHAPTER TEN

Marley

"This time it was only one flower, and it was left at the door," Bria says, walking through the front door.

I continue measuring out the cookie dough I've mixed in the kitchen as the oven beeps to tell me it's preheated. Music isn't working as an outlet right now, because Trent doesn't feel worth putting into words on paper, which leaves me with baking. Unfortunately, I inherited my mother's genes in the kitchen in every capacity, so there's a very good chance these cookies will turn out like shit, even if they look fine now. "I hope you're throwing it away."

"This one's pretty," she says, twirling it in her hands as she flops onto the couch. "Do you mind if I keep it?"

"Sure, if you want. Just because I don't want anything of Trent's, doesn't mean you can't reap the benefits of his apology tour."

"Understandably so, but does that include his room-mate?" Bria asks, and I scoop more dough onto the cookie sheet next to me.

"He lied to me."

She sighs, and I glance up now, spying the flower in her

hand. The lavender petals are beautiful, and I'm surprised Trent bothered to pick out something so beautiful *and* deliver it himself. Everything else has been extravagant bouquets of red roses, and the delivery guy has finally stopped looking surprised when I tell him I don't want them.

"What?" I ask, trying not to get defensive.

"Marley, I'm not trying to defend JJ, but what was he supposed to do? Tell you immediately after seeing you for the first time in two and a half years your boyfriend's cheating on you?"

"Yes," I say immediately. Rationally, I know he was put in a shitty position, but JJ still should have told me. I would have believed him.

"Well, then I think you should give him another chance. I saw how JJ looked at you when he first saw you, and he is the last person who would ever try to hurt you."

"He lied."

"Technically, he just didn't tell you. Unless you asked him if Trent was cheating, then JJ didn't lie," she counters, and sometimes it's really annoying having a best friend studying pre-law.

"Bria, I don't want to talk about him."

"I just think you should know JJ wants to talk to you," Bria says, and my hand slips, knocking the tray of cookies onto the tile floor with a clang.

"Shit," I swear, dragging my hands over my face.

"Five second rule?"

"No, they're ruined," I say, dropping down to start picking up the pieces.

Honestly, I'm pissed off about Trent, but that's not why I'm upset. I know I was going to the house to break up with Trent regardless of whether I caught him with another girl, but it's JJ who has my heart twisted into a knot I'm not sure where to begin untangling.

"They're not ruined—the cookies can be fixed, and if not, start over," Bria says, as I stand up, and I'm aware she's not talking about cookies anymore.

"Bria."

"Marley," Bria returns my scolding tone, and I throw the globs of dough in the trash can, washing my hands to get rid of the sticky feeling.

"There's nothing to say. You can argue he didn't lie all you want, but JJ didn't tell me the truth either. It's not fair for you to ask me to get over it already," I say, crossing my arms over my chest.

"I'm not asking you to get over it. What you choose to do with knowing JJ wants to talk to you is all on you, babe," Bria says simply, but it's not that simple.

I'm hurt, and I don't know if I can trust him.

"How do you even know JJ wants to talk to me?"

She twirls the flower slowly, the delicate petals drawing my attention again. I'm having a really hard time believing Trent could have picked out this flower. "Because I talked to him."

"When?" I ask, surprise getting the better of me. I shouldn't care Bria talked to JJ.

Bria pops the lid on her water, taking a long sip. "I thought you didn't care?" she muses, standing up and stretching.

Asher. It has to be because of Asher. Still, it doesn't help with the jealousy brimming under my skin. I really shouldn't care Bria saw JJ, but she needs to take a step back, or I might explode. I'm not an angry or brash person, and I don't like carrying this much anger.

"I don't," I snap back because I do care, and I instantly feel bad for snapping at her when this time, she falls silent. Bria's pushing my buttons on purpose, but it's what family does. Bria's as much my family as my own flesh and blood, and she's always been blunt and outspoken, exactly like her mother, who also has no problem calling it like it is. On the other end, I'm reserved like my parents.

I dry my hands off, exhaling softly. "I'm sorry, I shouldn't have snapped at you," I say, and Bria stands up, leaning against the counter next to me.

She smiles at me reassuringly. "Don't be sorry, Mar. I'm trying to get a reaction out of you, because it proves me right. You have feelings for JJ, even if you're trying to convince yourself not to have them."

"So you haven't talked to him?" I ask, and Bria grabs a spoon, dipping it in the remaining cookie dough.

"No, I have. We go running together in the mornings now."

They run together now? What exactly has JJ said to her? Shit, is it bad I want to know?

"Is he okay?" I ask quietly.

"Honestly, we don't talk about you, but JJ's not subtle. He wants to ask, but I think he's trying to be respectful and wait for you to come to him. He runs like the devil is hot on his heels, so take that however you will with how he's doing. Asher told me JJ knows he was wrong not to tell you right away, and he'd do everything differently if he could," Bria says, and I'm not sure how I feel right now. As if Bria can tell how conflicted I am, she continues, "I did learn another interesting bit from Asher, though. I guess since they've met freshman year, JJ hasn't so much as looked at another girl because he's been waiting to find you."

If anything, it only makes me feel worse because I waited for JJ too. I waited until . . . *I didn't.* I got in my head last year before I applied to Beaumont, and my friend, Leo, was with me. I was stressed and sad—neither of which was a good reason to do it, but I still kissed him anyway. One thing led to another, and it was awkward—*oh my god, it was so awkward*—we agreed to never, *ever* speak of it again. Then I met Trent in

April, and it had been two years by that point since I had seen JJ, so I tried to forget about the boy with vivid green eyes who asked me not to forget him.

I wish I had waited, because then we wouldn't be in this mess.

The terrifying thing is how badly I do want to see JJ, and maybe it's why I'm trying so damn hard to focus on how he didn't tell me. Maybe I need to remind myself he's human, and allowed to make mistakes, especially when it's obvious he wasn't hiding it maliciously.

I know I'm not entirely innocent, but I never crossed any lines. Being jealous of another girl talking to JJ and calling him to hang out is so different from fucking other girls while Trent and I were together.

"I—" The sound of a knock on the front door interrupts me, and I look at Bria in surprise. "Are you expecting anyone?"

"No, but if it's Asher trying to make a romantic gesture, tell him I'm not here," she says, retreating to the back of the apartment.

"Are you really hiding right now? Asher is like a golden retriever trapped inside a twenty-two year old," I say, rolling my eyes as I walk to the door.

I open the door, expecting Asher to be on the other side, but instead it's Trent, holding a bouquet of red roses, exactly like the rest of the bouquets up to this point. He thrusts them at me, stepping inside before I can slam the door in his face.

"Marley, babe, I'm so sorry. You have no idea how awful I feel. I love you so much and I've been miserable without you, but I wanted to give you space so you'd see how much better we are together. Those other girls meant nothing to me, and I can't imagine being with anyone but you. Please let me show you I'm different now. Don't throw away everything we've been building together because of a few mistakes. We can grow from this."

"Like further apart?" I retort back, absolutely stunned by everything coming out of his mouth. "I saw exactly how you managed just fine with other girls, and it didn't seem like there were any problems."

"I made mistakes, but that's all they were. Think of everything we could be if you just gave me another chance. I have never felt like this about anyone before, and I know you're not going to end us over a couple mistakes, right?" he asks, and I can't believe the audacity of Trent.

"I'm not giving you another chance, and it doesn't matter how much space you give me. I'm not changing my mind. We're over," I say firmly, hoping Bria can hear all this.

And then Trent smiles at me. "You don't mean that."

I hear Bria laugh behind me while I stare at Trent, wondering how I could have been so blind to see past his bullshit. "I actually do mean it, because if you truly want to be with me, you wouldn't have looked twice at another girl, which means you either wanted to use me as a fuck buddy, or you wanted me for my last name. I don't really care to find out which one it is, but we're done. I want you to leave, and take those with you, because I want nothing to do with you. Don't send any deliveries or leave any at my door," I say bluntly, and his jaw unhinges in surprise.

"I haven't left any at your door. I was trying to give you space, so everything I've sent has been through a delivery service," he says, ignoring the part where I said we're done. My heart stutters in my chest, realizing the beautiful lavender rose Bria found at the door is JJ's flower.

"It doesn't matter. Please don't send any others. You need to go," I say, doubling down.

Trent's jaw clenches, and I'm so ready to be done with him. "I think it does matter. Were you cheating on me?" he asks, and I shake my head.

"No. I never cheated on you. Get out," I say firmly, and he

attempts to cross his arms over his chest, but the obscenely large bouquet of flowers in his hands makes it difficult.

"I can't believe you're looking down on me like you're so much better than I am, when you were doing the same thing." Trent scoffs, tossing the flowers onto the couch.

"Marley told you to leave. Get the fuck out," Bria says harshly, and his eyes widen in surprise as if he can't believe she's speaking to him this way.

It's enough he backs up through the door, and I shut it, flipping the lock.

What the fuck just happened?

"You okay?" Bria asks, and I laugh in disbelief.

"Think there's any chance I can forget I ever dated him?" I ask, and she wraps her arms around me.

"I can pretend to have the memory of a goldfish if it makes you feel better," she says, hugging me.

"Actually, yeah, that would help," I say, but my gaze is stuck on the purple flower sitting on the counter.

It's midnight, and I still can't fall asleep. I've practically chewed my nails to nubs, and I'm sure I'll be horrified in the morning by the state they're in, but I've been lying here staring at the ceiling, waiting to fall asleep. I don't think it helps I've been replaying every moment with JJ in my head, starting from when I first met him, up until the present.

As annoying as Bria was this afternoon by refusing to let me hide from reality, I think she was right. JJ technically never lied to me about Trent, and thinking back on it, JJ was very deliberate with what he said and when he chose to be silent. What I can't figure out is why he thought I wouldn't believe him? If I were to believe anyone, it would have been him.

I roll over, fluffing my pillow, but it's no use. I can't think hard enough to magically come up with the answers, so I might as well go straight to the source.

The phone rings only once before he answers, and instinctively, I hold my breath. "Hello?" he asks, his voice laced with sleep, and I instantly regret calling. Of course he was sleeping, he probably has morning weights, and it's after midnight. "Marley?"

"Hi," I say. "I'm sorry if I woke you up."

"Don't apologize. Are you okay?" JJ asks, and my heart physically aches hearing his voice.

"Yeah." I don't know what to say now that we're actually on the phone together.

I hear him yawn and the rustle of his sheets. "I'm really happy to hear from you, and I'm definitely not complaining, but you do know it's the middle of the night, right?"

I spin the ring on my thumb, the hopefulness in his deep voice tugs at my heartstrings. "Why?" I blurt out. Until I have an answer, we have no shot of moving past this.

"Why what?"

"Why didn't you tell me? Why didn't you believe in me enough to know I would believe you?"

I hear him inhale, and I put the phone on speakerphone, resting it on the pillow. "Because I was afraid," he admits, but I need more.

"Afraid of what?" I ask, pressing for specifics.

"From the moment I learned Trent had a girlfriend, which ironically was the same day you came over, I planned to tell her he was cheating. But then it was you, and I couldn't believe I was finally in the same room as you until it dawned on me *why* we were in the same room again. I was afraid if I told you, you would think I was trying to break you guys up, but on the flip side, I was afraid you'd be angry at me for not telling you."

A soft laugh of irony bubbles from me. "I am angry at you for not telling me."

"Really? I couldn't tell," JJ muses. "I was coming back to tell you," he says, and I recall how he walked out of the house with purpose.

"I think I needed time to process. I don't know what I would have done if you had told me, but I still wish you had," I say, pulling the blankets up over my shoulders. "I would have believed you," I whisper.

"I'm sorry, Marley."

"I know you are."

"Is it a good sign you're calling me?" he asks, the same anxiety I'm feeling bleeding into his normally confident tone, and if there were anything on my nails left, I'd be chewing them.

"I don't know." My answer is honest, despite knowing it's not what he wants to hear.

"It's okay. I want you to take all the time you need. I'm here whenever you need me, or even if you don't need me. I'm here, Marley."

His words cause a smile to form on my face, my brain finally quieting from the madness of trying to decipher everything.

"Goodnight, JJ," I say, feeling a thousand times better than where I started the day.

"Goodnight, Marley," he says, and I wait for him to hang up, but he doesn't, and neither do I.

I fall asleep listening to the steady sound of JJ breathing.

CHAPTER ELEVEN

I'VE BEEN TRYING TO GIVE MARLEY SPACE, BUT IT'S harder than I thought, especially when she's the only person I want to talk to. After the first night, she's called me a couple of times over the last week and a half, giving me a second reason to sleep with my ringer at full volume after I hit the point of exhaustion when even my insomnia can't fight off sleep.

She opens up a little more with each call, and I think I'm slowly winning her forgiveness.

I still haven't seen her in person, but Bria made a comment a few days ago on our run that Marley seems more like herself, breaking our unspoken agreement to not talk about our roommates.

I'm glad she's doing better.

The only days Bria and I haven't run together was the day before our away game last weekend, and the day after because I couldn't move, even after taking my pills. I'm lucky Asher doesn't know she's running with me, or he'd be crawling out of bed to join us. I love the guy, but I don't feel like subjecting myself to an hour of his painful attempt at flirting every day.

Asher groans, tossing his controller to the side. "How the

hell are you winning? I never even see you play video games unless I ask you to," he grumbles, and I grin at him.

"Guess I'm just better than you."

"Shut the fuck up." He rolls his eyes, reaching for where he threw the controller. "Rematch, but this time, keep your hands where I can see them."

My hands have always been where he can see them, but whatever. "You think I'm cheating?"

"How else are you winning?"

"Maybe you just suck," I say, laughing at the stunned expression on his face as he presses start on the game.

"Maybe you're cheating," Asher insists, leaning forward to get into his ready position. Sometimes he makes it really hard to remember why we're friends. I shake my head, leaning back against the cushions as I try to remember which button on the controller does what.

Asher's head damn near explodes when I win, and he turns everything off. "This is bullshit." He scoffs, walking out of the room.

"Ash, come on! We could have played another round. I'll even let you beat me this time," I call after him, and his face is cherry red when he walks back into the living room, an energy drink in hand.

"That makes it so much worse, JJ. Now I'd rather lose than have you let me win."

"Dude, I don't know what to tell you then."

He sticks his tongue out at me. "You suck."

"You swallow," I reply.

Luka walks into the room, flopping onto a recliner. "Did Asher lose again?" he asks, glancing at the dark television.

"I hate both of you," Asher complains, pulling his phone out of his pocket.

"Don't worry. I won't tell Bria you can't beat me. I have a

feeling she doesn't date losers, but definitely not sore losers," I taunt, and he flips me off, causing Luka to laugh.

"Walker's right, but I bet he can't beat me," Luka says, tipping his head in my direction.

Yeah, I'm not falling for that. "I think Ash could use the practice instead," I suggest, knowing Asher can't turn down a challenge, even if it means getting his ass handed to him.

I like Luka, but he has awful taste in picking a best friend, because Trent would be the absolute last person I'd ever want to hold that title. I spend every day watching him do one of three things: one day, Trent misses Marley, and the next, he's claiming she cheated on him with some guy who left a flower at her door, or he's fucking his way through the cheerleaders.

It's taking everything in me not to beat the shit out of Trent when he talks about Marley. I don't even care if Trent finds out I'm the one who left the flower for her.

Purple roses signify love at first sight, and I can't think of a better way to describe my feelings for Marley. I've loved her from the moment I laid eyes on her, and I never stopped. I know what flowers mean in my family, and there is zero doubt in my mind Marley is my forever person. All I can hope is I'm hers, too.

I pass the controller to Luka as Asher turns the television back on, just as my phone rings next to me on the couch. I grab it, and the second I see the screen, everything around me fades into background noise.

Blocked caller.

It's him.

I stand up immediately, sprinting up the stairs to escape to my room. My fingers are shaking as I accept the call, my chest tightening painfully. "Bailey?"

There's a hoarse cough, and finally, I hear my little brother's voice for the first time in nearly four months. "Hi."

"Are you okay?" I ask, sitting at my desk. I grab the piece

of paper I tried—*and failed*—to write a letter on to Marley last night and my pen, straining to hear anything in the background I can tell the private investigator.

Bailey sighs, coughing again. "I'm okay. Sorry I haven't called. It took me longer than normal to get a phone."

He doesn't sound okay. "Where are you?" I ask this every time, hoping it will finally be the time he tells me.

Unfortunately, today isn't that day. "Somewhere safe," Bailey answers, but I'm not sure I believe him. I don't think he'd tell me if he wasn't safe, and the possibility terrifies the hell out of me.

"Bailey, *please*, tell me where you are."

"You know I can't tell you because you'll tell them. I'm not ready, JJ." He doesn't sound angry, he sounds tired.

I bet it's exhausting carrying around so much anger all the time.

"Mom and Dad miss you. They don't care about the past. They love you so much, B. They just want you to come home —*we all do.* Hunter and Mirabelle—"

I'm cut off by Bailey's now sharp tone. *"No."*

I feel my stomach twist, and I drag a hand over my face, feeling the stubble growing on my jaw after skipping shaving for a few days. *"Okay,"* I say, conceding before I push him too far. "Do you need me to send you anything? Money? Food? Clothes? A phone?" *Anything he wants, and I'll give it to him.*

"I'm fine, JJ. I don't need anything—just checking in."

I bite back the scream begging to escape my lungs. There's no way whatever money Bailey took with him has lasted this long. If he would accept just once, I'd stop feeling so damn useless because it'd give us a shot at finding him. Bailey's not stupid, though.

"I love you," I say instead, refusing to miss a chance of letting my brother know no matter what's happened, that hasn't changed.

"I love you too."

"Please, Bailey. Please come home," I whisper.

I hear yelling in the background on Bailey's end, but it's too indistinct for me to distinguish anything specific. "Shit, I have to go."

"Wait," I blurt out, panic flooding my system. I need more time. I'm not ready for the clock to restart.

"I'll call soon. Tell everyone to stop looking for me. I don't want to be found."

And then Bailey hangs up, ending the call as I sit there in pure agony, knowing I can't fix this. The pain is too much, and everything is too damn loud. I need it to stop.

I drop the pen on the unfinished letter, my chest tightening as I try to figure out what exactly I *have* to relay from his call, and what I can carry myself.

I spot the bottle on the corner of my desk, sitting in front of a picture of my family after one of Dad's games. I know I shouldn't, but I still pop two pills in my mouth to swallow them dry as the memory of that day taunts me, craving the sense of calm they bring. Grabbing the frame, I shove it in one of the drawers, slamming it shut before beginning the round of calls to inform my broken family I heard from Bailey.

I went through the motions at practice, muscle memory taking over as my mind was shrouded in the fog of recalling the sound of my parents crying when I told them Bailey called. The fog allows me to breathe without my lungs collapsing under the weight of guilt I feel telling Mirabelle I learned nothing new. It allows me to momentarily forgive myself when I tell my other brother, once again, his twin called me instead of him.

The pills can't be any worse for me than being trapped inside my head with no escape.

They still aren't enough to fix everything, though.

I could feel them start to wear off when I began my run, and as the fog clears, my feet slow to a stop as my knee throbs from the lengths I've been pushing it to recently. I'm not surprised to find myself in front of Marley's building, knowing I should keep running. I'm not supposed to be here, but it's also the only place I want to be. *Marley is my safe place.*

But I'm aware Marley isn't ready to see me in person, and it'd be selfish of me to go up there. I'm not sure I can be a big enough person to walk away after today.

I just need to see her, even if it's only for a second, and then I'll go back to waiting and writing, but I need Marley.

It's enough for me to rationalize climbing the stairs to knock on her door. I change my mind a dozen times before I knock, but once I do, I'm frozen in place.

Marley opens the door, a look of confusion marring her beautiful features. "JJ?" she asks, and I'm highly aware of my heart quickening in my chest. *God, she's fucking stunning.* I scan over her face, committing every detail to my memory to fill in the small holes of what I struggled to remember before in case this is the last time I get to see her.

Her olive skin has a slightly darker hue to it, and I wonder if Marley's been spending more time outside. It could also be the shadows from the lighting, though. More noticeable is the haircut Marley's definitely had, her brown hair hitting an inch or two below her collarbones, instead of falling down her back. She's wearing a large graphic tee with a faded snowman on it, reaching the middle of her thighs. *I wonder*—I force my gaze back up, dragging a hand over my jaw.

I'm all over the place. I'm trying to get Marley to give me a chance, not scare her off by being a creep. "I'm sorry. I said I wasn't going to push you until you were ready to see me, and here I am, fucking that up too," I say, taking a step back to put space between us. "I just . . . I needed to see you, and now that I have, I'm gonna go. I'm sorry for showing up like this. It was selfish."

"Wait, is everything okay?" Marley asks, crossing her arms over her chest.

It'd be so easy to tell her the same lie I feed everyone else, but I don't want to lie to Marley. Lies are what got me in this goddamn mess in the first place. "No, it's not," I admit. "I like your hair. You look beautiful," I whisper, offering the faintest of smiles. It's all I can muster right now.

I turn to go back the way I came when her arms snake around my waist, holding me in place as her body is pressed against my back. It takes a couple seconds for my brain to make the connection Marley's hugging me.

"You don't have to go," Marley says.

My willpower is weakening. *I should leave.* I got what I came for by seeing her for the first time in weeks, and it's enough. Having her touch me and say I don't have to leave is more than I deserve right now. She deserves better than me when I couldn't tell her the truth from the start.

Marley deserves someone who can give her the world instead of feeling crushed underneath the weight of it.

I wish I didn't feel anything at all right now, and I know exactly how awful that is.

"I should." *Fuck, it's better for both of us if I leave.*

Her arms tighten around me. "Please, stay."

And with two words, my willpower crumbles entirely.

"Okay," I agree. Marley unravels herself, grabbing my hand to pull me along with her into the apartment. *I'm not going anywhere, sweetheart.*

Marley mutes the television playing a sitcom in the background, taking a seat on one end of the couch as I stand awkwardly, aware of the layer of sweat on my skin. Her couch is really nice, and the last thing I want to do is leave a stain.

"You can sit down, JJ," she says, the corners of her mouth pulling upward. "The couch doesn't bite."

"I know," I say, relaxing a little. "I'm sweaty and gross, and I don't want to ruin your things."

Marley tilts her head, her gaze working its way down my body, before trailing up again. "I don't care, but I can tell you do," she says, standing up, only to take a seat on the ground a moment later. "Please sit down, it's making me anxious because I'm worried you might only be a figment of my imagination and disappear."

I slowly lower myself to the floor, wincing as my knees crack at the movement. "Thank you," I say, trying not to grimace as I stretch my leg out. It was a mistake not to take another one before running. "No Bria?" I ask, looking around the apartment to see if she's lurking behind a doorway to scare the daylights out of me.

"She's at the library, but you don't have anything to worry about. She likes you," Marley says, reaching up to play with her shorter strands.

"Don't tell Asher," I joke, feeling a faint smile tug at my mouth. "I really do like your hair."

I'm rewarded with her stunning smile, and Marley twists the strands between her fingers. "I needed a change," she says, and I nod, understanding where she's coming from.

"It looks good," I repeat, hating how thick the tension between us is. I don't know what to say, and I don't think she does either.

She crosses her legs before uncrossing them. If I didn't think my body would protest, I'd probably be crawling out of my skin, but I'm too damn tired. "Whatever happened . . . I'm sure it can't be as bad as you think it is. I don't want to push, but I'm worried, JJ."

I love her optimism, and I wish more than anything Marley were right. My mouth feels dry as I swallow the lump forming in my throat, and I focus on the blue hue in Marley's irises. "My brother called."

"The one who . . ." Marley trails off, her eyes widening when I wince.

"Yeah. Bailey," I say, feeling dizzy. I scratch the back of my neck, looking anywhere but at Marley. It's a struggle because the only thing I want to do is look at her, but do I deserve to feel better?

"Is he okay?"

Despite how hard I'm trying not to feel anything, tears well up in my eyes as I press my tongue to the roof of my mouth to keep them at bay. "He said he was, but I don't think he is," I say after a moment. "B still won't tell me where he is, but he did say we should stop looking because he doesn't want to be found."

I don't get it. Mirabelle and I have been over it a thousand times, and it still doesn't make sense.

"Did you tell your parents?" Marley asks, and I purse my lips, shaking my head.

"I . . . I think it would only hurt them more if they knew I thought he wasn't okay, so I lied, and I told them Bailey's safe." I resist the urge to claw at my chest, the visceral pain of knowing what my parents' hearts sound like when they break again is almost too much for me. I hate it more than anything. It's suffocating me, the sound wrapping itself around my neck like a noose to hang me for my failings.

Marley startles me, resting her hand on top of mine, squeezing reassuringly. "In this kind of situation . . . that knowledge can be invaluable, JJ."

"I don't know if it is. My parents are some of the strongest people I know, and they've been crippled by Bailey's choice to run away. I'm afraid I'm only giving them a false hope to cling to by hiding the worst from them, because I'm starting to think he might never come home." I haven't even admitted this to myself, afraid of even thinking it into existence, but I guess this is another piece of my soul that belongs to Marley.

Her entire face softens, as does her kind voice. "Hey, don't go there. You don't know what will happen. Bailey could come back in a couple of weeks for all we know."

"It's been nearly two years. If Bailey were planning on coming home, I think he would have by now." My breathing hitches, and I clench my fists as they shake from all the awful thoughts beginning to swirl in my head, but the ugliest one of all is trying to imagine what my future looks like if Bailey doesn't return. "What if he doesn't come back?" I ask, my voice cracking as my tears spill down my cheeks, blurring my vision.

What happens then? I can't keep counting the days between signs of life, slowly dying under the pressure. I can't keep hearing the disappointment in my parents' voices when I call them without an update, and the grief when I have one. I can't do this forever.

Tick, tock, tick, tock.

How long until I run out of restarts?

Hands touch the sides of my face, tilting my head up as I inhale raggedly, trying to catch my breath as I bite down hard on my lip to keep it from trembling. "JJ, hey, I need you to look at me," Marley says, and I'm paralyzed. "Fuck it," she mumbles under her breath, and then she's straddling my waist. "Look at me," she instructs firmly, and for her, I try.

"Marley, I can't. I just can't . . ." I trail off, full sobs breaking free as I lose control of the torrent of emotions inside me. She wraps her arms around me, holding me tightly as I rest my head in the crook of her neck, crumbling. As if Marley can understand how badly I need this, she doesn't let go, running her hand up and down my back.

"I've got you," Marley whispers.

CHAPTER TWELVE

Marley

I was wrong before when I thought I knew what heartbreak felt like. It hurt knowing JJ withheld the truth from me, but what I felt then is nothing even remotely close to what I feel now, seeing JJ fall apart because of the burden he shoulders for his family.

I can't even put myself in his shoes to understand what this feels like for him, and I hate I haven't asked sooner how he's doing. I've been punishing him for a crime that wasn't his to repent for.

JJ's whole body is shaking, but I don't let go. I couldn't just watch as he started to spiral, and I didn't know what to do. He was hyperventilating, looking as if he was trying to disappear into himself. This big, strong, beautiful man is falling apart in front of me, and the only thing I could think to do was hold him, because I have a feeling this never happens. Our conversations have helped me realize he's the type of person who is always there for other people, and never for himself.

I feel guilty for adding to the weight he carries, but everything before now doesn't matter. I can be there for him now.

We've shifted from me sitting in his lap to me leaning against the couch as he trembles in my arms, his head pressed into the crook of my neck. I can feel JJ's hot tears against my skin, and I rub his back in circles, despite his shirt being drenched in sweat.

How long was he running before he ended up at my door?

I was surprised and a little confused to see JJ, until I saw the pain he was poorly concealing. It was the way JJ looked at me like I was the oxygen he desperately needed to breathe, his emerald gaze combing over me with a hunger causing my heart to race in my chest.

I could tell something was wrong, and despite him trying to leave, every logical part of my brain was begging me to make him stay.

His hands are clutching my shirt with an unwavering grip, and I hum quietly under my breath, willing to try anything to help him calm down. It doesn't take long for the desired effect to take place, and JJ's breathing slows, his head shifting to rest on my chest.

I don't mind the slight smell of salt clinging to him, or the heaviness of his weight on top of me. *I'm not going anywhere.* I rest my chin on his dark hair, closing my eyes as I focus on the steady rise and fall of JJ's chest.

I'm afraid to even think the question, but the glimpse I saw of the hurricane raging inside of JJ tonight makes me wonder if anyone's taking care of him the way he takes care of everyone else?

I want to help JJ carry some of the burden on his shoulders—I don't think I'm afraid of wanting to be the one to take care of JJ anymore. I'm not sure in what capacity it would be, but I'm tired of fighting the desire to have him in my life.

He makes me happy, and all I want to do is make him happy in return.

~

I wake to the vibration of my phone next to my head on the couch, pulling me from a sleep I hadn't realized I'd drifted into. Reaching for it carefully, JJ inhales deeply in his sleep, and I hear the rain coming down outside.

"Hello?" I whisper, wishing I looked first to see who was calling. I don't want to wake JJ up over nothing.

"Yo, can you come pick me up from the library? It's pouring out, and I really don't feel like walking back in the rain," Bria says, and I look down at JJ, still peacefully asleep as he's sprawled out over me. His dark hair is falling onto his forehead, and I'm noticing just how long his lashes are. I haven't given myself the chance to really look at how handsome he is, because once I start, I don't know if I'll be able to stop. The other thing I notice are the bags under his eyes, and I wonder how much he's sleeping.

"Um, I think so. I just . . ." I trail off, hating the idea of waking him up, but I don't know how I'm supposed to get out from underneath him.

"Are you masturbating?" she asks, and if it were anyone else, I'd be surprised by the question.

I comb my fingers through JJ's soft dark locks, unable to resist the temptation. I remember what it was like to twist the strands through my fingers as he kissed me sweetly. Would JJ still be gentle, or would he devour me with the same intensity he stared at me with earlier? "No? Why is that the first thing your mind goes to?"

"Why else are you whispering?"

I'm really not sure how the two correlate, but I'm afraid to ask.

"Because you woke me up from a nap." It sounds better than the real answer anyway. *Oh, I'm whispering because the guy I'm still in love with just cried himself to sleep in my arms, and then I also fell asleep.* Bria's team JJ all the way. She might freak out if she finds out he's here, and I don't think he'll want anyone else to see him like this.

"Still doesn't explain the whispering," Bria presses, refusing to let it go. "Unless you're not alone . . ." she guesses, waiting for me to deny it, but I can't. "Holy shit, Marley. You're not alone! Who are you with?"

"It's not what you think," I whisper, freezing when JJ shifts, his arms tightening around me before he relaxes again.

Bria laughs, seeing right through my bullshit. "Okay, so if it's not what I think, then who's with you?"

I sigh, sweeping his hair gently out of his handsome face. *"JJ."*

She fucking squeals, and I have to move the phone away from my ear to keep from going deaf. "I knew it! I fucking knew once you gave him a chance, you'd realize JJ's the right guy for you. I know why you were being stubborn, but I'm so damn happy, I think I might cry."

"Bria, we're not together. We're just . . ." I don't know what to say because I genuinely don't know. I just got out of a relationship, and I know it shouldn't matter whether it's JJ or not, but it feels wrong to want someone so quickly after.

"Oh," she says. "I mean, that's okay too. You know, I don't think I need you to pick me up. I see one of my friends, so I'll ask them for a ride. Maybe we'll wait out the rain here just to give you some more time alone."

"No, it's okay. I'll leave no—"

"Nope, don't you dare," Bria says, hanging up before I can protest.

I peer down at JJ again as I comb my fingers through his hair.

JJ's green eyes open on their own accord, and I jolt in surprise.

"Sorry, I didn't want to scare you," he says, but it doesn't make the fluttering in my chest slow.

I reluctantly remove my hands from JJ's hair as he peels his body from mine, and it feels wrong to not have him pressed against me. My cheeks flush when JJ stretches, his shirt tugging up to reveal a sliver of his tanned skin, teasing the muscles underneath. *Holy muscle—* I sit up, forcing myself to look at his face because I shouldn't be staring at his body, especially after earlier. His eyes are swollen from crying, giving me a firm reminder he's here as a friend.

"How long have you been awake?" I ask, clearing my throat.

His gaze flickers a different direction, and his cheeks pink. "I'm, um, a light sleeper. I started waking up when you answered, but I wasn't fully awake until you said my name."

"Why didn't you say anything?"

"Can you really blame me? Mar, you were running your fingers through my hair while I rested my head on your . . . chest. It was nice."

I laugh in disbelief, shaking my head at JJ. "You are such a guy. I promise, a pillow would be much more comfortable than my boobs."

"Think whatever you want, but if I had to pick between a pillow and boobs, boobs would win every single damn time, no matter how much I might love pillows." JJ smiles at me, and it's such a drastic change from the broken expression on his face earlier before he fell apart, I'm hesitant to believe it. I suspect he's putting on a front, and I don't want JJ to feel like he has to with me.

"Yeah? How much experience do you have with them to answer so confidently?" I ask, playing along for a minute. It's still pouring outside, and the last thing I want to do is spook him into running away.

"None at all," JJ answers, and the ease in his body language as he tilts his head causes mine to spin.

I hate that I doubt whether he's telling the truth, but the idea seems so preposterous, it can't possibly be true. I know Bria said Asher told her JJ hasn't even looked at another girl, and Trent echoed something similar. Maybe I'm looking for reasons not to give in to whatever it is I feel for JJ, but I've seen JJ talk to other girls myself.

"Are you hungry? I have to use the restroom, but there's plenty of cookies in the cupboard by the microwave if you want any," I blurt out, deflecting because now I really do have to pee, but I'm also going to take the few minutes I'll be in the bathroom to collect my thoughts.

It's only after I'm washing my hands I remember the cookies probably aren't edible, and I'd really prefer to not poison JJ with my awful attempt at baking. I open the door, stepping out to see him putting the lid on the container holding the cookies.

"Wait!"

He startles, turning to look at me confused. "What's wrong?"

"Don't eat the cookie. I'm awful at baking, and I'm pretty sure they suck," I say, and JJ raises his dark eyebrows skeptically, taking a bite. I cringe when it takes him a moment to bite through the cookie, and I hold my breath, waiting to see if he drops dead.

JJ's slow to swallow, and I regret ever keeping the cookies in the first place. "Wow," he says, coughing, and I move to grab a glass to fill with water. JJ drains the glass, but a stray drip escapes the corner of his mouth, dribbling down his strong jaw to his neck before he wipes it away.

He clears his throat, and I think my entire body is redder than a tomato. "So what kind of cookie was that?" JJ asks, and I wish I could hide in the bathroom.

"It was supposed to be chocolate chip."

"Oh," he says, nodding his head thoughtfully.

Why didn't I throw them away when I realized they tasted like shit?

"That bad?"

JJ shrugs, his lips quirking up in another smile, and I grab the container, dumping all of them in the trash can. "You're not a baker, are you?" he asks, and I pluck the rock-hard cookie from his hand, tossing it with the others.

"Apparently not. I'm sorry, let me see if I can find something else. What do you want to eat?" I ask, my voice coming out slightly higher pitched than normal. Opening the cupboards, I look to see what Bria got last time she went grocery shopping.

"Marley," JJ says, and goosebumps prickle across my skin at the way he says my name.

"Yeah?" I ask, turning around to face him and lean against the counter behind me.

"I'd rather know what *you* want?" he asks, dragging a hand through his hair. As easily as he was joking around a few minutes ago, JJ's serious now.

The answer is simple, yet so complicated: *JJ. I want JJ to stay. I want to take care of JJ. I want him to be telling the truth when he suggests there has never been another girl.*

He's so *big*. It sounds stupid to think, but there's no other way to describe JJ from his height to his muscles. Sometimes it's easy to forget until he's right in front of me, but even the way he holds himself screams he's aware of his size.

"It doesn't matter to me. Whatever you want to do," I say, grabbing the counters for support in case my body decides to give out.

JJ tilts his head, looking at me in a way that feels as if he can see directly through my words to the ugly, stained truth I haven't been able to voice yet. It makes me dizzy, in an intoxicating way, and I don't know if it's good he holds this much control over me. "Sweetheart, the only thing I want is for you to be happy," he says, taking a step closer to me, and another, until my brain is malfunctioning at the proximity of how close JJ is without being close enough to touch me.

"JJ," I begin to say, but my throat catches. I could say it, but I'm not ready. I hold fast to the edge of the counter, but I refuse to let my grip waver when his fingers gently nudge my chin up to have our eyes meet.

"What?"

"I'm worried about you," I whisper.

His shoulders droop, giving me a glimpse of what I saw earlier, lurking behind the pretty smiles and the seemingly effortless charisma. JJ's eyes shut heavily, and his lips press tightly together.

"I don't want you to worry about me," he says, his voice hoarse, and I have a strong gut feeling I shouldn't let this go.

"I think you're hurting, and that's okay, JJ. I'm not going to lord it over your head, or hold it against you if you're not perfect, but I want you to tell me before it gets to be too much," I say, trying to be gentle with my delivery. There's a massive clap of thunder, and a bright flash of lightning through the blinds, causing a small gasp to slip from my mouth.

JJ's eyes immediately open at the sound, revealing the shattered windows to his damaged soul, distorting the emotion swirling in them. "I don't want you to worry about me," he repeats, leaning down to press his lips in a manner so gentle against my forehead it takes my fucking breath away. "Thank you."

"For what?"

He rests his arms on either side of me, and it still feels a little unreal JJ's here with me. "For not letting me leave, even when it wasn't fair of me to show up like I did—*especially how I did.*"

"Well, it's pouring outside, so I'm afraid I'm going to hold you hostage a little longer if that's alright with you." *Thank god for the rain. I'm not ready for him to leave.*

"Is that what you want?" JJ asks, watching me intently, and I can't think of anything I want more.

"It is," I say, very aware of how easy it would be for me to lean up and kiss him, just to see if it holds the same spark it did before. I think it's an excuse, though, because there is no doubt in my mind kissing JJ again would be as life changing as it was the first time. "You could also thank me for letting you use my chest as a pillow too," I tease, needing to lighten the tension between us. *Comedic relief, I think it's called, but it works.*

JJ blinks, stepping away from me to put space between us, a low chuckle sounding from his throat. "Thanks, Marley," he says, a smile on his face as he scratches the back of his neck.

"Well if I have to ask you to thank me for it, then it doesn't count," I point out, laughing again.

"My bad," he apologizes, his eyes crinkling happily at the corners, all traces of his sadness disappearing. *Maybe everything will be okay after all.*

I'm walking out of the business building, exhausted from the hour I just spent learning about the different marketing strategies utilized by businesses. Today was worse than normal thanks to having the worst cramps possible courtesy of my monthly reminder of how much it can suck to be a woman. *I just want to go home and curl up with a heating pad.*

"Marley!" A voice calls, and I hold back a groan as I turn to see Asher with the same girl I saw talking to JJ at that party.

He waves me over, and as tired as I am, it'd be rude to walk away, especially knowing I don't have anywhere to be until this afternoon. *I guess my date with my couch will have to wait.*

"Hey," he greets warmly, as if the last time he saw me wasn't when I was yelling at Trent in their house.

"Hi," I say, smiling at both of them. I'm a little skeptical of the girl, but Asher doesn't strike me as the type to fuck around with two girls at the same time. I'm not sure I can trust my judgement on this matter, though, considering I didn't realize my ex-boyfriend was the type to do exactly that.

She beams at me, practically bouncing on her toes with excitement. "Are you Bria or Marley? Wait, I want to guess," she blurts out, and it catches me by surprise.

I laugh, unsure what to do with my hands. "Okay," I say, and she scans me, turning to look at Asher quizzically before focusing on me again.

"You're Marley."

"How do you know?" I ask, and Asher groans.

"Charlie, could you please not embarrass me?" he asks, taking his hat off to drag a hand through his chestnut hair. It looks like it has a reddish tint in direct sunlight I haven't noticed before. I guess I haven't spent a whole lot of time around him in the first place.

"Where's the fun in that?" she asks, sticking her tongue out at him. "You can't be Bria because he's not acting like a lovesick fool around you, and Ash said Bria has the most beautiful grey eyes, but you have the brightest blue eyes I've ever seen."

I grin, looking at Asher who is pretending to look the other direction. "I'm Marley," I say, holding out my hand.

"I'm Charlotte, but the guys call me Charlie. I've heard a lot about you. You're a lucky girl. JJ's a catch," she says, and I feel my cheeks flush.

"We're not . . . um, thanks?"

"Don't you have a class you need to go to?" Asher asks her, shooting me an apologetic look.

Charlie groans, checking the time on her phone. "Shit, I do. Do you have plans later?" Charlie asks, looking at me.

"I'm supposed to call my parents later today, but I'm free after."

Another smile forms on her face. "Perfect, do you want to get my number from Asher? Maybe we could get together and hang out or something?"

"Sure," I say, trying not to overthink this. I have a feeling Charlie will push me out of my comfort zone, and it might be just what I need.

"Awesome." Charlie smiles at me, then hits Asher's arm with the back of her hand. "Don't be such a jerk," she says, walking away as Asher laughs.

"Sorry about Charlie. She's a lot at first—well, actually she's like that all the time. You just get used to it."

"It's okay. She seems nice," I say, and Asher flips his hat backwards.

"Nice until she's making fun of you," he grumbles, shoving his hands into his pockets. "Where are you headed? I'll walk with you."

"To the parking lot on the other side of campus. I didn't get here early enough for the one next to the business building," I say, and he grimaces.

"I think people sleep in that lot overnight to get a good spot for the next day," Asher jokes, and there's probably a very good chance people do that for one of the coveted spots.

"It wouldn't surprise me," I say, pulling my phone out of my back pocket. "I don't think I have your number, but if you want to text yourself from mine, you can give me Charlie's number."

"You know, you don't actually have to hang out with her.

She means well, but I don't want you to feel like you have to," Asher says, waving at someone across the sidewalk.

"She seems really nice, but how do you know her?" I ask, my curiosity getting the better of me.

"You didn't notice the family resemblance?"

"Family?"

"Charlie's my cousin. Our moms are sisters and both redheads, but I guess you can't really tell since mine is more brown than red." He laughs, pulling his hat off to show his hair, and I pick up more of the red tint to it now that I'm really looking for it. *Oh my god.* That's why JJ was talking to her at the party—she's Asher's *cousin.*

"Makes sense, but I could use some more friends here, so maybe it's a good thing she wants to hang out," I say and Asher shudders.

"You say that now. Wait until you've spent more than two minutes with her," Asher says, matching my pace as we walk. He bumps my arm with his elbow. "So how've you been? I haven't seen you around in a while, but I can't really blame you. Trent's an ass for what he did to you."

"I'm definitely doing better than the last time you saw me, but I'm not going to disagree with you," I say, laughing.

"You can do better than him." Asher scoffs, and I think I have a feeling where he's going with this. "The short hair looks good on you," he says, playfully tugging at one of the strands.

I swat his hand away, laughing. "Is this your subtle attempt to tell me your best friend is the right person for me?"

Asher shrugs, playing this better than Bria has been. Maybe it should say something everyone in my life is rooting for him. "I mean, if you came to that conclusion on your own, I'm not going to disagree with you," he repeats my words back at me, raising an eyebrow.

"How's he doing?" I ask, unable to help myself.

There's a flicker of hesitation in Asher's expression, and I can tell he's gauging how much to say. Asher's a good friend, and I'm glad he's in JJ's corner. "He's got some shit going on, but JJ's dealing with it in his own way. I can say he misses you."

I fidget with my ring, spinning it anxiously. I know JJ's dealing with it, but how? He didn't really seem like he was fine a couple of days ago. We spoke on the phone the last few nights, but I can't tell if JJ is putting on the front he wears so well, or if he's actually doing better.

"You're keeping an eye on him, though?" I ask, needing to hear Asher say it.

"I am, but can I ask you something?"

I tuck my hair behind my ears as the wind tosses it in my face. "Sure."

"How long are you going to make JJ wait for you? I know it's not my place to say this, but I think you should know he'll wait forever—even if it's only for a minute of your time." Asher's dark gaze is trained on me when I turn up to look at him.

I respect him for asking the question, but I wish I had an answer.

CHAPTER THIRTEEN

JJ

I'm trying.

I can stop if I want to, but if it can make me feel a little better tonight, then it might be worth it.

I promised Marley in the letter I wrote her that tomorrow I won't take any pills to make up for taking them twice today.

My hands are shaking as I drop them into my mouth, taking a swig of my water before swallowing. I can't sit still, but every move I take feels like my knee is about to buckle underneath me after today's game. I didn't do myself any favors with all the running I've been doing, and I'm wiped out.

"JJ, are you coming or not?" Asher asks, walking through my door without knocking. "Dude, you're not even dressed yet?"

I set the bottle back in the drawer, hopefully shutting it before he can see. "I'm coming. Impatient much?" I ask, pushing a smile on my face as I turn around to face him.

"Everyone else already left, and I thought you'd be a little more eager to celebrate the touchdowns you scored today. The guys on the team are taking bets on when you're going to set a new school record this season." Asher grins, completely skipping over the part where he made one hell of a block today keeping Trent from getting sacked. He's a good friend.

"Only because of the yards you helped us get," I add in, grabbing a shirt off a hanger in my closet, tugging it over my head. Turning around, I notice Asher's staring at the drawer the pills are in. *Did he see?* I clear my throat, dragging a hand through my hair. "Ready?"

His smile never falters as he makes eye contact with me again. "Hell yeah." *I must be imagining things. Ash would ask a hundred questions if he saw.*

"Are you driving or am I?" I ask, following behind him, grimacing as I force myself to walk normally. I just have to make it long enough for the pain to go away, but it feels like a dozen knives are being shoved into my knee, a new one added with every step.

"I got us a ride instead."

Somehow, that doesn't relax me, but it's taking more of my effort to appear fine, so I don't have it in me to ask questions. I swear, if this ride is an attempt to fix me up with someone, I'll go inside and spend the night waiting for Marley to call instead.

I'm even more confused once I see Charlie's car in the driveway, now a little irritated because he could have just said his cousin was picking us up. There was no reason for it to be a damn surprise.

Asher skips down the stairs, and I'm not sure what he has to be so damn giddy about. He nearly lost his shit when we ran into Charlie at that house party a couple of weeks ago. I like Charlie, but Asher's weird about his cousin coming around the team, and I can't blame him after hearing how some of them talk about girls.

"Shotgun," he calls, and my leg nearly gives out underneath me as I step down the stairs, causing a grunt of pain to slip from my clenched jaw.

"Are you good?" Asher asks, turning around to look at me.

I exhale sharply, forcing a smile that hopefully doesn't look as fake as it feels. "I'm fine, just a little tired from earlier."

"I've got just the thing to put some pep in your step," he says, and I'm surprised my answer is good enough for him not to inquire further.

Charlie honks the horn, and I shake my head, doing my best to get it together. Asher climbs into the front seat, but I freeze when I open the back door, greeted by the last two people I expected to be in this car.

"What's up, superstar?" Bria teases from the middle seat, but my focus is on the other side of her. Marley offers me a kind smile, lifting her hand up in greeting. God, she's fucking beautiful.

Every time I look at Marley, it feels like I'm falling in love all over again.

"JJ, are you getting in the car, or are we leaving you behind?" Charlie asks from the front seat, bringing me back to Earth.

As if I'd miss an opportunity to hang out with Marley for a night. I climb into the car, shutting the door behind me as I clear my throat. "Hey," I greet, my voice coming out rougher than intended.

Charlie turns to smile at me innocently, far from her usual mischief. "Have you met Marley and Bria?" she asks, knowing damn well I run with Bria every day, and Marley is . . . well, *Marley.*

"In fact, I have, Charlotte," I taunt, using her full name to get under her skin. She sticks her tongue out at me, turning around to reverse the car out of the driveway. "How exactly do you know them?"

"I saw Asher outside the business building last week, and

he introduced me to Charlie. We hung out later, and she met Bria," Marley answers, the soft lilt of her voice instantly captivating me. Everything about her demands my full attention. She's had it from the moment I saw her across the street, lost in a small town out of a fairytale in France.

"I see why you like her, JJ," Charlie says, winking at me in the rearview mirror.

I'm a little jealous Charlie's been getting to spend time with Marley when I haven't, but I promised I wouldn't see her again until she decided to reach out.

Is this Marley reaching out?

I adjust the collar of my shirt, trying not to get my hopes up, but sweet Jesus, I hope this is her reaching out.

She's the only thing making me feel like I can breathe.

We went to a different bar than the rest of the team, picking one that allows eighteen-year-olds in so Charlie and Bria could get in without having to use their fake IDs. Normally, I'd avoid this bar like the plague, but if this is the price of spending time with Marley, this place will be my new favorite spot.

I wish I had Marley all to myself the entire night, but I'm happy to be with her in general, even if it means having to share her. Setting another water in front of her, I can't complain because I finally have Marley to myself, taking the seat across from her at the high-top table our group claimed.

Bria is reluctantly dancing with Asher, but if I saw what I think I did, Bria's fighting a smile, and Charlie has disappeared with a friend from class.

My mood vastly improved after learning Marley was coming along tonight. Thankfully, the pills kicked in by the time our first round of drinks arrived, and everything wrong with me has disappeared without a trace.

"Thanks," Marley says, wrapping her hands around the base of the glass.

"Of course," I reply, smiling easily before taking a sip of my beer. The way I felt coming off the field tonight is nothing compared to this.

Marley taps her fingertips anxiously against the glass. "Does it bother you I don't drink?" she asks, looking at my bottle. *Why do I get the feeling this is something Trent made her feel like shit about?* If I didn't think it would open a can of worms I'd prefer stayed shut, I'd ask why the hell she stayed with him, but I think I'd rather not know. All that matters is she's here.

"Should it?" I ask, raising an eyebrow.

I remember the conversation when it came up after I offered to borrow a bottle of wine from my parents' wine cellar in France, and she explained a little about her mom's sobriety. The last thing I want to do is make Marley feel like shit about something she's trying to be proactive about.

A slow smile forms on her plump lips, which I'm trying not to stare at as Marley's eyes twinkle in the low lighting. "Nope," she answers, and a flush crawls up her neck. "You played amazing today."

"You went?"

Marley shrugs, feigning nonchalance as I grin. "I've heard a lot of hype about you, so I wanted to check it out for myself. All of it was deserved and true from what I could follow during the game."

"I wish I'd known you were there," I admit, chuckling under my breath.

"So you could do what? Make a dramatic grand gesture where you magically point to me in the crowd after running in another touchdown?" Marley asks, and there's got to be something wrong with me because this conversation shouldn't be turning me on as much as it is. *I want her in the worst way.*

"I guess we'll never know."

She leans forward, resting her chin on her hands, radiating pure fucking sunshine. "What would you have done?"

I wink playfully at her, feeling more like myself than I have in a long damn time, and this time, it has nothing to do with the pills numbing my pain.

"Sorry, sweetheart. If you want to find out, you'll have to come to the next one," I tease, loving how this time Marley doesn't shy away from me.

Marley laughs, shaking her head at me. *I love her laugh.* I take a sip of my beer, enjoying the moment with her. "If I have time in my schedule, maybe I'll go," she says.

"Well, you know where I'll be," I say, tempted to ask what it means that she's here with me, but ultimately deciding against it. I glance over at Asher shimmying toward Bria, shaking my head. "I will be shocked if she's interested in him after tonight."

"She's stubborn, but I think Bria likes how goofy he is."

"That's one way to describe him," I say, taking another drink as my phone vibrates in my pocket. My heart stutters. Despite knowing it's way too soon for Bailey to be reaching out, I check it immediately, but it's only a text from a guy I played with in high school, asking if I'm watching Hunter's game. I should be, but I think he'll understand when I tell him about Marley showing up.

"Everything okay?" Marley asks, and I set my phone down on the table, redirecting my attention to Marley.

"Yeah, all good," I say, but I feel exposed as she watches me closely.

"Are you sure? It's okay if it's not, JJ," she says softly, and I hate the look of pity on her face. I don't want to talk about this, but especially not tonight when things are finally feeling normal. I shouldn't have shown up at her door as upset as I was the night Bailey called, and I know it's only fair for Marley to be worried, but I want to just be a guy in a bar flirting with a pretty girl right now.

"Marley, *don't*."

She shifts her gaze away, choosing to look at the water in front of her as she taps her fingers on the glass. "Okay."

The single word hits me harder than a tackle on the field. *Fuck*. I stand up from my chair, taking the seat next to Marley instead. *"Mi dispiace."*[1]

"Non mi devi delle scuse o delle spiegazioni,"[2] she says, slow to look at me again.

"Lo voglio,"[3] I insist, reaching forward to brush a lock of hair behind her ear.

Marley exhales, her lips parting slightly as I drag my knuckles gently over her cheek, unable to resist the temptation of touching her. There was a reason I stayed on the other side of the table before. "You don't. I shouldn't have asked when it's none of my business. I'm sorry, JJ."

"Wait—why are you apologizing?" I ask, unsure of what's happening now.

"Because you already carry enough weight on your shoulders, and I never meant to add to it by being upset with you for not telling me about Trent cheating. You were in a difficult position, and I understand now. I should have heard you out, and I'm sorry I didn't."

"I mean this respectfully, but please shut up," I say, and her eyebrows jump in surprise. "I don't want you to apologize, because you have nothing to say sorry for. I was wrong. I should have talked to you about it when I took you home that first day. You did nothing wrong."

Marley does the last thing I expect by smiling at me. I will

---

1. I'm sorry.
2. You don't owe me an apology or an explanation.
3. I do.

literally never understand women. She holds her hand out in front of me, and I stare at it, trying to figure out what I'm supposed to do next. "JJ, take my hand," she whispers. I slip my hand into hers, her fingertips surprisingly rough to match the calluses on my palms. "Hi, my name is Marley Benson."

"Hi? I'm JJ Walker?"

"Is that a question or a fact?" she asks, shaking my hand.

What the hell is happening? "Fact," I answer, but when she smiles brightly at me, goosebumps prickle over my skin.

"It's nice to meet you."

"Sweetheart, what the hell are you doing?" I ask, causing her to sigh.

"We're starting fresh, which means this is the first time we've met. Do me a favor and play along, okay?" Marley looks so damn hopeful, I'm unable to help smiling at her. She is something else, better than I could have imagined in my wildest dreams.

"Okay," I whisper back, agreeing to her nonsensical idea.

"So, JJ, what do you like to do?" Marley asks, spinning the ring on her thumb.

"I like to talk to you, look at you, spend time with you, jump in fountains with you—all my favorite things are with you. What do you like to do?"

"I like to play my guitar, watch the sun set at the end of the day while the stars wake up, and I love to learn languages." She shakes her head, and a small laugh slips from her, clearly not believing me. No matter how corny my answer may be, it's the truth. I don't want to lie when I'm with Marley. "Be serious, please. I feel like we need a fresh start to move past everything, so tell me what you like to do."

"I am being dead serious. Marley, you make me feel like I've caught a life preserver after treading water in the middle of the ocean for days. What I like to do is be around you in any manner I can in whatever way you'll have me," I say, reaching for my bottle to take a drink, feeling her eyes on me after the little bomb I dropped.

"We're friends," she says, but I'm not sure who she's saying it for. I'm aware we're just friends, but the way Marley's looking at my lips doesn't feel like we're just friends.

"I wasn't hitting on you."

Marley scoffs, rolling her eyes. "Okay, then what exactly do you call it? Because I'm pretty sure someone who's a friend wouldn't call me sweetheart and say *All my favorite things are with you*." Marley deepens her voice to try and imitate me, but I just find it cute.

"I call it a fact," I say, smiling cheekily. "I could turn the same question around on you, though."

"Oh really?" she asks, and I nod. "How?"

I lean in toward Marley, close enough I can smell the intoxicating citrus hints of her perfume as her chest hitches. Her gaze falls once more to my lips, her eyes growing hazy with lust as my heart explodes into fireworks because I knew I wasn't imagining it.

"Because I'm pretty sure someone who's just a friend wouldn't be looking at me like they want me to kiss them."

"What?" she asks, blinking in surprise.

"You keep staring at my mouth. I'll kiss you if you want, but only if you ask me to."

Marley pulls her lower lip into her mouth as she stares at me. I want to know her thoughts, but it doesn't feel right to ask for them if I'm not willing to share mine.

"I probably shouldn't tell you this, because I'm terrified of scaring you off, but I care about you. I'm a patient man, Marley, and I'll wait as long as you need, but I hope you're going to ask me to kiss you," I admit, knowing how pathetic I sound right now. *I simply don't care.*

"I care about you too," she says, just loud enough for me to hear over the music playing in the background.

"Guys, I have an idea!" Charlie pops up out of nowhere, startling both of us. She looks back and forth between Marley and me, a smile forming. "Am I interrupting something?"

I can feel my heart pounding in my chest, forcing a chuckle. "What's your idea?" I ask skeptically, dragging a hand through my hair. I've heard Asher's stories about her ideas before, and I'm pretty sure nothing good is going to come from it.

"Will it be an adventure?" Marley asks, and I know wherever she goes, I'll go too—even if it's one of Charlie's terrible ideas.

"Absolutely." Charlie grins mischievously. "I have just the thing in mind."

CHAPTER FOURTEEN

Marley

JJ's strong arms flex underneath me, carrying me easily in his arms. "I'm sorry," I apologize again, stealing a glance at his handsome face.

"Unless you purposely landed wrong on your ankle after jumping the fence, don't apologize," he says, his emerald eyes flickering down at me. The color reminds me of the earrings my parents gave me for my fifteenth birthday. I wonder if either of his parents has the same color. God, and those lips . . .

JJ was right. I was staring at them earlier, wondering how he'd kiss me.

I saw him on the field earlier—all I could think about was how assertive and in total control he was. When JJ's with me, he's gentle and precise with everything he does. I couldn't help my mind drifting to wonder how it'd be. *Would I get the sweet or rough version of JJ?*

I know what it was like three years ago, but a lot can change.

A low rumble sounds from his firm chest, jolting me from my thoughts.

"Marley?" he asks, humor lacing his voice, and I wish I

could read his mind. Actually, I probably can. He told me he wants to kiss me, but he's going to wait until I ask. The only question is why haven't I asked?

"I didn't do it on purpose," I say, remembering what we're talking about.

"Then why are you saying sorry again?" JJ asks, the corners of his mouth pulling up. *Shit, that's the third time tonight I've been caught staring at his mouth.*

I can feel my fingers nearly twitching at the urge to chew on them. I hate the way they look, but it's a nervous habit I can't kick. "Because I feel bad you're carrying me. I can try to walk."

I'm lying through my teeth. I don't want him to put me down. I want to ask him to carry me all the time instead.

"Marley, you don't need to feel bad, and I'm not putting you down. Are we going to keep having this conversation?" JJ asks, shifting me further up in his arms.

How did I ever walk away from him in France?

I loop my arms around his neck, his skin hot beneath my touch. "JJ, I'm not sure what you're talking about. We only met earlier tonight, and I know nothing about you except I'm somehow your favorite person to spend time with, and you're much better at scaling a fence than I am."

The ache in my ankle is still there, but this conversation is a nice distraction.

He rolls his eyes but continues to sarcastically play along. "Right. How can I forget I know nothing about you, except your lack of ability to safely jump a fence."

"Rude," I say, pretending to frown. I totally deserve that. What was I thinking?

"Sorry, sweetheart. Will you tell me what you like to do?"

What I'd like to do is ask you to kiss me. "Nope. You're being sarcastic, so I don't want to tell you," I say, holding back a laugh as we approach Charlie's car.

"Can you reach in my front pocket for the keys?" he asks, switching gears.

"Oh, sure," I say. I slide my hand down between us, reaching blindly for the keys. Unfortunately, my hand has a mind of its own, completely missing the pocket to grab the front of his pants instead. JJ's grip instantly tightens as his breathing hitches. "Sorry," I mumble, really wishing I could curl in a hole right now and disappear. I just skipped way past not being able to ask him to kiss me to grabbing his dick. With the way JJ's holding me, it's a difficult angle for my arm, but finally after what feels like an eternity, I pull the keys from his pocket.

I unlock the car, and JJ silently helps me in. *Maybe if I ask nicely, he'll run me over with the car instead.*

What can I possibly say to make this less awkward?

I steal a glance out the other side of the window as JJ adjusts his jeans to hide the bulge, but it doesn't do much. I quickly look away, my cheeks burning as JJ climbs in the car. *Oh my god.* I should say something, but he beats me to it.

"Marley . . ." he trails off, his voice deeper now. Instinctively, I look at him before the lights in the car turn off, allowing me to see everything he isn't saying. "How is it?" JJ asks, and I blink in surprise.

What is *it* supposed to be?

"What?" I ask, trying to keep my eyes on his face.

"Well, I guess it's not hurting too bad if you forgot you twisted your ankle," he says, chuckling quietly.

I am an idiot. "Oh, right. Yes, my ankle, it um . . . hurts really bad." I stumble over my words, and his head tips back as a real laugh echoes through the car. I relax enough to smile because I'll take this sound any day over the sound of him crying. I'm not sure I'll ever be able to forget it.

"Marley."

"Why do you keep saying my name?"

JJ smiles, starting the car. "We should get some ice on it. I'll take you back to your place."

"Are you sure we should abandon our friends? What if someone calls the cops?" I ask, feeling guilty this is the first time I've even thought of them since we walked away.

"The friend Charlie saw at the bar? This is her apartment's pool. Nobody was breaking in, but that's what their bright idea was, and they're all going to hang here after so I said I'd bring the car back later."

"Are you telling me I jumped the fence for nothing?"

He winces as he pulls the car out, and I kind of wish I'd known this beforehand. "I did try to warn you before how breaking and entering into a pool to swim in our underwear wasn't the best idea, but you said you wanted an adventure."

I did say that. I love my parents, and I know they can't help who they are, but I always knew someone was watching me, waiting for me to mess up. I don't feel like that when I'm here, and it might be my favorite part about transferring. I'm finally getting the opportunity to figure out who I am.

"So we're going back to my place?" I ask, reaching for my necklace to play with it. It's the next best alternative to chewing my nails, giving me something to do with my nervous energy.

"I didn't think you wanted to go back to my house, considering your ex-boyfriend is one of my roommates."

Right. "Guess I didn't really think about that," I mumble, and he glances over at me, his expression softening.

"How are you doing?"

Perfectly fine because you're the one consuming my thoughts. I convinced myself it was easier to be mad at you for not telling me the truth than to admit to myself how much I want you. I'm mad at myself for not waiting for you.

Honestly, I'm surprised he's waited this long to ask. "Better," I say, because I'm afraid to admit the truth.

JJ nods silently in response, his hands tightening around the steering wheel.

Awesome, now I've made it more awkward than it already was.

I drag my hands over my face, sighing.

So much for a fresh start.

~

We stopped by the villa Tessa rented for the weekend so I wouldn't ruin the artwork we'd come here for, slipping away to go on an adventure afterward.

I should be more careful, but for some damn reason, I can't bring myself to leave his side. It's so out of character for me, but it's nice to exist without someone knowing all the dollar signs attached to my name.

I can't remember the last time I was this relaxed, and now I'm wishing Tessa and I weren't flying back tomorrow. I think I could stay in this meadow underneath the warm sun for the rest of my life and be perfectly fine. The array of freshly bloomed flowers in deep hues of purple and splashes of blue are surrounding us in the plush green grass.

"I wish I could live here," I admit, breaking the peaceful silence.

JJ props himself up onto his elbow to look at me. "You could."

"Oh, really?" I ask, amused by how quickly he came up with that.

"Yes."

"How?"

His head tilts, the corners of his mouth curling into a smile. "Well, my family has a house here, but I'd have to insist we get married if we're going to stay here."

"Should I be concerned about you?" I ask, wondering why

the fuck I'm not more freaked out by a guy I met a few hours ago suggesting we get married.

"Concerned about what?"

"You just said I could live with you and we'd get married. Do you need me to call someone for you? JJ, you barely know me."

He flops back onto the ground with a huff. "Haven't you heard of love at first sight?"

I can't help it. I snort. And then I'm so mortified by the sound coming out of my mouth, I cover my face with my hands as I wait for the sound of JJ laughing.

But it doesn't come. I peek between my fingers to see him staring seriously at me, and it throws me off. From JJ's easy smile, the constant stream of jokes, the confidence he exudes, seriousness is something I wasn't expecting. "You're not serious, are you?"

"I think I need another hour to decide, but just Marley, I think you're making me fall in love with you, and I think you're going to fall in love with me too."

See, now this should freak me out. A boy I met hours ago is telling me I'm making him fall in love with me and I'm going to fall in love with him too? It's pure insanity, but he doesn't look crazy. Maybe I'm jaded from the vicious social circles in New York where everyone is always angling for something, but he has no idea who I am. All I know is this level of honesty is refreshing.

I can't think of anything to say because my brain is so flabbergasted. So instead I focus on the sound of the grass swaying in the breeze for a while as we lie there, falling into a comfortable silence. His hand brushes against mine, and I inch closer to him until my arm is pressed against his. JJ loops our pinkies together, exhaling as he does. My heart is beating faster in my chest at pinky holding than it did the entire time I dated my last boyfriend.

What is it about JJ causing me to be affected like this?

"I promise, I had no ulterior motives when I approached you this morning," JJ says, breaking the quiet. I hold my breath, waiting for him to continue. "You looked lost and I wanted to help, but once I looked into your eyes, I knew I'd follow you to the ends of the Earth if you asked me to. It probably sounds stupid, but I'll tell you anything you want to know."

I try to make it a habit not to chew my nails in front of other people but especially now because I have no desire to break apart our pinkies. "Even if I wanted to know your last name?" I ask, turning my head to look into his vibrant green eyes almost the same shade as the grass his head is resting on.

"Anything does include my last name if you want to know it. I'm following your lead."

"What's something you've never told someone before?" I ask. He pulls his bottom lip into his mouth as he thinks, and honestly, if I didn't want to hear what JJ says, I'd probably lean over and kiss him.

"When I was younger, I think . . . around four, my parents were inside feeding my older sister and my little brothers. We had a pool in our backyard and I really wanted to go swimming, but I knew I wasn't allowed in the pool without my parents so I was waiting. Except I dropped the toy I was playing with in the water, and when I tried to grab it, I fell into the deep end." I inhale, concerned about the direction this story is headed in. Obviously he didn't drown if he's in front of me, but I guess he could be a ghost for all I know. It wouldn't be the craziest thing to happen today.

I reach over, pressing my hand to his forehead, and to my relief, JJ feels real. Then I pinch myself and I can definitely feel it. I am for sure awake.

"What are you doing?" he asks, seeming puzzled by my actions.

"Making sure you're not a ghost and I'm not dreaming."

JJ smiles widely, and it's beautiful. His smile transforms his *whole face from something handsome to dangerously beautiful "I'm not a ghost and you're not dreaming."*

I turn on my side to face him completely, holding tight to his pinky. "What happened next?"

"I didn't know how to swim, but I remember this woman helping me. She helped me swim back to the surface before lifting me onto the side of the pool. I swear I felt a kiss on my forehead and then she said goodbye. My parents came out and found me completely drenched, holding the toy in my hand on the concrete next to the deep end. They asked what happened, and I told them I fell in, but Carly saved me," he says, a wistful smile on his face.

"Wait—and she just left you there after helping you out of the water?" I ask, astonished by the direction this has taken. I really wasn't expecting this.

"I'm getting there," he says, chuckling. "My parents looked at each other in shock because Carly was my dad's mother's name, but she died when he was three in a car crash with my grandfather. So while I'm not a ghost, I do believe they exist, and you're the first person I've ever told. I know it probably makes me sound crazy, but. . ." JJ trails off, and if it were anyone else, I'd think they were lying, but I genuinely think he's telling me the truth. "Your eyes are a remarkable shade of blue. Stunning," he says, abruptly changing topics, and my cheeks flush in response. Doubt rears its ugly head, creeping into my mind.

"JJ, are you even real?"

I regret my question the moment he removes his pinky from mine to pinch himself. "Last time I checked."

"Guys don't say stuff like that! They don't lie in perfect picture meadows with a girl they hardly know, and they really don't tell the girl she's making him fall in love with her," I say, sitting up while feeling utterly ridiculous I'm letting a cute boy play me. I'm smarter than this. I stand, walking away before I

sink any further into this hole. I need to leave before I'm in too deep.

JJ's hand catches mine, stopping me despite his grip being loose enough I could pull away if I wanted to.

"Marley, I promise I'm real. If I didn't want to be here, I wouldn't be. For some unknown reason, I feel this connection with you, and I . . ." he trails off, doubt seeping into his confidence for the first time all day.

"You what?" My tone softens, and JJ drags his other hand through his hair.

"I like you. I can't explain it, but there is something about you, drawing me to you. Then I can't help but wonder if maybe there's a reason why. Maps don't just glitch, but yours did today at the same time I was sitting in that café," he says, laughing under his breath before dropping my hand. "I'm sorry. This is all too weird."

"Destiny," I whisper, all the dots connecting in my brain.

"What?" JJ asks, but I don't have an answer for him. I don't even have an answer for myself. I step closer, pulling his head down to meet mine. The second our lips touch, lightning strikes and I know nothing has ever felt more right than this. I can only assume JJ feels the same as he pulls me closer to him.

"Marley," JJ says, pulling me from my thoughts as we pull into my building's parking lot.

I turn to look at him, realizing as I replayed the moment I met JJ for the first time, I missed the entire rest of the drive and we're now sitting in the parking lot for my apartment building.

"Are you okay?"

"I was just thinking," I admit, wishing I could go back in time and tell JJ my full name. It's hard not to wonder how different things might be if I had, but I can't change it now. All we can do is move forward.

His head tilts as he wipes his palms on his thighs. "About?" JJ asks, and I can feel the tension filling the air as his pools of green meet mine, reading my unspoken answer. *I was thinking about you.* He clears his throat, turning off the car. "Stay in your seat, and I'll come around to get you. I don't want you to walk on your ankle."

He slides out of the driver's side before I can consider protesting, but I'm not sure I would. It's nice being held by JJ.

My door opens as I undo my seatbelt, and JJ offers me a hand to help me out of the car. This feels like overkill for a sprained ankle, but selfishly, I want him to hold me again. I take his hand, and once again, it feels just as right as interlocking the last piece of a puzzle.

"I can . . ." I trail off when JJ fixes his heated stare on me, dropping it. *Okay then.* JJ bends, looping his hands underneath my knees to carry me once more bridal style as my heart flutters in my chest.

We're halfway up the stairwell before I realize Bria has the keys to our apartment, but I'm also not a thousand percent sure the door is locked. "Do you have the keys?" JJ asks, pausing in front of my door.

"Um, not exactly, but there's a chance the door is unlocked."

A choking sound comes from JJ's throat, startling me. "I'm sorry, I really hope I heard you wrong. You don't know if you locked the door?"

"Kind of?"

JJ's jaw tightens in the dim light, and he sets me down, his hands lingering on me until I'm balancing on one leg. He reaches for the doorknob, testing it to see if we locked it, but the door clicks open. "Marley," he says, and I realize as young women living by ourselves, yeah, we probably should make sure our door is locked.

"It works in our favor, though, because we would have had to go all the way back to get the keys from Bria," I point out, trying to find the bright side, but he does not appear to be impressed by my logic.

"Wait here," he instructs, leveling me with a look that silences any argument I want to make. I think I like this side of JJ where he tells me what to do. I hold onto the siding to steady myself as JJ flips all the lights on and clears the apartment. It's sweet for him to do it, but totally unnecessary. His massive frame fills the doorway again as JJ offers me his hands to limp my way into the apartment. "You're lucky there was no one here. You shouldn't leave your door unlocked."

"I think you're being a little dramatic," I say, and JJ rolls his eyes.

"Except I'm not. You're hurt, coming back to an apartment where you left the door unlocked, and what exactly was your plan if someone broke in?" he asks, shutting the door behind me, making a point to flip the lock.

"I didn't need a plan because I have a six-foot-something tall guy with me who cleared the apartment of any bad guys who might've been waiting for me," I joke, trying to lighten the mood.

His mouth twitches, but his frown remains. "Six four. You had a six-foot-four guy with you who will always clear the apartment before letting you walk in, *especially* when you leave your door unlocked. I'm asking what your plan would have been if I weren't here."

"Did you know it takes more effort to frown than to smile?" I ask, changing the subject, but JJ doesn't stop frowning.

"I asked what your plan was," he says, taking a step closer to me as I lean against the door.

My plan? The only plan I have presently is to make JJ happy.

I wet my lips, taking a note from his playbook to fight smiling as his emerald gaze flickers to my lips. His mouth parts, and the air between us crackles with electricity. "My plan?" I whisper, hyper aware of how easy it would be for me to reach out and pull JJ closer.

"Yes, sweetheart," JJ says, the nickname rolling again off his tongue. He braces an arm over my head, and I suck in a sharp breath. *I like it when he calls me sweetheart.*

"To make you happy," I admit, and from our close proximity, I hear his breathing hitch.

"What?" His smooth voice has a hoarseness to it, and I stop fighting the urge to touch him.

My fingers brush across his jaw, feeling the dusting of stubble growing before cupping his cheek. His dark lashes flutter shut, a whimper escaping his lips I can't stop staring at. *Is this what it's like to be so completely and desperately wanted?*

"Marley, ask me to kiss you, *please.*"

I already was going to, but the sheer desperation in his voice makes my pulse skyrocket.

"JJ, will you kis—"

For all his talk about waiting to kiss me until I ask, JJ doesn't even let me finish the question, his mouth pressing against mine with a gentleness silencing me. My hand on his cheek slides into his dark waves, curling into the short, soft strands.

Time stands still, and my whole world has shifted on its axis.

I move my lips against his as my other hand reaches to pull JJ against me, and when he presses mine into the door, my entire body hums at the feeling of rightness. Despite how tender he might be with me, there's nothing soft about JJ's body, including his hard-on pressing into my stomach.

A soft moan sounds from the back of my throat, and he tilts his head, pressing his lips firmer against mine. I gasp, arching into him as our kiss morphs into something untameable, his tongue sliding against mine as he devours me. The tension between us has been explosive, and I'm blown away by how much more of him I want.

I'm not a person who makes reckless choices, but the magnetic pull I feel toward JJ doesn't feel reckless or like a choice. It feels like I've been spinning in circles, trying to fight it, but why? Why fight something that feels so right when I was trying to force something that never even felt half as good as this? JJ's breaking years of practiced discipline and inhibited desires.

JJ is my absolute undoing.

His hand skims the bare skin on the back of my thigh, pouring gasoline on the fire already threatening to consume me. I hook my arms around the back of his neck, refusing to let him pull away regardless of how my lungs are protesting for air.

With an assuredness I wasn't expecting, JJ's hands lift me into the air, and I take advantage of the opportunity to wrap my legs around his waist. A groan rumbles from his chest, and I feel like a fucking fool for not asking him to kiss me sooner. When my back is pressed against the door again, my body aches for more as our hips line up.

I want to know every part of him I've missed out on.

"*Fuck*," JJ mumbles, pulling away as he pants, his breathing shallow.

I can feel him pressing against me, and I twist his short hair through my fingers as my heart races in my chest. "*Wow*," I murmur, a little in disbelief at how easy it is to lose myself in him. Is it bad I want to kiss him again?

"Marley, I . . . fuck, sorry, I can't think holding you like this," he says, his cheeks flushing as a shy smile tugs at his lips, completely contradicting the caveman way he has me pressed against this door.

"You can put me down," I say, combing my fingers through his soft strands.

"I don't really want to do that either, but I think talking is a good idea," JJ says, but he doesn't move an inch.

"JJ?" I ask, choosing to make the first move by unwinding myself from around him, making sure my good ankle touches down first. He said he wants to talk, and I want to respect it. A breather is probably a good idea anyway.

It was no less special than our kisses in France, but just as we've both changed, the time apart seems to have only made the intensity between us grow from a slow flame to a raging wildfire.

He shuts his eyes, turning his head. "Need a minute, baby," he says, his mouth pressing into a thin line as his throat bobs. JJ draws in a ragged breath, and I would give anything to know what he's thinking.

When JJ's eyes open, focusing on me, all the air in my lungs is stolen away by the visceral desire I recognize in his eyes. He pushes off the door, taking a step back, it seems like it takes all of his effort, especially when he drags a hand over his jaw.

"I don't think we're very good at starting over," I say, trying to lighten the moment.

JJ tilts his head, a dimple appearing as his full lips curl into a breathtaking smile. "No, Marley, we're not, but that's okay because I don't want to forget a single second with you."

CHAPTER FIFTEEN

JJ

FOR THE SECOND TIME, I'VE BEEN ABSOLUTELY shattered by a kiss from Marley Benson. Trying to keep my hands off her is so damn hard, but I'm fighting every urge I have to take her into my arms and kiss her the way I desperately want to. I'm embarrassed by how carried away I got, losing the battle against my self-control when I heard the sweet sounds she made as I kissed her, pulling me closer.

In the two weeks since, I haven't allowed myself to kiss her again, despite it being all I think about. Especially when she looks at me, chewing on her bottom lip while staring at mine, and I can tell she's thinking about kissing me because I'm thinking about kissing her.

I'm trying to do the right thing and take it slow because even though I pressed Marley up against a door while kissing her senselessly, I don't want her to think the only reason I want to be with her is that I find her attractive. I didn't wait eight hundred and ninety-two days to find Marley again to ruin it all by becoming preoccupied with sex.

Is it weird for me to still be in love with her?

Probably, but it doesn't change the fact that I am deeply, madly, and hopelessly in love with Marley.

She's worth waiting for.

And then there's the fact I'm doing my best to not punch her ex-boyfriend in the fucking face. I'm not a violent person, and my temper doesn't run as hot as my siblings', but I am genuinely surprised I haven't hit him. The shit Trent says about Marley makes my blood boil to a dangerous temperature, and it's only a matter of time before I stop biting my tongue.

Perfect example would be when he started comparing his ex's blowjobs to the girl he was with last weekend, and my jaw was clenched so hard, I thought I might crack a molar. The only thing helping me keep my shit together was how disappointed I thought Marley would be if she heard I got into a fight with Trent over her, so instead I thought about how I spent my Sunday afternoon baking cookies.

One of us is going to have to learn how to make something edible if we're going to spend the rest of our lives together.

I can at least cook breakfast foods, but Marley? She can't cook anything to save her life, but I'll eat anything she gives me with a smile on my face, even if it kills me in the end.

I've spent at least some form of time with her every day since the night we kissed, but even with all the time together, we still talk on the phone until one of us falls asleep. It only took one time of waking up with my phone's battery drained entirely to ensure I plug it in before lying down. My anxiety can't handle the thought of missing a call from Bailey, and it scared me shitless to think about how careless I was with the only lifeline I have to him—*the only one we all have with him*—even if the reason was that I fell asleep talking to Marley.

The October breeze is a better change in pace than August and September where the heat is blistering underneath all my pads I have to wear at football.

I'm drained from practice, but I promised to meet up with Bria later to run intervals instead of for distance, and I think it's her way of trying to kill me. I'd rather die trying to digest any of Marley's creations.

I pull my phone out of my pocket and press my mom's contact, dialing her number. I almost think she's not going to pick up, but she does on the final ring. "How nice of you to call. How is my sweet California boy doing?" she teases, and I roll my eyes.

"Oh, Mom, you know I'm still a Carolina boy at heart. Sorry I haven't called much this week, there's just been a lot going on with football." It's a weak excuse, but it's hard for me to talk to my family knowing how far away they are. It was my decision to come here, but as much as I miss them, I hate the part of me that dreads making phone calls because of Bailey.

"You don't have to explain. I know how it is better than anyone." Mom chuckles, and I shift my bag on my shoulder, opting to walk to the house instead of catching a ride. "A little birdie told me it's not football consuming so much of your time, but I'll let it slide until you want to talk about it."

I'm going to kill Mira.

She's been in such a sappy mood since she and Henry got engaged. I kept her secret about being in love with Henry for years, and she can't keep mine quiet for more than two months?

Clearly, I'm the superior sibling.

"Oh, is this birdie newly engaged and a major pain in my ass?"

"Potentially. I would like to say she's also a major pain in my ass."

"Oh really?"

"You're all major pains in my ass. Don't think you're an exception," Mom says, and I can't help but smile.

"Right, okay, but I'm the *least* major pain in your ass."

"That is an awfully high presumption of you to make, JJ," Mom says, but she doesn't tell me I'm wrong. "So am I going to have to wait for news from tabloids about this girl like I did with Henry and Mira?"

I hate the idea of cameras capturing pictures of me and Marley. When I'm in California, they usually leave me alone, but when I'm home, I don't get it nearly as bad as Mira and Henry do. I don't mind the spotlight when it comes to football, but I've seen firsthand how invasive the media can be when it comes to getting the money shots they crave. It's the reason why there's naked photos of my sister on the internet forever. The thought of something similar ever happening to Marley makes the blood running through my veins turn to ice.

"We're not together or fake dating," I say, feeling the need to clarify the second part after Mirabelle pulled that stunt with Henry.

"Glad to know you're not following in your sister's footsteps, even if it did work out for her. So you have feelings for her? Come on, my birthday is next week, and I'd love to know if my present will be getting to meet this mystery girl."

I pause, considering how much I really want to admit here. I more than like Marley.

She's everything.

"JJ?"

"I bought her flowers," I ultimately decide to say, knowing that sentence is the only thing I can remotely say to try and explain what Marley means to me in a way my mother will understand.

Mom gasps. *"Alors, quand vais-je rencontrer ma belle-fille?"*[1]

"*Mom.*" I groan, but I can't deny the thought of Marley meeting my parents makes me smile. They'd love her, but I

---

1. So when do I get to meet my future daughter-in-law?

also think they'd scare the shit out of her. I love my parents, but their relationship is an acquired taste. "We aren't even dating, so maybe don't refer to Marley as your future daughter-in-law."

"Si tu lui achètes des fleurs, alors je suis confiante sur le fait qu'elle le sera,"[2] she responds.

"They're flowers, not an engagement ring." *Except in my family, flowers are essentially the equivalent to an engagement ring.*

"Bullshit. You know it means the same damn thing. I thought you had to be smart to get into Beaumont?" Mom teases, causing a bark of laughter to sound from me. Hilarious coming from her when she's asked me since middle school how much to tip at restaurants.

"I *am* smart."

"If you're so smart then why haven't you proposed to the girl you want to marry? If it's because you don't have a ring, I'd be happy to let you use mine."

I hear Dad in the background ask Mom who she's talking to, and then I'm placed on speakerphone to hear him more clearly. "Why is your mother offering to give you her wedding ring? I really hope you didn't knock some girl up because you didn't glove up first. We've talked about how condoms are important for more than one reason, including protecting both you and a partner from STDs and pregnancy," Dad says and I groan loudly, earning me a couple of looks from other people out enjoying the nice weather. It's hilarious, considering knocking someone up requires having sex, which hasn't happened.

"Because she's *delusional* and wants me to propose to a girl I'm not dating, who is *not* pregnant," I whisper-yell

---

2. If you're buying her flowers, then I'm confident that she will be.

because the last thing I need is for it to get around campus I've knocked a girl up and I'm proposing.

Oh shit, I probably shouldn't have called her delusional. Mom's quick to argue, "Bash, he's bought her flowers! I am not delusional!"

"Why is this the first we're hearing about her?" he asks, and I start thinking of ways I can get revenge on Mirabelle for opening her mouth.

"Maybe because I knew you guys would react like this," I drawl out. Honestly, they shouldn't be surprised I haven't told them, but maybe I should have after hearing how excited they are.

"Well we're coming to see your game in three weeks so make sure you invite her to dinner so we can get to know her," he says, immediately causing me to smile. I'd hoped they would, but between all the football schedules we juggle this time of year, I didn't know where they were going to end up.

"You guys are really coming?"

"We are! It's the same week as Hunter's bye week, so he'll be with us. Mirabelle's coming too, but Henry's going to fly out to meet us after since he'll play in Arizona Friday night," Mom says, and I really, *really* can't wait.

A couple of hours later, I jog up the stairs to Marley and Bria's apartment, already preparing myself to die while we run these intervals. A breeze kisses my bare chest as my shirt is preemptively tucked into the waistband of my shorts, knowing I'm going to sweat through it, so I might as well maintain my tan from all the surfing I did this past summer.

I knock on the door, glaring at the goddamn doorknob I'm hoping is locked. One twist tells me it's not, and I groan, walking in with every intention to pick another argument about how the door needs to be locked. Bria says it annoys her when she has to come let me in. *If the door is unlocked, just walk in,* she's said multiple times during the last two weeks since I started meeting her here for our runs instead of at the track. My counterargument is they're two girls living alone, and then Bria usually flips me off as Marley laughs.

This time, *six* sets of eyes meet mine, and I freeze in my tracks as the door shuts behind me.

"Who the fuck are you, and why are you walking into our daughter's apartment half-naked?"

My eyes nearly bug out of my head as I look down, realizing my preemptive plan was an awful idea. "Oh shit," I swear, pulling my shirt out of my waistband. *Did I get the day wrong?* "Um, hi, I'm JJ," I stammer, my eyes finding Marley, but she's staring at my abdomen, as are both of the women who look around my mom's age, their eyes widened in shock.

Bria gasps, drawing everyone's attention thankfully to her. "Oh my fucking god. We're supposed to run intervals. I'm so sorry, let me change and grab my shoes!" She mouths *sorry* to me on her way to her room, pulling her hair up quickly.

They're clad in expensive clothes that make me feel *extremely* underdressed. Everyone knows who Hayes Benson is, but even if I didn't, his eyes that match Marley's are a dead giveaway, and they're narrowed at me like I'm his next meal. I'm assuming the other one is Bria's father, and while his demeanor is slightly less terrifying, I'm wondering if I need to be afraid for my life.

"Dad, this is our friend, JJ. He's here because he and Bria run together, and she probably forgot to tell him you guys were visiting," Marley says, and all I can do is nod like a fucking bobblehead after tugging my shirt over my head.

The woman leaning against the counter with dark long hair tilts her head at me, a low whistle coming from her lips. "Hot damn, maybe I should have gone to college. None of the models I ever worked with looked like that," she says, and my face is on fire.

"Tessa!" The other woman laughs, and Marley covers her face with her hands.

I take a brave—or stupid—step toward Marley's dad, doing my best to look him in the eye as I hold out my hand. "Hello, sir, I'm JJ. Very sorry to be meeting you this way, but it is nice to meet you." It's a good thing I'm the biggest liar I know, because my voice doesn't shake once to reveal how terrified I am. He takes my hand, squeezing it tightly, and I'm highly aware of the threat it promises.

"Benson, be kind," a soft voice says, and he releases his grip on my hand.

"You as well," he says, and I turn to Bria's dad, offering him my hand as well.

His shake is firm, but at least he offers a slight smile. "Grayson, it's nice to meet you, JJ."

Bria hops out of her room, pulling on her shoe. "Fuck, sorry, JJ. I knew Marley's parents were coming, but I thought mine were in Italy, because that's what they told me last week. Ready to go?" she asks, giving me an escape I'm desperate for.

"Yeah, after you put more clothes on," her dad says, and Bria rolls her eyes.

"Dad, it's fine. It's the same thing I wear to practice, which is exactly what we're doing."

He frowns, and I feel a bead of sweat roll down my neck. "Bria—"

Bria hooks her arm with mine, pulling me out of the apartment. "We'll be back soon! Love you!" she calls over her shoulder, shutting the door behind us.

My jaw drops and I look at her in astonishment. "What the hell just happened? I can't believe you didn't tell me your parents were here."

"Yeah, 'cause you really care about meeting my parents,"

she teases, smirking over her shoulder before jogging down the stairs. "If it makes it better, I really did forget we were supposed to go running after my parents showed up, but how was I supposed to know you'd show up shirtless?"

"You think this is funny?" I ask, following her quick pace.

"Actually, kind of. The look on your face after Hayes asked who you were was priceless. I promise he's not always scary," Bria says, laughing. I think we'll have to disagree, because I feel like he could crush me under his shoe like a bug without thinking twice about it. "You have nice clothes here, right?"

"Yeah, why?"

"Because I know for a fact you earned yourself an invitation to dinner tonight. Wearing something nice could help erase the fact you walked in shirtless."

"Maybe if you locked your door, I wouldn't have walked in," I grumble under my breath. Maybe I'll get lucky and these intervals will in fact kill me before Marley's father can.

CHAPTER SIXTEEN

Marley

LYING IN JJ's ARMS, FOCUSING ON THE STEADY RISE and fall of his chest is the most relaxed I feel I've been in a while. One of the reasons Bria's mom brought me on this trip was to give me a chance to breathe without feeling the weight of everyone's attention on me.

Every couple of years, there's rumors that pop up from a close source of our family claiming my mother has relapsed, and while I know they're not true, they bring up awful memories for me of the last time she did.

I'm proud of my mom and the progress she's made over the last six years, but it doesn't get easier to hear the media speculate about her drug addiction.

"What are you thinking about?" JJ asks, the low timbre of his voice reverberating through me.

"Do you really want to know?" I ask, curling my fingers in the soft fabric of his shirt. It's tempting to stay here forever—hiding in the mountains.

"If you want to tell me, but you don't have to," he says, and I want to laugh at how easy it is to be with him. It would be my *luck I would meet the perfect guy, but somehow I have to be perfectly content with never seeing him again after tomorrow.*

I've never told this story before. I haven't needed to. My circle of trusted friends in New York are all children of my parents' friends, and they were all around then when it happened. Everyone else knew what happened from the gossip magazines and countless articles detailing the worst day of my life thanks to the cleaning crew who saw everything after hearing me scream. My dad was too busy scrambling for the Narcan he kept hidden away, hoping he'd never have a reason to use it, to send them home.

"It's not a pretty story."

JJ's fingers twist through the ends of my hair. "Not all stories are. They don't have to be perfect, but if it's real, it doesn't matter. The right people will still want to hear it."

It's a different side of him, and I guess I'll know if he scares easily, but there's something telling me JJ doesn't. Being here with him feels like I've found something I never even knew was missing, and even if it's only for tonight, I want to be myself.

"I was twelve when I walked into my parents' bedroom and found my mom unconscious on the floor from a drug overdose. She's an addict, and she'd been clean for a really long time. Mom aggravated an old injury, and didn't want to take the time to rest, so she saw a doctor who prescribed her a couple pills without knowing her history, and that was that."

"I can't imagine what that would have been like, especially at twelve. Is she doing okay now?"

"She is, but people like to bring up her worst moments to tear her down when everything is going well." Maybe I should be used to people using my family's pain as another way to get ahead, but it never gets easier. I guess I haven't grown thick enough skin yet. "I feel like I'm right back in the moment, but my mom just smiles and shrugs it off like it doesn't bother her.

Then I feel selfish letting it bother me when she doesn't, but I don't know how to pretend it doesn't."

"Why do you have to pretend like it doesn't bother you?" JJ asks, his voice a soothing rumble.

It's a good question, but I don't have an answer. "I'm not sure," I admit. "I think because I don't want her to feel like I'm worrying about her. I don't doubt whether she can stay clean, but I do worry about her."

"I think all it means is you love her, and there's nothing wrong with that."

I lift my head to look at JJ, and I'm not sure how I ever could have thought going with him this morning would be a bad idea. In fact, it feels like I've found something I never even knew was missing.

"Thank you," I whisper, and JJ tilts his head to look at me.

"For what?" he asks.

"For listening," I say, curling my fingers in the fabric of his shirt to rest my head against JJ's solid chest.

~

I can't believe JJ walked in shirtless earlier. Once I got over the initial shock, I wanted to laugh, especially after Tessa whistled —*because honestly, same*—but the look on Grayson and Dad's faces easily helped me repress the urge.

For the first time since I cut my hair shorter, I regret it. I did it for a change, but I'm starting to wonder if I did it for the wrong reasons. Looking in the mirror, I twist my fingers through the ends, and it's healthy, but I wish I'd waited.

"Second guessing it?"

I turn, jolted out of my daydream to see Tessa leaning against my doorframe.

The corners of her mouth pull up into a smile as her grey eyes crinkle. "Sorry, I didn't mean to scare you, but I saw you pulling at your hair. I like it, but I'm sure it's taking some getting used to."

"No, you're okay. I was just thinking about something."

Tessa walks up behind me and rests her hands on my shoulders. It's crazy how much Bria looks like her mother. "Like?"

"Our trip to France when we went to that tiny town in the mountains," I admit, and confusion twists her striking face.

"Not that it wasn't a great trip, but why are you thinking about it now?" she asks, pulling a dress the same green shade as JJ's eyes off the bed and holding it up. "This is really cute. Are you going to wear that tonight?"

I shrug, taking a seat on the edge of my bed. "I'm not sure."

"The dress or the trip?"

"Both? The trip just . . . I was reminded of it."

Her eyes narrow in scrutiny, and I know I'm not making any sense. She one hundred percent knows something is up with me.

"We'll have to go back. I love Italy with all my heart, but France is almost as beautiful—especially the countryside. I bet I could get another commission from the artist, and we can bring Bria with us." Tessa smiles at me before carefully laying the dress flat on my comforter. She runs her fingers over the smooth material, giving me a reprieve from her watchful gaze. "Does this have something to do with the young man earlier?"

I look away to one of my favorite pieces of art hanging on my wall. I didn't want to leave it in my room at home so I insisted it come here with me. It's a painting of the night sky, and probably one of the least valuable pieces in my family's collection, but it means the world to me because it reminds me of that night.

I've always loved the stars, but since then, they've held a special meaning.

No matter where I was in the world, I could look up and know JJ would be seeing the same stars. It was comforting when I had no idea where he was or how he was doing.

"Everything has to do with him," I admit, my voice a whisper as I force the words out. "I don't know what I'm doing."

She rests her hand on mine. "None of us do. Sweetie, I've made so many mistakes in my life. Some I wish I could take back and some I don't regret, but all of it has led me to where we are now. That's the beauty of life."

"You're right."

"Obviously," Tessa says, her quiet laughter lightening the air. "Do you feel better?"

"Kinda. I'm nervous about tonight. Do you think Dad will be nice to JJ?" I ask, and this time she snorts.

"Oh, hell no. He's going to give him the third degree and rake him over the coals, but after the bullshit your last boyfriend pulled, I think it's understandable."

"He's not my boyfriend," I say, but I wish he was.

"*Yet*," Tessa corrects. "He wouldn't be subjecting himself to tonight if he didn't have feelings for you."

CHAPTER SEVENTEEN

JJ

Every single manner my parents ingrained in us is saving my ass tonight. I feel like every move I make is being scrutinized by her family, and for the first time in my life I'm worried I might not be enough.

I started off the night by showing up at Marley's apartment with flowers in hand, this time waiting until the door is opened for me. Immediately after Bria and I finished earlier, the first place I went was to Hope's Flowers, getting an assorted bouquet of different types of purple flowers from Eddie. With the hope they'll forget earlier so I can get on the right track with the parents, I also have boxes of chocolates for everyone else.

However, not even the lull of the drugs in my system can help calm me now.

"So, JJ, how did you and Marley meet?" Marley's mother, Sephine, asks from where she sits next to me, watching me with interest.

Thank fuck we're starting with an easy question.

"We met a little over two and a half years ago in France. She was lost, and I helped give her directions. We never exchanged numbers, but I was happy to see her again on campus." I feel like it's for the better if I don't bring up the fact that I saw her again because she was dating my roommate.

"France, you say?" Bria's mom questions, her eyes lighting up as she looks at Marley, whose face is turning bright red. Bria snickers in her seat, and it is so tempting to ask why she didn't invite Asher to this. I have a feeling her parents would be very interested to learn about him, and it might take some of the pressure off Marley. But I also happen to like my balls where they are, so I might wait to play that card.

I nod in confirmation, clearing my throat to draw the attention back to me. "My family has a house in the Jura Mountains near Baume-les-Messieurs we've owned since before I was born. It's one of my favorite places on Earth, and I love to go back every chance I have. Unfortunately, my football schedule doesn't allow me to visit as often as I'd like."

Bria tries to hide her laugh by coughing, and before I can ask her what's funny, Marley's dad finally speaks to me for the first time since we sat down, commanding my attention. "You play football?"

"Yes, sir. I'm a tight end for Beaumont."

"I played lacrosse my first two years at Beaumont as well until I injured my knee. It forced me to medically retire, but sports were never my future—only a hobby," he says, but I hear the underlying tone of what he's getting at: sports aren't forever. I let it roll off my shoulders because it's not the first time someone's hinted at it or even flat out said it to my face. I'm well aware of how few college players make it through their eligibility in college and then are drafted.

"I tore my ACL and meniscus last season, but thankfully, I made a full recovery thanks to our incredible athletic trainer. I'm sorry you weren't able to continue, even if it was only a hobby," I say, and with a quick glance to the side, I see Marley smile as she takes a sip of her sparkling water. I clearly said the right thing causing his demeanor to soften.

"And you're still playing?" Grayson asks, sounding impressed. God, I hope he's impressed, or at least doesn't think I'm stupid for continuing to play.

I chuckle softly. "I am. I'm getting my degree in mathematics in case playing professionally isn't in the cards for me. It's always good to have a backup plan."

"Is playing professionally your goal?" Hayes asks.

"If I'm fortunate enough, yes," I answer, trying not to sound like a pompous asshole.

"That's really nice, JJ," Sephine says, offering me a smile. "I hope it happens for you."

"Thank you, ma'am."

"I know you're trying to be sweet, but you're doing a fine job of making me feel old by calling Sephy over here ma'am when I'm older than her," Tessa teases, and I can say with the utmost certainty, she and my mother would get along perfectly.

"Oh, would you stop already. We all know neither of you looks a day over twenty-five, and people are more likely to think you're our older sisters instead of our moms," Bria says, stabbing at her salad.

Grayson chuckles, his arm resting on the back of his wife's chair. "You'll be thanking us in about twenty years for the phenomenal genes you received instead of rolling your eyes."

A waiter takes everyone's orders, and I'm grateful for the slight reprieve from the questions I've been answering. I listen to everyone interact with a familiarity rivaling my parents' inner circle. The one thing I've noticed is how Marley seems to fade into the background of everyone else's bold personalities, allowing them to speak instead.

Since getting to know her better, I've started to realize she's more reserved in large groups, but I didn't think it'd be the case with her family. She seems like she's enjoying herself, but she's barely joining the conversation.

Marley's hair has natural sun-kissed highlights from the sun, and she's straightened it to where it falls just past her collarbone. The pale green dress contrasts nicely with her olive skin, and I'm having a hard time taking my eyes off her. I'm not sure there's a universe in which she'd ever be the first person in a room I wouldn't notice first.

Her eyes dart to meet mine, catching me staring at her, and her tempting lips lift into a smile. Out of all my favorite things about her, I think her smile is my most favorite. I'm not even sure if it makes sense, even if it's only in my head, but I think that's the best part of love. It's not supposed to make sense.

I wink at her, hoping to make her laugh, but the sound of her father clearing his throat shuts that down unfortunately. Probably not my smartest idea trying to flirt with her in front of him, but it's a risk I'm willing to take.

"JJ, what do your parents do? Are they supportive of your hope to play professionally?" he asks, and I realize I've never actually told Marley who my parents are. It didn't seem important before to say, *Hey, by the way, I know your parents are super rich and famous, but so are mine so I don't care*, but maybe I should have said it.

"Dad," Marley protests, and I smile at her, shaking my head to silently tell her not to because it's okay. I don't mind, and it's not like I'm in a position where I can really say no. I would be wary of any guy coming near my daughter after the way Trent treated her . . . and then there's the *great* impression I made earlier I'm still kicking myself over.

"No, it's really okay. I'm happy to answer." I wipe my sweaty palms on my chinos, and I regret not taking a drink of water when I had the chance. "They've made it clear they'll support whatever career I choose to pursue, but there is a little bit of jealousy from my dad that I didn't follow in his foot-steps by becoming a quarterback. He retired a couple of years ago from the NFL, and my mom freelances as a photographer, but she owns a couple of galleries in the States and a few more in Europe."

I see it in Grayson's face when he connects the dots, and he drags a hand over his jaw. "Holy shit. You're one of Sebastian Walker's kids."

"Yeah, that's me," I confirm, feeling my cheeks flush.

"Wait, who?" Sephine asks, and Tessa shrugs as Marley and Bria share similar looks.

"I don't know either."

"The football player who won sexiest man of the year the year after me," Hayes explains and now all the women gasp, looking at me differently than before.

"That makes so much sense," Tessa says, and Bria groans, covering her face.

"Mom, you're embarrassing. Please stop."

I laugh, shaking my head as Sephine gasps. "Your mother is Thalia Walker. I have one of her portraits hanging in our living room. I love her work." *Well screw the flowers I was going to send her on her birthday. I think she'd rather know billionaires have her work in their home. Her ego will skyrocket.*

"Her work is spectacular, but I haven't seen anything new for a while. Is she still taking photographs?" Tessa asks, and for the first time this evening, I falter.

Since Bailey ran away, I've only seen Mom pick up her camera a handful of times. It doesn't seem to bring her the same joy it used to.

"She's been taking some time off recently," I say, keeping it vague because while Bailey's absence has been noticed by the media, somehow, we've managed to keep the truth out of the tabloids. The last thing our family needs is to be put on blast again.

"How's the company doing?" Marley interrupts, and I turn to look at her in surprise. *What is she doing?*

Her dad smiles, and everyone's attention slides to her, including Bria who looks as confused as I am. "It's doing well. Maddox is taking charge of winning some of the board members over, and I'm just glad it's not me having to kiss their asses," he says, and Bria shakes her head.

"I don't think you or my dad know how to kiss anyone's ass," Bria says, but I'm too busy trying to figure out who the fuck Maddox is, and why I'm just now learning about him? I have no right to be jealous, but when Marley smiles, I am.

"Bria," Marley says, laughing, and I reach for my water, taking a drink.

"Are you learning anything interesting in your classes?" Grayson asks at the same time Bria leans over to whisper to me.

"You don't have anything to worry about with Maddox," she says, her chest shaking with silent laughter, but I'm still not sure why I haven't heard of him before.

"Sure," I agree, trying to pay attention to what Marley's saying about her classes.

"Relax. She's never looked at him that way, it'd be really weird if she did," Bria continues, and I hate I'm this predictable. I'm jealous of a guy I just learned about when it comes to the girl I'm in love with but not dating. *Why aren't we dating again?*

"Am I that obvious?"

She doesn't even try to hide her smile, her silver eyes lighting up with mischief that should scare me. "You have been from the moment you two saw each other again."

"What are we whispering about?" Tessa asks, and I feel like I've been caught with my hand in the cookie jar.

"Oh, nothing, just telling Bria my hamstrings are tight from not stretching enough before our intervals today."

"He was asking who Maddox was," Bria corrects, thankfully leaving out my feelings for Marley. I'd prefer if she didn't advertise that to everyone before Marley and I even get a fair chance to discuss it. If it ever ends up happening that is, but she's not the only one with cards up her sleeve.

"Has Bria mentioned introducing you to my roommate, Asher? I swear, he talks about her all the time," I retort, throwing her under the bus in response. Her mouth unhinges and Marley laughs.

"Who's Asher?" Tessa asks, looking at her daughter who is too busy glaring at me to notice.

"Exactly how close are you to our daughters if you don't know Maddox is her uncle?" Hayes asks, and when I look at him, his eyes are narrowed in scrutiny, and I'm back to square one.

"I might not know who Maddox is, but I know plenty. Bria has no problem voicing her opinion, but she can be forgetful. She's the kind of girl who will kick your ass if you need it, but she's loyal and a good friend." I take a breath, trying to gather my thoughts, but I don't need to. I need to speak from the heart. "Marley chews her nails when she's nervous, but when she doesn't want you to see, she spins her ring on her thumb. She loves to play the guitar and sing because it allows her a way to express her emotions without discussing them, but it's also the same reason she doesn't share her music with anyone. She's incredibly smart, caring, and the kind of person you meet once in your life, or in my lucky case, twice."

Hayes blinks, his cerulean eyes widening, and I have a feeling he's not caught off guard very often. But sitting to his right is the girl of my fucking dreams with tears shining in her eyes and the most beautiful smile.

~

My phone trills, signaling an incoming text to pull me out of the light sleep I've been drifting in and out of. I blink, trying to get my eyes to adjust to the bright screen in my dark room.

MARLEY

Are you awake?

I'm not missing a chance to talk to her. I'd much rather speak to her over the phone than text, so I call her and it doesn't even have a chance to ring once before she picks up.

"I'm sorry if I woke you up. I just really needed to talk to you and I—" she rambles, speaking too quickly for my barely awake state.

"Sweetheart, take a breath, it's fine. I was kinda awake already," I say, rubbing my eyes as I sit up in my bed. "What's on your mind?"

"How . . . how do you remember all these things about me? The water you remembered to grab for me at the party, that I play the guitar, the music therapy, learning Italian, and everything else. How, JJ? *Why?*"

Okay, I guess the middle of the night is an appropriate time for this conversation although I'd prefer to have it in person. I wasn't honest with her about the one thing I should have been honest with her about, but I can be honest about this. "Why? Marley, do you even need to ask?" I laugh, not because it's not funny, but because it's the easiest damn question I could ever answer. "Because I'm in love with you, sweetheart. I've loved you from the moment I saw you, and I can't imagine ever not loving you. I know it doesn't make sense, but I've had a lot of time to think about this, and I think not being able to understand how it happened is part of the beauty. All I need to know is what you mean to me and that's enough. I've replayed our hours in France so many times, memorizing everything so if I ever saw you again, I could show you what you mean to me instead of telling you." I swallow the lump forming in my throat, hoping I didn't take it too far. *At this point, go big or go home.* "I didn't think I'd see you again because of your ex-boyfriend, but I'm glad he convinced you to transfer here."

I don't know why I hold back the letters. Maybe it's because I know if I tell her, Marley will want to read them, and some things are better left forgotten in the box I've kept them in. There are sins written I'm not ready to atone for by losing Marley.

Marley's subtle gasp of air is the only reason I can tell she's still there. She exhales a shuddering breath, and I wish I were next to her right now. "Wow . . . um, there is a lot to unpack, and some I think we need to talk about in person, but your last point is something I can clear up right now. I didn't transfer to Beaumont for Trent. I met Trent in April after I'd already been accepted and decided I was transferring here. My dad went here, which you know after dinner, but my transfer was already in motion when I met him."

What?

Oh fuck, I'm an idiot. Why the hell did I believe Trent? I should have known better, because it's not something I think Marley would do, but I wish I'd asked about this sooner.

"Tomorrow," I blurt out, eager to have this conversation with her. Hell, I'd drive over there right now if she asked, but I also want to give her a second to process everything. *Shit, does she need more time than tomorrow?* "If it's not too soon, we can talk tomorrow," I say, trying to backtrack a little to take some of the pressure off Marley.

"JJ, don't you have a game?" she asks.

"Bring your family to the game. They can use my family's tickets to sit in the suites, so no one really bothers them."

My eyes are slowly drifting shut as I lie back into my mountain of pillows.

"I'll see what I can do, but they might've already made plans."

"It's no problem if you can't make it, but I'll leave them at the ticket booth anyway if you guys can. I'm sorry, but I do have to get back to sleep," I say, my heart filling with hope. "Goodnight, Marley."

"Goodnight, JJ," she says softly, and even though she didn't say anything about her feelings in this call, I still fall asleep with a smile because her face at dinner said everything she's left unspoken.

CHAPTER EIGHTEEN

Marley

I BARELY GOT ANY SLEEP LAST NIGHT. I SPENT THE entire night replaying every look, touch, and word from JJ. The bags under my eyes show how exhausted I am, and it doesn't matter how many cups of tea I drink, I'm exhausted.

He told me he loves me. Actually—not only that he loves me, but he's in love with me.

The thought makes me giddy, but also sick to my stomach with nerves because . . . I love JJ too. *How could I not?*

I've never been one for sports, but at his game today, I couldn't take my eyes off him. JJ was incredible, his reflexes like lightning. I could have sworn he looked right at us a few times, but with the distance and the helmets, it's hard to be sure.

My mom and Tessa came with me and Bria, but my dad had to stop by the West Coast offices, and Grayson went with him. They're supposed to be back tonight, but once the moms learned JJ wanted to meet with me after the game, they were practically shoving me out the door. I think it's a safe bet JJ won them over.

The butterflies in my stomach are fluttering with excitement as I walk up to the ice cream shop we agreed to meet at. JJ's sitting outside on a bench, fiddling with a small bouquet of daisies in his lap, and I melt like an ice cube in the Sahara, any nerves quickly disappearing.

He stands up, wiping his hands on his thighs as he smiles at me.

Everything standing in our way before seems to have failed to reduce the love I think we have for each other: *time, distance, and even last names.* None of it matters.

I can only hope love will be enough.

JJ leans down, brushing his lips over my cheek as he pulls me into a hug, and I've never felt more safe. "Hey," he murmurs while I sink into his embrace.

"Hi," I say, inhaling the smell of soap and citrus.

"These are for you," he says, offering me the flowers after pulling away.

I wonder if he knows what his love language is, because I would have initially said words of affirmation, but now I want to say it's acts of service. "I love them, but you didn't have to buy me another bouquet. You already gave me flowers last night," I say, holding them in one hand as he opens the door for us.

"I know I didn't have to, but I wanted to."

He hovers next to me as we stand in line, looking at all the different flavors when I reach for his hand, hooking our pinkies together. JJ looks down at me, a sweet smile curling his lips up, and I think I might go into cardiac arrest. His smile combined with sweet words is a lethal combination for my heart. I can already hear the music in my head, perfectly emulating this moment.

"I feel like I should have brought you flowers. You were incredible today," I admit, and his smile widens.

"Thank you, Mar. It means a lot coming from you, and even more you were able to make it not just to the game, but also here."

My cheeks flush under the weight of his focus. "I wouldn't have missed either," I say, the conversation pausing as a scooper asks what flavors we want.

JJ's already handing over his card before I can offer to pay, leading us back out to the bench he was on when I arrived.

"How did you sleep?" he asks, angling his body to face me, and I look down at the flowers in my lap, next to my cup of cookies and cream.

"Not the best," I admit, and JJ's arm rests on the back of the bench, his knuckles brushing against my shoulder. "I had a lot on my mind." I take a bite of my ice cream, glancing at JJ who is only watching me with what I can describe as concern.

"Even after we spoke?" JJ asks, prodding gently for me to attempt untangling my thoughts. The flowers in front of me suddenly become very interesting again. I don't know why this is hard for me to talk about. It shouldn't be. I think my feelings for JJ is the least complicated thing in my life and it's still difficult to vocalize. "Marley?"

"I'm not good at talking about my feelings," I say, my confidence waning as I struggle to find the right words to say. Give me a piece of paper and I can write them into song lyrics, or a guitar and I'll find the right chords to speak the unspoken. Me trying to vocalize my feelings is a different thing entirely.

He smiles at me, and it feels exactly like the first day of spring after a long winter. "It's okay."

Maybe it doesn't matter if I have the right words. Maybe it's about trying to be vulnerable.

"I thought about you all the time after I left France. I went back and forth between regretting not giving you my full name or phone number, and being glad I didn't." JJ flinches, and I shake my head, quickly elaborating. "It's not that I didn't want to see you again, but everything about our time together was perfect. I was afraid if I saw you again, it would somehow ruin it."

"And has seeing me again ruined it?"

"No," I answer quickly, and JJ's shoulders relax. "JJ, you're like a breath of fresh air, filling my lungs instead of suffocating them. If anything, you're better than I ever could have hoped for." I reach over to take his hand, trying to reassure him because I'm not sure I'm making any sense. "It scares me how comfortable I am with you because I don't let people in. My entire life, I've seen and experienced first-hand how cruel people can be. But you, JJ? You have made it so easy for me to be in love with you from the moment I met you. I feel like my existence has been separated into two categories, and every single moment before you came into my life pales in comparison after meeting you. That's what I thought about all night."

It feels like a weight has been lifted from my chest, finally admitting my feelings for him.

"I-I . . ." JJ trails off, his eyes shining as he stares at me.

"You okay?" I ask, and this time, his smile is bright enough it could light up the darkest night.

He brushes his thumb over the back of my hand, the gentle gesture causing my body to react with a shiver. "My words are failing me right now," JJ admits, his voice a quiet rumble.

"How about, I love you too?" I suggest, and he chuckles.

"I do—*so much.*"

JJ and I sat at the ice cream shop as long as we could, but unfortunately, Bria could only stall for so long. It worked out fine because JJ had plans with the team, and I'd rather not scare him off by subjecting him to my father's line of questioning for the second night in a row. Unfortunately, when JJ kissed me goodbye, one kiss turned into two, and then I lost track until Bria called to ask where I was.

I step out of my car with my flowers in hand at the same time my dad and Grayson climb out of theirs. If the tension I can clearly see in my father's shoulders didn't clue me in to something being wrong, the scowl on his face says everything.

My hand lingers on my car door as I strain to hear what they're saying.

"I'm so sick of this shit, Gray. Do they really think because headquarters are in New York, they'll get away with anything they want?" Dad asks, tugging a hand through his salt and pepper colored hair.

"I can draw up the paperwork tonight, but I can't file it until we get back. I trust my associate, but I'd prefer to handle this myself," Grayson says, and Dad shakes his head. I should interrupt, but I want to know more.

"No, you rarely take time off. I'm not having you do any more work than I already have by asking you to go with me today. It can wait until we're back."

What is going on?

Grayson scoffs, shutting his door. "Hayes, I'm volunteering. Tessa will understand, and I'm sure the girls are ready for us to give them a break. If you need it done tonight, I'll get it done." If my dad will listen to anyone, it's Grayson.

"I can't wait to fucking retire, but I hate this is Marley's future. There's no question she'll thrive, but the fucking people. They make the job a thousand times harder than it needs to be," Dad says, his shoulders drooping.

I know there's nothing I can do to jump into the future, but I feel guilty I can't take over the company yet. Dad's given me everything and more, including supporting me when I told him I needed out of the city. It might not be my dream, but I want to do this for him.

"Have you thought about delegating more to Maddox?

I'm sure he'd be happy to help more," Grayson suggests, and Dad loosens his tie.

"No. His kids are young, and I can't ask him to change his mind about taking on more until they're in school. Maybe Dean had the right idea—getting out before he was in too deep." Dad pauses and I can only imagine everything he's leaving unsaid.

My uncles—Maddox and Dean—are half-brothers, and they've both worked for the family company at one point or another in their lives. My Uncle Maddox is currently the Chief Operating Officer, working as my father's right-hand man until he becomes mine, but both of his kids are still under the age of five. I remember overhearing my parents talk about how Uncle Maddox told my dad he was afraid of missing out on time with his kids while they were young, and my dad promised him he wouldn't have to.

My Uncle Dean was initially being groomed for the position prior to Uncle Maddox taking on the role when he abruptly quit to join the fire academy twenty years ago. I've always envied my Uncle Dean for making a choice to defy his birthright as a Benson in the way I'm afraid to let myself dream about. Sometimes, I think my father feels the same way.

"You could alwa—" Grayson starts to say before Dad levels him with a sharp look.

"No, and I don't want Marley to know anything about this either. I'll just plan on making more trips out here to help with the transition of the new head of this branch. At least there's a bright side of getting to see my kid more."

I hate seeing him like this, but what I hate even more is how he's trying to shield me from it instead of letting me carry some of the load.

"It's only a couple more years, right?" Dad asks, dragging his hands over his jaw.

Yeah, Dad. It's only a couple more years.

I shut my car door loud enough for them to hear, plastering on a smile to pretend I didn't hear everything they just said. Dad's face lights up, but I see right through the exhaustion he's trying to hide. "There's my girl. How was the game?"

"It was super fun. JJ was a rockstar, but how was the visit to the branch today?" I ask, fishing a little to see if he'll tell me.

Dad ruffles my hair. "It was fine, but why aren't you inside? Did you go somewhere after the game?"

My cheeks flush because I'm an open book when it comes to JJ, and Grayson eyes me the same way Bria does. "You were with JJ, weren't you?" he muses, and I can't help smiling.

"We went to get some ice cream." I steal a look at my dad to gauge what he's thinking, but I can't get a read on him. "What did you think of him?"

"He's not good enough for you," Dad answers, causing Grayson to snort.

"You never think anyone is good enough for me," I counter as we start walking up the stairs.

"I liked him. I thought he held his own against the interrogation last night," Grayson says, and I agree. I was mortified when Dad asked what his parents do, but I can admit I should've asked JJ sooner. I mean, I assumed his parents were wealthy based on his clothes and the second house in France, but I didn't realize they were famous as well. He told me Mirabelle was engaged to a football player, but I didn't think much about it.

"Hayes, you have to admit this kid is better than the previous asshole."

I nod quickly. "Exactly. JJ's a good guy."

"I'll believe it when I see it," Dad says stubbornly, but I have no doubt in my mind JJ will be able to win him over. He's a sucker when it comes to making me happy, and if JJ makes me happy—*which he does*—then I know Dad will learn to love him.

When we step into the apartment, Mom, Tessa, and Bria are sitting on the couch, staring at the door. "Finally! So?" Bria asks, nearly bouncing in her seat with anticipation.

"So, what?" I say, walking to get a glass of water from the kitchen.

"Oh, come on, we've been sitting here for over an hour waiting for you to get back to grill you on how it went with JJ," Tessa says, patting the open spot on the couch next to her. Mom's eyes are bright as she watches me, and it's nice to have them rooting for him.

Dad groans, shrugging out of his blazer to sit on the other side of Mom. "I don't want to hear about this."

"Plug your ears then," Tessa says, and Mom laughs.

"Okay, you two, play nice. Benson, just look at Marley. She's practically glowing, and I want to hear what the young man did to make her so happy. You heard him talk about her last night—it was so sweet. I hope you haven't forgotten what young love is like in your old age," Mom teases, reaching for his hand. Instead, he wraps his arm around her, pulling her into him. He presses a kiss to her cheek, and I melt, watching them.

"I'm four months older than you. Watch who you're calling old," he grumbles, before sighing. "Go ahead, Mar, tell us what the boy did—keep in mind I can ruin his life in a couple of phone calls if he hurts you."

I roll my eyes, acting as if this annoys me, but I love how happy my parents are together. They ground each other and balance out in the best way. Kind of like me and JJ.

A picture pops into my head of JJ and me in twenty years, sitting the same way my parents are after a long day of work, whispering secrets to each other in different languages. The idea makes my smile wider as I enjoy torturing my father to the delight of everyone else with details of my time with JJ today.

CHAPTER NINETEEN

I'M ON TOP OF THE FUCKING WORLD.

I wipe the small stream of beer off my chin that escaped while the guys and I were shotgunning. Between the conversation I had with Marley and this morning's game, I feel on fire. The drugs and alcohol have numbed the twinge of pain in my knee to nothing.

The only thing I would change about this moment would be having Marley here, but with her parents being in town, it's okay she's not, especially when I know this isn't her scene. I know she's missed them, and I feel bad I unintentionally crashed their dinner last night.

Her dad is fucking terrifying, but I think I held my own.

I catch sight of Asher jumping into the pool with all of his clothes on, and everyone else follows suit. The pool is no match for the flood of people, and it quickly becomes a mosh pit. I wouldn't touch it with a ten-foot pole.

I drop my empty can in a nearby trash bag hung up on the back of a chair before heading inside to grab another drink. A couple of people clap me on the back in congratulations, but I don't bother taking note of their faces. I know everyone and everyone knows me.

A group of cheerleaders I know passes me a shot in the kitchen, and I don't think twice before throwing it back. I mean, why the hell not? It's okay to let loose sometimes. I'm not in any danger of missing a call from Bailey. It's only been a month since his last call, and I deserve a night where I don't carry the weight of everything on my shoulders.

The only problem is I've lost track of how much I've had.

Is it a bad idea to call Marley? I want to talk to my girl—

A hand taps me on the shoulder, and I turn, my vision swimming as a girl throws her arms around my torso, knocking me off balance. "You run so fast, like a cheetah!" she says, and my back hits the wall behind me. I blink rapidly, my brain slow to connect the dots. *Why is this chick hugging me?*

"Hey, don't touch me," I slur, pushing her gently off me as the music rattles every bone in my body.

This is wrong, I took it too far.

My vision clears enough I can place her as a cheerleader, but her name is lost in the oblivion. "JJ, I was just congratulating you?"

"I-I . . . I have a girlfriend. Don't touch me," I say, trying to remember if Marley and I defined what we are earlier, but it's not coming to me. I don't think we did. I would remember, but regardless, she's the only one for me.

"You must be *really* drunk if you think you have a girlfriend. I thought you didn't do relationships, or do you just tell everyone that because you're gay?" she asks, crossing her arms over her chest.

"What?"

"Are you? It's okay if you are, but you don't have to hide it. Sure, it'd be disappointing, because holy hell, have you looked in a mirror? Half the cheerleaders totally want to hook up with you," she rambles on, and my brain can't even comprehend this conversation right now.

"I'm not gay," I say, stumbling over my words.

"Wanna prove it to me?" she asks, stepping forward to rest her hand on my chest, sliding it all the way down to my pants, copping an unwanted feel before I can react. I jerk back from her touch, hitting my head on the wall.

"No. *No*, I have a girlfriend," I insist, wincing as my head throbs.

A familiar blonde comes out of nowhere, stepping between us. "He said no," I recognize Charlie's voice, but all I can think is how I've messed up everything.

"Call me when this psycho bitch isn't here."

I shut my eyes for a moment, resting my head against the wall, until there's a slap across my face, snapping my eyes open. *Oh shit. She looks pissed.*

"How much have you had to drink?"

"Charlie?" I question, struggling to make sense of what's going on. The girl—*Marley.*

"Yes, dumbass. C'mon, we need to get you out of here while you can still somewhat walk," she says, wrapping my arm around her shoulders to help support me. We stagger toward the exit, shouldering our way through people as my eyelids fall further down.

"M-Marley," I slur, reaching for the phone in my pocket.

"Yeah, sorry, but you're not calling her while you're like this. What the hell were you thinking getting this fucked up?"

I *wasn't* thinking. *I don't think I have been for a while.*

I wake up on the floor of an unknown bathroom, my shirt soaked through with sweat and a stain that looks like vomit after closer examination. A loud pounding slams against my skull as I focus on my hands shaking in front of me.

My stomach rolls and I lean forward into the toilet, heaving.

What the hell happened last night?

I wipe my mouth on a piece of toilet paper, trying to piece everything together. *I know I was at the party, but everything after is a blur.*

When my stomach stops churning, allowing me to stand, I rinse the aftertaste of vomit from my mouth. However, as I try to cup the water, a majority of it slips through my fingers from how badly they're shaking. I can feel a disgusting sheen of sweat covering me.

The pills—*they'll fix it.* They'll fix *me.* I rapidly pat my pockets, feeling for the extras I've started carrying, but panic begins to course through my veins as I try to think of where I would have put my emergency ones because I'm not feeling them.

The thought of calling them emergency pills results in a dark laugh slipping from me. I'm a fucking mess. *Emergency pills? What happened to the promise you made to stop taking them, JJ?*

I wince, another round of nausea threatening to bring me to my knees as the pressure in my head increases. Holy shit— my jacket. I put them in my jacket.

Shielding my eyes from the harsh white light, I glance around the bathroom, but if I don't even know where I am, how the fuck am I supposed to know where my jacket is.

Bracing myself over the sink, I splash more cold water on my face before reaching into my back pocket for my phone, but I swear, my heart stutters in my chest at the empty pockets.

My phone is my lifeline to Bailey. If he gets into trouble and by some miracle calls me, only I don't answer because I got too fucked up at a party. I don't know how I would ever forgive myself.

Reaching for the handle, I stagger out of the bathroom into a dorm room, clearly belonging to a girl, and I feel even worse than I did before. What the hell have I done?

I drag my hands through my hair, feeling like I'm gasping for air as I search through the messily made bed for my phone. I can't have missed a call from Bailey, and Marley—oh god. *Marley*. My vision blurs as my chest constricts at the thought of hurting her because I took it too far mixing alcohol and pills.

The tears slipping down my cheeks echo the cracks breaking me apart from the inside out. *Why am I like this?* I clutch at my chest, dropping to my knees as the pounding in my head only grows worse. How could I be so reckless and stupid?

I need to stop taking the pills—this can't happen again.

Marley deserves better than this. I know I wouldn't cheat on her, but I'd be stupid if I didn't consider the thought that it could have happened and I'd have no idea. My fist hits the hard floor as I choke on a sob, bowing my head, and *everything* aches.

I'm done. I'm so done with all of this—the crushing pressure everything will fall apart if *I* fall apart, and I'm nearly killing myself to keep up with it. *It's fucking exhausting.*

A hand rests on my back, startling me.

"JJ, *oh my god*. What happened? What's wrong?" Charlie's voice asks as I lift my head, gasping for air.

"What the fuck is wrong with me?"

Charlie wipes my cheeks, helping to clear some of the tears from my vision, shaking her head. "Take a deep breath with me."

"I-I can't," I stutter over my words, panic refusing to release its grip on me.

I thought I'd hit a low point when I broke down in front of Marley, but if that was a breakdown, then I don't know what to call this. My nervous system is in *fight or flight* mode, tempted to let the boulder sitting on my chest finally crush me.

She grabs my face, forcing me to look at her. "You can—in through your nose, out through your mouth," she says, and I try, feeling the hot tears continue to stream as I inhale raggedly. "Again."

I continue, feeling the panic slowly recede, but my body continues trembling. "Thank you," I whisper, and Charlie brushes my tears away again.

"Dude, what is going on?"

"I'm . . ." My voice falters, chickening out at the last second. "What happened last night?"

"I found you in the kitchen with a cheerleader still trying to feel you up after you pushed her off of you. You were in rough shape, so I brought you here because the party was just down the street from the dorms. JJ, do I need to call someone? Asher?" Charlie asks, and it feels a little easier to take a breath now, knowing even out of my mind, I was right about wanting nothing to do with another girl.

"Where's my jacket and phone?" I ask, rubbing my eyes.

She squints, staring at me. "Are you insane?"

"Charlie, I need my phone. My brother—*he* . . . I'm the only one he calls. I need my phone," I say, and I can feel my heart begin to race in my chest again.

Charlie pushes herself up and grabs the jacket hanging on the back of the door, tossing it at me. "Your phone is in the pocket," she says, and my breath catches. *She would have said if she found my pills.* "You took off the jacket when we got here last night, but I kept your phone. I didn't think you should be calling anyone in the state you were in."

I reach in the pockets, and I hate how the second my

fingers graze over the pills that somehow lasted through everything last night, I relax. Instead of grabbing them, I pull my phone from the other pocket with my keys still in it, quickly turning it on to see the only call I missed was from Marley. "Shit," I mumble.

"When I saw Marley texted, I let her know you had too much to drink and I brought you back here."

I look at her, embarrassed, but grateful for how she took care of me last night. Charlie's a better friend than I deserve.

"Thank you, Charlie. I'm sorry," I say, my mouth feeling like it's been stuffed full of cotton.

She pulls a lock of her strawberry blonde hair over her shoulder, twisting it around her finger. "You didn't answer my question," she says, and I'm not sure there's a chance in hell I can play this off without giving Charlie something.

"Which one?"

Her mouth flattens. "Do I need to call my cousin?"

"I don't know," I admit, hating myself for it even more when her eyes widen. I recognize the fear in them because I know what it's like to be afraid. I'm even more ashamed when I remember we're in the dorms because Charlotte's only eighteen.

I've known her for a couple of years now since her folks live in the area, and Asher started bringing me with him to visit when we got sick of dining hall food freshman year. I think part of it was because he could tell I was homesick.

"It scared me last night how out of it you were. I mean, I've seen you drunk, JJ, but it was a different level. And this morning? I . . . I don't even know what to say," Charlie says, and I look away, my hands gripping tightly into fists.

She's a kid—it's not her burden to shoulder.

"I just had too much. I promise I'm fine, Charlotte." I reach to ruffle her hair while using the wrong name, hoping to make her smile a little. *She doesn't.*

"I don't think you are, but I hope you know Ash and I are here for you if you're in any kind of trouble."

"I'm sorry," I say again, because I'm not sure what else I can say.

Charlie stands up, catching me by surprise when she wraps her arms around my torso. "Don't be sorry, just don't do it again, okay?"

"Okay," I agree, returning her hug.

She steps back, wrinkling her nose. "Sorry, but you smell awful. I don't think you should let anyone come near you without showering first."

I lift the collar of my shirt up, grimacing at the stench hitting me a second later. "Gross," I mumble, tempted to just take it off to dump it in a trash can, and wear only my hoodie on my walk back to the house.

"Do you want me to take you home?" Charlie asks, and I shake my head, mustering a smile.

"I think the fresh air will do me good. Thanks again for looking out for me," I say, but honestly, I'm starting to get nauseous again.

I know I look like a fucking wreck, but thankfully, it's early enough in the morning that most people are still asleep, I can complete my walk of shame without too many prying eyes on me.

Showering helps me feel a little better, but I'm not sure there's anything possible to change how disappointed I am in myself for putting Charlotte in that position last night. I should wake Asher up to talk to him, but I know once I open my mouth I can't take it back. It'll change everything.

So instead, I sit at my desk and I write to the girl who makes me want to be the guy she believes I am, haunted by the bottle of pills sitting in the drawer a few inches away.

CHAPTER TWENTY

Marley

MY SONGBOOK IS LYING FLAT IN FRONT OF ME OPEN to the song I'm working on as I strum the chords of my guitar a few times. I've been stuck on it for the last hour after getting off the phone with Kaden, and all the phone call accomplished was making me miss my little brother, especially after seeing everyone else this weekend.

"*I've tried to fight this feeling.*
The one making my knees weak and my head spin.
I didn't understand before.
But I understand now.
It's only been you.
It's only ever been you, even before you," I sing softly, strumming the chords while following along with the scribbles and notes in my songbook, trying to find my footing.

"*I think you're the only one, the only one that's ever seen me.*

Now I'm here, singing a stupid song about stupid you and stupid me . . ." I trail off, dropping my guitar next to me as I flop backwards into the pillows of my bed. I groan, dragging my hands over my face as my door creaks open.

I jump half out of my skin, nearly slipping off the edge of

the bed as I turn to see who's there. I instantly smile at the sight of JJ, his massive frame filling the doorway, my heart skipping a beat as he fixes his smile on me. I knew he was coming over, but I must have lost track of time.

"Personally? Your song about stupid me and *pretty you* might be my new favorite, but I think I have a bone to pick with the writer who never locks her front door," JJ says, crossing his arms over his chest as he raises an eyebrow.

"Would it make you feel better if I said I unlocked it specifically for you?" I ask, sitting up as JJ takes steps toward me to close the distance between us.

"No. I'm perfectly capable of standing out there by myself until you come let me in. You and Bria need to start locking your door."

I stick my tongue out at him. "You'll be happy to hear my dad has a locksmith coming by in the morning to install one with a five-minute auto lock timer, ergo, problem solved."

"You could have led with that, sweetheart," he says, taking a seat next to me, leaning in to brush his lips over my cheek, his stubble scratchy. "How was your night?"

"It was fun. My dad and Tessa made dinner, and then Bria got a text from Asher when her dad had her phone," I say, a quiet laugh bubbling from me.

JJ laughs, shaking his head. "Of course he did. What did it say?" he asks, and I try not to get distracted by the bags under his eyes.

"Something along the lines of she's the most beautiful girl in the world, but it's pretty obvious he's not the best at drunk texting," I say, and JJ laughs, the sound a deep rumble from his chest.

"Sounds like something he would do. What did Bria say?"

I raise my eyebrows skeptically because JJ's spent enough time with Bria to know exactly what she did next. "Denied everything, of course." I roll my eyes because she's acting ridiculous, but after what our fathers put JJ through, I don't blame her. "How was your night? It sounded like you had fun." I didn't expect him to answer last night when I texted, but I wanted him to know I was thinking about him. Charlie said he spent the night sleeping on the bathroom floor.

JJ smiles, but it looks forced. He reaches for my hand, and I'd be lying if I said anxiety wasn't creeping in. "Honestly, I would rather have been here with you," he says, a soft exhale escaping his lips. "I'm sorry I wasn't."

"Are you okay?" I ask, wondering if there's more he's not saying.

His thumb swipes over the back of my hand, and he nods after a moment. "Better now that I'm with you," he says, and JJ lifts my hand, pressing his lips to my knuckles. "Didn't mean to interrupt you, but I couldn't have my girl calling herself stupid in a song." JJ's eyes twinkle, meeting mine through his dark lashes, and I feel a flush crawl up my neck. My god, I'm not sure which wreaks more havoc on my heart—being called his girl or sweetheart—but either way, they do a number on me.

"It's still a work in progress," I say, willing myself to not hide this part of me from him.

JJ glances at the open songbook, and I reach for it before he can try. I've written too many songs about him to have it sitting out. I have no doubt if I asked him to leave it alone, he would in a heartbeat, but if I knew JJ had a notebook lying around with songs he'd written about me, I can admit it'd be tempting.

"Do you write a lot of songs about me?" he teases, and I roll my eyes, trying to feign nonchalance when my heart is actually galloping at the speed of a racehorse.

"Don't flatter yourself," I say, getting up to move the guitar to its stand in the corner, setting the songbook on the shelf nearby. My queen bed somehow looks small with JJ sitting on it, watching me with his dark hair waving messily in a way to make me want to tangle my fingers in them while I kiss him.

Will being with him ever stop feeling like a dream?

I have never wanted anyone the way I want JJ. He's the only thing I've ever dared to let myself want. I love music, but it'll only ever be a hobby. I can't think of it as anything else, no matter how tempting it might be to let myself consider more.

I'm honestly not even sure I know who I am, but the way JJ makes me feel like it's okay to color outside the lines to find out means more to me than he could ever know.

I love the way he's my biggest cheerleader, and how he makes me feel like I'm the center of his universe. *It's an addicting feeling to be loved by JJ.* I'm done worrying about how soon it is or what anyone else thinks because *fuck them* if they can't understand the way I feel when I'm with him.

The most beautiful thing about JJ isn't how physically attractive he is, but rather how big his heart is for the people lucky enough to be loved by him.

"Marley," JJ says, and his throat bobs as he swallows, the energy in the room shifting.

"What?" I ask, my voice breathy. My fingers fidget with the bottom of my shorts, but I can't look away from him.

"If you're waiting for permission to kiss me, this is my explicit consent begging you to kiss me whenever you want." JJ's smile is lopsided and beautiful. "I'm yours, Mar. I always have been."

The happiness he makes me feel is more than I could have hoped for.

He reaches out the instant I'm in front of him, tugging me closer, his hands sliding over my hips. I straddle his strong thighs as I loop my arms around his neck, leaning in to press my lips against his. JJ's nose bumps against mine as he kisses me back, his fingers pressing into my lower back through my shirt. *I want to know what it feels like to have him touch me everywhere.*

"I'm yours too," I whisper against his lips. The audible hitch in his breath makes my heart sing, and I can't believe what a fool I was for naively believing one day in France could ever be enough. It should terrify me how much I want JJ, but it doesn't.

"I've never wanted anything more," JJ says, tilting his head to kiss me again. His lips are soft as they move against mine, and it feels so damn right, my heart might explode.

My shirt rides up a little as I shift, wanting to be closer, and his touch is featherlight as his fingertips dance over my skin. It makes every part of me yearn for more. I part my lips, and JJ follows my lead, deepening the kiss. His tongue tangles with mine, and I curl my fingers in the short strands on the back of his head.

More. Please, more.

I reach down to the hem of my shirt, my pulse racing, but before I can start to pull it off, JJ angles his head back. His eyes are hazy as they scan over my face before finding mine as he inhales a ragged breath. "Are you good?" JJ asks, his voice hoarse.

"I'm good. I was just . . . I was going to take my shirt off? Are you okay?"

"Definitely—nowhere else I'd rather be."

It gives me the boost in confidence needed to pull my shirt off, acutely aware of the rise and fall of my chest from how hard I'm breathing. His full lips part as he stares like he's committing the sight of me wearing a sports bra to memory. Slowly, JJ lifts his head to look at me, pure desire shining in his handsome features.

"You're breathtaking," JJ says, shaking his head, chuckling to himself. "If you only knew how many times I pictured this moment over the last two and a half years."

"What did you picture?" I ask, my breath trembling as JJ's fingers skate higher up my side.

"I'd rather show you."

Yes, *please.*

I nod eagerly, and JJ rolls us to lie on top of me, bracing himself over me. His pelvis presses perfectly against me, and I can feel how hard he is.

His eyes are normally such a clear green, but right now, they're a hazy moss. I don't think I've ever seen them this color before. I cup his face, feeling the prickle of his stubble. "JJ," I whisper, tracing the curves and edges of his face. I want to memorize every detail.

"Marley."

I'm so irrevocably gone for this man.

I shift restlessly underneath the weight of his body, needing more friction, and JJ chuckles. "I pictured kissing you here," he says, leaning down to kiss the corner of my mouth. "Here." His mouth presses against the curve of my jaw and then where my pulse races. I tip my head back into the comforter, my eyes tempted to flutter shut when JJ lights me on fire. "Eyes on me, sweetheart." I look at him, my head dizzy and he tilts his head to the side, resulting in my head nearly exploding when I realize he means for me to watch in my full-length mirror.

Holy shit.

"Keep going," I say, locking eyes with him in the mirror.

His mouth is soft on the skin above my collarbone, and a quiet moan slips from my lips when he teases the sensitive spot with his tongue. "I thought about here," he mumbles against the swell of my breast, and seeing JJ positioned over me while feeling his lips on my skin is sensation overload. I twist my fingers through his hair causing a groan to rumble from him. "And I've really thought about here," JJ says, pressing a searing kiss directly on my nipple through the sports bra. *It's not enough.*

"Please, JJ—" No sooner than his name leaves my mouth, JJ's silencing me with a desperate kiss making my toes curl. He grinds his hips against me, and I bunch the fabric of his shirt in my fists, holding him close. I need more of him.

He pulls away, dropping his head to rest in the crook of my neck. "Marley, I'm trying to control myself."

I laugh, wrapping my arms around him. "Have you considered maybe I don't want you to?"

"If I've learned anything, it's that good things come to those who wait. If they didn't, then I wouldn't have you," he says sweetly, pressing another kiss to my neck.

"You're right."

JJ slowly pushes up, creating a clear separation of where I end and he begins, taking the spot next to me on the bed. It makes me feel a little better when he readjusts himself, but I'm envious of his self-restraint. His head turns, catching me staring at the obvious bulge in his pants. *There's not enough readjusting in the world to hide that.* JJ rolls on his side, tipping my chin up to look at him. "I promise, it's not because I don't want to. *God, do I want you.* Maybe I'm just a romantic or whatever, but there's no rush. I'm not going anywhere, and I hope you aren't either."

"I'm not. I believe you, JJ," I say, relaxing a little. I mirror how he's lying, my knees bumping his, and a warm smile forms on his face. "Did you . . ." I trail off, unsure if it's okay to ask.

"Did I what?"

"You said you pictured this moment. Did you mean it?"

"I mean every word with you," JJ says. "It was actually thirty-one months, but who's counting?"

I smile, chuckling. "It sounds like you have." A blush crawls up his neck and into his cheeks, but I don't want him to be embarrassed. "I think it's cute," I say, but now JJ raises an eyebrow.

"You think it's cute I've been counting since the last time I was with a girl?"

My brain glitches, not understanding. It means . . . I mean, I know what Trent told me about never seeing JJ with anyone, and Bria told me what she heard from Asher, but when JJ never said anything, I didn't know what to think. "But that's when we met in France?"

"Trust me, I know." JJ snorts, dragging a hand through his hair. "Marley, you're the last girl I kissed. I mean, I'm not saying I didn't kiss other girls before I met you, but there hasn't been anyone since you."

"But you're *you*. How?" I ask, stumbling over my words because JJ has set the standard to another level when it comes to *if he wanted to, he would.*

"What does being *me* have to do with anything?" he asks, an edge to his voice.

Oh shit, that is so not how I meant it.

JJ sits up and I follow suit. "I didn't mean it like that. I meant because—well, honestly, you're the type of hot guy most girls wouldn't even try to hide taking a picture of to send to their friends. You're kind, charismatic, and a football player —" I scramble to explain, but JJ cuts me off.

"So because I'm hot and play football, it means I'm a man-whore who can't keep it in his pants like Trent?" *Oh my god, he looks so hurt right now.*

"JJ—" I try to interrupt.

"Look, I don't care if you were with other people. Trust me, I'm aware of how slim the odds were of us running into each other again, but having sex with someone means something to me. I didn't want to be with just anyone—I wanted to be with you." JJ exhales sharply, looking away from me. *How could this have gone so wrong so quickly?*

I reach for his hand, holding it tightly to keep JJ from pulling away entirely. "*Amore mio*[1], I'm sorry," I say, silently begging him to look at me. "It came out wrong. If anything, I feel bad for not waiting for you too. I wish I had because it's not a bad thing, and I'm truly sorry if I made you feel like it was. I know you're not Trent. It just caught me by surprise."

"I don't want you to feel bad for anything, but it was more than just waiting for you. I never felt anything remotely close to the connection we had, and it never felt right," JJ admits, turning his head to fix his soft gaze on me. I just did to JJ what I've always hated people doing to me. I assumed because of his sport, appearance, and easy-to-love personality he was a certain way, when the reality couldn't be further from it.

Fuck, I really messed up.

I wrap my arms tightly around him. "I'm so fucking sorry. I didn't mean it that way at all." I only feel slightly better when his arms immediately wrap around me, instead of pushing me away.

"It's okay, sweetheart. I know, I just . . ." he trails off, pressing a kiss to the side of my head as I bury my head in his shirt.

"I hurt your feelings," I say, knowing for a fact I did. If the roles were reversed and JJ had said that to me, I'd be crushed.

JJ takes a deep breath, and I feel his chest expand. "I'm not going to lie, it stings hearing you say it, even if I know it's because I caught you off guard. So, maybe this one is on me because it should've been a conversation we had before now."

I just can't get over how unbelievable JJ is. He saved that part of him for me or for himself—either way, it doesn't really matter. His hand strokes my back soothingly, and I know this is exactly where I'm meant to be.

"You're the only person I've ever said I love you to," I

---

1. My love.

whisper, closing my eyes as I inhale the crisp smell of his laundry detergent, the same smell I could breathe in forever.

"Not even to Trent?" he asks a moment later, a vulnerable wobble to his deep voice.

I sit back so JJ can see I'm telling the truth. "Not even to Trent. He said it to me, but it always felt like a form of manipulation, and I never said it back. I didn't feel that way for him, and I refused to lie because I couldn't figure out how to love him when I was still utterly in love with you."

It starts slow before his face breaks wide open into the most earth-shattering smile. "You know, Marley, for someone who claims to be terrible at expressing their feelings, you just did a pretty damn good job."

I return his smile with a relieved one of my own, lean forward to press a sweet kiss to his cheek. "Only for you. Are we okay?"

"We were never not okay. If I've learned one thing from my parents, it's the relationships worth having are the ones that take work. I'm not going anywhere just because you hurt my feelings. It's going to take more than hurt feelings to get rid of me. I'm afraid you're stuck with me," JJ reassures me, and I breathe a sigh of relief because there's no one else I'd rather be stuck with.

And then, breaking the moment, JJ's stomach rumbles loudly, and a blush crawls up his neck. I laugh, covering my mouth to attempt to stop, but I can't, especially not when JJ begins laughing too.

"Are you hungry?" I ask, smiling wider as his dimples poke through.

"I guess so. I'm not really sure the last time I ate," JJ admits while I pull my T-shirt back on.

I slide off the bed, offering him my hand. "Then let's get you some food. There should be leftovers from last night to eat."

He takes my hand, but instead pulls me back to him to kiss me deeply, taking me by surprise. "I'd much rather eat you," he says after pulling away, leaving me craving more. JJ stands up, his hands skating down my sides to linger at my hips.

I can honestly say I've never met anyone like JJ. I don't want to mess this up.

His stomach rumbles again, protesting his statement. I laugh, patting his stomach. "I think a different part of you would prefer real food."

JJ raises an eyebrow. "I can think of a couple parts of me that'd be plenty satisfied with just you, but you might be right. To the kitchen we go," he says, confusing me as he bends down and suddenly I'm hanging upside down over his shoulder.

"JJ!" I shriek, holding on tightly to him.

"Yes, dear?"

"What are you doing?" I ask, laughter spilling from me as JJ starts to walk out of my room.

"I'm going to the kitchen. What are you doing?" JJ asks, turning my question around.

"Staring at your ass because you're holding me over your shoulder like a caveman," I retort, taking the opportunity to ogle him.

"Good thing it's a great ass," he says, and my smile doesn't fade the rest of the evening.

CHAPTER TWENTY-ONE

JJ

"Dude, I think Bria might agree to go out with me," Asher says, waggling his eyebrows, and I roll my eyes.

"Pretty sure you said the same thing last week too," I retort, adjusting the strap of my backpack as my stomach turns. *Just a couple more hours. I can do it.*

"Has she said anything to you?" he asks, looking like a damn lovesick puppy.

"Marley?" I ask, playing dumb to distract myself from how shitty I'm feeling.

Asher shoves his hands in the pockets of his sweatpants. "I meant Bria, but if Marley's said anything about my chances, then by all means feel free to share."

Sometimes I have a love hate relationship with this campus and how spread out everything is, especially when walking back from the library to the nearest lot is a mile away. "Not really. Bria and I don't talk about that stuff, and the one time I asked for you, Marley shut me down citing '*girl code,*'" I say, wiping at the sweat dripping down the back of my neck. "If you really want her to go out with you, maybe don't hit on Mirabelle in front of her this weekend."

Asher laughs next to me, and I catch sight of one of the fountains Marley and I splashed around in, and some of the tightness in my chest eases.

I'm trying to cut back on the pills, but it's causing my anxiety to skyrocket, forcing me to feel everything they block out. Tylenol works to an extent for my knee, but I've been in the training room every day this week with Billy, and I haven't been able to run nearly as much. My insomnia has only gotten worse, and I spend half the night staring at the ceiling or the drawer the pill bottle is in as my mind runs rampant.

But, even with everything, the only time I've caved and taken enough to feel normal was during our away game last weekend where we beat the crap out of the University of Northern Washington in Seattle.

Asher nudges my arm, and I glance at him. "What?"

"You're not listening, are you?" he asks, giving me a look.

I open my mouth, planning to say I was, but we both know I'd be lying. "Yeah, I wasn't listening."

"I asked how things are going with your family?" Asher asks, and I push a smile on my face.

"They're good," I say, and I can tell he doesn't believe me because I wouldn't believe me either. "They're happy Mirabelle's engaged because it gives them something else to focus on. Mira's PI hasn't found anything, and neither have my parents."

"I'm sorry," he says, but I don't like the way he's looking at me. *Did Charlie talk to him about the party?*

I look at the ground, noting the cracks in the pavement. "It is what it is," I say, keeping it vague because talking about Bailey is honestly the last thing I want to do right now. It only makes my cravings for the euphoric feeling of forgetting stronger.

Maybe I'm like cracked pavement, pieces of myself slowly being chipped away. I wonder how long I have until the tiny chips split to create a substantial crack—or maybe they already have.

"How are you doing with it all? Has he . . . *you know,* called you recently?"

I swallow the lump forming in my throat. "Why are you asking?"

"Because you're my best friend, and I'm worried about you."

Tell him, my brain screams at me, but the thought of how differently Asher would look at me after knowing the truth makes me more nauseous.

"Thanks, but I'll be okay," I say, trying to believe the words coming out of my mouth.

The truth is I'm lying to both of us.

I walk into the living room, looking for where I left my sneakers, when I run into Trent camped out on the couch with his laptop. Turning around to leave would make it more obvious I'm avoiding him. Even before Marley was in the picture, I wanted nothing to do with him. Trent is the kind of guy who thinks the zeroes in his bank account give him an excuse to act like a douche, and I'm irritated I've tolerated it as long as I have simply because he's my teammate.

Trent looks up, tipping his chin in acknowledgment. "Hey, Walker. Haven't seen you around much the past few weeks," he says, stretching.

"Yeah, been busy," I say, scratching the back of my neck, glancing around for my shoes. I stopped by the flower shop yesterday after Asher and I got back from study hall. I was helping Eddie unload a new shipment, and he kept making comments about how long my hair was getting. I told him he was being rude, especially when he wasn't paying me to be there, but the old man wasn't wrong. It's longer than normal since my mom usually cuts it, but I figured it'd be better if she thought I was taking care of myself before they come this weekend, so I didn't cancel the appointment Eddie scheduled for me this afternoon. I'm not going to make it on time if I can't find my shoes.

"I heard your family is coming to the game this weekend," he starts, and I can feel the tension in my body start to coil.

He's not seriously going to—

"If you need any extra tickets, you can have mine," Trent continues, and I blink in surprise, the offer entirely catching me off guard.

"Thanks," I say, hating the twinge of guilt surfacing in the pit of my stomach. I have no reason to feel guilty after the way he treated Marley, but a part of me is wondering if I'm the asshole in the situation now for not saying anything to Trent. "They have season tickets, but I appreciate the offer."

Trent shrugs, closing his laptop to rub his temples. "No big deal. Just wanted to let you know you could have 'em."

"I appreciate it," I say, scanning the room again before spotting my sneakers under the couch. I must have kicked them underneath when I went upstairs earlier. I pull them out, loosening the laces to slip them on.

"You heading out again?"

I glance up, meeting his curious gaze. "Yeah. I thought I'd get a haircut before this weekend."

Trent cracks a smile, shaking his head. "Man, if I didn't know better, I'd think you were seeing someone with how often you're gone."

I force a wry smile to match the laugh coming out of my mouth. "Funny," I remark, standing up as my knee twinges.

"There's more to life than football, Walker. Hell, you might even play better than you already are if you just loosen up a little," Trent says, pulling his phone out of his pocket.

"Yeah, we'll see," I say noncommittally.

"Whatever you say, but your loss is my gain."

It's ironic how accurate his statement is if it were flipped around because Trent's loss of Marley was one thousand percent my gain.

~

"How are you going to get your homework done if you're staring at me?" I ask without looking up from the equation I'm calculating.

"It's boring," Marley complains.

"I'm not sure it's supposed to be fun, but it still has to be done," I tease, setting down my calculator to write down the answer on my paper. I look up at Marley, finding her watching me with a smile to make me feel like I hung the moon.

She spins the ring on her thumb, and she's too far away from me. I'm not sure I trust myself to keep my hands off Marley if I'm next to her, though.

"What if I just didn't do it? I could throw it out the window and say my boyfriend's dog ate it, and my professor would be none the wiser," she says, her eyes twinkling like stars.

"I don't have a dog," I point out, and Marley scoffs.

"I know, JJ."

I push my homework to the side, standing up from the loveseat to sit by Marley on the couch. Her smile grows, reminding me of a ray of sunshine, and I'm just lucky to have her light shine on me.

"Hi," she says, turning off her tablet to face me.

"Sweetheart, you still have to do your homework," I say, and she frowns, her eyebrows furrowing.

"I don't want to."

I chuckle, shaking my head. "I know you don't want to."

Marley raises her hand and her fingertips graze across my cheek to the shorter strands of hair on the side of my head.

The barber Eddie sent me to called it "a messy crew cut," after making sure to leave the hair on the top of my head long enough for it to still wave. It's a neater version of what Mom normally does, but Bria nodded her approval when I got here earlier. I believe her exact words were, *You look like a Hemsworth, but hotter*, and I felt like a million bucks when Marley's jaw dropped after she walked out of her room. It was certainly enough to make me forget about my interaction with Trent earlier.

"I like your haircut," she says, now running her fingers through the longer strands on top, and a quiet sigh slips from my lips. "When you told me you were getting one, I was worried I wouldn't be able to run my fingers through your hair anymore." The corners of her mouth tilt up, pulling my attention to them, and it was a bad idea to move by Marley, especially when she's combing her fingers through my hair. It'd be so tempting to lean forward and kiss her. I might have restraint, but I'm not a saint, and the number of times I've replayed the moment in her bedroom is embarrassing. I've had two and a half years to fantasize about all the things I want to do with Marley. I want to know what it feels like to press my lips to her skin, and what it feels like to have hers on me. Mostly, I just really want to kiss her. "Hey, JJ?" she asks, and I slowly lift my gaze to meet hers. *God, she's so fucking pretty.*

"What?" I ask.

"You're looking at me like you want to kiss me, *amore mio*[1]." And just like the first time I met her, Marley's whole face breaks into a smile capable of knocking all the air from my lungs.

"That's my line, sweetheart, but yeah, I do," I say, leaning

---

1. My love.

forward to kiss her. She's still smiling when my lips press against hers, and her nails scratch over the back of my head, causing a rumble to rise out of me. *Kissing Marley is dangerous because it makes me want to lose control.*

I cup her face in my hands, reluctantly pulling away. Marley's nose bumps against mine as our breath mingles in the space between our mouths. "Why'd you stop?" she whispers, and my throat catches.

"Because I don't trust myself to if we keep going," I admit, stroking her cheek with my thumb.

"Are you okay with that?" Marley asks, leaning her head back to look at me, her cerulean orbs watching me.

I'd be more than okay with it, but at the same time, I'm afraid I'll disappoint her. I saw how surprised Marley was when she learned I'd waited for her. I'm aware *anything* with Marley will feel like heaven to me, but I want *everything* to be good for her.

"JJ, we don't have to do anything. I'm happy to just be in the same room as you," she says, sincerity ringing in her lyrical voice.

"I love you," I say, and Marley smiles.

"I love you too."

I pull Marley to me, kissing her again as she leans in, meeting me halfway when the lock on the door flips. Marley turns away at the same time Asher and Bria walk in the front door, their conversation halting when they see us.

"Sorry, were we interrupting?" Bria asks, not even bothering to hide her grin.

"Dude, you look like a Hemsworth. *Nice*," Asher says, and Bria laughs, smiling at him.

"I said the same thing," she says, and he visibly melts.

"Get a room." I groan, mildly irritated we've been interrupted.

"In his dreams." Bria scoffs, but her cheeks grow pink.

Asher smiles a dopey smile in her direction, his eyes never leaving her as she perches on one of the bar stools. "I can promise you are in every single one."

Marley chuckles, squeezing my hand as she whispers in my ear. "We can pick this up later?" she offers, and at the risk of sounding like Asher, Marley is all of my dreams coming true.

"Deal."

CHAPTER TWENTY-TWO

Marley

"ARE YOU SURE YOU'RE OKAY WITH MEETING MY family this weekend?" JJ asks, walking out of my bathroom.

"Should I not be okay with it?" I ask, pulling the covers back before climbing into my bed. Everything I've heard from JJ about his family makes it clear how much he loves them, and since hearing the phone call when his sister told him about her engagement, I've been excited to meet her.

JJ's gaze is smoldering as he looks at me, shaking his head. "They can just be . . . a lot. They have big personalities, and I don't want to overwhelm you."

My heart flutters in my chest, and I smile at him. "I'll be fine. I'm excited to meet them," I reassure him, and he studies my face before nodding.

"You'll let me know if you're not okay?" he asks, moving closer to the bed.

It's tempting to roll my eyes, but I appreciate his concern. JJ seems to be the only one who can read me like an open book.

"I promise I will let you know if I'm not. Now will you please get in bed?" I ask, patting the spot next to me. His eyes glimmer, and his fingers skim the bottom of his shirt. *What is he waiting for?*

"I get hot in my sleep. Is it okay if I take my shirt off?" JJ asks, looking at me with those beautiful eyes of his. I think green might be my new favorite color, but only the exact shade of his irises.

JJ surprises me more than he knows. He's asking for permission to take his shirt off, but he had no problem telling me to watch him kiss his way down my body in the mirror? It certainly keeps me on my toes.

"Whatever makes you comfortable," I say, trying not to seem too eager. I don't want JJ to think I asked him to stay the night because I have expectations of anything. Honestly—I want to know what it feels like to fall asleep next to *him* instead of holding my phone. It's really just an added bonus he has a body belonging to a marble statue.

He grabs the back of his shirt, pulling it over his head in a smooth motion, revealing every inch of his perfect physique. I play with my thumb ring, trying not to gawk, but I'm afraid the sight of JJ will never cease to amaze me. I didn't think it was possible for someone to exist with as pure a heart as JJ, who also looks like he belongs on the cover of a magazine.

JJ climbs into bed after turning off the lights, a quiet laugh slipping from his lips as he rolls to face me. The dim lighting coming through my slanted blinds is enough for me to see his handsome features as the corners of his full lips tug upward into a smile. "Sorry, I just . . . sometimes I have to pinch myself to make sure I'm not dreaming," JJ says.

"Yeah?" I ask, mimicking how he's lying.

"Yeah. I don't know if I've said it, but I'm really happy to have been lucky enough for our paths to cross a second time."

Maybe I need to pinch myself. "Even though I was dating your roommate at the time?" I ask, and JJ cringes.

"Maybe we can forget about him," he says, a fuller laugh rumbling from his chest.

"I wish." I scoot closer to JJ, and his body heat is radiating like a furnace in the middle of winter. His arm wraps around me, tucking me closely to him, our bodies lining up perfectly. JJ hisses through his teeth when my feet brush against his legs.

"Your feet are like icicles," he says against the curve of my neck, tangling our legs together as a chuckle slips from me.

"Sorry," I apologize, trying not to laugh as I rest my head on his bicep. I didn't think I was this tired, but there's something so relaxing about having JJ's arms around me.

The subtle fragrance of my body wash lingering on his skin makes me smile as I close my eyes. Lying in his arms feels better than waking to the sound of rain on a spring morning. *I wonder if JJ can feel how fast my heart is beating.*

There's a comfort in the silence, simply enjoying the intimacy of letting sleep slowly pull us under together.

Is this what forever feels like?

~

I'm awoken by the sound of banging and the lack of JJ's body heat as he climbs out of bed.

"What time is it?" I whisper, a pit in the bottom of my stomach as I throw the covers back, moving to follow him.

"It's almost two," he says, moving toward my bedroom door as more banging sounds. "Stay here, Marley."

As much as I want to stay here and hide, I'm not letting him answer the door by himself, and Bria's here. "No, I'm coming with you," I insist, and thankfully, JJ doesn't try to stop me.

"For fuck's sake, do you have any idea what fucking time it is?" Bria yells through the door as JJ flips the kitchen lights on, illuminating the darkness. The expression on Bria's face is murderous, but the pounding from the other side of the door doesn't stop.

"Bria, who is it?" JJ asks, his entire body coiled as he stalks toward the door.

"I don't know. They covered the peephole with their hand!" Bria smacks on the door a couple times in return. "Fuck off, you fucking coward! I hope you choke on your own dick."

I'm sure later this will be funny, but at the moment, it feels like my heart has leaped to my throat.

"Should we call the police?" I ask, and JJ falters, seeming to contemplate the suggestion.

"Dial it just in case, but don't call until we know who it is. It's closing time at the bars on a Thursday night. Could just be some drunk kid thinking this is his apartment," he says, and it makes sense, even if it doesn't make me feel any better. I'm definitely glad Dad had a locksmith change the lock.

"If you call the police it's because I'm going away for murder. Some of us actually need sleep," Bria shouts at the door again, and JJ's hand hovers over the lock as the pounding increases.

"You're not helping by yelling through the door," he says, and she scoffs, disappearing into her room to return with her phone in hand.

What if it's not some drunk guy at the wrong apartment? I just have a bad feeling this is all about to go horribly wrong. A part of me wants to tell Bria to call anyway because it's exactly what we'd be doing if JJ weren't here.

He glances back at me, worry twisting his features, and I hold my breath as he flips the lock, opening the door. To my surprise, Trent falls against the opening door, grabbing the frame to catch himself.

"Marley, I'm so fucking sorry," he slurs, and I gasp in

surprise, but he's also the only person I know crazy enough to do something like this.

"Trent?"

JJ looks at me in shock, clearly not expecting this either.

Trent's brown eyes find me, then Bria, and I see the confusion in Trent's expression. My stomach drops when Trent finally looks at JJ, still holding the door partly closed as the muscles in his arms bulge under the pressure from Trent's body leaning against the door.

"Walker? You're here?"

Oh shit. This is really not good.

"What the fuck are you thinking showing up here, drunk off your fucking ass to bang on the door where two women live alone? What the hell is wrong with you?" JJ asks, his voice low and trembling with a rage I haven't heard from him before. I won't even argue with him if he tries to say *I told you so* later—I'm just so damn glad he's here.

"I want to talk to Marley," Trent says, rubbing his eyes as his balance wavers.

"No," JJ and Bria say at the same time.

"C'est bon. Je vais lui parler,"[1] I correct them, stepping forward.

JJ frowns, clearly disagreeing with me. *"Je ne te laisse pas seule avec lui quand il est comme ça."*[2]

"Please, babe," Trent pleads from where he stands.

I nod to JJ, silently telling him it's okay to let him in. *Bad idea, Marley. Don't do it.* I drag my hands over my face, taking a step closer to JJ as Trent stumbles into the apartment. My nose immediately wrinkles, protesting the smell of booze following him. Bria pops a squat at one of our barstools, scowling at Trent as she does.

---

1. It's all right. I'll talk to him.
2. I'm not leaving you alone with him when he's like this.

"You wanted to talk to her, so fucking *talk*," Bria seethes, crossing her arms over her chest.

"She's got a lot of bite, JJ. Watch your dick so you don't lose it," Trent says, making the mistake of taunting Bria. I don't have a chance to see her reaction because I'm focused entirely on how JJ bristles at his comment.

"I'll chop yours off and spoon feed it to you, Trent," Bria threatens, and it feels like we're teetering at the edge of a cliff, and it will only take one more thing to send someone over the edge.

"I'm not here for Bria," JJ says, moving to stand protectively in front of me. "No offense."

"None taken, pretty boy."

Trent looks at me, and then at JJ's positioning between us, his eyes widen for a moment before he laughs. "Oh, this is fucking great. I knew you were a cheating bitch, but my *roommate*? What'd you do? Sneak out of my room and go to Walker's for seconds? I should have known. While we all thought JJ was just getting busy with his hand, it turns out he was screwing my girlfriend behind my ba—" His hurtful words are cut off as JJ moves faster than lightning, shoving him up against the wall, his forearm pressed against Trent's throat. My hands fly to cover my mouth as Trent grunts, trying to move, but JJ has the advantages of being sober and possessing more muscle mass, along with the element of surprise.

"*Watch your fucking mouth.* You don't get to talk to her like that. You don't talk to *any woman* like that," JJ seethes, and I'm shocked. "Marley never cheated on you. I knew you were an asshole, but I didn't think you were pathetic too—showing up in the middle of the night drunk to talk to your ex, only to belittle her when *you're* the cheating bitch who couldn't keep it in your pants."

JJ's arms bulge at the force required to pin Trent as he tries to get free while JJ leans in closer.

"If you come near her again, none of daddy's money can help you in the draft if my family blacklists you. Don't look at Marley, don't speak to her, don't contact her," he says, and Trent's face is turning red. *"Do. You. Understand?"*

He struggles to nod, and JJ releases him, causing Trent to fall in a heap on the floor. I don't spare Trent a second look when my whole world turns around to look at me, nothing but concern showing on his face as tears flood my vision. His arms wrap around me, pulling me into the safety of his embrace as Trent coughs before the door slams shut a moment later.

Even in the worst moment, it doesn't feel quite so awful knowing JJ's by my side. I feel his lips press against the crown of my head, and the feeling of being loved by JJ now makes every moment we spent apart over the last three years worth it.

CHAPTER TWENTY-THREE

JJ

I LEAN DOWN, HUGGING MY SISTER'S SHORT FRAME. It's a relief being in the same room as her again, even if I've been fraying at the edges trying to predict what it's going to be like with my family here. I've been worried I won't be able to keep my shit together without the pills numbing everything.

Factor in the bullshit with Trent last night, and the practice from hell we had today, I'm barely keeping it together as it is. I thought Coach's head was going to explode at practice earlier because of how out of sync our offensive line was today. We ended up having to run suicides before Coach dismissed us, and my knee is feeling every one.

"JJ, you won't believe how glad I am to be with you again. Everyone else is crazy," Mira whispers, and I smile at her as she pulls away.

"What about Henry?"

"He's the craziest of all. Dude must be insane for wanting to be stuck with me for life," she says, holding up the sparkling emerald cut diamond on her finger.

"Must be quite the workout wearing a rock this big on your finger," I tease, but I couldn't be happier for them.

"Lord help him because he's going to need it. I can't wait for him to take you off my hands," Dad says, and Mom hits his arm with the back of her hand.

"Shut up, Bash. You were just whining last night about how she's not your baby girl anymore." She rolls her eyes, winking at me. They seem like themselves, and as nice as it is, it only furthers my anxiety that I shouldn't trust my mom—*or Mira, let's be honest*—not to say something unhinged in front of Marley.

It's a little painful to see Hunter because seeing only him standing there without his twin is a stark reminder that Bailey isn't here. Still, I love my brother, refusing to let anything else show as I embrace him tightly. He's nearly as big as I am, his sandy blond hair an unkempt style of mess. Oceanside has been good for him. "Hey, bro."

"You're getting skinny. Think I can outlift you by now?" Hunter says, keeping the mood light. I think it's something we've all learned to do because if we acknowledge the void left by Bailey's absence, the mood sinks faster than the Titanic in the ocean.

"You wish." I step back toward Marley who was hovering behind to let me greet my family. I interlace my fingers with hers, immediately feeling centered by her gravity. "This is Marley—my not fake girlfriend." I clarify the second part, causing Mom to smile and Mirabelle to roll her eyes.

Marley gives me an odd look, and it dawns on me I've never told her how Henry and Mirabelle's relationship started. "Definitely real last time I checked, but it's lovely to meet you. JJ talks about you all the time." Marley smiles, and I have no doubt they're going to love her.

"Hi, Marley. I can only hope you don't believe everything he's said—or maybe believe everything. JJ's the most likely to say something nice," Dad teases, and his dark eyes glimmer as he smiles.

Maybe I've been worried for nothing.

Mom's gaze bounces from Marley to me, her short blonde hair swishing over her shoulders. *"Elle est belle."*[1]

Marley's audible inhale is the only reaction she gives, but I'll leave it up to her if she wants to explain she's fluent in French. Mom's not wrong—the blue sundress she's wearing today brings out her eyes, and it stands out nicely against her warm olive skin. *"À l'intérieur comme à l'extérieur,"*[2] I say, squeezing Marley's hand.

"Welcome to the family," Mom says, smiling at Marley.

"Could you come up with something more disgustingly sweet?" Hunter asks, pretending to gag, and I snort, giving him the finger. *Way to ruin the moment, Hunt.*

"Ignore him, he's grumpy because his girlfriend, Kaitlyn, couldn't come with us," Dad says.

Marley giggles next to me, giving my hand a squeeze of her own. "How was your flight?" Marley asks, changing the subject as I reluctantly let go of her hand to hug my mom.

"Just so you know, I could always use an upgrade on my ring if you want to propose with mine," Mom whispers, and I feel my cheeks heat because I like the idea a little too much for someone who hasn't been dating my girlfriend longer than a week.

"Mom."

"I wanted to sleep, but someone talked the entire time," Hunter says, and I see the pointed look he sends in our sister's direction after pulling away from Mom, just as Mirabelle begins bouncing on the balls of her feet.

"Do you have to pee or something?" I ask, but she ignores me.

"Can I hug you? I feel like I've known you for years from

---

1. She's beautiful.
2. Inside and out.

everything JJ's told me," Mira blurts out, staring at my girl-friend. *Oh jeez. I clearly jinxed myself by thinking everything would be fine.*

Marley laughs, her smile growing brighter. "Yeah," she barely says before Mirabelle is throwing her arms around her, nearly knocking them both to the ground. I'm aware it's just Mirabelle, but I still feel a lurch of protectiveness as Marley wobbles, before stabilizing them both.

"God, Mira, I think you missed your calling as a lineman. Take it easy," Dad jokes as Mirabelle leans up to whisper some-thing to Marley, then turns around to stick her tongue out at him.

"Absolutely not. I prefer to sit pretty on the sidelines, but we'll meet you at the car. We have things to talk about," Mirabelle says, hooking her arm with Marley's to pull her toward the parking lot of the private airport, conveniently leaving her bag on the ground before I can say anything.

"I guess we're past how excited you are to see me again. Do you have the keys for the car?" I ask, looking at Dad. It's crazy how much can change in two months, but I swear he has more grey streaks in his salt and pepper colored hair.

"The crew slipped me the keys after we got off the plane, and the car is in the lot," Dad explains. "I'm going to make sure we're set for our flight back on Sunday first. I wouldn't leave Mira alone with Marley for long, so you guys go ahead."

He's probably not wrong about leaving them alone. I'm glad Mira wants to make Marley feel welcome, but holy shit, I'd appreciate it if she didn't scare the shit out of her at the same time.

"Is Asher joining us for dinner?" Mom asks, and there's honestly not a chance in hell he'd miss it. I wonder if Marley would want to invite Bria? *Wait—no.* This is supposed to be about my family getting to know Marley, not Asher having another opportunity to strike out with Mirabelle while staring at my dad with stars in his eyes. He's going to kill me, but he'll have to get over it.

"Nope. It'll just be us," I say, begrudgingly grabbing Mira's bag as Hunter grabs his. "You have the address, right?"

"We'll be fine. Go save your girlfriend," Mom says, and Hunter doesn't need to be told twice to start walking toward the car.

"How are things going with the team? Oceanside is ranked pretty high," I say, looking at my brother who tugs a hand through his blond hair.

"We'd be ranked higher if you transferred—you're having one hell of a comeback season. How's your knee holding up?" he asks, turning it around on me without answering my question. I guess things still aren't going well with the running back, but I guess the same could be said for me and Trent at the moment.

"Have you thought about transferring here? Our quarterback graduates this year, and you're twice the player he is." *I swear, I'm not just saying this because I can't stand the guy.* Hunter made a name for himself when Oceanside started him as a freshman over their senior captain from the previous season *and* led them to their first Bowl game in five years. This season, they only have one loss on their record so far, even with the tension between Hunter and his teammate.

I'm great at football, but Hunter has started to show he has the type of talent that only comes around once in a generation. There are whispers of him being on the shortlist for the Heisman as a sophomore, which is practically unheard of, but we won't know until December when the finalists are announced.

"Is your college right on the beach?" he asks, and I have to admit, that is a perk Oceanside has over Beaumont.

"No, but it's a top five ranked university in both academics and athletics," I point out as we get close enough to the

Jeep to see Mirabelle and Marley. I can't help the smile tugging at the corners of my mouth because I actually can't wait for them to get to know each other. I know it's sappy, but Mirabelle's my best friend.

"Have your coach call me if the campus moves within walking distance of the ocean," Hunter says, and I shake my head. It's geographically impossible. It only takes twenty minutes by car to get to the beach from Beaumont, but I understand the appeal Oceanside has being located *on* the beach, while still having a top-notch athletics program.

Aside from Hunter transferring to Beaumont, the only other thing I would change right now is having Bailey here. The clock is ticking on when he'll call next, but knowing we're anywhere near the window of possibility has me crawling out of my skin from the anxiety.

Fuck, I shouldn't be thinking about Bailey right now.

"JJ?" Hunter asks, and I clear my throat.

"Sorry, wasn't paying attention. What'd you say?"

The sadness in his green eyes contrasts with the smile he forces, and it's like looking in a mirror because I recognize the expression from all the times I've seen it on my own face. "It's fine. Doesn't matter."

It hurts that this is what our once close relationship has become, but as long as I'm the only one Bailey calls, I'm not sure we stand a chance at fixing it. I hate how when I look at Hunter, I'm also looking for Bailey.

I think we've all put our lives on pause in some manner for Bailey, but eventually, we have to start living. I only wish living didn't also feel like dying.

I made sure Trent wasn't going to be here, but honestly, he wants to see me right now about as much as I want to see him.

Luka didn't bat an eye at Marley walking in with me, but he did leave a few minutes ago. I texted Asher from the airport to let him know he'd be on his own for dinner, and was surprised by his response saying it was fine. I really thought he'd put up more of a fight, but it made sense when I saw Bria's car in the driveway. I wasn't expecting to see them playing Uno, or for him to look so damn happy about losing, but I think he was just happy to be spending time with her. He barely gave Mira a second look aside from saying hi before refocusing on Bria.

If only Bria knew what a momentous occasion this was.

Mira snuck off to my room a few minutes ago to call Henry before his game later, and I'm hoping she doesn't help herself by going through all of my drawers. I fight the urge to kick Mirabelle out of my room, desperate to relieve the anxiety I can't seem to shake. I'm doing my best, but I can't stop thinking if I just take a few more pills this weekend to get through my family's visit without revealing how perfectly not fine I am, I'll go back to cutting how many I take. I've been doing really well since the scare at the party, but right now, I'm on edge, and it's the last thing I want to be.

Almost as if Marley can sense something is wrong, she rests her hand on my thigh, and it's the perfect distraction because instead of thinking about how badly I want to take something right now, all I can think about is her hand on me.

She looks at me, her ocean eyes scanning over my face, appearing to ask if I'm okay, but before I can even try to reassure her, Asher's voice grows excited as he and Bria continue their very exaggerated and detailed description of my reunion with Marley in this living room.

"And then JJ was all like, 'She's my girl, stop macking on her,' and then they started speaking in Italian or something to each other. I don't remember how many languages Marley speaks, but it's a *lot*," Asher says, and Bria snorts, rolling her eyes. Well, looks like Mom is about to figure out Marley understood what she said at the airport.

"Oh my god, don't listen to him. It wasn't like that. The only thing he's right about is the Italian, though. It was more of a *you're mine* look JJ gave her, and they're lucky nobody noticed except for me and Asher," Bria corrects, and Mom's piercing eyes find me.

"Since when do you speak Italian?" she asks, and it feels like the temperature in the room has gone up twenty degrees. Marley turns to look at me, and I feel nauseous.

"Honestly, I've been thinking about picking up a second language as well," Hunter chimes in, trying to have my back. I guess he'd know better than anyone how things have slipped past our parents after Bailey. Their focus has been on finding him, and they shouldn't feel bad about it.

I felt guilty enough for the attention I took away from Bailey after my knee surgery last winter. "It's not a big deal," I say, forcing a dry laugh. "I took it both semesters freshman year for my language credit and picked it up easily."

Mom's face falters and my lungs constrict in my chest. *Fuck.* I press my hand against my chest as my heart rate quickens, and I can't quite catch my breath.

"Hunter's right. Once you learn one Romance language, the rest of them are easier to understand. I can only speak Italian and Spanish, but Marley's fluent in French, Italian, Portuguese, Spanish, and I'm not sure where she's at with Mandarin. It's annoying when they start whispering to each other in French because they know I can't understand, which makes me think . . ." I can't hear anything Bria says over the struggle of taking breaths, unable to look away from the poorly concealed heartbreak on my parents' faces as they share a look. *I'm fine.* I'm *supposed* to be fine. They can't know I'm the furthest thing from it.

"JJ," Marley murmurs quietly, her hand squeezing my thigh, trying to get my attention.

"I'm going to see what's taking Mira so long," I interrupt, desperate to escape. I pull away from Marley's touch, and I can't bear to look at her because I think seeing all the questions I don't have answers for will actually send me over the edge.

Instead of going directly to my room, I pivot toward the bathroom Asher and I share, locking the door behind me as I try to catch my breath. *What the fuck is wrong with me? Why am I like this?* I stare at myself in the mirror, and I'm honestly impressed by how fine I look on the outside, despite how broken I feel.

Pull yourself together, JJ. Talking about how you want to be fine isn't going to fix a goddamn thing if you can't make it happen.

I turn the sink on, splashing the cold water on my face as I make myself inhale a ragged breath and then another, my heart rate beginning to slow as my lungs fill with oxygen again.

Giving myself another moment before I leave the safety of the bathroom, I realize I don't actually know why Mirabelle needed privacy to make this call to Henry.

I really hope they're not having phone sex in my room. The thought alone is enough to break some of the waves crashing over me, giving me a glimpse above the surface.

I still knock on the door before walking in just to make sure, and Mirabelle opens the door. "What?"

"Are you planning on coming back down anytime soon?" I ask, but then my gaze lands on my desk, and the answer seems so simple. They might be the wrong answer, but they'll make everything easier.

"I'll be down in a second," she says, pulling my attention back to her. Mirabelle tilts her head, her dark eyes narrowing as she sees right through my bullshit. "What's wrong?"

"I just need something from my room."

Don't ask questions you don't want answers to, Mira. You're not going to like what you find if you do.

"No, there's something wrong. Are you okay?" she asks, stepping aside to let me in my room, and in an instant, water floods my lungs again.

Would it be better to finally tell someone how thoroughly fucked in the head I am?

The decision is made for me as Henry says something incoherent, and she gives me an apologetic look. "Sorry, Henry's superstitious. Just give me a sec and . . . sorry, I'm still here," she says, putting the phone up to her ear again. "It's JJ. He needs something from his room. No, I'm fine, but I probably do need to go in a few."

I can feel her watching me as I walk toward my desk, my hands shaking as I pull out the Tylenol bottle I've hidden them in. After the way Asher eyed my desk a few weeks ago, I got paranoid he'd look to see what was in it, but thank god I did, or the jig would be up.

I throw one back before I can second guess myself, shoving the bottle back in the drawer.

"Actually, babe, can I call you back?" she asks, and my heart rate goes through the fucking roof. *"Je t'aime aussi."*[3]

"Sorry, you didn't have to hang up on him," I say, making my way toward the door, but Mirabelle darts in front of me, stopping me in my tracks.

"What'd you just take?"

"Tylenol," I answer smoothly. "Is it a crime to have a headache?"

Lies. I'm lying through my fucking teeth and she knows it.

Mirabelle tilts her head, crossing her arms over her chest.

---

3. I love you too.

"Is your knee bothering you? You weren't wearing your brace last weekend."

I roll my eyes, but the truth is, it's never not bothering me. Whether it actually hurts or I've tricked my brain into thinking it does, I'm always reminded it'll never be the same as it was.

"Mira, let it go. I'm fine, call your fiancé back," I say, trying to play it off, but Mirabelle is the one person who might know me better than I know myself. *Why did I think coming up here was a good idea again?*

"Why don't I believe you then?"

"If there was a problem, I'd tell you."

She purses her lips, shaking her head. "No, JJ. I don't think you would."

Mirabelle's bluntness doesn't often catch me off guard, but this time it does. I blink, staring at her in surprise.

"Then do me a favor and pretend I'm fine like I do, so I don't give our parents another kid to worry about," I say, nearly choking on the words as they come out of my mouth.

"JJ—"

"Hurry up. Everyone's waiting," I mumble under my breath, moving her out of my way to retreat downstairs where the sound of laughter greets me pleasantly. I avoid Mirabelle's watchful stare, hoping she won't say anything in front of our parents.

CHAPTER TWENTY-FOUR

Marley

I ADORE JJ'S FAMILY. HIS PARENTS HAVE AN interesting dynamic, but it's obvious how in love they are. It's crazy how much each of the Walker kids resemble their parents —*I mean, yes, I look like my mother with my father's sun-kissed complexion and blue eyes*—but there is zero doubt who gets their striking features from whom. JJ looks so much like his dad, and his brother is the spitting image of his mother. I knew Mirabelle was beautiful from when she followed me on social media, but now I'm wondering if she's even human because it's really not fair to look so pretty after spending five hours on a plane.

Everyone was really nice and welcoming, but I'd be lying if I didn't admit I have even more questions about Bailey than I did before. I'm just not sure if there will ever be a right time to ask them.

JJ seemed off last night, but Mirabelle appeared to be the only other person who noticed based on the way I kept seeing her eye him throughout dinner. JJ didn't say much to her which seems highly unusual given the way he's previously talked about their relationship, and I'm not sure what to think of it. Everything seemed fine at the airport, but after JJ came back from going upstairs, it was like the energy between them changed when she followed behind him.

JJ seemed to relax as the night went on, but I didn't get a chance to ask him about it last night because he looked like he might fall asleep while walking me to my car at the end of the night. I don't think he slept much the night before, but I'm not sure it was possible after Trent showed up in the middle of the night, so I'm hoping he was able to rest after I left.

I woke up to a direct message from Mirabelle asking if I wanted to get breakfast with her this morning, and while it was one thing to be alone with her for five minutes at the airport, after last night, I'm not sure what to expect.

I beat Mirabelle to the local diner known for their cinnamon rolls, grabbing a table in the corner while I wait for her. It's only a few minutes before she walks in wearing a maroon hat, but it's the large man behind her who pulls everyone's attention to them. He pulls his hat lower, ducking his head as Mirabelle smiles at me, heading our way before anyone can approach them.

"I'm sorry, Henry wasn't supposed to get in until after breakfast, but he caught an earlier flight, so I hope it's okay he's joining us," Mirabelle says, smiling apologetically as she slides into the seat across from me.

"It's fine," I say, giving him a little wave. "I'm Marley, it's nice to meet you."

"Sorry for crashing your breakfast," he says, the corner of his mouth ticking upward into a ghost of a smile. I almost wish he didn't have the hat on so I could see the differences in his photo for the league Bria showed me and in person. Either way, I can tell he's handsome just by the way he holds himself.

"No problem, but we might need to order more cinnamon rolls," I say and Mirabelle chuckles.

"Absolutely," she agrees, nodding as Henry rolls his eyes.

"I'll just get a coffee, but feel free to pretend I'm not here," he says, his voice a rich, deep rumble.

"No, you're less grumpy when you're not hungry, and we're going to a football game today with my family. You're delusional if you think you won't be recognized, and I'd prefer if Stacey didn't add more things to your schedule to make up for any negative press today," Mirabelle says, leveling her fiancé with a look causing his face to blanch.

"Extra cinnamon rolls please," he says, tapping his fingers on the table.

"Good boy," she says, reaching up to pat his cheek. *Oh my god, Mirabelle has him wrapped around her finger.* "Thanks for meeting us here."

"Of course," I say, smiling, but I'm not sure if I should be afraid of her or not.

She adjusts her hat, seeming to need to do something with her hands and I know the feeling all too well. It's taking everything in me to fight the urge to chew my nails. "Are you excited for the game today?" I ask after a moment, needing to break the silence.

"Yeah, it should be a good one," Mirabelle says, as the waitress approaches with the plate of cinnamon rolls, and I ask her for a second order. I want her to like me, but I'm not sure what to say. "Listen, Marley, I'm sorry, but I'm going to cut to the chase because I don't know how else to say it."

"Mira . . ." Henry murmurs, but she doesn't look away from me.

"Say what?" I ask, my appetite seeming to fade despite the mouthwatering cinnamon roll in front of me.

"How's JJ doing?"

I chew on the inside of my cheek, trying to decide how I want to answer this. JJ's made it clear he doesn't want his family to know he's struggling with being the one Bailey calls, and he doesn't want anyone to worry about him. If anything, I think JJ needs more people to worry about him. I'm honestly relieved she's asking, but I don't want to betray his trust.

I can't blame JJ for not wanting to worry his parents, especially after seeing how confused his parents were to learn he speaks Italian. I'm not trying to pass judgement, but how invisible has JJ made himself for the sake of his family?

"I'm not sure what to say." I try to keep my answer vague, even if it feels wrong.

She takes a deep breath, shaking her head. "I hope you know I respect you more for not just rolling over and telling me what's going on with him. I know I'm a lot and we only met last night, but please believe me when I say I love my brothers and I would do anything for them," Mirabelle says, staring at me with so much emotion, there's no way I couldn't believe her. "JJ's my best friend, and I need to know if I'm making a big deal out of something in my head before I make it everyone else's deal."

This family has been through hell.

I've been trying to understand why JJ wouldn't say anything to anyone about how he's doing, but it's all starting to make more sense after meeting everyone. He wears his smile like armor, but not to protect himself—it's to protect his family from the storm raging inside of him.

"I don't think you're wrong to worry about JJ," I admit, my gut telling me it's the right thing to do.

Mirabelle seems to be processing this as the waitress delivers more cinnamon rolls, which Mira pushes in front of Henry after I smile brightly at the waitress. "Is it his knee?"

"No, at least, I don't think so," I say, wiping my sweaty palms on my jeans. "It's Bailey."

Henry chokes on the drink of coffee he's taking, and Mirabelle's mouth falls open before she can compose herself, glancing around the table to see if anyone is within earshot of us.

"You know about Bailey?" she asks, her voice wavering over their brother's name. Henry coughs into his elbow, finally clearing his throat before reaching for Mirabelle's hand.

"I know he only calls JJ, and it's taking a toll on him."

Mirabelle's eyes shutter as a pained expression flickers across her striking features. She's slow to open them, and I don't miss the warning glance Henry directs my way before she does.

"Thank you," Mirabelle says, mustering a faint smile.

I don't think either of us feels better, though.

Mirabelle was right about their family being recognized at the stadium despite all of them wearing hats and sunglasses. They're not exactly an inconspicuous bunch with JJ's dad, Henry, and Hunter towering over most of the people we walk by.

At first, it started with people staring, but it quickly became pointing, and then it felt like I was back in New York City on display with my family.

Mirabelle hooks her arm with mine, a smile pasted on her face. "I give it five minutes in the box before we're on the Jumbotron," she whispers, and I raise my eyebrows skeptically.

"Are you sure?"

"Absolutely, and the first thing I'm doing when we get up there is getting a drink at the bar. If I don't have one in my hand at all public outings, headlines will run tonight speculating how far along I am," she continues.

"I wish everyone would just mind their own damn business," I mumble, recalling all the headlines speculating my mom's sobriety when I was growing up.

Mirabelle's dimples pop when she turns to look at me.

"Marley, if Hunt's girlfriend wasn't Henry's little sister, I'd say you're going to be my favorite sister-in-law."

After breakfast this morning, it feels like Mirabelle and I are on the same team, and the conversation took a much lighter tone when I asked why everyone kept making jokes about fake relationships. Mirabelle's cheeks flushed and then she explained how her and Henry's relationship began, and I'm starting to understand it's not only JJ who's a hopeless romantic. All of the Walkers are.

"We're not engaged," I remind her.

"He bought you flowers. Hate to break it to you, but you're basically engaged in my family's eyes," she says, her eyes glimmering with humor.

All of us barely fit in the elevator, but it's a short ride up to the boxes where I sat with my mom, Bria, and Tessa a few weeks ago. Bria and Charlie wanted to sit in the student section, insisting I needed time alone with JJ's family.

I end up sitting between Hunter and Mirabelle, and it reminds me to send a quick text to Kaden letting him know I miss him.

We're close, but our schedules are polar opposites with us being on different sides of the world, so our communication has been in the form of long emails recapping our weeks. I prefer to write mine in class when I'm not paying attention to my professors.

His last email told me he'd be back for Thanksgiving and Christmas, so I'm looking forward to holiday breaks.

"Do you want anything from the bar?" Mirabelle asks, and I shake my head.

"I'm okay. I don't drink," I say, waiting for the automatic response I usually get from others, wondering how I do it, or asking why.

Instead, Mirabelle doesn't bat an eye at my answer as she turns to Henry sitting between her and her dad. "Can you grab me my usual and a water for Marley please?" she asks, and his whole face softens for her. He nods, leaning forward to kiss her cheek as he gets up.

Unfortunately, Henry's not back by the time Mirabelle's proven right and our box is blown up on the Jumbotron as the teams warm up on the field. My phone vibrates with a text thread from Bria and Charlie.

CHARLIE

the amount of girls who sighed around us is hilarious

honestly, all the guys are freaking out too

BRIA

how does it feel to be surrounded by football royalty?

MARLEY

you guys are ridiculous

. . . intimidating because I know nothing

"So you're a quarterback?" I ask Hunter, and he turns off his phone.

"Yep," Hunter says, tugging his hand through his blond locks. "Dad would have died if no one took after him," he jokes and Mirabelle snorts.

"I think you mean Uncle Owen's ego wouldn't have been able to handle it if both you and JJ took after Dad after Henry already did," Mirabelle corrects.

"Thank god one of you did, or I never would have heard the end of it," Thalia chimes in as Henry returns with three drinks in hand.

"End of what?" he asks, handing one to Thalia who smiles warmly at him.

"My brother's fragile ego if JJ didn't want to be a tight end like him."

Henry laughs, passing me the water bottle. "Remind me to thank JJ later," he says.

"Maybe you can help me convince him to transfer to Oceanside," Hunter says, but Henry makes a face as Mirabelle takes her drink from him.

"Dude, you're lucky I even have an Oceanside shirt. I'm not helping you convince JJ to transfer."

"What's so bad about Oceanside?" I ask, but I can't say I'm keen on the idea of JJ transferring universities unless it's something he wants.

"Absolutely nothing but a dumb rivalry." Hunter rolls his eyes as Sebastian scoffs.

"There are so many things wrong with Oceanside," Henry adds, and Mirabelle laughs under her breath.

"Let's not get into this again today," Thalia suggests, as the stadium starts to come alive, signaling the start of the game soon.

"We all went to Duke, but because my dad is a donor for the football program, the optics wouldn't have looked good if JJ and Hunter committed there. It wasn't a problem for JJ, because he wanted to come here, but Hunt wanted Duke," Mira whispers, stirring the little straw in her drink. "I think he committed to Oceanside as a *fuck you,* showing them that he was good enough there wouldn't have been a problem with him starting. Supposedly he's on the short list for the Heisman as a sophomore. I don't know what you know about football, but to even be considered as an underclassman is practically unheard of."

"Honestly, I don't know much about football," I admit, and she waves it off.

"Totally fine. It's basically this award you win for being the best player in college football. My dad won his last year at Duke, and Henry was runner-up his senior year. It basically solidifies you as a first-round draft pick if your name is associated with it."

"Shut the fuck up about the Heisman, Mira," Hunter grumbles, checking his phone. "Kait says you might want to start sipping on your drink instead of holding it in your hand. There's already posts online trying to guess whether you're pregnant or not."

"For fuck's sake." Mirabelle groans, lifting her drink to her mouth with one hand while holding her middle finger up with the other. The Jumbotron chooses this exact moment to pan to our box again, and Mirabelle's middle finger is blown up for a few seconds before flipping to the student section. "Oh goodie, maybe they won't show us again," she says, huffing, and I honestly can't blame her. I would love to do it with her.

"I bet they won't," I agree, leaning forward to see if I can catch a glimpse of JJ on the field.

"Is it like this with your family too?" Mirabelle asks, and it's the first time since they've arrived that my family's been brought up, which I honestly appreciate, because I feel like it's the first thing people want to talk about.

"Yeah. At my last school, the press would try to follow me to class. Part of the reason I wanted to transfer here was to get away from it all to figure out who I am outside of the city. It's part of the gig, but it usually gets crazier whenever rumors pop up about my mom relapsing, and it takes a few weeks before some other scandal happens and distracts everyone." I lean back in my seat, and then I realize everyone's fallen quiet. "Oh, it's never the truth. She's been clean for nine years," I add, refusing to let the memory of the day I found her on the bathroom floor ruin today. I was twelve and it was the worst day of my life to date.

Oh god, I made this awkward. Great job, Mar! You just made a very loud group of people fall silent, and I have a feeling this never happens.

"That takes a lot of strength. I'm glad she's doing well," Thalia says, directing a reassuring smile my way, helping me to relax.

"Thank you," I say, smiling back at her.

"Are you liking Beaumont?" Sebastian asks, and I smile, nodding.

"I do. My dad went here for his undergrad, so my brother and I have spent a lot of time here over the years. It makes me forget sometimes who I am, and it's just a nice feeling," I say, and Mirabelle reaches over to squeeze my hand reassuringly.

The game starts a few minutes later, and it's clear before the first quarter is over that it's not going well. I'm not sure I've ever heard this many swear words in such a short amount of time.

After another play leaves JJ standing wide open, our offense is jogging half-heartedly off the field as our defensive line replaces them.

"What the fuck is he waiting for? JJ's been open the whole fucking time!" Hunter swears, yelling at the field right alongside his mom.

Mirabelle shakes her head, taking a sip of her drink. "He's throwing the game," she says, as the other team's quarterback throws the ball, finding a man open, and my jaw falls open when they score again.

"What?" I ask, and Mirabelle stares at the scoreboard, showing the ugly score I hope we can recover from.

"Your quarterback is throwing the game." She points to the sidelines where the coach is yelling at Trent as the band thunders, trying to pump up the crowd. "He's not running the plays the coach is calling."

"He wouldn't," I say, trying to give Trent the benefit of the doubt, because regardless of how pissed he might be at me and JJ, he wouldn't do that to his team.

Except he proves me wrong when not a single defensive

member of their team blocks JJ on the next play, and instead of passing it to JJ, Trent throws it directly into the hands of the other team. The crowd is deafening as it yells at Trent and the offensive line exiting the field.

"Did something happen between them this week?" Mirabelle asks, looking at me for answers, confirming my suspicion this is about the other night at my place.

"Um, kind of," I say, chewing on the inside of my cheek. I don't have any nails left to bite. "JJ was staying the night at my place a few days ago, and Trent showed up drunk, banging on the door. He wanted another chance, but realized JJ and I are together, so he said some shit . . ."

She raises an eyebrow, waiting for me to continue and I sigh.

"JJ pinned him against the wall, and basically told Trent if he comes near me again, no team would touch him if your family blacklisted him."

"Holy fucking shit," Mirabelle swears, a quiet laugh escaping her. "For JJ to threaten him . . . *Wow*. I mean, he's not wrong, but what the hell did Trent say to you?"

"For the record, Trent and I had been broken up for a few weeks before anything happened between me and JJ, but he might have called me a cheating bitch—*which is really ironic considering he couldn't remember how many times he cheated on me*—and asked if I would leave his room at night to go to JJ's for seconds." My cheeks are burning, and I can barely look at Mirabelle. *This is beyond embarrassing.*

"He *what?*" Hunter asks, his voice low, and I didn't realize he was paying attention.

"It's fine, everyone was fine. I think his ego is bruised or whatever, and this is his tantrum for not getting his way, but—"

"*But nothing,*" Hunter interrupts, his outburst pulling everyone's attention. "It doesn't matter what the circumstances are, he shouldn't have said any of it to you, and as an athlete, he should know better than to bring his shit onto the field. JJ said he was a dick, but he didn't explain why."

"What happened?" Sebastian asks, and I wish I could turn invisible right now.

"Marley dated the quarterback before JJ. He found out they're together this week, and obviously, he's not taking it well," Mirabelle explains, and I hate how awful it makes everything sound. If anything, JJ is the innocent one in all of this. I didn't do anything wrong, but I'm aware of how everything can be perceived. Unless people know about JJ and me meeting two and a half years ago, it doesn't sound great I ended up dating my ex's roommate a few weeks after we broke up.

"If Hart keeps it up, he'll be pulled before half. There's nothing we can do right now, so let him dig his own grave," Henry says, and I fidget with the ring on my thumb as our offense takes the field again.

"Yeah, but it's also not making JJ look great either," Mirabelle adds.

"Fuck, this is a ranked team getting slaughtered eighteen nil in the second quarter," Hunter says under his breath, shaking his head. He rubs his eyes and mutters something under his breath about his contacts, but I forget what I was going to ask as I look for JJ on the field while the teams line up again.

I really need to ask JJ to explain football to me so I'm not clueless. I want to understand the game he loves.

"Holy shit," Mirabelle says, grabbing my arm. "He's passing it to JJ!"

"Finally," Thalia says, as my gaze lands on JJ with his arms stretched out to catch the ball.

The victory is short lived when he's hit from the side by another player, my throat catching as we watch him go down.

CHAPTER TWENTY-FIVE

JJ

Trent avoiding me is something I don't mind, except when he's also doing it on the field, throwing off the balance of our team.

Coach Dixon, our head coach, is losing his fucking mind on the sidelines, but I'm right there with him, barely keeping a grip on my temper. I haven't touched the ball the entire fucking game, but I think the only thing to possibly make this worse is if I got in Trent's face for letting personal shit affect football. After throwing an interception while trying to get it to our wide receiver who has been double teamed all day, he's making it painfully obvious to everyone who he has a problem with. The Colorado Cougars defense isn't even bothering to cover me with anyone, and Trent is still choosing to ignore every play involving me.

It's embarrassing and it makes both of us look bad. I clench my hands in my gloves as our crowd jeers at Trent, clearly frustrated with the numbers on the scoreboard.

"What the fuck is he thinking?" Asher asks, lowering his voice. "Is he really going to blow this game rather than get the damn ball to you?"

I thought the end of it would have been the shitty practice yesterday.

"Apparently," I answer, trying to keep myself composed before I make everything worse.

I didn't mean to pin him against the wall—actually, even thinking that is a lie. My only regret is it happened in front of Marley. Despite nothing happening while they were still together, I know she feels guilty for the timing of everything. We haven't exactly had a chance to talk about the other night because she was pretty shaken up after Asher came to get Trent, and then my parents got here.

I know how big I am, and I try to be nothing but gentle with her because I know how intimidating I can come across, but my temper slipped hearing the shit he was saying to her. I don't want her to be afraid of me or think I'm capable of being violent, but I'm going to protect the people I love.

I couldn't stand there and listen to him berate her for something that never happened because us being together isn't wrong. She's the only thing in a long time to make sense to me.

I glance up at the box my family is in today, and I can only imagine how pissed off my family is. This clearly wasn't the game for them to come to, but nevertheless, I'm glad they're here.

"Fuck this," I mumble under my breath, spraying water into my mouth.

"Whatever the fuck happened between you, fix it," Luka says, moving to stand next to me.

"How do you want me to do that?"

He smacks my back, a grunt slipping from my mouth. "You're supposed to be the smart one. Figure it out because our shit is getting rocked out there."

I scoff, walking toward where Trent is watching the field further down the sideline. I guess our offensive coordinator is done yelling at him until the next time we come off the field. He catches sight of me and immediately turns away, but I'm sick of this.

"Look, we don't have to like each other, but you're screwing everyone over by not getting the ball to me. I've been wide open the entire game after you made it clear to the other team you have a problem with me. Grow the fuck up and leave your shit off the field, or do everyone a fucking favor and don't bother going back out there."

He turns to stare at me, a hard expression on his face. I'm not interested in anything he has to say, though, so I walk away, antsy to get back on the field.

This is a fucking nightmare, but it only further proves Trent is a piece of shit who was never good enough for Marley. Hell, I'm not even sure if I'm good enough, but I'm willing to try.

Shaking off the fact we're down eighteen points is hard, but if we can get our shit together and give our defense a break, we might be able to come back from this deficit.

I listen carefully, awaiting the play to be called, and I try not to react when Trent actually calls a passing play involving me. *Maybe he does have some common sense after all.*

The minute the snap occurs, I take off, pumping my arms and legs as no one covers me, trying to set myself up correctly for Trent's throw. Turning my head, I catch sight of the perfect spiral heading my way. I reach out, but as the ball hits my hands, I'm hit hard from the side.

All the air is immediately knocked from my lungs as I land on the ground hard, my knee twisting underneath me as the other player lands on top of me.

The knee I should have had safely enveloped in a brace to protect it, but I stubbornly thought I was fine.

The ball is cradled to my chest, but I see stars in my vision from the pain coursing through my body. The other guy climbs up, and I hear whistles blown as my lungs try to refill with oxygen. My jaw is clenched, trying to keep any sound from escaping as I roll, trying to give myself a second before attempting to get up. *No pop. There wasn't a pop.*

"Walker, did you hit your head? Can you get up?" Billy's voice asks next to me.

I gnash my teeth together, inhaling sharply before sitting up. "As much as you deny it, I knew you cared about me, Billy," I joke, mustering a smile as she kneels next to me. I'm momentarily blinded by the light she shines in my eye, checking for signs of concussion, and I push her hand away. "I didn't hit my head," I say, and she frowns, reading between the lines.

"Is your knee okay?" she asks, and this time, I don't deflect from the question when answering. Billy has the authority to pull me from this game in a heartbeat if she wants to.

"I'm fine—honestly. I just got the wind knocked out of me," I say, and Billy purses her lips.

"I'm pulling you this half."

"Billy—" I protest, but she crouches down, slipping my arm around her shoulders to help me up.

"Do *not* argue with me if you even want to think about re-entering this game, Walker."

I snap my mouth shut, rise to a standing position with the help of Billy, and my knee is already protesting. *I'm fine. It'll be fine.* I take a step, grimacing at the pain I feel, but I also feel immense relief because it's not torn, even as I limp with Billy's help. Everything will be fine.

I take a seat on the bench, pulling my helmet off as Coach Dixon hovers to observe Billy's examination of my knee as the game continues.

"Does this hurt?" Billy asks, rotating my knee in. It doesn't feel great, but it's not the worst pain in the world.

"It's fine. Just get me an ice pack and I'll be fine."

She twists it outward now and a yelp slips through my clenched teeth as my hands grip the bench tightly. "Motherfucker! When you twist it like it belongs on a doll, it's obviously going to fucking hurt."

"Language!" Billy corrects, shooting me a sharp look as our offensive coach glances in our direction.

"Billy, will he be able to go back in?" Coach Dixon asks, his head turning to look at the scoreboard.

She looks at me, her eyes surprisingly sympathetic before shaking her head. "Not this half. I want to take him back to the training room to do a more thorough evaluation—ice, heat, all the works. Walker might be able to go back in after halftime."

"I'm fine," I protest, but I'm ignored.

I could scream, except no one would listen. No one is ever listening to me because I'm the one who's supposed to keep everyone together. *I'm the one who's supposed to be fine.*

It was risky, but I snuck an extra pill during the chaos of halftime which helped everything fade away, including my anger toward Trent, but I'm not wasting any more time on him.

There's no sign of a limp in my step, but I still didn't go back in. By the time Billy was done examining me, their lead was too great, so the coaching staff decided it'd be better for me to rest than risk an injury by allowing me to go back in. While I understand their reasoning, I could have helped.

Ash bumps my shoulder with his as we exit the locker room to meet my family.

"You good?" he asks, raising an eyebrow.

"I'm fine," I repeat for what feels like the umpteenth time today.

"Yeah. You look fine. Almost like you didn't get hit at all," he muses, but it's the nonchalance in his tone making my heart rate spike.

I bump him back, eager for my parents to see I'm fine. "You know Billy, she works miracles."

Asher grabs my arm and pulls me off to the side of the hallway, waiting until some of our teammates pass. "What are you on?" Asher asks, his voice low. I feel all of the blood drain from my face, but it doesn't stop me from trying to recover with a half-ass smile.

"C'mon, Ash. Is this supposed to be a joke?"

He doesn't smile back at me. "JJ, what the fuck are you on? You've been popping pills for months, and I don't exactly believe you're suffering from chronic headaches all of a sudden like you've been claiming. I saw your leg twist earlier when you went down. You should at the very least have a limp right now, but you're somehow perfectly *fine*."

"I took Tylenol," I say, lying through my fucking teeth.

Asher scratches the back of his neck, shaking his head. "For fuck's sake, don't lie to me. I saw you take something in the locker room, and I talked to Charlie. She told me how messed up you were at that party because it scared the shit out of her, and she wanted to know if it had happened before. What are you taking?" The words hang in the air like a guillotine, ready to hand me my death sentence. "Don't make me go to Coach," he whispers.

"You wouldn't."

"I will if you don't tell me the truth."

I drag a hand through my hair, still damp from my shower in the locker room. "Oxy," I mumble, nearly choking on the truth. "I don't take them very often. It's just what I have left over from my surgery." *Lies.* I've lost track of how many refills I've managed to secure. At some point they'll probably stop writing the prescriptions, but as long as I say the right things and I have cash, I haven't had a problem yet.

"Do you think I'm stupid? Your surgery was last December." Asher's eyes widen after realizing what he's said, and white hot *shame* floods every fiber of my being as his face softens. "JJ, have you really been taking that shit since December?"

"I . . . I can stop," I whisper, feeling pathetic even trying to claim I can, because if I could, wouldn't I have stopped already?

"Can you?" he asks, and I never wanted to know what it felt like to have someone look at me the way my best friend's looking at me now.

"You're not . . . you aren't going to tell anyone, right?"

"You should tell your family. They can get you help," he says, but I shake my head.

"No. I'm done. I'll get rid of them. Please, Asher, I can't tell them. Not with Bailey still gone," I say, the panic rising in me at the thought of them knowing how not okay I am. "Please," I beg, and he stares at me for a moment with an unreadable expression before slowly nodding.

"You'll get rid of them?"

"I'll get rid of them," I promise, but I can tell he's hesitant to agree.

"All of them," he says, leaving no room for argument.

"All of them," I agree, knowing time is running out on how long my family will wait before coming to find where we are. I'd rather they not find us in the middle of this conversation.

"I don't like this," he says, and I take a shallow breath.

"That makes two of us."

❧

My family and Marley relaxed once they saw I was perfectly fine, and I hate how my brain immediately used it to justify taking the pills.

Not even swimming in the pool at the house my parents rented for the weekend has helped me relax, but it's probably because I haven't been able to look away from Marley in her lilac bikini. It's about the only thing distracting me from the conversation with Asher after the game. The water doesn't sing to me the same way it does to Mira and Hunter, but it's a soothing familiarity helping to ease some of the anxiety in my chest.

Dad is grilling as Hunter and Asher take turns jumping off the diving board to see who can make the bigger splash. Henry's supposedly judging, but I'm not sure he's actually paying attention because the last few jumps have all been a five out of ten.

Marley is sitting in the water on the stairs with my mom and Mirabelle talking about Mira's ideas for the wedding. I think it's hilarious to even ask if she has any ideas considering she's been planning her wedding to Henry since kindergarten, but it's whatever.

I've noticed Asher keeping an eye on me, but he's been subtle enough about it that no one else has noticed, or at least, no one's said anything.

"Four," Henry says, his tone flat as he takes a sip of his beer, and Hunter glares at him.

"It was bigger than the last one," Hunter argues as Asher grins.

"I can make it a three if you want me to re-evaluate my score?" Henry counters, and Hunter swims to the edge of the pool, pulling himself out without further complaint. "Why the hell did they ask me to judge this?" he grumbles, shaking his head.

"No idea. I'm just glad they didn't ask me," I say, laughing as my attention is pulled back to the brunette with ocean eyes and a smile brighter than the sun.

"You doing okay?" Henry asks, his voice quiet as water sprays the side of my face from Asher jumping in.

"Why wouldn't I be?" I counter, maintaining my poker face better this time than I did with Asher earlier. It helps I have sunglasses on now, though.

He shrugs, leaning against the edge of the pool. "I just want you to know it's okay if you're not."

"My knee's fine," I say, dragging a wet hand through my hair.

"Not talking about your knee, but I'm glad it is," he says, and I can't have this conversation for a second time today. "I mean up here," Henry clarifies, tapping a finger to the side of his head. "It's not fair you get all the pressure of being the only one B talks to."

"It is what it is," I say, trying to gauge if there's an underlying meaning to this I'm not catching on to.

"It's not, JJ. I know they all think it, but if they haven't said it, thank you for answering when he calls. I'm sure it's not easy."

"He's my brother."

Henry's smile is sad as he adjusts his shades. "I'll tell you the same thing I've told Mira—he's your brother, but you're not his keeper."

"What are you saying? I shouldn't answer when he calls?" I ask, my anxiety trembling at the idea of letting it go to voicemail.

"No. I'm saying regardless of how this all shakes out, you're not responsible for Bailey's choices," he says as Hunter hits the water with a smack, the rotation of his flip too slow, and my back stings watching it happen. Mirabelle laughs from the end of the pool, and I hear Marley's quieter one join in.

"Hunt, I'm not even going to dignify that with a rating. Do better," Henry says after Hunter surfaces.

"My name's Henry and I got my degree in English so I can use big words no one understands," Hunter mocks, causing Henry to chuckle.

"If you don't know what the word dignify means, maybe you should read more instead of insulting my degree. Aren't you getting a little old to throw temper tantrums?" Henry asks, his tone teasing.

I slip under the water for a moment, popping up in time to hear Hunter's response. "Aren't you getting old in general?"

Henry laughs, the sound a full belly one. "Kaitlyn's rubbing off on you," he says, a rare full smile showing, and I shake my head.

"Better than rubbing him off," Asher quips, too busy laughing at his own joke to see how Henry's expression changes, but I do. *Holy fuck, please tell me he didn't just say what I think I heard.*

Hunter's face turns flaming red, and he gapes at Asher while my eyes nearly bug out of my head.

My best friend's smile fades, finally realizing how everyone is looking at him. "What?" he asks, but no one says anything, too stunned to speak. Shit, I better not be guilty by association. "Obviously, I stuck my foot in my mouth, but it's a joke."

Mirabelle coughs, trying to cover up her laugh. "Um, yeah, a joke you just made about Henry's little sister giving her boyfriend a hand job."

"Oh my god, sometimes I hate being in this family," Hunter says, dragging a hand over his face as he walks to the cooler by the grill where our dad is shaking his head, laughing silently.

"His girlfriend is your sister?" Asher's head snaps to look at Henry, his face paling. "Would it help if I said sorry?"

"No, it really wouldn't," Henry says, his jaw flexing as he crosses his arms over his chest. "How about you don't talk about my sister in general."

"Great advice."

"Dinner's ready," Dad calls out, and I bet Asher's wishing it were done a few minutes ago. I take the seat next to Marley, reaching it only a second before Mirabelle does. I stick my tongue out at Mira as she rolls her eyes, plopping into the seat next to Dad instead as Henry grabs another beer.

"Did you really just stick your tongue out at your sister because you got to sit by me?" Marley asks, her eyes glimmering in the sunlight.

"Absolutely, sweetheart," I say, leaning over to kiss her cheek chastely as her cheeks flush.

"Henry used to be the one stuck in the middle," Mom teases, the corners of her eyes crinkling as she smiles.

"Apparently I'm old news now, haven't you heard?" Henry says, the dry tone causing Dad to laugh.

"You're not old news, babe," Mirabelle says.

"If Henry's considered old, your father is ancient then," Mom says, winking at Dad.

I can feel Asher's gaze lingering on me, and he's going to make it too damn obvious something's up.

"Maybe let's hold off on arguing so we don't overwhelm Marley?" Dad suggests, setting down the plate piled high with hamburger patties and hot dogs.

"It's okay, really. I love this," Marley says, and I feel my whole heart melt at the idea of her fitting in with my family. It's one thing to hope they'll get along, and another thing to actually see it happen.

"Us arguing?" I ask, snagging a patty to set on my open bun. Marley really is one in a million if she can see the arguing for what it really is—*love.*

"Yeah. It reminds me of me and my brother with Bria," she says, her smile taking my breath away.

"Just wait till you come visit back home. It feels like all we do with each other is argue, but it used to be worse when Bailey was there. He and Mira would go at it until they were blue in the face," I say, chuckling at the thought.

The only response is silence, and my throat seizes, choking me as I realize what's slipped from my mouth. My parents' smiles fade, and Mirabelle's eyes fill with tears.

No, I wouldn't have—*except I did.*

Marley's hand finds mine, squeezing. "I'd love to visit," she adds, her voice seeming to shake everyone from their spells, and Mom's smile looks forced.

"You're welcome anytime, honey. We have plenty of room." She clears her throat, standing up from the table as my stomach fills with guilt. "I'm sorry, I'll be right back."

Dad doesn't bother apologizing before following inside after her, and I can't believe I was so careless I would say his name in front of them.

"If you think her reaction to hearing his name is bad, try being the identical twin and knowing everyone is wondering what Bailey looks like now when they look at you. They can't even look at me sometimes without tearing up," Hunter says bluntly, and no one says anything because there's nothing to say.

CHAPTER TWENTY-SIX

Marley

"I'm sorry," I mumble again, pulling the blanket over my face as more cheering sounds outside our building.

Leave it to me to end up with the worst sinus infection on Halloween, while also having my period. *Talk about a double whammy.* "What are you apologizing for?" JJ asks, wrapping his arm around my shoulders, and I don't even have it in me to try to pull away.

"Because you're here instead of the party we were supposed to go to. And because I don't want you to get sick again," I say, pressing my fingers to my sinuses as if it will do anything to relieve the pressure. JJ's been pushing himself especially hard the last week and a half since his family left, despite the fact he's supposed to be taking it easy after the hit to his knee, not to mention the stomach bug he came down with last week. I suggested he should maybe see a doctor, but JJ insisted he was fine.

Aside from getting sick, I'm worried he's not fine. Asher's been glued to his side since his parents left, but I suspect part of it's because it gives him an excuse to be around Bria.

JJ kisses the side of my head, pulling the blanket tight around us. "Sweetheart, there is nowhere else I'd rather be than next to you."

"Mar, are you sure you don't want anything to eat?" Bria asks from the kitchen, and I moan as my face throbs. "I'll take that as a no," she says, assuming correctly.

"So what movie are we watching?" Asher asks, and I'm jealous of how lively he sounds. I came down with the sinus infection over the weekend while they were in Arizona for a game, but my period started yesterday so the cramps are killing me.

"It's Halloween. What do you think we're watching?" she asks, and JJ chuckles, his fingers twisting through my hair.

"*Ghostbusters*?"

He couldn't be more wrong, but it's part of what makes them so perfect for each other. I'm pretty sure he spent the night last night, but I've also taken so much cold medicine I could be delusional. I tap JJ's chest, hoping to get his attention without having to move too much.

"Yeah?" he whispers.

"Did he stay here last night?" I ask, keeping my voice quiet as Bria informs Asher we're going to watch a slasher movie instead.

"Yep," JJ murmurs, and I smile, curling my fingers around the soft fabric of JJ's shirt as I focus on the steady rise and fall of his chest. I totally called them getting together. Kaden is never going to believe me when I tell him it's happened.

Bria's always been a hard nut to crack, and sometimes I wonder if she gives Asher a hard time just to see what he's willing to put up with. To determine if he actually wants her instead of the idea he might have of her.

I think I understand it a little, because part of me wondered if there was a chance JJ was more in love with the fictional version of me he'd created in his head, but every moment with him has made me regret even considering the thought that his love wasn't genuine. Maybe it's why I fought so hard against forgiving him in the first place for not telling me the truth about Trent.

I know it wasn't very long ago, but it feels like an eternity has passed since then.

"Can't we watch something less . . ." Asher trails off, and Bria snorts.

"Suck it up, buttercup," she says, and I can only imagine the look on his face.

"Halloween is her favorite holiday," I say, wishing I could have a little more enthusiasm, but I am so tired. If I hadn't looked like death attending classes yesterday, I'm sure my professors would have assumed my emails written in a drug-induced haze were actually from a Halloween-sized hangover.

"Marley, maybe you should go to bed?" Bria suggests, but even the thought of moving hurts.

"I'm fine," I say, wincing as my uterus cramps, but then because I moved my face, I'm reminded of the pressure in my nose.

"Yeah, you look fine," Bria says sarcastically and JJ combs his fingers through my hair gently.

"Earlier, you said she looks like a corpse," Asher chimes in. *Seriously, someone needs to talk to him about the time and place to say certain things.*

"I also told you where the door was, and not to let it hit you on your way out."

JJ's chest shakes with silent laughter underneath my cheek, and I can feel myself drift closer toward the lull of sleep as I breathe through my mouth, listening to the intro of Bria's favorite movie I've seen a hundred times.

I stir when JJ shifts, slowly opening my eyes to focus on the sight of Asher sitting with his arm tucked around Bria as her face is lit by the screen of her phone. "JJ, have you seen this?" she asks, scrolling.

I hear JJ yawn as screams sound from the television. "The movie? Yeah," he says, and I don't want to get up to go to the bathroom, but I know I need to.

"Oh shit," Asher says, peering over her shoulder, and I feel my insides cramp again. I can take more medicine if I get up too. I swear, being sick on your period makes it a thousand times worse than usual.

I sit up slowly, my head spinning as the congestion in my face shifts. "You okay?" JJ asks as I pull myself up.

"Yeah, just need to use the bathroom," I say, standing up to head toward my room.

When I step out, the lights are on and the movie's forgotten in the background as JJ paces on the phone and Bria types furiously.

"Mom, I'm going to kill her," JJ says, tugging a hand through his dark hair, his gaze landing on me a moment later. "Gotta go. Love you too," he says, hanging up.

"What's going on?" I ask, cringing at how nasally my voice sounds. "Who are you going to kill?"

"My sister," he says, sighing. "Um, you remember how she flipped off the cameras during the game while they were here?"

"Yeah," I say, not following.

"He's tiptoeing around the fact you guys made the papers after everyone caught a glimpse of you sitting between America's favorite Olympian, and the next golden goose of the NFL. The press's words, not mine, just to be clear. Honestly, I'm kind of shocked it took them this long to piece together who you are."

"Is that it?" I ask, feeling woozy again, grabbing the doorframe for stability. JJ's at my side in an instant, sliding an arm around my waist to help support me.

"I'm taking you to bed," he says, a note of finality in his tone.

"If you insist," I relent, accepting my fate. I can think of worse fates, though.

JJ pulls the covers back on my bed, and I climb in, a smile pulling at my lips when I see how many pillows are on the side JJ's inadvertently claimed as his. He's a pillow princess, and I'm starting to wonder if I need to worry about him stealing mine out from under me in the middle of the night.

"Do you need anything else? Heating pad, or water?" he asks, tucking the blankets around me. I shake my head and pull at the covers on his side.

"Just you if you're still not worried about getting sick," I say and JJ flips the lights off, the bed dipping a few moments later as he climbs in next to me.

"You can get me sick anytime, Marley," he says, and I curl into his arms again.

"You wouldn't be saying that if you had as much pressure in your face as I do right now," I say, laughing miserably. "I'm sorry your Halloween was hijacked."

"I'm not," he answers without hesitation, and I'm honestly not sure what I did to deserve JJ, but I know I'll do anything to keep him. "Does it really not bother you about the press?"

My brain is only working at sixty percent capacity, but I'm functioning enough to know JJ and I haven't had a conversation regarding what a relationship will actually look like outside our bubble here at Beaumont. Maybe I've been avoiding it because I don't want to scare him off, but based on the way everyone reacted in regard to his family while they were here, I've been hopeful he won't care.

"Sure, it's frustrating, but it's not anything I'm not used to already. Here, we're in a bubble, and no one really cares who we are or what we do, but I figured it was only a matter of time before the rest of the world learned about us," I mumble, hoping I'm making sense to him.

"I hope it goes without saying, but I'm not with you for your money," he says, his arms tightening around me.

I wish I weren't sick so we could talk more about this, but I'm hanging onto consciousness by a thread. "It went without saying, *amore mio.* Thank you for staying."

"I'm here as long as you want me to be."

CHAPTER TWENTY-SEVEN

JJ

I HAVE NEVER HATED SCHOOL MORE THAN I DO right now, and I normally love it, so I think it says something.

Marley is finally feeling better from her sinus infection, and quite frankly, I didn't really care if I got sick, but she did. I know she thought I was sick the week before, but the truth is, withdrawals fucking suck.

She wasn't able to make it to our game last weekend, but she sent me a picture of it on her television, and I laughed when I spied "the rules of football" search on her computer screen caught in the bottom of the photo.

She has a huge chemistry exam in a few days, and I have a deadline coming up for my statistics project where I'm analyzing individual player stats and the effect they can have on a team's performance as a whole. Our upcoming game is away, so I have to get it done before we're scheduled to leave Thursday night.

I'd much rather take Marley to the beach to watch the sunset over the water.

The last thing I want is to be stuck on opposite ends of the room because I'm not sure I can keep my hands to myself if I'm sitting next to her.

"Oh, how the tables have turned," she says, laughing quietly as she looks at me over the top of her laptop.

"And what exactly is that supposed to mean?" I ask, raising an eyebrow at my cheeky girlfriend, who apparently thinks she's a comedian now.

Marley smiles, her eyes sparkling. *"It's not supposed to be fun, but it still has to be done,"* she mocks, and I roll my eyes, regretting saying it in the first place.

"It does need to be done," I relent, momentarily hating I chose a degree where I actually have shit to do instead of coasting through my classes without a second thought. *Why did I do this to myself?*

"I know, but you look so upset," she says, laughing again at my misery.

"And it's funny?"

She shakes her head, biting her lower lip to attempt to hide her smile. "Not funny at all. It reminds me a little of a toddler throwing a temper tantrum, though."

"I hate math." *Yeah, I'm definitely throwing a temper tantrum.*

"No, you don't."

I scoff, stretching as I fight every urge telling me to abandon this project to kiss the sass right out of Marley.

"I don't hate math, but I hate it right now," I grumble, looking away from her to the numbers swirling on my screen. I pinch the bridge of my nose, closing my eyes to try to get my mind right. *Responsibilities first, then everything else.* Numbers have always made sense to me, their reliability something I fell in love with growing up, but right now, I can't make sense of the equations in front of me.

The sound of footsteps getting closer causes me to look up, and it's really unfair how beautiful Marley looks wearing my Beaumont football sweatshirt. Her fingers curl around my laptop, pulling it away to tap a few things on the computer before closing it. "Marley," I say, intending to complain, but instead, it sounds like I'm begging.

"It's okay to take a break," she says, resting a hand on my shoulder to straddle my lap as my pants become uncomfortably tight. *If I touch her, it's game over.*

Marley lifts her hand to comb her fingers through my hair, the feeling of her hands on me better than drugs. My eyes flutter shut, a moan slipping from the back of my throat. My grip on my willpower slips completely when her lips graze over mine, and I grab her hips, pulling her against me entirely.

She gasps, and the sound is pure fucking music to my ears. "Sweetheart, I'm a lot of things, but right now, I'm not sure I can be patient," I warn, cupping the back of her smooth neck.

"JJ, have you considered I don't want you to be patient?" she asks, shifting her hips against mine, and *fuck being responsible.*

The only thing I want is Marley.

I tug her closer, slanting my mouth over hers as Marley slides her hands over my chest to hold onto my shoulders. There's nothing gentle about this kiss as I take what I want. She bites at my lower lip, lighting my body on fire as she rolls her hips, grinding against my stiff cock, desperate for more contact through our layers of clothing. *My god, I'm fucking gone for her.*

She could ask me for the moon right now, and I'd find a way to make it happen.

I'd do anything for Marley because there is no me without her.

She moans into my mouth when my tongue slides against hers, and I'm not sure I've ever heard a prettier sound. I move my lips to press them against the hollow of her neck, and as she rocks her hips against mine, a low moan breaks free from me. My grip on her hip tightens, lifting her up slightly to create space between us, because this is quickly going to become embarrassing if she continues.

"You okay?" she asks, out of breath, and I smile at her, appreciating the question even if I'm better than okay right now. Being with Marley is the only thing making me feel anything close to okay these days.

"Perfectly okay," I answer, reaching up to pull her hair loose from the clip holding it back, the caramel tresses falling onto her shoulders. "You're the most beautiful girl I've ever seen—inside and out."

A red hue crawls up her neck as Marley's cheeks flush under the compliment. "I've never met anyone like you."

"I find that hard to believe," I say, leaning forward to press a kiss to her throat.

"You're kind, sweet, and gentle. So gentle, sometimes in my head I call you my gentle giant."

"I love you." I lift my head to meet Marley's piercing gaze, knowing my walls have completely crumbled. Everything is laid bare, and if she asked me for the truth, I'd give it to her. "No matter what happens, Marley, I'll always be yours."

Every single damn letter I wrote her has a piece of me in it, and all of them are hers.

"I love you doesn't feel like the right words to accurately describe how I feel about you," she says, her entire face softening. "You were right, JJ. This is fate, and it makes me believe we're soul mates—as stupid and cliché as it sounds—but I feel like there's no possibility of a lifetime where I don't know you and your love."

I regret none of the days I spent waiting and hoping I would find Marley again.

My heart thumps in my chest, and I wonder if Marley can feel it.

I lean up, pressing my mouth to hers with a gentle kiss.

Marley's nose bumps against mine as she angles her head to press her lips more firmly against mine, her hand on my chest bunching the material of my shirt. "Marley," I mumble against her sweet mouth, my hands sliding to cup her ass.

I squeeze the soft curves as she inhales a ragged breath, tipping her head back. "*More*," Marley whispers, and I pull her closer, erasing the space I'd created between our bodies.

"Tell me what you like," I ask. "Tell me what you want, sweetheart."

"I like . . . I want you to touch me, and I want to touch you," she says, kissing my jaw as my body trembles at the idea. I can confidently say I'm an idiot for making us wait this long before doing anything more than heavy petting, but my patience has disintegrated. I stand up, holding Marley up as I do, a squeak escaping her. "JJ, what are you doing?" she asks with a laugh, holding onto me as I carry her to her room.

"I'm giving you what you want," I say, pushing her door shut behind me with my foot, to set Marley on her bed.

"Are you sure you don't want to go back to doing home-work?" she teases, leaning back on her elbows, her lips pulling at the corners in a smile. Her hair is messy and her cheeks are glowing, but I think this might be my favorite version of her because no one else gets to have Marley like this.

"Fuck homework, I want to make my girl happy," I say, grabbing the back of my shirt to pull it off.

"Yeah?" Marley asks, her eyes drifting down to my torso, landing on the bulge in my pants.

"Yeah." My throat bobs as I stare back at Marley, my chest filling with pride at the sight of her wearing *my* sweatshirt. She can have my whole damn closet if it tells everyone I'm hers. "Where do you want me to touch you?" I ask, my voice hoarse.

She pulls off my sweatshirt, and my jaw unhinges at the realization Marley isn't wearing anything underneath it. "Anywhere you want. There's no rush, just do what feels right to you."

I hover over her, bracing myself to keep from crushing Marley, as the bed dips under my weight. I kiss her lips, my hand sliding up to the smooth skin of her stomach, feeling her shiver under my touch. "You're perfect," I say.

My knuckle grazes underneath Marley's breast, daring higher to brush over her hardened nipple. I feel Marley's breathing hitch, and this time I circle the peak with the pad of my thumb, applying more pressure. Her hands find the back of my head, guiding me. "I like my nipples played with," she says, and I smile, glancing up at her.

"Yes ma'am."

I flick my tongue over the stiff peak as her fingers grip my hair, the sting only making my cock ache for something to relieve the pressure. Closing my mouth over her nipple, I suck, rewarded by the honey sweet sound of Marley moaning. She arches into my mouth, and I reach for her other breast, making sure to stimulate both of them as her breathing hitches again.

"*JJ, yes,*" she says, and the sound of her saying my name is too much for my restraint. I shove my other hand into the waistband of my briefs, wrapping my hand tightly around my thick length. *Get a grip, JJ. This is about Marley.*

Marley shifts underneath me, growing restless as her nails drag against my scalp when I drag my tongue over the sensitive skin, wishing I could see the look on her face right now. I switch to the other side, repeating the same pattern before applying more suction. "Use your teeth please," she instructs, her voice shaking and I stroke myself once, loving how she's telling me what to do.

Fuck, this is amazing.

I tentatively drag my teeth over her nipple, following Marley's directions. I squeeze my cock until it's borderline painful to keep from bursting, turned on more than I think I ever have been before. A guttural moan slips from me, and I lift my head to blow on her pretty pink skin.

Flicking my tongue once more, I can't help myself from jerking my hand down my length again, before taking her nipple between my teeth carefully, smiling as she grabs my hair again. I switch, having tried to keep track of what she liked, focused entirely on making her feel good as her hips shift again, seeking more. With my hand paying special attention to her other nipple, I roll the peak between my fingers, my mind exploding as her hand closes over mine, pinching my fingers tighter as her back arches.

Before I can even try to stop it, I come hard enough for stars to fill my vision, spilling in my hand as I shudder, groaning against Marley's sweet skin. "Fuck," I mumble, my face heating with embarrassment as I pull away. "Sorry," I apologize, pulling my hand out of my pants. *I guess it's a good thing I started keeping spare clothes here.*

"What are you apologizing for?" she asks, out of breath as she sits up, her swollen nipples on full display as I grab a tissue to wipe my hand off.

"I didn't want to come before you."

"JJ, I don't care if you came first. I care about you enjoying yourself," she says, reaching for my arm, and I take a seat next to Marley on the bed, trying to hear her words instead of believing the anxieties in my head I didn't even know existed before now. "Were you enjoying yourself?"

"I think touching you might be my new favorite thing," I admit, meeting her gaze. "I was trying to pay attention to what you liked, and I got lost in the moment."

"I did too," Marley says, and her gaze drops to the stain on the front of my dark grey sweats. "I know you don't think so, but I really liked watching you come."

"Yeah?"

Marley chews on her lower lip as she nods, her eyes slow to meet mine again. "I didn't think I'd like telling you what to do as much as I did. I've never felt comfortable enough to ask for what I wanted before."

I'll be damned.

It really is this simple.

"I liked you telling me what to do," I admit, feeling far less self-conscious than I did a few minutes ago. "Do you want to stop or keep going?"

Marley stands, moving in front of me, her ocean stare locked on mine as she pushes her shorts down, leaving her in only her underwear before lowering to her knees. "Take off your pants, *amore mio*," she says, and my eyebrows raise in surprise.

"But—"

"I still haven't gotten to touch you, so you don't get to touch me again until I touch you."

I lift my hips, sliding them down to my thighs, and Marley helps pull them the rest of the way off, tossing them to the side as my cock is already hardening again. Marley's mouth parts as she looks at me, and I feel my cheeks flush under her stare.

She wraps her hand around the base of my cock, and I've changed my mind. *Marley touching me is my new favorite thing.* "Holy shit, you're not even fully hard yet," she says, and my hands grip her comforter tightly. "JJ, I mean this in the nicest way possible, but you're *huge*. I mean, I assumed you would be given how tall and muscular you are, but . . ." Marley trails off, sliding her hand down the length to brush her thumb over the tip, causing my hips to jump from sensitivity.

"*Sweetheart*," I say, my voice strained, trying to keep still and she beams up at me.

"Am I the first person to touch you?"

I nod, swallowing as I try to keep my thoughts straight. "Besides myself? Yeah." *This is infinitely better already.*

The only warning I have is the slight smile before Marley gives me a taste of my own medicine, flicking her tongue over the tip, much like I did to start with her nipples. A strangled moan fills the room and Marley watches me through her dark lashes as she drags her tongue along the underside, her hand holding the base.

"*Fuck*," I say through clenched teeth.

"Not today. Good things come to those who wait," Marley teases, taking the head between her lips to swirl her tongue at the same time as my hips lift. Her other hand grabs my thigh as she lowers her head taking me further into her mouth. *I'm really starting to hate how she uses my words against me.*

The filthy words running through my mind are stolen by the heaven of Marley's mouth. She looks so fucking pretty with her lips wrapped around me.

"*Marley*," I choke out her name as she hollows out her cheeks, and I fight to keep my eyes from shutting in pleasure, not wanting to look away for a second. If she keeps this up, I'm going to come again.

She pulls away, her hand still stroking me and I'm trying really hard to keep my thoughts straight. "Are you okay?" she asks, resulting in an incredulous laugh to escape me.

I release my grip on the comforter, my fingers stiff as I reach for her wrist, pulling Marley up to me. "Am I okay? I'm fucking *perfect*, sweetheart. I also feel like an ass because you haven't come, so let me get on my knees and worship your body the way you deserve," I say, daring her to argue with me.

"If you insist," Marley says, mirroring my position on the bed as I drop to a kneeling position in front of her. I pull her to the edge of the bed, opening her legs around me as I see the damp spot on her underwear. My mouth waters at the idea of tasting her, eager to find every way to make her pull at my hair.

My knee protests before I can do anything, reminding me of its presence.

"Can you hand me one of those pillows?" I ask, and Marley freezes, her eyes widening.

"Nope, get up. You have a game in a few days, and I will not let this be the reason your knee is so sore you can't play," Marley says, crossing her arms over her chest.

"Sweetheart, I'm fine. I'd crawl from the other side of the room to you if it would convince you I'm fine. I'm only trying to be careful," I say, resting my hands on her thighs, pressing my lips to the inside of her thigh.

"Are you sure?" she asks, but her legs fall further apart. This time, I drag my tongue up the inside of her thigh, getting closer to where I desperately want to put my mouth as her breathing hitches. "Fine, pillow it is," Marley mumbles, and I lift my head as she reaches to hand one to me. It feels a million times better already.

"Thank you," I say, glancing up at my beautiful girl.

I might not be skilled, but I'm sure as shit not going to rush this. If Marley's not dripping and begging for me to touch her by the time my mouth touches her underwear, I'll have failed at my job.

I take my time kissing my way up her thigh, alternating between nipping and sucking at her sensitive skin until I reach her upper thigh. I can smell her arousal, and just before my nose brushes against the material of her underwear, Marley shifts closer, my name falling from her lips. "JJ, please," Marley whimpers, her hand finally resting on the back of my head.

I press a kiss to the damp material, pushing the fabric to the side to graze my fingertip over her core, immediately feeling how wet she is. "God, you're soaked," I say, lifting my head as I find her clit, circling over it as her thighs quiver from the effort to hold them open.

"Yes," she gasps, looking prettier than ever as she plays with her nipple. *"More, please,"* she begs, and this time, I watch her face as I push my finger into her, pumping slowly as Marley bites her lower lip, her eyes shut in ecstasy. She's beautiful, and she's mine.

"Show me how you like to be touched," I say, barely recognizing my own voice, too focused on watching Marley.

Her eyes blink open slowly when I pull my hand away to squeeze my aching cock again. "You're doing fine," Marley says, and I loathe the word fine. *I can do better than fine.*

I hook my fingers around the waistband to drag it down her golden skin, baring Marley completely to me. "Show me," I repeat as it takes everything in me not to lean forward to see what sounds I can coax from her.

I groan, watching as she dips two fingers into herself, and despite wanting to watch, I can't help myself from joining her, pressing my thumb to her clit again. Marley gasps again, her hand still on my head, dragging through my hair when I circle the sensitive nub, committing the sight of her fingers coated in her arousal to memory, and I'm *done*. I wrap my hand around her wrist, pulling her fingers from her as they shine to wrap my lips around them, tasting Marley for the first time. I look up at Marley as her eyes stare at me widely, watching me suck her fingers clean.

"JJ, holy shit," she swears, her chest rising and falling rapidly.

"So pretty and pink," I say, leaning in with every intent to devour Marley until she comes on my tongue. I lap at her pussy, pinning one of her thighs down to hold them open after they start to close when my thumb resumes the slow circles around her clit.

"Oh fuck," Marley says, grinding against my tongue while she holds my head in place, the sound of her moans music to my ears. I swirl my thumb faster and she gasps, trying to pull

away as I hold her close. "Too much," she cries out, causing me to freeze as she sighs, her body relaxing under my touch. "Don't stop, just . . . slower," Marley instructs, her fingers combing through my hair, tugging on the strands causing a rumble of approval to rise from me. *"Good boy, perfect,"* she praises, sighing as my cock throbs.

Gripping her thighs, I hook her legs over my shoulders, taking a gamble by moving my mouth higher up to suck her clit between my lips. I slowly flick my tongue over it as her thighs start to shake, but she's not trying to shift away so I'll take it as a sign to keep going. "Fingers," she begs, and I'm quick to push two fingers into her core, feeling her clench around them as my brain imagines what it will feel like to thrust into Marley.

Remembering she asked me to use teeth on her nipple, I scrape my teeth over the hard nub at the same time I curl my fingers inside her. Marley's thighs snap shut around my head, squeezing tightly as her legs shake, arching against my mouth as she cries out my name.

My cock throbs painfully, begging to be touched as her body relaxes, giving me the chance to fill my lungs with air again. I grip myself, my fingers still slick from being inside Marley, trying to hold off on coming. "Fucking incredible," I breathe out, as her eyes blink open to meet mine, hazy with lust. She slides off the bed, landing on the ground next to me, and her hand wraps around mine.

"Let me help," she says, jerking our hands together. Marley pulls my head to hers, locking our lips in a messy kiss, capturing my moan as I come again.

I lie back on the floor, pulling Marley with me, unable to find the energy to move up on the bed as the room is filled with the sound of our heavy breathing. "One hell of a study break," she says, her hand resting on my chest.

"I'll say," I agree, laughing as I wrap my arm around her stomach.

"Are you sure you haven't done this before?" she asks, and I shake my head.

"Nope, but I've figured out you pull my hair when you like what I'm doing," I say, inhaling a ragged breath as she laughs. "Give me a minute and I'll grab a towel to help clean you up," I say, turning my head to press a chaste kiss to the side of Marley's.

"You're the best," she mumbles, yawning, and I'm too tired to argue with her.

It dawns on me later after she curls around me that for the first time in a really long time, I didn't even think about taking a pill.

CHAPTER TWENTY-EIGHT

Marley

"I SWEAR, THIS BOUTIQUE HAS THE CUTEST clothes," Charlie says, the added skip in her step causing her strawberry blonde hair to swing behind her. It doesn't feel like November, despite the days getting shorter.

"If you want clothes, you could always go shopping in Bria's closet. She doesn't wear anything other than athletic clothes, but she has all these samples from brands trying to convince her to model for them," I say, and her head whips around.

"Are you serious?"

I chuckle, wondering if I should ask whether she has whiplash now. "Ask her about it later."

Charlie grins, spiking my curiosity. "Did I tell you what Asher told me?"

"No?"

"He said he asked Bria to be his girlfriend, and she said maybe! His goal is to get her to a game this season wearing his jersey," she says, and I love the idea of Bria wearing a football player's jersey, especially after how she complained about them being jocks—*not athletes*—at the beginning of the semester.

"I'm not sure I understand the fascination football players have with seeing their girlfriends wearing their jerseys, but I wish there was a way to accurately describe the look on JJ's face the first time I put his on," I say, laughing as she leads me down the sidewalk.

A smile forms on my face as I recall the way he looked at me the other day when I was wearing his sweatshirt. I've been trying really hard not to compare my fumbling disaster with Leo and my times with Trent against the afternoon last week with JJ, but there isn't anything to compare. JJ was perfect in every way—listening when I liked and didn't like something, and as someone who hasn't made a whole lot of choices when it comes to being asked what I want, JJ's eagerness to please made me feel so *wanted*.

"I'm afraid I'll never know what it feels like because Asher would pull the overprotective cousin act if I even looked in the direction of a football player," she says, but after everything with Trent, I can't say I blame him. "Hey, isn't that JJ's Jeep?" Charlie asks, pointing out the blue Wrangler parked on the curb. For a moment, I almost say it can't be his because the top is on, but I remember JJ telling me he was putting it on today since we're supposed to get rain the next few days.

"Yeah, I think it is?" I say, trying to remember if he mentioned anything about going shopping when he was done with classes. I know he's picking me up later tonight for our date, but I can't remember if he mentioned anything else.

"*Hope's Flowers*," she reads out loud, looking at the sign above the store he's parked in front of. Is this where he gets all the flowers from? "Let's go inside," Charlie says, hooking her arm with mine, changing our direction.

"What about the boutique?" I ask, letting her lead me into the store.

"Why would I spend my own money when I can shop for

free in Bria's closet? We're basically cousins-in-law, so what's hers is mine," she says, and I snort.

"Yeah, I probably wouldn't call her your cousin-in-law just yet. You might send her running in the other direction."

"Noted," Charlie says, opening the door for us to step inside. It looks like they're in the middle of remodeling the store, or at least moving things around, because there's buckets of flowers displaced everywhere.

"Sorry about the mess, I'm not as young as I used to be, and my help isn't much help," an elderly man says from behind the counter.

"I heard that, old man. I'd like to see you assemble these shelves and move them by yourself," a deep voice calls from the back of the store, causing my skin to pebble involuntarily. I'd know it anywhere.

"Mind your manners, boy," he says. "What brings you ladies in today?"

"Eddie, are you talking to yourself again?" JJ asks, walking from the back of the store, a streak of dirt smeared across his glistening chest on full display. He falters, his eyes widening as they land on us, and then his handsome face transforms into a breathtaking smile. "Sweetheart, what are you doing here?" he says, closing the gap between us to press his lips to my forehead.

"Don't mind me, just standing right here," Charlie mumbles, her voice laced with sarcasm.

"Hey, Charlotte," he greets, and she rolls her eyes, giving him the finger as Eddie stands, tapping his cane on the ground.

"No kissing the customers."

JJ laughs, the hearty sound rumbling from his chest as I lean into him. "This is my girlfriend, and the reason I'm keeping your business open with all the flowers I buy from you." JJ looks down at me, the healthy glow radiating from him causes an automatic smile to form on my face. "Marley, meet Eddie. I come here and help him sometimes with projects he can't do."

"Can't do," Eddie mocks, scoffing. "I can do them."

"Yeah, well I do them for free," JJ adds, laughing, and my pheromones are going crazy as I breathe in the scent of JJ's sweat mixed with soil and notes of floral.

Eddie is slow to come around the counter, offering his hand to Charlie. "I hope you're not also his girlfriend," he jests, and JJ's hand slides to rest on my lower back. Even just an innocent touch has my body craving more, especially after he was gone this past weekend for an away game.

"*Gross*, he's like family," Charlie says, wrinkling her nose.

"I'm honored," JJ says, as Eddie turns in our direction, his dark eyes crinkling as they train on me.

"You're too pretty for him, but it's nice to meet you. I guess you're the one I need to thank for giving Jonathan a reason to come into the store."

My curiosity skyrockets as JJ sighs behind me. "Eddie, we've talked about this. I have two first names, and I don't go by Jonathan. It's *JJ—just JJ*," he says, turning to wink at me.

"Jonathan?" I ask, not letting my boyfriend, whose name I apparently *don't* know, try to distract me. "But your dad's name isn't Jonathan so how can you be a junior?"

"I'm confused, what does JJ stand for then?" Charlie pipes in, and JJ's cheeks flush.

"It's embarrassing," he says, scratching the back of his neck, and I try not to get distracted by how his bicep flexes. "My parents couldn't agree on what to name me, and my mom wanted to name me Jonathan, but my dad wanted Jacob. I think I went without a name for the first three days, my mom calling me Jonathan and my dad calling me Jacob before my uncle called me JJ, tired of hearing them bicker, and it stuck."

Charlie sputters, laughter spilling from her. "So your name is Jonathan Jacob Walker?" she asks, and I giggle, because I can totally see them doing that.

The corners of JJ's mouth pull up as he chuckles. "Actually, it's Jonathan Jacob Alexander Walker. Alexander was my great-grandfather's name, but talk about giving your kid the longest name on Earth to learn how to spell."

I look at Eddie, curiosity getting the better of me because how have I never thought to ask what JJ stood for? "How do you know this?" I ask, astonished by this kernel of information.

"He didn't believe how tall I was, so he asked to see my ID." JJ snorts, his thumb dragging back and forth over my shirt, his fingertips grazing my skin.

"I thought your generation was supposed to be all interested in serial killers and stuff, and you didn't think to ask for his ID?" Eddie asks, and JJ scoffs, but I mean, he has a point.

"Do I look like a serial killer?"

"I feel like his point is most serial killers don't look like serial killers, so maybe you do, but I'm also literally never calling you JJ again as payback for all the times you've called me Charlotte," Charlie says, beaming as Eddie chuckles.

"I think she means it," I whisper, and JJ's chest rumbles.

"Probably," he agrees, stepping away toward an assortment of roses, plucking a lavender colored rose to pass to me. *"Une belle fleur pour ma chérie."*[1]

I recognize the flower immediately as the same one Bria found outside our door, confirming my suspicions it was JJ all along.

His green eyes twinkle like stars in the night sky, and Eddie's cane taps the floor again. "I'm taking it out of your pay," Eddie says, but there's nothing but fondness in his tone.

---

1. A beautiful flower for my sweetheart.

"You're not paying me, Eddie," JJ says, shaking his head as he leans toward me, his mouth kissing the corner of mine fleetingly. "I need to finish up here, and in the nicest way possible, I won't be able to focus with you here. I'll pick you up later?"

"Can't wait," I say, my heart turning to straight mush. "Charlie has some shopping to do in Bria's closet. It was nice to meet you, Eddie. You have a beautiful shop," I say, smiling at the old man.

"It was nice to meet you both," Eddie says, and on our way out the door, I smile, hearing JJ and Eddie's conversation continue before the door shuts behind us.

This time, I'm the one with a skip to my step as we walk back to my car.

"Are you going to tell me what the plan is?" I ask as JJ stops at a red light.

I caved and ended up texting him to ask what the plan was for tonight, but JJ kept his answer vague, saying to wear something casual and comfortable. It didn't really help much, but I'm learning to adapt from the expectations of the city to find my own sense of style, despite how many people have been staring at me on campus since my relationship with JJ made headlines.

I picked a pair of denim shorts and a cute cropped top Charlie pulled from the back of my closet earlier, insisting I wear it tonight to bring out the blue in my eyes. I kept my hair natural and went light on my makeup, but I'm dying to know what JJ has planned for this evening. It honestly doesn't matter what we do because the fact that he took the time to plan tonight means more to me than where we end up.

"We're almost there," he says, patting his hand resting on

my thigh, temporarily distracting me. "You're impatient tonight."

"I'm curious," I correct, causing JJ to chuckle. "You're being secretive."

"Is it so bad I want to surprise you?"

"When you don't tell me where you're taking me, it could be, especially if you're a serial killer. Maybe Eddie had a point earlier," I muse, loving the blush crawling up his neck as he shakes his head.

"Even if I were a serial killer, you'd have nothing to worry about because you would never be a victim of mine."

I laugh, this conversation taking an entirely different spin than I ever thought it would. "Thank you for the reassurance," I say, smiling as I rest my head against the headrest to watch JJ drive. If he isn't going to tell me where we're going, I might as well take the opportunity to check him out.

His white T-shirt hugs his biceps, and it's really not fair how effortlessly attractive he is. JJ's dark hair, prominent cheekbones, and green eyes are a lethal combination, making it impossible not to stare at him.

I can't explain it, but there's something different about JJ since his family visited, and I can't put my finger on it. I thought he seemed really anxious the first few days, and then my brain is a little foggy from being sick, but I've noticed since his anxiety ceded a little, he's more at peace? Maybe I'm crazy, but whatever the change, I think it's helping him deal with some of the weight he carries.

"Sweetheart, I have to focus on the road, and if you keep looking at me like that, I'm going to want to watch you smile, and I'd really prefer to not crash my car." I bite my lower lip, trying to hide my smile, but JJ gives me a quick side glance. "I didn't say you had to stop smiling—I said I want to watch you smile."

"Don't they mean the same thing?"

"No, it does not mean the same thing."

Scoffing, I shake my head. "I'm pretty sure it means the same thing, JJ."

"I would never ask you to stop smiling because it's my favorite part of you. I love watching you smile, but I have to focus on the road," JJ says, but his explanation only makes my smile wider. "*Marley*." He groans, and despite the fact he's making no sense right now, I turn away to look out the window again.

"Your logic is flawed, but I'd also prefer if you didn't crash the car so I'll go with it," I say, laughing again.

JJ pulls off into a small parking lot for beach access a few minutes later, and I spot Asher's car next to us.

"We're going to the beach?" I ask, turning to look at him and the intensity of his emerald gaze steals all the oxygen from my lungs. I'll never have to doubt the way JJ feels about me because I don't believe anyone could fake the tender expression on his face.

"Is that okay?"

"JJ, I don't care where we are because it only matters to me I get to be with you."

He smiles, drawing my attention to his mouth, and I can't help myself as I lean forward to press a gentle kiss to his lips. JJ's quick to pull me back for a second kiss, his eyes scanning over my face afterward. "I'm sorry I wouldn't tell you where we were going, but I brought a hoodie for you in case you didn't have a jacket. Can you wait for me to get your door?" JJ asks, unbuckling his seatbelt after turning off the engine.

I nod, knowing even if I had brought one, I'd still choose to wear JJ's hoodie instead.

JJ opens my door, but my jaw drops when he kneels, and I think my brain momentarily explodes. His eyebrows knit in confusion as he looks up at me, before laughter spills from him. "Marley, I'm not proposing. I'm just going to take your sandals off so you don't get them all sandy," he says, a goofy smile transforming his face.

My entire body burns from the mortification immediately following his clarification because, of course, he isn't proposing. "Definitely makes more sense," I say, knowing my cheeks are bright red as he wraps his hand around my ankle, being so very careful as he undoes the buckle of my shoe before finishing the next.

"You'll know when I'm proposing. There won't be any question about it."

If it were anyone else, I'd run for the hills, but I'm honestly impressed JJ's gone this long without it being brought up considering that within hours of meeting me the first time, he was asking me to move in and marry him. So I'd consider this progress.

After leaving our shoes in the backseat and grabbing his hoodie, JJ's quick to intertwine our fingers together as we walk toward the sound of waves rolling in. The sand is still warm from the day beneath my feet, and a figure lounging in the sand stands up as we approach, waving.

"I hope it tastes as good as it smells," Asher says, passing by us to head in the direction we just came from.

The final pieces of JJ's plan fall into place when we arrive at the blanket, weighed down on the corners with stones and the picnic basket in the middle.

A lump forms in my throat by the sheer thought JJ put into this, and this is . . . *I don't even have words.*

"Do you like it?" he asks, and I don't know why he would think I wouldn't?

"I love it. Thank you," I say, my voice wobbling as I blink back tears, squeezing his hand. "It's perfect. What are we having?"

"Baked macaroni and cheese. I'm sorry it's not normal

picnic food, but at least it's not breakfast? I'm trying to branch out from my comfort zone," JJ says and I sit on the blanket as he opens the bag to pull out the containers, passing one of them to me with a fork.

I crack the lid open, and Asher was right. It does smell good. "You made this?" I ask, impressed.

"Yeah." JJ's cheeks flush as he pulls out two small bottles of lemonade, and he cracks the seal on one before offering it to me. "I figured one of us should be able to somewhat cook so we don't starve."

"Hey, the eggs I made last week were edible," I say, pointing out the breakfast I made him, and his expression wavers. "What's the face for?" I ask, and he scratches the back of his neck.

"I love you, but they were crunchy."

"Crunchy? Like eggshells were in them?" I ask, gaping at JJ as he nods, taking a bite. *I'm sorry, what?* "JJ! Why didn't you say anything?"

"You just looked so proud of yourself, and I didn't want to make you feel bad."

"Oh my god." I groan, covering my face with my hands. *I was proud of myself for not messing them up, but I can't even cook eggs right.* "But you still ate them? What if you got sick?"

"Marley, it's fine," he says, smiling, and I'm mortified. "If it makes you feel better, I only had a few bites before you went into the bathroom, and I hid them in the trash can. I think the shells are supposed to add extra nutrients anyway."

"I'm so sorry," I say, but holy shit, I think JJ might be insane. Who the hell eats eggs with *eggshells* in them because they don't want to make their girlfriend—*who can't cook to save her life apparently*—feel bad?

"I'm not. It meant a lot to me you even tried," JJ says sweetly, and I hear the music start to come to life in my head already as I look at him.

It feels cliché to think, but everything about tonight is perfect, right down to the person I'm with.

I slipped into his hoodie after eating, greedily inhaling the addicting scent of citrus and detergent clinging to the fabric while JJ insisted on packing everything up to run it back to the car quickly so we could watch the sunset. I guess he had asked Asher to help him set up and watch over everything while he picked me up so it would already be ready when we arrived.

JJ found me again at the edge of the water, my toes slowly disappearing into the sand. The breeze tousles his dark hair, lifting the short strands out of his face as the setting sun casts a soft glow on his devastating features when I look up at him.

"Do you ever think about how many times we were in the same place without ever knowing?" I ask, feeling JJ's fingertips brush against mine, causing sparks to dance across my skin before hooking his pinky around mine. The simple touch threatens to pour fuel on the simmering fire in me, but the burn is one I'd welcome since JJ's already consumed every fiber of my being.

"I looked for your face in every face of every place I went during the eight hundred and ninety-two days until I saw you again. I would have known in my heart if we were in the same place at the same time," he says, his voice smooth like crushed velvet as my heart skips a beat. "For the longest time, I thought I was meant to only love the memory of you, and now I can't help wondering if I'm dreaming," JJ says, his gaze sliding to meet mine, and I think I fall in love with him all over again. "It doesn't feel real being here with you, but I'm so damn glad it is."

Just when I think he can't get any better, JJ goes and says the most romantic thing I think I've ever heard. "I felt the same way the first time we met," I say, wishing I could say more, but I can already feel the tears welling in my eyes, threatening to fall from the sheer power of his love.

"You asked if I was real," he recalls, a soft chuckle rumbling from his chest.

There is no doubt in my mind JJ has replayed our time in his head as many times as I have from every minute detail he's been able to pull out from seemingly nowhere at any given moment.

"And you promised me you were, just like I'm promising you I'm really here with you."

I wonder if there's a limit to how many times I can fall in love with JJ?

"I love you," JJ says, squeezing my hand in return.

"I love you too, Jonathan Jacob."

JJ tips his head back, a beautiful laugh spilling from him, and I *cherish* the sound of it. I grin at him, and the pure joy radiating on his face is more breathtaking than the sky above us ranging from hues of yellow, burnt orange, and purple.

"You're my favorite person," I say, watching as the intensity of his expression shifts into something resembling surprise while he turns to face me, his full lips parted. "I haven't had many choices in my life, but if choosing you is the last one I get to make, I wouldn't change a single thing."

JJ's throat bobs as he watches me, his hand lifting to brush my hair out of my face with a tenderness that makes me feel like I'm floating on cloud nine before cupping the back of my neck. I reach up, holding his arm, happy to have finally said something to make him the same way he always makes me feel.

I recognize the look in his eyes, and my gaze drops to his mouth, taking my time on the way back up. "Hey, JJ?"

"What?"

"You look like you want to kiss me," I tease, smiling cheekily at him.

"I absolutely do," he says, leaning down while his other hand curves around my lower back, tugging me closer to him. "I can't tell you how lucky I feel to be your favorite person."

"It's not luck. It's *you*."

Everything feels so right when JJ leans down as I rise up to meet him, his lips slanting over mine.

CHAPTER TWENTY-NINE

JJ

MY EYES FLASH OPEN AS MY SHOULDER IS SHAKEN, pulling me from sleep. "JJ, your phone," Marley says, and the tightrope I've been teetering on to stay clean the past few weeks snaps, sending me headfirst into the chasm below. There's only one person who would call me in the middle of the night.

I note the blocked caller ID on the screen as she hands it to me, answering it before it disappears. "Bailey?" I ask, while Marley flips her lamp on, casting the room in a soft glow.

"Yeah, it's me," Bailey says, followed by a quiet sigh. "I'm sorry for calling so late."

"No," I blurt out. "Don't ever apologize for calling. I'm here anytime you need me." *Please don't hang up, Bailey.* Give me something—*anything.*

"Thanks for answering."

"Always, B," I say, the nickname rolling off my tongue, feeling tears prick my eyes. "Are you okay?"

"I . . . I'm okay." His hesitation causes the hair on the back of my neck to stand up. *Something isn't right about this.*

The sheets pull back as Marley moves, and I reach out to snag her wrist, stopping her. *Don't leave me alone*, I beg silently, hoping she can read my mind. Marley nods, placing her other hand on top of mine in silent reassurance.

"Where are you? Is there anything I can send?" I ask, following the script we've crafted over the last nineteen months, praying this time something is different. I'm desperate for something to be different because I can't keep doing this.

"JJ, you know I can't tell you," he says, nothing having changed from the last time I spoke to him.

"Please. *Please just come back.* Mira and I never told Mom and Dad what you did. No one has to know—"

"*Don't.* I can't. There are people who need me, and I can't leave them," he says, and for the first time since he left, I feel an anger so hot, I can't suppress the explosion.

"What about your family, Bailey? We all need you and you left us pretty fucking easily."

"You don't need me—none of you do. You're dating a Benson, Mira's engaged to Henry, and Hunter has Kaitlyn. You're all fine without me, just like I knew you would be."

A bitter laugh escapes me, and Marley's hand squeezes mine. Seeing the concern shining in her eyes is the only thing stopping me from asking him to tell me again how fine I am when all I think about is numbing everything with pills. This isn't how she should find out. "How can you even think that? None of us are fine, but I guess if it's what you need to tell yourself to feel better about leaving, then *fine.*"

"You don't get it. I thought you of all people would. You're the best of us, JJ. You always have been." Bailey pauses, coughing and my heart stutters, realizing my mistake. Fighting with him isn't going to convince him to tell me where he is. "When I call, you always offer money, food, clothes, and whatever else I could ever ask for. When you see people on the streets, living under overpasses and in camps, do you offer them the same? Or do you make sure the doors of your car are locked, and pretend they don't exist by not even sparing them a second glance?" Bailey's voice wobbles as he utilizes his best weapon: *his words.* "What makes me better than them? Because I come from a privileged family? I am not worth more than any of the other people out here. My life is *not* worth more than theirs."

Despite the torrent of emotions wrecking me, I tuck away the first scrap of information he's given me since the calls started. He's living on the streets. I feel like I'm going to be sick, but I need him to confirm it for me. "So come back and do something about it. Use your *privilege* to help those who need help because living on the streets is not the answer."

"Neither is coming back."

"Bailey—"

"I have to go," he says, and panic grips me as my chest tightens, making it difficult to breathe. Before I can say anything, the line clicks as Bailey hangs up.

No.

He didn't say goodbye. Bailey always says goodbye and he'll call soon. He didn't this time.

I didn't tell Bailey I love him. What if this time was the last time?

I try to inhale, but my lungs aren't cooperating, refusing to take in the air I need to live. Hot tears blur my vision, and this has to be what dying feels like, and I can feel everything without the pills numbing me.

He's living on the streets. How am I supposed to tell my parents their son would rather be homeless than come home?

I'm not sure what's worse—*knowing the clock is restarting and it's a waiting game until he calls again, or not knowing if he'll call again.*

"JJ, you need to breathe," Marley says, but I can barely hear her over the chaos in my head. Everything is spinning out of control, and I don't know how to stop it. I hate no matter how hard I try, I can't seem to fix any of this or my family, so how can I hope to fix myself?

I can't tell them this. I can't tell them he's on the streets. It will obliterate any piece of them still remaining.

"JJ," Marley says more urgently this time.

I choke, trying to take a breath as my stomach rolls. *There are people here who need me, and I can't leave them.* I need him. I need my brother to come back.

I can't do this.

Run.

My hand presses against my chest, and I can't breathe. I would have rather learned nothing at all than what I did this time. If I had just kept my shit together, and I didn't push, maybe he would have said he'd come home.

I try to force air into my lungs, the pressure growing unbearable as black spots dance at the corners of my vision, and I'm vaguely aware of hands brushing my cheeks. *"JJ, baby,* snap out of it," Marley says, and the death blow comes when I see her beautiful eyes glistening with unshed tears. Her thumb swipes under my eyes again, cupping my face, and I can't do this to her.

Marley deserves to be with someone who isn't barely holding on to their sobriety. She deserves to have someone who thinks about her more than they think about numbing the pain with pills. *She deserves better than me.*

When she finds out what I've become, it's going to destroy her. The last thing I have ever wanted to do was hurt anyone. I need to be okay, and right now, I don't know any other way, even if it destroys me in the process.

I pull away from her completely, stumbling off the bed to reach for my duffle bag in the corner. I drop to my knees, digging for the pocket inside the bag. My fingers close around the pill hidden, and I hate myself for it, but I hate causing Marley pain more. I found this one in my travel bag a few days after Asher went through my whole room with me, watching as I flushed all of the pills. I told myself I wasn't going to take it, but I think I've already proven I lie to myself as much as I lie to everyone else.

I force it down before I can talk myself out of it, my whole body shaking as I grab socks and shoes while the best thing to ever happen to me kneels next to me, trying to push my hands away to stop me.

"You can't go anywhere right now. You can't even breathe. Baby, please look at me," Marley begs, but I know how to make it stop. I know how to make all of it stop by running until I don't feel like this anymore, because I won't feel anything at all.

"I need to run." I choke on the words, and she shakes her head.

"You need to stay here. It's three in the morning. You can't leave," she insists, and I close my eyes as my stomach twists.

"Please, just let me go," I whisper, my voice cracking, and then there's a knock on her door.

"Are you guys okay in there?" Bria asks, and Marley doesn't look away from me.

You're the best of us feels like a sick joke because I'm not. I struggle to breathe, desperate to escape the feeling of my world crumbling underneath me. "Bria goes with you, and you promise to come back," she says, and I nod, crawling out of my skin to not feel anything.

"Hello?" Bria calls again.

"Promise," I say, inhaling a gulp of oxygen that feels more like shattered glass, and Marley pushes away my hands again, but this time to tie my shoes for me.

It's reckless for her to love me because the only way I see

this ending is with our hearts broken in a way we won't ever recover from.

Bria's standing on the other side of the door, her eyes widening as I resist the urge to claw at my chest while Marley asks her to go with me.

Marley's arms are crossed over her chest as she watches us leave, and I know she's upset with me. I don't blame her for it either.

I should stay here and explain exactly how not okay I am.

Instead, I walk out the door, listening to the soft padding of Bria's footsteps as she runs behind me until I can't feel anything at all.

I overdid it. *Surprise, surprise.* I ran for so long last night even Bria was struggling to keep up, but I forgot how incredible it was to feel nothing at all. The only reason I stopped when I did, is because I thought my lungs were going to give out, only that time for the right reason.

The pills did exactly what I wanted them to. They numbed everything, including the pain in my knee that was crystal clear this morning when I woke up from the brief sleep I got.

I couldn't face Marley and Bria this morning, not after the way I fell apart last night, so I left before everyone else was awake.

If I weren't focusing so damn hard on trying not to give away how much pain I'm in—*physically and mentally*—I'd probably care more about how the only thing Asher's said to me since I arrived for weights was, *"Not here."* Bria probably called him and I'm sure he connected the dots. He has every right to be upset with me.

I underestimated how much taking one pill would make

me crave another, so despite my brain screaming for another, I'm not giving in. I don't *want* to take another, even if it means having to feel everything.

It might mean I'm screwed for our game this weekend unless Billy can work a miracle, but I'm done with the pills. My knee aches, but it's only a dull throb now instead of a sharp reminder of how badly I fucked up last night, like it was before the ice bath I just endured. My mind tried not to replay the conversation with Bailey the entire time. Naturally, I couldn't think of anything else.

Asher's leaning against my Jeep, his arms crossed over his chest and his hat flipped backward, letting me see exactly how pissed off my normally easy-going best friend is. *Fuck, I'm really not ready to do this right now.*

I roll my shoulders, exhaling as I approach. "Ash, can we do this later?" I ask, the exhaustion from everything catching up to me.

"No. Give me your keys," he says, holding out his hand expectantly.

"What?" I ask, blinking in surprise. *He wants my keys?* "I'm not giving you my keys."

"Give me your keys or I'm walking in there and telling Coach to drug test you," Asher says, his mouth flattened into a hard line as a slow drizzle begins. "We both know you'll fail, but the choice is yours."

Funny. It doesn't really feel like a choice.

I reach into my pocket, tossing the keys at him. "Happy?"

Asher's dark eyes meet mine, and for the first time in a long time, I feel small under the weight of disappointment in his expression. "No, JJ. I'm not fucking happy. Get in the goddamn car."

I swallow the lump forming in my throat, climbing into the passenger seat of my car without arguing. When we pass the turn to our house, and then to Marley and Bria's, I start to get nervous. Asher doesn't have the radio playing, and I'm aware of every breath I take as we merge onto the highway out of town.

"Where are we going?" I finally ask, shifting in my seat as my anxiety wins out. I don't like not being in control, and there's nothing about this I feel good about.

"A meeting," he answers, giving me no other inclination as to what it could imply.

"A meeting? What?"

"The next town over has an open morning Narcotics Anonymous meeting."

I sputter, choking on my sharp inhale. "Wait—what? *Narcotics Anonymous?* Seriously?"

"You promised," Asher says, his voice shaking.

"I tried." It's a weak defense. If I really had tried to kick it, I wouldn't have kept one hidden. I would have thrown it away with the rest of them.

He scoffs, scratching his jaw as his other hand clenches on the steering wheel. "Bullshit."

"What do you want me to admit? I'm a liar? Fine, Asher. You win—I lied, but it doesn't mean I need to go to an NA meeting." *Please make me go. Don't listen to me.*

If only the words coming out of my mouth could match the ones running through my head.

"I want you to admit you're an addict."

It feels like a punch to the gut and a breath of fresh air to finally have someone say the ugly truth I've only admitted in my letters to Marley. His gaze flickers over to me before settling on the road again as we exit, and I say nothing because I don't know how I got here.

How did I become this person addicted to painkillers?

I know better. I know the risks with taking them, but it

started as one refill to help me sleep through the night from the physical pain keeping me awake, and then I kept asking for more because I realized it was better to feel nothing at all than to feel everything at once. They didn't say no, and I started bringing cash to make sure they didn't start to.

Asher pulls up to a small church, and a pit forms in my stomach at the thought of going in and admitting I'm an addict to a room full of strangers who could easily recognize me. I know it's supposed to be anonymous, but would it be enough to stop anyone inside the room from going to a gossip site and posting something? My face is everywhere right now with Marley's.

"I get it," I murmur. "It won't happen again."

"I don't believe you."

I turn to look at him, trying to swallow the shame threatening to overwhelm me. "My brother called, and I slipped. I'm trying, man. I really am, but it was a bad night." *Don't listen to me.*

"What happens on the next bad night, JJ? Do you have some other stash I don't know about? I mean, god, the fact we're even having this conversation right now is exactly why you need to go in there. You need *help*."

"I'll do bette—"

"How would you feel if I were the one waking Marley up to go running in the middle of the night while I'm messed up and on drugs?" he asks, the words hanging heavy in the air. Ash drags his hands over his face, shaking his head. "I know how you feel about your family and not wanting them to worry about you, but don't involve my girl in it again. Next time, call me instead."

God, I hope there's a day I can return the level of kindness and friendship Asher is extending to me when he has every reason to be angry with me. I've lied to him countless times over the last year and still, he drove me here instead of giving up on me.

"There isn't going to be a next time," I say, unbuckling my seat belt. I feel nauseous, but maybe this is the push I needed to accept this might not be something I can do on my own. "Will you come with me?" I ask, my voice shaking.

"Whatever you need." He offers me a smile I don't deserve.

CHAPTER THIRTY

Marley

I'M WORRIED, AND I DON'T THINK I'M WRONG TO BE.

JJ scared the hell out of me last night, and I would do anything to take some of his pain to carry myself. He left without waking me up this morning, and I've been stuck in my chemistry lab all afternoon, my head spinning as I try to sort through the chaotic mess in my brain.

Bria sent me a text earlier asking how he was today, but the only messages from JJ I've gotten were to tell me he was with Asher, and a follow-up a few minutes later asking if he could come over tonight.

I only heard JJ's half of the conversation, but from what it sounded like, his brother is homeless. I have so many questions, but I'm terrified to ask JJ about Bailey in case it affects him the same way the call did last night.

Maybe I shouldn't have done it, but I reached out to Mirabelle before my class, asking her if she could call me because I think the only way to help JJ is by having the full picture to fully understand what's going on with him.

She times it perfectly, though, calling me the second I step out of the building. "Hey, Mira," I greet, resisting the urge to yawn despite the third cup of coffee I finished a little bit ago.

"Do I get to call you my sister yet?" she asks, and a laugh slips from me.

"I'm not sure I even want to ask what you mean by sister?"

Mirabelle laughs, and I feel bad knowing I'm about to ruin her afternoon, especially after the way everyone reacted when JJ mentioned Bailey in front of their family. "You'll know soon enough I'm sure."

"If you say so." I put in an earbud so I can walk without holding my phone up to my ear, tucking my hands into the sleeves of the hoodie I kept from JJ, with zero intention of giving it back. "Listen, I'm sorry to do this over a phone call, but I need to ask you about something I'm not sure I can ask JJ."

The jovial tone in Mirabelle's voice drops immediately. "Is everything okay? What happened?"

I can't tell her about JJ's . . . episode last night without revealing the call from Bailey, and I don't know if JJ's told his family about it yet. I think it's safe to assume he hasn't after the way this call started.

Tread carefully, Marley. "Everything's fine," I lie, immediately feeling guilty for doing it, but I'm caught between a rock and a hard place right now. *What was I thinking calling Mirabelle? This was dumb.* "He mentioned it's getting closer to the time Bailey calls, and I can tell he's more anxious, so I wanted to ask if you could tell me more about Bailey?" *I hope she doesn't push harder.*

Her sharp inhale is another punch to the gut, but I have to know. Mirabelle clears her throat, and I cross my arms over my chest as I turn toward the far parking lot. "So JJ, Henry, and I have a lot of theories about why everything went down the way it did with Bailey, but what we've speculated is Bailey found out about a gap in our parents' relationship none of us knew about, but we think the information he discovered was wrong. I don't know why he didn't talk to our parents about it himself, but he was mad at me at the time for hiding my relationship with Henry. I think there were probably other things going on we don't know about too, but we didn't know how bad things were until it was too late.

"Bailey set the house we grew up in on fire. The only reason we know now is because Bailey told Henry and me after we found him in front of another fire at the beach house my parents currently live in, the day before he ran away while my parents were in Europe. He said something about Hunter lying about Kaitlyn, and Henry admitted he knew Kaitlyn and Bailey kissed at some point, but he didn't know anything more. Maybe it's wrong of us, but we've kept Hunter in the dark because what good will it do to make him feel guiltier about his twin leaving?

"Honestly, I've replayed the conversation in my mind a thousand times, but Bailey was really specific about JJ being the only one who hadn't lied to him, which is why we're assuming he's the only one B calls."

I'm impressed they've managed to keep this out of the press as long as they have. "I'm really sorry you guys are going through this," I say as Mirabelle sniffles.

"He'll come back, so there's no reason to apologize," she says, but all I can picture is the look of despair on JJ's face when he admitted to me how he believes if Bailey were going to come back, he would have by now. Everything is starting to make a lot more sense now, especially JJ's anxiety about the calls.

Mira and I never told Mom and Dad what you did, is what JJ said last night.

"Your parents don't know about the fire, do they?" I ask, connecting the dots as I turn toward the parking lot at the far end of campus. I almost wish I had early morning classes to have an excuse to get here earlier to find better parking before it's all gone.

"No, they don't know. I mean, you saw their reaction when JJ said his name. Hunt wasn't wrong when he said they look for Bailey in him."

I hate this for all of them, and I wish I could say if I were put in their position, I'd do things differently, but would I? If Kaden were the one to run away, and I was the only one he spoke to, would I be able to look at my parents and tell them he's living on the streets?

All I know for certain is I can't blame JJ for beginning to suffocate under the pressure he puts on himself.

CHAPTER THIRTY-ONE

JJ

T**ODAY WAS A FUCKING NIGHTMARE, EVERY** horrible moment replaying on a loop in my mind. The way I did everything possible to try and help my team today, but the reality is with my brace on, I'm not anywhere near as fast as I need to be. It's the worst game I've had in a long time, and the other team took full advantage of our missed connections on the field.

My hands clench, and I need to hit something. I need to feel something because the urge to feel nothing has me by the throat, especially after my slip.

I know it's going to take time for my knee to fully recover, especially after the hell I've put it through the last few months. I can't expect it to be perfect like it was when I couldn't feel anything.

My anger bubbles over despite the shower I hastily took with the hope of it helping me shake my mood before I go to find Marley. My teammates have given me a wide berth since we entered the locker room, and I'm disappointed in myself for letting them down.

It's fine. I'm fine.

I ignore the looks from my teammates. I'm not one to normally get heated over games, but right now I'm struggling to find what my new normal is. It was different last season because I couldn't do a damn thing about it while recovering from my surgery, but this time I could have made a difference, and we still lost.

"You good?" Ash asks from my left, and I grab a shirt out of my locker, pulling it over my head.

"Perfect."

He snorts. "Yeah. You and everyone else in here. Are *you* good?" he asks again, emphasizing his words carefully as if I don't know exactly what he's asking.

I look at him, lying straight through my fucking teeth. "I'm good." *I'm clean, but I'm not good by any means.*

"JJ, you did your best. Anyone could see it," he says, clapping me on the back.

I nod tersely, not trusting my voice right now.

"Go find Marley. Seeing her might help," Asher suggests, and for once he actually has a good idea.

"Thanks, man. You had a good game," I say, offering him the faintest of smiles. It's the best I can do right now, but I'm starting to think my best isn't good enough.

Marley and I have been meeting in the same spot after every game since we got together, and I could really go for a hug from her right now. I grab my things, waiting until I'm out of the locker room and the view from lingering eyes before pulling my phone out to search for any meetings in the area I can slip away to. I'm trying to do the right thing.

Asher started driving me to one every day, and as hard as walking into the first one was, I think he's right to make me go. As much as I'd love to listen to the part of my brain screaming I need the pills, I don't *want* to take them. I haven't shared at a meeting, but the way everyone simply listens and doesn't judge the other people makes me want to hit a point where I feel comfortable in the uncomfortable by sharing.

I'm working on finding a way to explain everything to Marley, but I'm terrified of what it might mean. Still, I'm aware it needs to happen sooner rather than later.

To my relief, Marley is still waiting for me. However, my heart drops to my feet when I realize Mirabelle is standing next to her. They're deep in conversation and haven't noticed me.

What is she doing here? I didn't ask Mira to come. I need more time clean before I break my family's hearts, and I'm not in the right headspace to deal with it now.

I don't have time to wrap my brain around my sister's presence when Marley catches sight of me. Her eyes light up and Mirabelle turns to see me. She's quicker to move than Marley, running and throwing her arms around me. "I know it slows you down, but I'm really proud of you for wearing the brace today. Your knee will be better before you know it."

This feels like a sick joke.

I leave my arms motionless at my sides, and she moves back to look at me. "JJ? What's wrong?"

"*What's wrong?*" I ask, a bitter laugh escaping me. "What's wrong is I would have been good enough today if I weren't wearing the brace. I wouldn't be the way I am, stuck with everyone telling me I did my best today, knowing fully well I'm nowhere near the player I was before picking a fight with some asshole on the field after he described how he'd like to —" I cut myself off, and Mirabelle's brown eyes widen. "Why are you here?" I ask, my mouth growing dry as if it's been stuffed with cotton. *Does she know Bailey called?*

She straightens and Marley's stare is heavy on me. *Everything feels heavy.* I don't have it in me to pretend I'm okay. Right now, it's easier to blame Mirabelle than it is to blame myself for being the way I am.

"Why am I here? Do you really have to ask? You're my best

friend and my brother. I love you, and I miss you." Mirabelle steps back, her eyebrows knitting as she crosses her arms over her chest. "Finish what you were going to say. What fight are you talking about? What was he saying?"

I swallow, shaking my head as my anxiety runs rampant, taking advantage of my mood. "You shouldn't have come. I don't want you here," I whisper, consumed by the guilt of what I know.

"JJ," Marley says, and Mirabelle's jaw drops.

"No. I'm sorry, I can't do this right now."

And I walk away, hating I've become this person who lies to the people I love.

I'm trying to be better. *I just wish they knew it.*

CHAPTER THIRTY-TWO

Marley

JJ HASN'T RESPONDED TO ANY OF THE TEXTS I'VE sent him since he walked away from me and Mirabelle at the stadium earlier this morning.

Mirabelle texted me late last night to let me know she caught a last second flight to see JJ's game and grab lunch before her flight tonight to Minnesota where Henry's game is tomorrow, but her flight was moved up due to expected weather in Minnesota. We stopped on our way to the airport to grab a quick bite to eat, but it was a quiet meal, both of us shaken from the interaction with JJ.

I wasn't expecting Bria to be at the apartment when I returned from dropping Mira at the airport, but she's sitting at the counter doing homework when I walk in.

"I thought you were supposed to be with Asher?" I ask, hanging my keys on the hook by the door.

"He said something came up with JJ, and he had to take him somewhere." She looks up, her mouth turning down in a frown. "Are you okay? You look exhausted."

I feel some relief knowing JJ's not by himself, but I am

exhausted. I've been wracking my brain trying to figure out what's going on with JJ, but I can't help thinking there's more to this than anyone knows.

"I'm wiped. This feels like the longest week ever."

"Right? I'm so ready for a week at home. Kaden texted a little bit ago to ask what day we're flying back. I should tell him Saturday, right?" Bria asks, pulling her hair back into a messy bun. I got the same text, but I haven't responded yet.

"I think that's what my dad said at least."

I wish I was excited to go back to New York, but I'm not. I told my dad I wanted to dip my toe in the water, so I asked if I could go to work with him for a few days. It took some convincing, but I figured if I'm already going to be home, why not start getting used to what lies ahead for me?

"So where did Ash and JJ go? I'm surprised you're not with them," Bria says.

I flop down on the couch, staring at the ceiling as my head spins, trying to put the pieces together still. "I'm not sure where they went. JJ isn't responding."

Where would they have gone?

"Is everything okay?" she asks, hesitating, which is so unlike Bria, it only further confirms my suspicion everything is not okay.

"I don't know," I admit, wishing I knew the right questions to ask so I did know.

I'm not sure I know anything at all anymore.

Bria left a little bit ago to stay the night at the guys' house, and I finally heard back from JJ. He asked if he could come over so we could talk, which has only made me spiral while I wait because I don't know what to expect.

There's a knock on the front door, and I spring to my feet, moving quickly to flip the lock and open the door before he can disappear again.

JJ's standing there, his hands in his pockets, looking as worn as I feel. "I think I'll have to thank your dad for getting this automatic lock," he says, trying to joke, but there's nothing funny about the blatant fear lurking in his eyes.

"I'll let him know you like it," I say, stepping back to let him in, the questions I've come up with over the past few hours running through my mind at lightning speed.

I sit down on the couch, but JJ doesn't sit next to me, instead choosing to hover before sitting on the other end of the couch, out of reach. *What is JJ so afraid of? Was I right to spiral?*

JJ stares at his hands, and I shift, restless from the silent tension in the air. I tug at my necklace, twisting the diamond pendant between my fingers.

"*Amore mio*, you're making me nervous," I say, and he turns to look at me, revealing the unshed tears shining in his eyes. "Hey, whatever it is, I-I'm sure it's fine," I stammer, and he exhales, shaking his head.

"You're going to hate me, and I'm selfishly not ready for the way you look at me to change."

How could he ever think I'd hate him?

"JJ—"

"Sweetheart, I love you. I'll understand if you don't believe anything I've said to you after I tell you, but you have to know I've never lied about my feelings for you. I've loved you since before all of this," he says, faltering as he wipes his eyes. "And I can only hope you'll let me love you after. I'm sorry, Marley. I'm so fucking sorry."

I want to move closer to him, hold his hand to reassure him there's nothing he could say to change that, but JJ obviously sat on the other end of the couch for a reason. I feel my own tears pool and I wait for JJ to continue, and it slips into my mind these may be our last moments before everything changes.

JJ's gaze returns to his hands. "I went to a meeting earlier. I just listened, but they were talking about the steps, the first one is admitting you're powerless. I am, and I hate that I am. I wish I was better and stronger, but I'm just . . . I'm not."

Why does this sound familiar?

"Meeting?" I ask, the question slipping out of my mouth before I can stop it.

His hands brace on the back of his neck as his large frame coils with tension. "For addicts."

"But you're not an addict?"

"Except I am."

"*What?*"

My entire world shifts on its axis, and I stare at JJ, dumbfounded, my brain struggling to process the information. I don't know what I was expecting, but it wasn't this. This doesn't make any sense?

He can't be . . . but maybe, it *does* make sense. This is the final piece of the puzzle I've failed to fit together, the edges not lining up until now.

Oh my god.

"I'm sorry. I'm so sorry, Marley," he repeats, the words propelling me into motion. I move closer to JJ, erasing the space between us to wrap my arms around his torso, feeling his body tremble. "I'm trying. I promise I am."

How did this happen?

Except, I don't need to ask the question to know the answer because it's so glaringly obvious. It was the injury to JJ's knee. That's what he meant earlier when he said *I wouldn't be the way I am.*

It was the same for my mom. She injured her shoulder, and instead of taking time off to recover, she tried to push through with the pills a doctor prescribed for her until it was too late. I bet if I asked JJ, he'd confirm that his doctor prescribed the pills, but the truth is, all I care about is that he doesn't take any more of them.

If anyone should have realized what was going on with JJ, it's me. Maybe my first instinct should be to leave, but I know what it's like to love an addict, and because of that, I know it's possible for them to change.

"It's okay," I say, pressing a gentle kiss to the side of his head, my heart racing in my chest. "It's not your fault."

"Isn't it?" he asks, his voice cracking. "I should have stopped taking them sooner. It was just . . . it was nice to have a break from everything, to not feel anything at all. I'm sorry."

It was a perfect storm brewing inside him.

"Oh, JJ," I whisper, rubbing his back, wracking my brain for the right thing to say.

"I haven't taken any since Tuesday, but I almost made it a month before then. I don't want to be like this anymore. I know you deserve better than to have another addict in your life. I want to get better, so even if this means you hate me now, I need you to know I'm trying to be the man you thought I was. I'm trying to be someone worthy of being loved by you."

Tuesday morning is when Bailey called, and JJ went off the deep end, only I didn't realize until now how far he fell. If I'm understanding correctly, he was clean before Tuesday, which explains the change I noticed in him.

I feel my tears slide down my cheeks, as I close my eyes, resting my head against JJ's. "I could never hate you. I'm not leaving you. You're sick and you need help, but you're going to get better," I reassure him, swallowing the lump in my throat as I run countless moments through my head. "One day at a time, okay? You're going to get better."

"Do you really believe that?" JJ asks, and the vulnerability shining in his question makes my heart threaten to shatter completely.

"I do," I say, because the alternative is unthinkable.

CHAPTER THIRTY-THREE

MARLEY IS FAST ASLEEP, CURLED INTO MY SIDE WITH her hands clutching my shirt like it's her lifeline when my eyes flutter open. My head is clear—well, about as clear as it can be after telling my girlfriend I'm a drug addict, I guess.

I have a couple of texts from Asher, checking in to ask how the conversation with Marley went, and another from Hunter, asking if I've reconsidered transferring to Oceanside. I'm not surprised I have nothing from Mira, but I'm hoping it's because she's angry at me and not because she's trying to understand everything.

Maybe it's selfish of me to keep it a secret from them, but I have no intention of telling my family about my addiction. What good will it do? I'll go to meetings and focus on my sobriety, but I can do it without making them feel worse than they already do because of Bailey. I can't be another source of heartbreak for my parents.

Carefully extracting myself from the hold Marley has on me, I make my way into the bathroom, catching a glimpse of myself in the mirror. I hardly recognize the person staring back at me.

I wish the first thought in my head wasn't one telling me to get the pills, and a follow-up one trying to seduce me into thinking everything will be fine if I do.

Splashing some water on my face, I hear Marley's words echo through my head, *You're going to get better.*

I feel guilty enough for asking Marley to bear the burden of carrying my secret, especially knowing how her mother's addiction made her feel after what she told me about it in France. There's more for us to discuss, but it feels like some of the weight has lifted from my chest, making it easier to breathe already. If she can still believe in me, maybe there's still hope for me after all.

Marley is sitting up in her bed, rubbing her eyes when I step back in, the light from the bathroom casting enough of a glow for me to see the soft smile pulling at her lips. I love her smile. "Hey, how are you feeling?"

"Better," I say, reclining into the pillows stacked on the side of her bed I've claimed as Marley moves closer, leaning into me. "I'm sorry if I woke you up."

"I'm not."

I wrap my arm around her instinctively, tugging the blankets up over Marley. "It's the middle of the night. You should be sleeping."

"I could say the same about you, PP." Marley sighs, the sound a gentle puff of air as she rests her head on my chest.

A short laugh escapes me. "I'm sorry, what did you just call me?" I ask, causing Marley to laugh as well.

"PP—short for Pillow Princess," she explains through giggles, and I shake my head.

"You're ridiculous."

"So is the number of pillows you like to sleep with. We're basically reclining, JJ."

PP sounds like a bad dick joke. "Reclining into a cloud," I correct, appreciating the lighter topic.

"Maybe if half of them weren't intended to be used for decor, it would be like a cloud instead of an uneven lump of pillows," Marley says and I feign a gasp, causing more of her laughter to fill the darkness.

"Take it back, sweetheart," I warn, letting myself be in the moment instead of holding myself prisoner to the shackles of my guilt.

"Nope," she teases, twisting to lie on top of me, her soft curves pressed perfectly against the ridges of my body. "I guess I should be thanking you for not stealing the covers. Maybe I'll get you some better pillows for Christmas."

"Getting to be yours is the greatest gift I could ask for, but in the same breath, I wouldn't complain if you wanted to get better pillows."

"My bank account has to be good for something so let me see what pillows I can find," Marley says, pressing her lips to my quickening pulse. "Do you have a list or something?"

Honestly, it's easy to forget who Marley is and the amount of zeros in her accounts until moments like this. "A list?" I ask, unsure what she's asking for.

"Yeah, a list of one-liners, because the amount of times you have the perfect thing to say in the perfect moment can't be a coincidence," she says, and I'm grateful it's the middle of the night so she can't see the blush crawling up my whole neck and face.

Maybe it's a good thing Marley doesn't know about the letters.

"Nope, just spent too long wishing you were next to me, and now that you are, I'm going to make sure you know how appreciated you are," I say, promising myself and Marley I will never take her love for granted.

"Do you know when you're leaving for break?" Marley asks, causing my entire body to inadvertently tense.

We have Thanksgiving week off this year, but Hunter plays

the rivalry game against Duke on Thanksgiving, and Henry against the Vegas Mambas on Black Friday before I'll fly back Sunday. I feel bad it does, but the thought of going home in less than a week to face my entire family threatens to paralyze me.

"I think Friday," I say, feeling my throat tighten. I was awful to Mirabelle earlier, and all I can do is hope she doesn't tell our parents. "How upset was Mira?" I ask, and when Marley hesitates before answering, it says everything I need to know.

"She was . . . she's worried," Marley says, and I hate how my anxiety spikes. I would have preferred to hear that Mirabelle was so mad she threatened to sic Henry on me, but hearing she's worried means she'll ask questions. I should've been more careful with my words because she's not the type to let it go, especially after the way Mirabelle watched me during their visit after I snapped at her the first night.

"Do you think I could borrow your phone to call and apologize? I don't think Mira will answer if I call from mine."

"Are you sure she's still awake?"

I'd be shocked if she weren't awake. "Family of insomniacs, remember?" I try to joke, but it falls flat. Maybe I'll be lucky and Mirabelle will be asleep, so I can apologize in a voicemail.

Marley rolls for her phone to unlock it for me, and the bright light is blinding since my eyes have already readjusted to the darkness. "Do you want me to go?" she asks, and I love her for it, but I'm not sure I should be left alone for this conversation. I'm not sure I should be alone for any difficult conversations for a while, so I swallow the lump in my throat to reach for her hand.

"Don't let me run," I whisper, and she grips my hand tightly.

Mirabelle proves me right, answering on the second ring.

"Hey, I'm sorry I forgot to let you know I landed in Minnesota. I was trying to make it to Henry before his curfew. Have you talked to JJ?"

I clear my throat. "It's me."

"Oh." Mirabelle's tone is completely different now.

"I'm sorry."

"Fuck you, JJ," Mirabelle says, and I flinch, realizing it's not better to be on the receiving end of my sister's temper. It's definitely what I deserve, though.

"Mira—"

"No," she interrupts. "Seriously, *fuck you.* I understand how much it sucks to lose, but it doesn't give you the right to speak to me the way you did. You don't get to just walk away after telling me I shouldn't have come across the country to see you, and if you're really apologizing, you can start by telling me what really happened when you hurt your knee."

Marley squeezes my hand, offering silent reassurance, and it means more than she'll ever know. My heart rate slows, and I exhale a shaky breath. "I really am sorry, but there's nothing to tell. You didn't deserve to be the person I took my anger out on, and I wish I could take it back."

"We're family. You don't walk away from family, okay?"

Her choice of words only reminds me of Bailey and the ugly secret I'm keeping.

"I won't."

"Promise me," she says, her voice cracking,

"I promise," I agree, hoping I can keep it.

By the time the call ends, my brain is screaming at me, begging for a reprieve.

Just one won't kill you. It'll make everything a little easier, and all this pain and agony will fade away.

"You okay?" Marley asks, breaking the silence as I shove the thoughts to the back of my head.

"No, but I'm hoping I will be," I admit, seeking out the

comfort holding her brings, and she settles against me once more. "I know it's not fair of me to ask this, especially at the last moment, but is there any way you'd want to come to North Carolina with me for break? I-I need to find a way to tell my family about the call from Bailey, and I don't . . ." I trail off, feeling guilty for asking. Her brother is supposed to be back from Italy, and I'm sure her family has shit planned. "Actually, it's okay. I'll be fine. Forget I asked."

"Hey, don't do that. If you need me there, I'll be there," she says, yawning, and I fold my arms around her again. "I love every part of you—especially the imperfect parts, JJ."

Hearing this from Marley after she knows the truth means *everything* to me. "I love every part of you too, Marley," I whisper, closing my eyes once more, finally beginning to see a way through the darkness.

CHAPTER THIRTY-FOUR

Marley

JJ TALKED TO HIS PARENTS ABOUT BAILEY THE FIRST night we were here, and I think it's for the best he got the conversation over with. I hoped he would tell them about his drug problem too, but after the way his mom began crying, I don't blame JJ for not being able to.

It helps me understand a little more why he broke down the way he did at my front door the last time Bailey called, and why the phone call two weeks ago sent him spiraling in the first place.

I'm sitting on the wraparound deck of his parents' beach house, flipping through the pages of my songbook, trying to find which one I want to give to JJ for his birthday. When Sebastian asked JJ at dinner last night what he wanted for his birthday since they weren't going to be able to go to France with everyone's schedules, I felt stupid for not realizing his birthday was the same day as Christmas.

I definitely need to get him something better than a pillow, and hopefully one of the songs I've written about him isn't too cheesy of an idea.

Picking one is proving to be harder than I expected it to be, though.

"When you asked if I wanted to run with you, you failed to mention we'd be running at a sprint the entire five miles." A deep voice groans from the bottom of the stairs.

"I think what you mean to say is *Thanks, JJ, for offering to help keep me in shape*," JJ says, his familiar laugh tugging at my heart strings.

"I'm plenty in shape—you're fucking insane if you think this is fun."

JJ's dark head of hair appears as he jogs up the wooden stairs, his defined chest glistening from perspiration, and I don't even try to pretend I'm not staring at him. Hunter appears a moment later, clutching his side while he groans, his entire shirt soaked through with sweat despite the chilly breeze coming off the water.

"Hey, sweetheart," JJ greets, and I manage to tear my gaze away from his torso, happy to see his green eyes sparkling.

"How was your run?" I ask, shutting the songbook, and his eyes linger on it, an easy smile forming.

"Would have been better if he hadn't complained the whole time."

"Shut the fuck . . . up," Hunter says, struggling to breathe.

"Getting any inspo from the ocean? If you sit here long enough, you might spot a mermaid," he says, and Hunter keels over, panting as he flops onto his back, staring up at the sky. From how hard he hit the deck, I'm wondering how it's supposed to make him feel better. "You definitely have a close-up of a dead fish."

"Just looking through old songs," I answer, biting my lip to keep my laughter from slipping out.

JJ shakes his head, laughing as he leans down to kiss my cheek. "I like seeing you here," he whispers, going back for seconds to kiss the corner of my mouth as I smile.

I like being here.

"What did you do to him?" I ask, and JJ shrugs, opening the back door to step inside, returning a few moments later with a water bottle in each hand.

"We went for a run, and Hunt had a problem with the pace," he says, taking a seat in the chair next to me, but despite how he's not panting, he chugs what I'm guessing is nearly half the bottle.

"When the hell did you start running like the devil is chasing you?" Hunter asks, pouring water on his face instead of drinking it.

The light in JJ's eyes dims a fraction, and he scoffs, his hand resting on his knee, rubbing circles on the joint. "I think the better question is when did you get so out of shape?"

"You're annoying."

"So are you," JJ fires back, before the back door opens, and Thalia pokes her head out, eyebrows raised as her gaze bounces from Hunter to JJ.

"Do I even want to know?"

"Probably not," I chime in, and she chuckles.

"I was coming out to ask if anyone heard from Henry and Mirabelle to know if they're coming over for dinner tonight, but I might just call her again and leave you boys to your bickering. Marley, I don't know if you need rescuing, but you're welcome to join me inside if they're being too much for you," Thalia continues, a soft smile directed my way before the door closes again.

JJ tilts his head, leaving it up to me, which I appreciate, but it would be nice to get to know her better.

A strangled cry sounds from the ground, causing us both to jump. *"Shit, motherfucker, make it stop,"* Hunter begs, shoving his fist in his mouth as he grabs for his leg.

"Dude, what the hell is wrong with you?" JJ asks, looking at Hunter. "I thought I was the one with the bum leg."

"Charley horse," he says, his voice strained. "Can you massage it?"

"Okay, I'm out, this is weird," I say, laughing as I grab my songbook, and JJ follows.

"Yeah, no thanks, but you can call your girlfriend to do it."

"You so did this on purpose." Hunter moans, and I shake my head as I open the door into the spacious dining room off the kitchen.

"Are you good if I slip out for a bit?" JJ asks, and I turn to look at him, trying not to let my head fill with worry.

"Yeah, I'll hang out with your mom. You okay?" I ask, and JJ reaches for my hands, squeezing them briefly, his cheeks turning pink.

"Yeah, there's just a meeting nearby I want to hit. I won't be gone long," he whispers, glancing away as if he's embarrassed by the admission.

He's trying. *He's really trying, and I couldn't be more proud of him for it.* "I'm proud of you," I say, and his emerald gaze is slow to meet mine. "I love you and I'm proud of you," I repeat, to make sure JJ knows I mean it.

JJ's hand leaves mine as he slides it into my hair, pulling me to meet him halfway for a kiss making my toes curl and tempting me to beg for another. "Thank you," he says, lifting his mouth to kiss my forehead again. "Thank you for seeing me, and still loving me."

"Loving you isn't a choice, JJ. It's part of who I am."

His smile is blinding when he steps back. "Now who has the one-liners?" he teases, winking playfully at me.

"Shut up, I'm never going to say anything romantic ever again if you're going to give me shit for it."

JJ's shoulders shake as he turns around. "That's okay. I'll come up with enough of them for both of us."

~

My jaw falls open as JJ steps out of the bathroom, a towel slung low over his hips and his ridiculously chiseled chest on full display. I close my journal, shamelessly staring as his eyes find me. My head is telling me I should finish getting ready so we can leave for Hunter's game, but every other part of me is telling me to put my mouth *all* over him.

He laughs, his smile wide as he looks at me. *I wonder if he can read the filthy thoughts running through my head?* "Close your mouth, sweetheart, unless you plan on using it for something else," JJ teases, and apparently, he can read my mind. *JJ, if you can read my mind, drop the towel.*

"Is that a challenge?"

A familiar blush crawls up his neck, turning his cheeks a rosy color. "We'll be late."

"Do you care if we are?" I ask, and JJ looks torn.

His family left earlier while JJ was attempting to give me a surfing lesson, but I was hopeless. Any athletic ability I had vanished when I quit dancing years ago.

"Marley," he says, and I stand up, walking closer to JJ, hyperaware of the distance between us I fully intend on closing.

"*JJ,*" I reply, reaching out to wipe away a drop of water trailing down his chest, before deciding to let it linger. "Tell me to stop."

He swallows and I press my hand directly over where JJ's heart lies in his chest, feeling the strong heartbeat. "I'm powerless when it comes to saying no to you," he says, and I lower my hand until it reaches his, holding the towel in place.

"Are you saying no?" I ask, giving him an opportunity.

"I'm saying please *don't* stop."

I beam at JJ as I pull his hand away, looking down to watch his towel fall to the floor, his thick erection jutting out toward me. Before JJ, I would have said I didn't care about sucking a guy's dick, and it always felt like more of a chore than anything. With him, it's different.

I want JJ to enjoy this, and I'll take him any way he'll let me have him.

My gaze lifts to watch JJ's face when I wrap my hand around him, thrilled when he pulls his bottom lip between his teeth to bite back a groan as his head tips back.

I lower to my knees, and when I close my lips around the tip, JJ releases a breathy moan. Electricity shoots through my veins as I take more of his cock in my mouth, using the lubrication of my saliva to help my hand move easier as I stroke him.

"Pillow," he says, his eyes struggling to stay open and I'm confused.

"Did you say pillow?"

"It's more comfortable for you." JJ strains to get the words out as I tighten my grip, jerking him off firmly the way he showed me he liked, taking him in my mouth again, my hand bumping against my lips as I moan around him. *Only JJ would think of a pillow right now.* "Let me grab one, *please*," he begs, his hips bucking forward, surprising me by forcing more of him into my mouth than I'm ready for, and I gag, my eyes watering.

"Fuck, I didn't mean t—"

"I'm fine, really," I interrupt, smiling at JJ so he believes me.

"Pillow, nonnegotiable or I say stop."

Is JJ serious? "You realize you're stopping me in the middle of a blowjob because I'm not kneeling on a pillow?" I ask, and JJ's jaw tightens before he nods.

"I think you seriously underestimate how much I care about you being comfortable," he says, cupping my cheek in his hand. "I'm actually disappointed I didn't think of it sooner."

I can't help smiling when JJ steps away before retrieving a pillow from the mountain of them on his bed, bringing it back with a pleased smile on his face, but I do my best to make him smile for a completely different reason a minute later.

~

JJ and I are the last ones to arrive at the stadium, and I didn't think it would be obvious until we stepped into the box and every single person in the room turned to stare. This time, the box doesn't only consist of JJ's family—I was prepared to be surrounded by people, but not *this* many people.

"JJ, who are all these people, and why is everyone staring at us? We made it before the game started," I whisper through my smile, willing it to stay in place instead of shrinking under the weight of everyone's stares.

"Because everyone thought you were a blow-up doll I was toting around in public."

My head snaps quickly to look at him. "I'm sorry, *what?*"

JJ laughs, his smile bright as he looks down at me. "I'm kidding, sweetheart."

"Damn, I thought you wouldn't show until after the game started," a tall man says, walking up to us. I recognize him from some of the pictures around JJ's parents' house, but I can't put a name to the face.

"It's good to see you too," JJ jokes, removing his hand resting on my lower back to hug him. "Marley, this is my uncle. Uncle Owen, meet my girlfriend, Marley."

The name sparks in my brain, and my anxiety becomes an afterthought as I gasp. "You're the one who came up with the name JJ!"

His green eyes light up as he grins. "I couldn't let my nephew go by Jonathan Jacob for the rest of his life. Could you imagine how awful it would be?" he teases, and JJ groans.

"I can't imagine," JJ drawls sarcastically.

"Well, you owe me twenty dollars, so let me know how you want to send it to me. I take cash, check, Bitcoin, and I think there's a ne—" Uncle Owen starts counting off with his fingers, and I laugh as JJ looks at him, confused.

"I'm sorry, what exactly do I owe you money for?" JJ asks, pulling me back to his side, this time slipping his hand into the back pocket of my jeans. My breath catches at the simple touch and I turn to look up at him, tempted to pull him somewhere private so we can continue what we started back at the house.

"There was a betting pool on when you would show up, and because you got here before the game started, I'm out twenty bucks."

"Yeah, I'm pretty sure you don't need my money after your contract renewal last year. Who won?"

"Me," Thalia chimes in, winking at me. With them standing next to each other, the family resemblance is undeniable. "I see you still haven't called animal control for the squirrel hiding on your face. Do you need me to?" she asks, looking up at her brother who is as tall as JJ is, but lacks the muscle mass. I cough, trying to cover my laugh as JJ sighs next to me, and I think it's safe to assume this is a frequent occurrence.

He touches his short beard, frowning. "What is so bad about me growing facial hair? Bash also has one for No Shave November, and I haven't heard you threatening to call animal control on him."

"Can't you just accept you're not meant to have facial hair?"

"Mom, be nice," JJ chides, but I think this is hilarious.

"Blake likes it," his uncle argues, and Thalia crosses her arms over her chest.

"Does she?"

"Okay, we're going somewhere else now before your bickering can scare Marley off," JJ says, pulling me in the opposite direction. "I'm sorry, my family is ridiculous, but my uncle was kidding about borrowing money from me. He's one of the highest paid head football coaches in the league and was giving me shit because he thinks he's funny."

"Who all do you think was in on this betting pool?" I ask, and a set of arms wraps around my shoulders, recognizing the scent of Mirabelle's signature vanilla perfume a moment after.

"Every single person in this room. I put money on you not making it at all, but I'm happy you're here," Mirabelle says, pulling us toward where Henry and a few other guys are sitting.

"Marley, obviously you know Henry, but this is Wilson and his boyfriend, Jason. Henry and Wilson play for my uncle, but Jason is a left wing for the Carolina Dolphins."

"It's nice to meet you, but I'm not sure why anyone thought we wouldn't make it?" I ask, and she smirks, glancing from JJ to me, and in the process, I can feel my face burn, absolutely giving away what JJ and I were doing before leaving the house.

Mirabelle laughs, moving to sit next to Henry. "Don't worry about it. As long as they don't walk in on you, no one's going to complain about consenting adults doing consensual adult *activities*."

JJ swears under his breath, and my eyes bug at the thought of someone walking in on me giving JJ a blowjob.

"Um . . ." I trail off, stalling until I figure out what I'm supposed to say here.

Henry grimaces, resting a hand on her knee. "Mira," he warns, "maybe let's not talk about this in a room full of people?"

"Are you telling me you weren't doing something along the lines of whatever it is we all suspect you were doing?"

Mirabelle continues, looking to JJ while his face turns as red as mine. *Oh my god, we're never going to live this down.*

"I think I would die," I mumble under my breath.

"Don't worry. It's pretty fucking awkward to be the one walking in on it too. I lived with Henry, and I'm convinced they were trying to see how many times they could get caught," Wilson says, laughing, and for the first time, I see Mirabelle's cheeks tint.

"I'm officially team Jason," Mirabelle adds, sticking out her tongue at the handsome man as he turns to look at the blond man sitting beside him, his warm brown features softening in the process.

"I really can't blame you since I'm also team Jason."

"You're being mean. Cut them some slack. Mira didn't make fun of me when I showed up to Pilates last week already out of breath," he says, and Wilson smiles, chuckling.

"Jace, you have no idea what it was like to live with them. I'm surprised my eyes still work, but nothing was as bad as walking her parents out to the pool and finding them naked."

"No." I gasp, covering my mouth.

"This is my version of hell," JJ says, grimacing, and I seriously can't imagine. I would never be able to look JJ's parents in the eyes again.

"I don't know how many more times I can apologize for the pool." Henry groans, and Mirabelle snorts.

"The answer is you can never apologize too many times for the pool."

"What about a pool?" A tall girl who seems around my age appears on the other side of me, her honey eyes lighting up as they meet mine. "Hey, you guys made it. I'm Kaitlyn."

I return her smile, noting the similarities between her and Henry. "Marley," I say, noting a small spatter of what looks like orange paint in her brown hair. I brush it out without thinking twice, catching her by surprise, and my face heats. "Sorry, you had some paint in your hair."

She laughs, combing her fingers through her hair. "All good. That's actually pretty normal for me these days. Painting is a new hobby I'm trying out, but I haven't quite figured out how to keep the paint on the canvas and off me."

"I think that's really cool you're trying new things," I say, and she shrugs.

"I guess it's a perk of not knowing what you want to do with your life, but since you guys are here now, I think it means Thalia won the bet," Kaitlyn says, turning back to Henry. "Why do you need to apologize about a pool?"

Mirabelle goes to open her mouth, but Henry covers it with his hand quickly before she can say anything. "Mirabelle thought she saw a mermaid in the pool. I didn't tell you about it?" he asks, giving Mira a look as she bats her eyelashes innocently at him.

JJ turns, leaning down to whisper in my ear, "I'm so sorry about them."

"A mermaid? Why are we—" Kaitlyn tilts her head before her eyes widen. "Ew, gross. Forget I asked, I don't want to know."

"*Si tu veux vraiment me faire taire, je peux penser à autre chose que je préférerais dans ma bouche, mon cœur,*"[1] Mirabelle says and JJ scoffs.

"*Sérieusement? La moitié de cette salle parle français!*"[2]

The roar of the stadium becomes almost deafening as fireworks go off and the teams take the field, all the attention in the box moving toward the game.

"Oh thank god, I thought the game was never going to

---

1. If you really want to shut me up, I can think of something else I'd prefer in my mouth, my heart.
2. Seriously? Half this room speaks French!

start," JJ says, taking the opportunity to pull me away from everyone else. "Are you okay? I'm sorry about, well, everyone actually."

"Flustered and slightly mortified, but I'll survive." I reach for JJ's hands, his much larger ones engulfing mine as he exhales, and I search his face for any sign of the mask he so easily slips into. "You okay?" I ask, trying to be careful with my words.

"I'm good, I promise," he reassures me, leaning down to kiss the corner of my mouth. "Thank you for being here."

"Of course," I say, wishing more than anything I could have turned my cheek to kiss him directly. "We better go back and make sure everyone can see us before they suspect we're doing something else over here." JJ's smile meets his green eyes, crinkling at the corners, and I smile right back.

"They can think whatever they want, but I've been looking forward to explaining football to you. Might even be a test later," he whispers, and my heart thumps erratically in my chest at the suggestion. This time, his soft lips graze over mine with the gentlest touch and the promise of more. "I'm eager to show you just how well I've been paying attention."

"Remind me again how long games last?" I ask, my breath catching.

"Long enough to make the wait worth it."

CHAPTER THIRTY-FIVE

"Have you changed your mind about telling me what happened with your knee?" Mirabelle asks, plopping down on the couch next to me, having no idea she's only twisting the knife I plunged into my own chest. I thought after everything was fine at the games the last two days, she'd drop this, but I guess not.

"Don't you have your own house now?" I ask, getting up because I don't want to talk about this right now. I want her to drop it, but she's like a bloodhound once catching a scent.

"Sorry for giving a shit about you. I wonder what Mom and Dad would think if they knew there was more to it than you've said," she mumbles under her breath.

"There isn't. Let it go," I say through gritted teeth. *Why does she have to push?* I stand up, fully intending to walk away before we can get into another argument.

Marley left earlier this morning to fly to New York for an investment meeting at their company's headquarters after asking me a thousand times if I was okay with her going, but I can handle the last thirty-six hours with my family. I think she was also stalling when it came to packing, but I didn't want her to go either.

She must have given Asher a heads up because he texted a little after Marley left to let me know he was there to talk if I needed him.

"Too damn bad. You've been acting differently for months. What the hell is going on with you?" she asks, pulling on my shoulder to get me to turn.

"*Nothing*."

"Nothing, *right*." Mirabelle scoffs, shaking her head at me. "Or you can stop lying and tell me what's happening. I get you don't want Mom and Dad to worry about you, but maybe they should. We don't need another Baile—"

And then I explode, Bailey being thrown at me after the hell I've put myself through takes it a step too far. "You have no idea what you're talking about. Just because you're older doesn't mean you know everything, Mira. I don't have to tell you every single part of my life, but it doesn't make me Bailey. *I'm fucking fine*," I snap at her, immediately regretting it when Mira takes a step back from me.

"You're very clearly not because the JJ I know would never speak to me the way you just did," she says, her voice trembling.

Hunter appears at the bottom of the stairs, and I feel sick. "What's going on? I can hear you from all the way upstairs."

Mirabelle looks at me like I'm the one supposed to respond here. Her face falls when she realizes I'm not going to say anything. "JJ was just reminding me I have my own house. See you later, Hunter."

Hunter pushes his glasses further up on his nose, staring at me in disbelief as Mirabelle walks by him. She ignores whatever he whispers to her before shaking his head at me, saying nothing else until the front door slams. "You're lucky Mom and Dad aren't here because they'd be so disappointed."

"Hunter, I'm trying to protect her!"

His whole face changes, and I drag a hand through my hair, wishing Mirabelle had never made the trip to California. If she hadn't been there while I was struggling to figure out my next step, I would have been more careful with what I said.

"What do you mean you're protecting her?"

This is such a mess. "Do guys say shit about Mira to you?" I ask, and his jaw tightens telling me everything I need to know. Out of everyone, Hunt would be the one to understand.

"I mean, sometimes," he admits, shrugging. "I try not to let it get to me, but what does this have to do with what's going on between you guys right now?"

I swallow the lump in my throat threatening to choke me. "The game I hurt my knee, the linebacker who hit me was trying to get in my head, and I didn't give him a reaction until he started chirping about those fucking leaked pictures and how he'd like to pass Mirabelle around their locker room since she likes being on display. I shoved him after calling him on his bullshit, and on the next play, he took me out. It wasn't an accident."

"JJ, what the fuck? Why didn't you say anything?" he asks, moving closer, and I hate the look of pity in his expression.

A short laugh falls from my mouth because it should be obvious. I haven't said much of anything about the shit that matters because I don't want them to worry. It honestly makes me wonder what Hunter's kept to himself too, because I can't be the only one with secrets.

"What was I supposed to say? Mom and Dad were worried enough about the injury without me ripping the scab open by making Mirabelle feel like shit again for something out of her control. I didn't have to react. I could have let it go, but because I didn't, I'll never be the same."

In more ways than anyone could know, that moment

changed my life forever. If I hadn't reacted, maybe he wouldn't have hit me as hard, and I would have been able to get up. I wouldn't have needed the surgery, and I wouldn't have been in a vulnerable position to get hooked on pills. *I would be JJ Walker, rising football star, instead of JJ Walker, drug addict.*

"Dude . . ." Hunter trails off, surprising me by pulling me into a rare hug. He's not a fan of physical touch unless it's on his terms. "I'm sorry."

"It is what it is. I didn't mean to let it slip. She caught me by surprise on a bad day after an awful game, and I wasn't in the right headspace, but I caught myself before I said anything. Mira's pissed I won't tell her the real story."

"You're still a great player, but that's not the only thing you are. You're a good person, and an even better brother," Hunter says, but I'm not convinced he'd still say it if he knew the truth.

I'm slow to wake up from my nap that I hadn't meant to take after getting back from another meeting. I didn't get a whole lot of sleep last night, but I didn't think I was tired enough to fall asleep at my desk while writing a letter to Marley.

I tug on a sweatshirt, heading down the stairs to the kitchen for a snack as my stomach grumbles for food. My parents are in the kitchen and seem surprised to see me here.

"Why are you looking at me like that?" I ask, yawning while I open the fridge to see what's inside. I have another recipe I want to try before I make it for Marley, and the ingredients are pretty standard.

"We thought you were out with Hunter," Dad says.

"He's at Kaitlyn's, but I was sleeping," I explain. He asked me if I wanted to go, but I was leaving for the meeting, so I made some excuse about going to look for a Christmas present for Marley. I didn't feel good about lying to Hunter, but I'm not ready.

Mom appears next to me, resting the back of her hand against my forehead. "Are you feeling okay? You never take naps."

"I'm fine. Just tired, I guess."

"It's been a while since I stretched my arm out. Do you want to throw the football around?" Dad asks, and I have a funny feeling there's more to this that they're not saying. *Did Hunter say something about what I told him?*

"Sure, if you want to," I say, shutting the fridge to see Mom frowning at Dad.

"Bash, I don't think he feels good," she says, and now I know something's up.

"What's going on?" I ask, crossing my arms over my chest as they share a look.

Mom's hand drifts up to tug at the necklace she wears. "I talked to Mirabelle, and she mentioned you guys got into an argument earlier. Is everything okay? I can't remember the last time you fought with her."

I force a chuckle, scratching my jaw as my head spins, trying to find a way out. "I don't know. You know how Mira gets when she doesn't get what she wants," I say, trying to play it off like it's nothing, because the last thing I want is more questions being asked.

"No, JJ. I don't know how she gets, but I do know you're not acting like yourself right now. Do you care to tell us what's going on with you?" Mom asks, and I blink, caught off guard. *How would she know if I'm acting like myself?* My chest starts to grow uncomfortable, and I press my hand to my chest.

"No, not really," I say, for once choosing to not be invisible. "You haven't exactly cared the last two years, so you don't need to start now."

The bullet has been loaded for a long time, but I never thought I'd pull the trigger. Mom's eyes widen as the truth echoes louder than I think any of us would like it to, her demeanor cracking to show how deeply my words have landed.

I'm afraid to look at my dad, and the pressure on my lungs grows heavier. My eyes land on the door located on the far wall of the dining room, the escape calling to me louder than anything.

I walk past them, refusing to stop until my bare feet touch the cold sand, giving me something else to focus on instead of the panic sinking its claws into me. Marley would tell me to breathe in through my nose and exhale out my mouth. The first one feels impossible, but I keep trying.

Sitting in the sand, I watch as the waves beat mercilessly against the shore. The ocean is angry today, and I understand it because I'm angry too. I know I shouldn't have said it, but I wasn't wrong, even if my delivery could have been better.

God, it feels like forever since Marley left, and it was only this morning. *What a nightmare of a day.*

I think I'm starting to understand what everyone at the meetings talks about when they say getting clean is the easy part, because right now, I think I'd give anything for a few minutes of bliss where I feel nothing. I just keep fucking everything up.

They're my parents, and I love them, but I feel like they don't even see that I've been so busy trying to make sure everyone else is okay that I've completely lost myself in the process.

Out of the corner of my eye, I see my dad lowering himself into the sand. He doesn't say anything, but he doesn't need to.

"I'll apologize to Mom when I go inside," I say, trailing my fingers through the sand, trying to ground myself.

Dad sighs, and I hold my breath, waiting for the lecture

I'm about to get. "Good. You should apologize to her, but right now, we're just going to talk."

My fingers brush over a shell, and I pick it up to throw it into the water, watching as it disappears among the waves without a trace. "About what?"

"Anything you want to."

It sounds so simple when he puts it that way—except it's not.

"You don't need to humor me by asking now. I'm fine."

"You're not fine, but it's okay. You don't always have to be okay," Dad says, throwing his own seashell into the abyss.

"But I do. I have to be okay because everyone else gets to be upset about Bailey, except for me. I'm not allowed to be upset because he talks to me. It's only on his terms, but still." *I'm not allowed to be angry or scream about how unfair it is, because what good would it do anyone?*

"JJ, you absolutely do get to be upset about Bailey. Just because he only calls you doesn't mean shit," Dad says, but it's almost two years too late.

"Dad, can you honestly remember the last time you called me on the phone, and you didn't ask if I'd heard from Bailey?" I point out, looking at him with all of my walls down. His amber eyes drag over my face, finally seeing past the facade I've had up for so long. I can practically see the gears moving in his head as he thinks back, but based on the way his mouth turns down, I don't think he can. *I'm not sure I even know at this point.* "Every single time he's called, the first thing I do after he hangs up is call you and Mom. I call and listen to the sound of your hearts breaking all over again, and it makes me feel like I don't exist for anything other than to be the one Bailey speaks to. You guys didn't even know I learned Italian, or how I'm—" I cut myself off quickly, wiping my eyes blurring with tears as I look back to the water.

"You're what?" he prods when I don't continue, and the cold breeze stings my cheeks.

Is this it?

Is this the moment where I come clean about everything?

"I'm lost, Dad," I whisper, wondering if I'll escape the whirlpool I'm caught in, or drown first.

He falls quiet, and I'm wondering if this conversation will be another one of those things my family doesn't talk about when I'm done making waves. "I know . . ." he falters, clearing his throat. "I know we've spent a lot of time focused on Bailey and finding him, but it was never our intention to make you feel invisible. I can't change anything, but I'm going to try to be better from now on. No one is perfect, and we've never expected you to be, JJ."

"Then why haven't you ever told me that?" I ask, turning to face the man I look so much like.

Dad looks as tired as I feel, his expression shadowed by emotions. "Because I thought you already knew it, and I'm ashamed I haven't told you already." He drags a hand over his stubble, and I wish we'd had this conversation sooner. Maybe things would have turned out differently. "JJ, you are so good at hiding your emotions—*much better than I thought you were*—and I'm sorry for not looking harder. Your mom isn't perfect, and I'm so far from it, I'm not even sure where to begin with the list of mistakes I've made."

"I don't expect you to be perfect, I just want you to put in the same amount of effort with me as you do with Mirabelle and Hunter." I wipe my nose on the sleeve of my sweatshirt as Dad's eyes begin to shine.

"I'm sorry, JJ. I'm so sorry I haven't seen how lost you've been."

"It's fine."

"*Don't lie.* Don't tell me it's fine when it's not," he says and I look away, my fingertips searching for another seashell to throw.

"I don't know what you want me to say."

"Sometimes there isn't anything to say."

We sit in silence, the tall grass blowing noisily behind us in the wind as the waves crash onto the shore just mere feet in front of us, the salt spraying our faces. I can't remember the last time I sat with my dad like this, but I'm not willing to ruin the moment by elaborating on exactly how lost I've been.

I feel like, for the first time in a long time, my dad is listening to me.

CHAPTER THIRTY-SIX

Marley

I NEEDED TO ESCAPE THE LOOMING PRESSURE OF MY future after attending a slew of meetings with my father after my flight landed, so I'm hiding at my family's penthouse in the heart of the city, trying to pretend I'm still in North Carolina with JJ. I'm also avoiding packing to go back to school, but that's a later problem.

I can't blame my dad for asking me to come, especially after I bailed on our original plan for me to go into the office with him all week. It gave me a good chance to practice my Mandarin since one of the investors originated from Singapore, but I'm nowhere close to being fluent. The investor did seem delighted I could converse a little before I became lost, and we switched to English. I haven't practiced Mandarin hardly at all since transferring to Beaumont, but yesterday was a stark reminder I should make it more of a priority.

I love learning new languages and taking trips to practice with native speakers, picking up on the things I can't learn from a tutor.

It's not that I don't want to be at home with my family, but I'm not ready to act like I'm excited to do this for the rest of my life. Six months ago, it would have been easier, but transferring to Beaumont has changed me more than I ever could've imagined it would. I'll go back soon to spend some time with them before Bria and my's flight is scheduled to depart later this evening, but I need a little more time to myself.

I'm camped out on the couch, working on a song I started to put together in my head a few days ago while I wait for takeout from my favorite hole-in-the-wall Chinese restaurant to be delivered.

I looked to the sky
Wishing for a sign
You're everything I wanted
But everything I thought I'd never have
A shooting star I was lucky to see
Burning bright in the night

The elevator dings, pulling my attention to the entryway, and I'm dreading being found already. I thought no one would think to look here, but I'm a creature of habit, seeking comfort in the familiar.

The door slides open, and I'm pleasantly surprised to see my Uncle Dean standing there. Last I heard, his kids were sick with the flu, and they had to skip out on Thanksgiving this year.

"How did you know I was here?" I blurt out, my song-book abandoned as I stand to meet him halfway.

"I thought I'd at least get a hello, but I guess not." He smiles, pulling me into a hug. "It's good to see you, Lee."

I roll my eyes, but I don't protest the nickname. Anyone else I would, but not my uncle. He's the only person in the world I would ever let call me Lee.

"How are you here? Kaden said your kids were sick, so I didn't think I'd get to see you before I leave later."

"They're on the mend, but Tori said she had it handled so I could come check on you," Uncle Dean explains, his blue eyes twinkling as he ruffles my hair.

"But I'm fine? Why do you think you need to check on me?" I ask, tilting my head.

"Your dad called me last night, come cook with me in this beautiful kitchen going to waste," he says, changing directions to head toward the state of the art kitchen we barely use. I'd rather he explain why my dad called him, but I recognize I'm not going to get my way in this, and it's easier to follow Uncle Dean into the kitchen.

"If you want it to be edible, I suggest you have me do all the washing and drying while you cook," I say, spinning the ring on my thumb, trying to avoid picking at my cuticles since I tore them to pieces during the meetings yesterday.

"Everyone should be able to cook at least one meal," he says, and I snort.

"You've met my mother, right?"

"Except her. It's a good thing she married your father, or I'm afraid she would have starved by now," Uncle Dean says, and he's not wrong. "Lucky for you, Hayes keeps this kitchen pretty well stocked, and we have all the ingredients we'll need."

It's nice he's trying to give Dad credit, but we both know there's a housekeeper who comes by twice a week. The first time she stops by, she drops off groceries and tidies up. The second trip, she donates whatever hasn't been used to a local shelter for survivors of domestic violence.

"What are we making?"

"An Alfredo sauce from scratch, but I'll take pity on you by letting you use dry pasta instead of also making it from scratch," he says before tilting his head toward a cabinet. "Grab a medium size pot and a saucepan please."

I follow directions, not surprised he knows where everything is here. Once I have the pot filled halfway with water I salted over a lit burner, Uncle Dean begins clapping. "Congratulations, you know more than your mother, and I'll bet you'll even take it one step further by proving you can't burn water," he teases.

"What's next?" I ask, and he shakes his head.

"I've got it from here, I want to be able to eat it when it's done," Uncle Dean says, and I pull myself up to sit on the counter.

"Probably a good choice. I tried making my boyfriend eggs last month, and I was mortified when he told me they were crunchy."

My uncle stares at me, his dark eyebrows raised. "He complained to you they were crunchy after eating them?"

I laugh, shaking my head. "Yep. JJ actually ate them still with a smile and planned on never telling me, until he mentioned on a date he was learning to cook so we don't starve. I tried to use the eggs as an example of how I can cook, and he told me it meant a lot to him I even tried to make something for him."

"Sounds like he's a keeper, and a thousand times better than your old one," he says, nodding his approval. "When you find someone like him, don't let him go."

"You know, if everyone just told me what they really thought of Trent when I was dating him, maybe I would have dumped him sooner," I say, giving Uncle Dean a pointed look.

"Lee, you know we were all just trying to be supportive. You have to make your own decisions, even if it means making mistakes along the way. It's part of being an adult," he says, offering me a smile to go with the wisdom. I feel like there's a double entendre there, but Uncle Dean will get to his point when he wants to. "It seems like you're enjoying Beaumont more than Columbia," he says, and I watch as he turns the saucepan to a low simmer, dropping some butter in the pan.

"I love it. Columbia wasn't the right fit for me," I say, and the distinction between the two has never been more clear after the last twenty-four hours. Everything there was about who your parents were, and how much money was in your bank account. Beaumont still has plenty of people with wealthy connections, but it's a different vibe entirely.

"I'm proud of you for transferring. I know it probably wasn't an easy decision, but you seem happier."

It wasn't an easy decision, but it was the right one.

After my freshman year, I tried sticking it out a second year at Columbia, knowing it was important to make connections there, but no matter how hard I tried to make myself fit the mold and meet people's expectations, I couldn't.

"I am happier there. I've made some really great friends there, and I'm learning a lot about myself," I say, shaking my head and spinning my ring again. I chew my bottom lip as Uncle Dean turns away to push the garlic he's been mincing into the pan before adding the box of noodles to the boiling water. "Uncle Dean?"

"Yeah?" he asks, looking over his broad shoulder at me.

"Why did my dad call you?"

He offers me a smile riddled with sympathy more than anything. "You'll have to ask him yourself if you want to know. I'm not the go-between for anyone anymore. I stopped doing that when I left the corporate world twenty years ago."

"Did you really hate it so much you just quit?" I ask, curiosity getting the better of me, and I know I'm more interested in his answer than I should be.

Uncle Dean leans against the counter, crossing his arms over his chest. "I did, even though I was good at it—actually, I was really fucking good at it. It's the family business, and it might sound silly now, but all I ever wanted was to feel like a

Benson. I thought working for the company would fix it, but I hated it. I was pretending to be someone I wasn't, and your dad knew it," Uncle Dean explains, and I try to picture him in the meetings I sat in yesterday, but I can't. "He told me life is too fucking short to spend it doing something you hate. I applied to the fire academy, and realized he was right. I loved running into burning buildings for a living, and I met two of the most important people in my life while doing it. I'm a firm believer that everything happens for a reason."

"Sounds like something Dad would say," I say, and my uncle tilts his head.

"Are you excited to work at the company?" he asks, and I swallow the dread rising in me.

"Yeah, I am."

He laughs, and I push a smile on my face, hoping it helps my answer be more convincing. "Then why do you look like you swallowed a lemon?"

"I do not!" I glare at him, regretting I even opened the door to this conversation. Curiosity kills the cat, and in this instance, I'm the cat.

"You do, and you can continue to deny it, or you can tell me what you really think. Up to you," he says, turning to add heavy cream and shredded Parmesan to the pan, using a whisk to mix them together.

"It's different for me than it was for you. I don't get to quit," I say, not wanting to talk about this. I have two years left in school and another two of shadowing Dad before I'm eligible to take over. *Only four years of freedom.* It used to be a bigger number but I've forgotten as time passes, the number shrinks. It's easier to pretend when I'm not here. "You and Uncle Maddox were never expected to take over the company, but I've grown up knowing my future, and it's not an option for me to quit. I sat in those meetings yesterday, pretending I didn't want to crawl and hide under the table like a little kid, and it feels selfish to not want it. I know how long my dad has wanted to retire, and I would rather spend the next thirty years pretending to be someone I'm not than disappoint him," I admit, wondering what great words of advice my uncle will have for me now. "How dare I complain about the billion-dollar company I'm going to inherit?" I mumble, mocking myself because it's a ridiculous conversation to even be having.

"Lee, you always have a choice. You don't have to run the company if you don't want to," he says, his voice softer now. I don't need to be coddled for this, and I shouldn't be hiding here. "What would you do if you could do anything in the world?"

It's not a fair question because I can't answer it. It's easier to lose something you never had than to lose something you've spent time dreaming of. I shake my head, tears of anger threatening to spill over. "No. I want to. I want my dad to be less stressed, and this is the only way. I want . . ." my voice falters and I shove my feelings deep inside. This time when I speak, my voice is unwavering. *"I want to run the company."*

Uncle Dean stares at me with his piercing blue eyes proving his lineage as a Benson. "All I am saying is you don't have to."

Except I do.

The one thing I feel like's a choice is being with JJ.

CHAPTER THIRTY-SEVEN

JJ

"HEY," BRIA SAYS, SMILING AT ME AS I WALK UP THE stairs as she holds the door for me on her way out. "Marley's in her room."

"You off to see your boyfriend?" I ask, and she rolls her eyes, but her smile doesn't drop.

"Asher isn't my boyfriend."

I laugh, shaking my head at her. "Yeah, whatever you want to tell yourself."

"He's not."

"I believe you," I say, giving her a quick hug. "Did you have a good break?"

"I did, despite you stealing my best friend and forcing me to suffer through a hundred questions at Thanksgiving dinner about your roommate by myself," Bria says as we trade places with me entering the apartment.

"Sorry."

She scoffs, shaking her head. "You could at least pretend to look sorry. Tell Mar I'll be back in a couple hours."

"Have fun with your boyfriend," I tease as Bria starts down the stairs.

"Not my boyfriend!" she calls out over her shoulder, throwing her middle finger in the air.

I lock the door behind me, chuckling to myself as I slip out of my shoes. Charlie told me earlier how Asher wouldn't shut up about Bria the entire time and made multiple declarations to his entire family about how he was going to marry her. They are the very definition of opposites attract because I honestly think Ash would propose today if he thought she'd say yes, and she won't even admit he's her boyfriend.

It feels good to be back here, some of the weight lifted from my shoulders after the conversation with Hunter and my parents. It's easier to breathe, and it helped give me the courage to share for the first time at a meeting this morning. I'm three weeks clean, and I successfully made it through a trip home without searching for pills.

Marley and Bria's flight got in before mine yesterday, and Marley was asleep by the time I got back to my house, but I'm eager to be in the same room as her again. She makes everything easier.

I'm about to knock on her door to let her know I'm here, when I freeze at the sound of a guitar and Marley's melodic voice as she sings on the other side.

Carefully opening the door, I hover in the doorway, selfishly wanting to listen for a moment. She looks beautiful wearing one of my sweatshirts, her caramel hair pulled back in a clip as pieces hang in her face while she looks down at the songbook in front of her.

"Without a doubt, you're the only choice. The one I've dreamed of, the only thing I need," she sings softly, and not to be narcissistic, but I hope it's about me. *"Everything fades awa —"* Marley stops, her eyes widening when she sees me. "JJ?"

"Hey, sweetheart," I say, stepping in the room, and she pushes the guitar to the side to jump up, throwing her arms around me.

"I missed you," Marley says, and just like in her lyrics, everything does fade away.

How did I get so fucking lucky?

I fold my arms around her too, enjoying the blissful feeling of holding Marley. "I missed you too," I say, and with her arms still hooked behind my back, Marley pulls me to her bed.

"Not as much as I missed you. Can I play you something?" she asks, her blue eyes sparkling as she sits down on the bed, reaching for her guitar.

"You want to play for me?" I ask, my heart stuttering in my chest.

"It'd be better than hovering in the doorway like a creeper," Marley teases. "Unless you don't want to?"

"No, I do," I blurt out, not needing to be asked twice. I sit, facing her as she takes a deep breath, strumming the guitar.

"A shooting star, a rare glimpse in the night," she starts, her voice shaking as she peeks up at me. I'm not even sure if I'm breathing. *"Gone in the blink of an eye, too fast, too soon. It felt like a dream, but one worth chasing. You're my once in a lifetime. I looked to the sky, wishing for a sign. You're everything I wanted, but everything I thought I'd never have."*

I feel tears welling up in my eyes, but I don't wipe them away, afraid that if I move, Marley will stop singing.

"I lost my way, but I never stopped searching. For the light in the dark, wishing you'd appear. Without a doubt, you're the only choice. The one I've dreamed of, the only thing I need. You're my once in a lifetime. A shooting star I was lucky to see, burning bright in the night, on your way back to me."

Marley continues strumming, but she stops when her gaze meets mine. *"Amore mio,* what's wrong?" she asks, setting her guitar down.

"Absolutely nothing," I say, my voice choked up as I feel the tears fall, overwhelmed by how much love I feel for Marley.

She moves closer to me, swiping my tears away as I stare at her, unable to find the right words.

"Are you sure?"

I nod the best I can with her hands cupping my face, trying to swallow the lump in my throat so I can speak. "I love you."

"It's not quite done, but I wanted to play it for you."

"It was perfect," I say, meaning every word. "Thank you."

Marley is glowing, and it feels like the easiest decision I'll ever make to lean forward and kiss her. I could kiss her forever and never grow tired of it. She moves away a moment later to recline on her pillows, pulling me with her as my mind races.

"No matter what happens, JJ . . . I'll always find my way back to you. You're my once in a lifetime," she whispers, gazing up at me, and I know in my soul there is no ending to our story where we aren't together.

Marley completes me in a way nothing else ever has or ever will.

There is no me without Marley.

This time when I kiss her, there's an urgency to it. She hooks her leg around mine, pulling me directly on top of her, pressing our bodies together with too many layers of clothing between them. I can taste my tears on her lips as our mouths move in tandem.

I pull away, my entire body trembling with need, my heart cracked wide open for Marley, scars and all.

"JJ, what is it?"

My hand is shaking as I brush her hair out of her face, collecting my thoughts into words.

"You don't have to say yes simply because I'm ready, but I don't want to wait anymore."

CHAPTER THIRTY-EIGHT

Marley

"You don't have to say yes simply because I'm ready, but I don't want to wait anymore," JJ says, and I can feel his hand brushing my hair from my face shaking.

"Are you sure?" I ask, wanting to make sure he means it. I respect him for not wanting to rush things, and I have no problem letting JJ take the lead in how slow or fast we move physically.

He was right when he said he's not going anywhere.

JJ's green eyes are smoldering as they gaze into mine. "Never been more sure of anything. I want you."

"So take me."

His lips curl into a smile, and I can feel how badly he wants me pressing against my thigh. *God, do I want him.* What JJ lacks in experience, he makes up for with his eagerness to please.

He leans down, pressing a kiss to my cheek. "I think you're dazzling."

"Dazzling? Really? Are you okay?" I ask, and a wavy lock of JJ's dark hair falls into his face as his eyes twinkle like stars in the night sky.

"Exquisite." This time, JJ presses a kiss to the corner of my mouth. My breathing hitches while I impatiently wait for him to press his lips where I want them most. "Enchanting." He skips right over my mouth, landing on the other corner.

"JJ," I whine, causing him to chuckle.

"You're being impatient."

"And you're teasin—" I'm cut off by JJ finally kissing me, and the outside world disappears. I hold the back of his neck as JJ and I explore each other as if it were our first kiss again. My other hand slides under his shirt, my fingertips gliding over the hard lines of his body, and JJ's groan reverberates through my entire body.

I can't get enough of him, but I also want him to know it's okay if we don't have sex today.

JJ tilts his head away, his breath mingling with mine as his nose bumps against mine. "Do you believe me now?"

"Huh?" I ask, dazed and unable to really focus on anything but how right it feels to have JJ's body pressed against mine.

"I have never been more at peace than I am with you, so do you need to ask me again if I'm okay, or do you believe I mean everything? I don't know everything about your relationship with Trent, but I know he was a piece of shit to you, and I want you to know while I'm wildly attracted to you, your body is the least interesting thing about you." My eyes widen and JJ frowns, shaking his head. "Wait, I don't like how that sounded—it sounded better in my head. What I mean is, even though you're definitely the most beautiful girl I've ever laid eyes on, your heart is my favorite thing about you. You're so careful with who you shine the light of your love on, and I'm honored to be one of them. I'm not just trying to get you into my bed."

I love how he understands me so well, without me even having to say anything. The effort JJ puts into our relationship, compared to the one with Trent, is like night and day. They're not even worth comparing.

"Sweetheart?" he prods, staring directly into my eyes.

"Yeah?"

"I'm waiting for you to say you believe me."

I am so in love with him. He makes me feel seen in ways I *never* have before. "I believe you."

JJ kisses me one more time—so sweet, tender, and full of love—I sink into him, wondering how I could have ever made it as long as I did without him. I'm hyperaware of everything right now. The way JJ's touch sends electric shocks through my body. The cool kiss of air on my skin as JJ tugs the sweatshirt I'm wearing up, his calluses scraping deliciously over my smooth skin after pulling it off. How warm his body feels pressed against me after he pulls his own off. The way his kiss grows more desperate when his mouth slants over mine again, and how much more of JJ I want as he rocks his hips against my pelvis.

"I *need* to touch you. Is that okay?" JJ asks, his voice shaking after breaking our kiss as my chest rapidly rises and falls underneath his stare and I nod without hesitation.

"Please touch me," I say, nearly begging when he finally cups my breast with his large palm, dipping his head to drag his tongue up the crevice between them.

JJ takes my nipple in his mouth while simultaneously rolling my other between his fingertips.

I hook my leg over his thigh, shamelessly grinding against him. The teasing scrape of JJ's teeth causes a whimper to slip from me, turning into a moan when he bites down, having taken notes and his attention to detail only adds to the moment before he soothes the sting away with his tongue, pressing a sweet kiss after.

"Je ne te laisserai jamais être un presque,"[1] he whispers against my skin, and I wish I had enough sense to ask what the significance of the word *almost* is to him. Instead, JJ torturously blows air on my wet skin, causing me to grab the sheets.

"More, please."

"Tell me what to do, baby. I want to be a good boy for you," JJ says, and I smile at the beautiful man above me.

"Kiss me."

Before JJ, I never would have thought a kiss would feel like gasoline being poured on a raging fire, but it causes my body to burn brighter and hotter than before. Much to my delight, his hand slips between us, dipping beneath the elastic band of my lounge shorts and underwear. JJ circles my clit with slow, teasing circles, and I tip my head back in pleasure to gasp, breaking our kiss. JJ's mouth moves to my jaw, and then my neck as my grip on the sheets tighten.

I think he's making it his personal mission to know my body better than I do.

The crescendo in my body builds as JJ shows me exactly how well he's been paying attention. "*Good boy,* keep . . . going, please," I beg as JJ dips his fingers into me, maintaining pressure on my clit with the heel of his hand.

"I love how polite you are, even when I'm fucking you with my fingers," he says, and my hips roll in response.

JJ takes my nipple in his delicious mouth again, and my body falls over the cliff, a cry slipping from me as I tangle my fingers in his dark waves, holding him close.

My breathing is heavy when JJ looks up at me, a pleased smile on his pretty face. "What?" I ask, and he shakes his head.

"I love you."

"I love you too." I smile at him, chuckling as I brush a

---

1. I will never let you be an almost.

stray dark wave out of his face. "Are you okay?" I ask, and JJ nods, his cheeks pinking.

"Just thinking about how far I need to dig my grave."

Grave? What? I shift, sitting up to look at him, noting how his green eyes drift to look at my breasts, his jaw clenching. "What are you talking about?"

"I'm not sure how long a guy is supposed to last, and what if I accidentally hurt you? I try so hard to be mindful of how much bigger I am than you, and I want it to be good for you, but what if I'm so bad at sex you want to break up with me?" JJ admits, and my breath catches. I can't believe I didn't think about JJ being nervous and having performance anxiety.

I reach up and cup his face in my hands. "*Amore mio,* there is nothing you could do to make me want to break up with you—especially sex. I don't care how long you last because I only want to feel close to you. You're doing a pretty damn good job of making it good for me if you can't tell," I say, but he still looks unsure. "We don't have to do anything else if you're not ready, but it's never crossed my mind you might hurt me. If I don't like what you're doing, I promise I'll tell you if you promise to do the same."

JJ nods, and I lean forward, kissing him gently on the forehead. "I promise too. I want to be with you," he says, sliding his hand into my hair to pull my mouth to his again.

Shedding the last of our clothes, I reach into the drawer of my nightstand, grabbing a condom from the box. I try not to drool as I let my gaze roam over JJ, enjoying the work of art that is his body. Without a doubt, everything about JJ is proportional from his large frame to his hands—everything.

"Do you want to put it on?" JJ asks, stroking his cock, his hungry eyes never leaving mine when I rip open the packet. A hiss escapes him when I replace his hand with my own to position the latex over the tip, slowly rolling it down his thick length. Despite having wished I'd waited for JJ, I'm a little glad it's not my first time, because I think I'd be more nervous about whether he'd fit. JJ is still bigger than both of my previous partners, but since he already made me orgasm, I'm not worried.

"How do you want me?" I ask, my body practically vibrating with a need for JJ to be inside me.

"On top," he says, his voice rough, and I rest my hand on his chest to push him back into the pillows.

"You're definitely a Pillow Princess," I say, causing him to laugh until I climb over him, positioning my knees on the sides of his hips to lean down and kiss JJ again. His hands glide up the outside of my thighs before grabbing my ass to move me forward, and I curl my fingers on his chest as he slides against my opening without penetrating me.

"Please," JJ whispers against my mouth, and I reach between us to wrap my hand around the base of his cock, lining our hips up.

I bite my lip as I sink down, feeling him stretch me in a way no one else has. My body sings in pleasure, but I don't dare shut my eyes at the feeling because I refuse to miss a second of the look on JJ's handsome face. "Fuck," he mutters, his fingertips digging into my skin as he grips my hips. "You can take it, sweetheart. Make it fit," he says through clenched teeth.

"Oh my god," I say, doing my best, but it's too much on the first try, my body not accustomed to something so big. When I lower myself for a second time, his eyes flutter shut in ecstasy, a groan slipping from his addicting lips when I bottom out, holding still for a moment while my body adjusts to the feeling. The strong column of his neck exposed as he tilts his head back into the pillows. He looks straight out of a dream.

"You feel . . ." he trails off, and I agree. There are no words for how right this feels.

"Oh fuck," I swear, rising up most of the way, taking all of JJ again, my hand on his firm chest for balance. I feel so full.

My heart is racing in my chest as he thrusts up, meeting me halfway, and I gasp, our movements growing smoother as we learn how our bodies work together. JJ's hands leave my hips as I rock them, fully seated to grind my clit against his pelvis, before cupping my breasts, his thumbs pressing against my sensitive nipples again.

I arch into his touch, a gasp escaping me as he thrusts up into me. I can feel the pressure in my body start to grow again as JJ plays with my nipples, tweaking them as his movements grow less controlled. *"Yes,"* I pant, looking down between us to watch him thrust into me, the sight adding to the heightened sensations until he lifts me off him completely. I look at JJ, my jaw slightly ajar, wondering what the hell he's doing.

"I want you on your back," JJ says, rolling us to flip our positions. My mouth waters as he kneels between my legs, my body aching to be filled by him again.

"JJ, please," I whimper, shifting restlessly.

"There you go again using that word," he murmurs, hooking his hands around the back of my thighs to pull me closer to him.

I open my mouth to ask what's so wrong with the word please, but JJ pushes into me, and I moan instead. I wrap my legs around his waist, doing my best to meet his strokes as he leans down, kissing me with a desperation I didn't know existed. JJ's mouth is hot and demanding, and I respond with just as much enthusiasm.

He groans, the sound echoing through every inch of my body as I drag my nails over his wide shoulders. JJ turns his head, breaking our connection as my thighs tremble. "Fuck me, *please*," I say, and my taunt is rewarded with a rumble from JJ, his lips latching onto my neck as he thrusts roughly, the room filling with the sounds of our moans.

"Oh fuck," JJ mumbles against my throat, and I love feeling him lose control. JJ's grip tightens as his hips jerk, holding me close as his cock throbs inside me, his strong body shuddering as he comes. I smile when his body sags against mine, my heart racing in my chest. "Perfect. You're perfect," he says, out of breath, but as JJ eases off me, his hand slips between my legs, circling my clit.

I sigh in relief, turning my head to look at JJ as he watches me with a relaxed smile. I chase my impending orgasm, teetering on the edge as I keep my eyes locked on JJ's as my hand joins his, my legs falling open more.

"Come for me, sweetheart," he says, and my back arches up at the same time my breathing hitches, my orgasm sweeping over me as my toes curl.

I fall into the dream of forever as JJ leans in to press the sweetest kiss against my lips.

Only . . . I didn't know how different our forever would turn out to be.

CHAPTER THIRTY-NINE

JJ

Between finals and my football schedule, the last three weeks have flown by. I feel a little guilty for not spending my birthday and Christmas with my family, but I'd feel worse about not spending the time with Marley.

She ran herself ragged with projects, and for a few days there, I think Marley was sleeping less than I was.

I'm not even sure she knew how much nervous energy she was projecting, but I think after the meetings she went to New York for after Thanksgiving, she's wavering in her determination to take over. As a result of her hesitancy, it seems like Marley has thrown herself into overdrive to prove to herself she wants to take over.

I understand her commitment to taking over for her father as the CEO in a few years, but I also hate saying nothing as a bystander to her misery. Thankfully, I'm smart enough to understand it's not my place to say anything, no matter how much I might want to. Marley's been there for me countless times over the last few months, and while I wasn't happy about the circumstances, I was glad to finally be able to return the favor of being there for her.

I'm even trying to learn Mandarin so Marley can have someone to practice with, but I'm finding it's entirely different from learning Italian. Hasn't stopped me from making flashcards and listening through my headphones to practice during my walks to and from class, though. It's nice to have a different way to distract my brain from the cravings that are still rearing their ugly heads inside me.

Thankfully, my parents weren't upset about me coming to New York early for the holiday, since I have to be here anyway for my team's bowl game a few days after Christmas. While I was overwhelmed at first by how nice the Benson's townhome is, it definitely helped seeing her dad walk around in sweatpants and an old Beaumont Lacrosse sweatshirt, making him seem a little more down-to-earth than when he's wearing his full suits.

It's still one thing knowing how many zeroes are attached to the Benson name, and another thing to see it firsthand.

Marley is brushing a comb through her tangled, damp hair on her bed when I step out of the bathroom, pulling my clean shirt into place. There's just something about airports that makes me want to shower before doing anything else, and knowing this, Marley asked if I wanted to join her, but I didn't trust myself to keep my hands to myself.

Her cerulean eyes find mine, and a stunning smile peels across her face. "You know, it would've saved water if we showered together."

I chuckle, shaking my head at Marley. "As much as I love an excuse to touch you everywhere, I highly doubt it'd be faster," I say, sitting next to her as her comb catches on a knot. She sighs, tugging it through, and it just looks painful. "Can I help?" I ask, and Marley turns, her eyebrows raised.

"Help with what?"

"Comb your hair."

"What? Why?" she asks, and I shrug.

"I like taking care of you."

Marley's mouth parts, her breath catching. "Okay," she agrees, her voice soft.

I pluck the comb before she can change her mind, starting at the ends like I've seen Mirabelle do so many times before. I take my time to work my way up—more time than necessary —until the comb is able to glide through her caramel hair.

"You're good at this," she says, tilting her head back.

"I told you, I like taking care of you," I say, enjoying being helpful. "Thank you for inviting me to come with you."

"Thank you for coming. It means a lot, especially knowing everything going on with your family." Marley twists, turning her whole body to face mine as I set the comb down on her comforter. "I'm really happy you're here."

"Happy to be here, Mar." It's so tempting to lean forward and kiss Marley, but instead, my eyes shift to my open bag in the corner of her room. "I know it's not Christmas for a few more days, but can I give you a present early?"

It's honestly a miracle I've kept it to myself until now. Bria went with me to pick it out, and I have been so excited to give it to her.

"Right now?"

"Why not?" I ask, standing up to grab the little box from my bag.

She chuckles, her cheeks rosy as Marley smiles at me. "Because it's not Christmas yet," she says, shaking her head.

"So? I have another one you can open on Christmas, but humor me a little," I tease, my heart beating fast in my chest as I hand her the small, wrapped box. "Merry Christmas, Marley."

She takes it from me with a smile, carefully peeling back the wrapping paper instead of ripping into it like I would've to reveal the velvet box inside. Her brilliant blue eyes lift to meet mine before she opens it, emitting a soft gasp.

"JJ."

"Do you like it?" I ask, trying not to let my nerves get the better of me.

Marley covers her mouth with her hand, nodding as she looks up at me with tears in her eyes. "It's perfect."

"My family has this tradition of sorts about flowers, and it stems all the way back to my great grandparents. My great-grandfather always bought flowers for my great-grandmother —for any occasion, but most of the time without a reason— and this in turn translated to my grandfather when he met my grandmother. My dad's made sure all of us have kept their memory and the tradition alive by teaching me and my siblings how flowers are meant for the most important people in your life," I say, as Marley lifts the dainty gold flower pendant from the box. I picked gold because I noticed the rest of the jewelry she wears is gold, and I wanted it to match. "I wanted you to have a permanent flower because you're the most important person in my life."

"That's why you buy me flowers?" Marley asks, sniffling.

"Sorry I didn't tell you the reason sooner."

She launches forward, knocking me backward on the bed when she wraps her arms around me. "I love you, *je t'aime, ti amo.*"

"I love you too," I say, holding Marley close.

"So how did the end of your semester go?" Marley's father asks me as I help him set the table for dinner. He offered to teach me how to make Marley's favorite dish, a creamy Tuscan chicken, and I'm not sure I'm skilled enough to attempt it on my own, but I definitely plan to practice.

"I think I started dreaming about numbers by the time I took my final exam after all the studying I did, but I'm hoping it paid off. I'm waiting for the score of my project from my statistics class to be entered, but I have a good feeling about it," I say, glancing to Marley as she brings silverware to the table. "It helps I had a great study partner."

Yeah, Marley didn't help me study at all, but she made sure I took breaks to keep from losing my mind. If anything, I had to try to keep her on task more than anything.

Kaden sets the pan on the table, a short laugh escaping him. "Mar must really like you if she willingly looked at numbers with you. She doesn't even lik—" he stops talking when he realizes the look Marley is giving him, and I feel bad for inadvertently opening this can of worms.

Marley looks like a deer caught in the headlights as her dad looks at her, and she forces a laugh, passing out the plates. "Dude, you're being dramatic. I love numbers, so of course I would help JJ study," she says, pasting on the fakest smile I've ever seen her attempt. She's too busy glaring at her brother to notice how Hayes frowns, and I can only guess he's also aware of how bad Marley is at lying, especially when it comes to this topic.

I don't want to push her, but she's obviously miserable in all of her classes, and she avoids any topic involving Benson Pharmaceuticals like the plague. I'm not the only one noticing either.

Sephine walks into the dining room, her movements practiced and graceful. "Something smells good," she says, smiling.

"For once, it wasn't all me," Hayes says, tipping his head in my direction. "Thanks for the help," he says, and I wish I could enjoy the praise, but I'm too busy watching Marley to see if she's okay.

"Of course. I'm not sure how much help I really was, but thanks for showing me how to make it," I say, realizing I should probably respond.

Once we're all seated and dinner's been dished out, I'm only half-listening to the conversation Kaden is having with his parents about some art auction he's going to attend with Bria's mom. I can't stop watching Marley. The way she's been spinning her ring nonstop tells me Marley's overthinking something, and I'm willing to put money on it being the exchange with her brother.

I bump her leg under the table with my knee, causing her to glance in my direction. I lift my eyebrow, hoping she can understand my wordless question.

Her mouth tilts into a smile—one growing wider when my gaze dips to see the necklace I gave her on her neck. She bumps my leg back, and I smile back, loving how some of her tenseness seems to ease.

A throat clears, and both our heads turn to see her parents and Kaden staring at us. "Anything you want to share with the group?" Kaden asks, a shit-eating grin on his face.

"Actually, yeah," I say, looking at her dad. "I've been meaning to thank you for having the new lock installed on their apartment."

Hayes chuckles as Marley groans next to me. "Well, I thought it would be for the best if more shirtless men weren't able to waltz into the apartment because it was unlocked."

"I whole heartedly agree with you," I say, grateful he didn't murder me then.

"I get it, I need to be better about locking the door."

Kaden sputters, choking on his water. "I'm sorry, you don't lock your door? Are you stupid?"

"Kaden," Sephine says, giving him a look.

"Dad fixed it by getting an automatic lock, so it's not a problem anymore," Marley says, rolling her eyes.

"Mar, I feel like you're missing the point here," her brother argues, and it's nice to know I'm not the only one who feels strongly about this. "You and Bria live alone, and you know exactly why you should be locking your door."

"JJ and Asher are there ninety percent of the time, so I'm pretty sure anyone who thinks about breaking in will run for the hills after one look at the sheer size of them," Marley grumbles, and then her cheeks heat as I cough, trying not to choke on the bite of chicken in my mouth.

Kaden turns his attention to me, sizing me up, and I mean, Marley's *not* wrong. Even just one of us there would probably be enough to at least make an intruder second-guess coming through an unlocked door, let alone two of us.

"Can you crush someone's head between your thighs?" he asks, and this time, I do choke.

Hayes swears under his breath, low enough I can't hear. Marley drops her fork on her plate to cover her face with her hands, and I'm really not sure what the right way to react is when Sephine starts laughing.

I clear my throat, taking a sip of my water to help, but my voice is still hoarse when I speak. "I can't say I've ever tried, or I'd let an intruder stick their head between my legs?"

Marley erupts into a fit of giggles, joining her mom and she shakes her head. "I'm sorry, it's not funny," she says, peeking at me before more laughter spills from her.

Honestly, it is a little funny to picture, but it's a good thing Marley doesn't have thighs the size of mine, or I'd be a goner from all the time I like to spend between them.

Oh shit, definitely not the right thoughts to be having at the table with her family.

"I'm going to pretend I didn't hear any of this," Hayes says, taking a bite of his chicken. "I think I miss how quiet it is when they're gone," he muses, and Sephine rolls her eyes.

"And I think you're a liar."

A leg nudges mine, and I glance in Marley's direction,

finding her blue eyes crinkled with happiness at the corners, and I can't help but smile.

Regardless of what lies ahead for us, I'll never stop trying to be the man she thinks I am.

CHAPTER FORTY

Marley

"So?" JJ asks, bumping his hip against mine.

I look up at him, my cheeks cold from the freezing chill in the air. "So what?" I ask, waiting for further clarification.

He motions around us, the blankets of snow covering the ground as we walk through Central Park, a soft glow cast on his face from the twinkling lights strung up. This is one of my favorite times of year, and while I might have a love-hate relationship with New York, I love how magical the city becomes for the holidays. "Has this date been everything you hoped it would be? You got the whole restaurant to sing happy birthday to me, we have the hot chocolate, the Christmas lights, the snow, the perfect boyfriend. Pretty sure we've checked everything on your list for tonight."

He's not wrong—JJ *is* the perfect boyfriend.

"Everything and more," I say, smiling up at him. He seems good. JJ's been going to meetings consistently, and he's holding himself differently, almost like he's starting to believe in himself again.

"I'm glad. You deserve the world, but I'd give you the entire universe if I could. Thank you for giving me the best birthday," JJ says, wrapping an arm around my shoulders, leaning to press a kiss to the top of my head as I melt into him.

He makes it so easy to love him.

"I know I haven't been the most fun to be around the last few weeks, but I really appreciate how patient you've been with me," I say, adjusting my grip on the cup of hot chocolate in my hands, grateful for my gloves.

"If there's one word to describe me, it'd be patient," he jokes, while we walk through the light layer of snow collecting on the sidewalk.

I chuckle because he's not wrong. I've never met someone like JJ before, and I probably never will again. "Fair point. I guess what I'm trying to say is it means a lot. I know you've got a lot going on, and I just . . . I love you. Thank you for making me feel seen."

"Sweetheart, you're the first thing I look for when I step into a room. I always see you," JJ says, his smooth voice deepening, and I wrap my arm around his lower back in return. "I wasn't always this person everyone had to babysit to make sure I wouldn't break. I used to be reliable, and not someone who has to fight the urge to numb everything wit—" he falters, and I refuse to let go of JJ while he clears his throat. "With pills. I don't like being like this, but I'm trying to be better."

"You are reliable, JJ. Your addiction and the pills don't define you as a person, and you've been working so hard to stay clean. I'm so proud of you, *amore mio*," I say, looking up at him. I wish I could take away all of JJ's struggles and pain because I can't think of anyone less deserving to carry the weight of the world on their shoulders than the man in front of me.

There are a few snowflakes collecting in his dark lashes, and his eyes are trained on me, trusting me with his bruised heart.

I wonder if Bailey has ever regretted leaving, because

speaking from experience, JJ's not an easy person to walk away from, let alone his entire family. I can't help but think there's more to it than any of the theories they suspect.

"You have a way of making me feel seen too," JJ murmurs, and my gaze drops to his soft lips before drifting back up to his emerald gaze.

His hand lifts to brush his thumb over my cheek, the cashmere material tickling my skin. "Do you ever think about how crazy it is we found each other again, and now we're here celebrating your birthday?" I ask, and his smile is a gift I once only dreamed of.

"I never had a doubt about finding you, Marley. You're my once in a lifetime too," he says, and the fact he remembers the lyrics from the song I sang to him means more to me than anything else. I feel like my heart might explode from the depth of my feelings for him.

To stop my tears of happiness from falling, I stick my tongue out to catch a snowflake, elated when JJ joins me.

I'm convinced it can't get better than this.

My body is on fire from the way JJ has me pressed against the wall of the elevator on our way up to the penthouse. The sheer desperation of this kiss makes my body crave the feeling of JJ's pressed on top of me.

His lips clash passionately against mine, both of us fighting to lose ourselves in this moment and in each other. We're both wearing too many layers, and I shift to move closer to him, but the rail is digging into my back. I groan, pulling away to laugh softly, and JJ gives me a questioning look.

"I'm sorry, I promise it's not you I'm laughing at," I say, untangling my hands from where they'd ventured into his dark hair.

JJ offers me his slanted smile I love so much. "No, it's definitely me and it's okay. I know I'm funny looking, and you're the pretty one in this relationship."

I lean up, kissing his lips once more. "No. The bar is digging into my back," I explain as the elevator chimes before the doors open. JJ steps back to drag a hand through his already mussed hair, pausing to frown at the bar as if it will make it disappear.

I kick my boots off by the door, shedding my coat, gloves, and scarf as JJ does the same before following me further into the penthouse.

"Should I put a movie on?" I ask, feeling his presence right behind me. I pause in the living room, sucking in a breath when he pulls my hair over one shoulder to press his lips to the side of my throat.

"Do you really want to watch a movie?" he asks, and the hoarseness in JJ's voice that wasn't there before causes shivers to crawl up my spine.

"No," I admit, unashamed of how badly I want JJ. He's already seen every part of me—there's no reason to pretend I don't. My gaze shifts to see the hot tub sitting on the patio overlooking the city. "We could take a dip in the hot tub?"

"I don't want anyone else to see what's mine, and I'd rather show you how well I pay attention to see how many orgasms I can bring you too," he says, kissing my throat again. My breath catches, and his deep chuckle against my throat is distracting.

"But it's your birthday," I protest, but it's a fight to keep my eyes from rolling to the back of my head from the gentleness of his touch.

"I promise you, getting to touch you is a gift, and I'd like to see if I can get you to crush my head between your thighs," he teases, causing an abrupt laugh to slip from me.

"I can't believe Kaden asked you that," I say, but when JJ turns me to press his lips against mine, I forget all about it.

We leave a trail of clothes on our way to my bedroom, and I'm confident there isn't a part of my body he hasn't touched. Shedding the last of my clothes, I look up at JJ, only to find him already staring at me.

"See something you like?" I tease, and his mouth tilts into a smile.

"I see everything I love." JJ drags a hand through his hair, causing his dark waves to fall onto his forehead. *He's beautiful.* My hands twitch at my sides, eager to touch him as I watch him stroke his hard cock, and I sit on the bed, watching as his abdomen flexes and a bead of pre-cum forms on his tip. I slip my hand between my legs, biting my lip to hide my smile when his throat bobs as I touch myself.

"Sweetheart, do you have any idea how pretty you look right now?" he asks.

"Funny, I was thinking the same about you," I say, dipping my finger in me before bringing it up to my nipple, coating the sensitive skin with my arousal, and JJ's patience snaps. He's quick to close the gap between us, pressing a bruising kiss to my lips not nearly long enough before he moves to close his mouth over my nipple, sucking eagerly.

"I like the way you think," JJ says, and I moan when his fingers drag over my aching core, but they never push into me, instead tracing a matching circle around my other nipple. I move to touch him when in one smooth movement, JJ catches my wrists, and holds them above my head against the pillows.

"You're not going to let me touch you?" I ask, raising my eyebrows at him.

"It's my birthday, my rules, sweetheart. If you can't keep your hands to yourself, I'll make you," he says, before swirling his tongue around the path his fingers took. I gasp, arching into his mouth, and he holds my hands in place, but his grip is loose enough that I could definitely pull them free if I wanted to. Except, I don't because as much as I like telling JJ what to do, it's sexy seeing this other side of him.

I twist underneath his firm body as he continues painting my skin with my arousal before lapping it up with his tongue. "More," I beg, cracking when once again, he doesn't put an end to my misery. I know I'm not the only one desperate for more.

"Keep your hands up there," he instructs, and I nod, because I'll do anything JJ wants right now if it means he'll tip me over the edge instead of continuing to let me teeter on it. He gives me a wicked smile before his mouth trails down my body, and he sucks my clit into his sinful mouth.

I cry out, but as my eyes flutter shut from the intense amount of pleasure, I remember to keep my hands above my head. He finally pushes two fingers into me, but it's when he curls them inside me, I see stars as the pressure builds in me. "Fuck yes," I moan, my head twisting as I fight the urge to grab JJ's hair as he circles my clit with his tongue.

"Can you take another?" JJ asks, and my hips arch, seeking more. "Gotta make sure your pretty pussy is ready for me to fuck you."

Oh my god, I love hearing JJ unfiltered. I feel myself stretch as he adds a third finger, curling them at the same time he applies pressure to my clit, and my body implodes from the inside out. My breathing is heavy, but I smile when JJ kisses my lips. "You did so good."

"Can I touch you?" I ask, and he shakes his head.

"Not yet," JJ says, stroking himself, the swollen head glistening from his pre-cum, and I ball my hands into fists. "See how hard you make me?"

"JJ, please. I need you inside me."

He bites his lip, gripping himself. "Oh fuck, Mar," he chokes out, his control starting to wane. JJ tears open a condom, rolling it on before looking up at me, his eyes hazy with lust. "You okay?"

"Fuck me, please," I say, and he laughs, shaking his head.

"What have I told you about the word please?"

I grin, knowing full well how he feels about it. "What are you going to do about it?"

"Roll over, and get your ass up, face down, sweetheart. I'm going to fuck the word out of you."

Oh hell yes. I roll onto my knees holding my ass in the air as JJ's hands find the curves of my hips, and my head drops as he starts to push in, the full feeling threatening to overwhelm my senses, but then JJ thrusts deeply, a low moan slipping from him. I look over my shoulder to see his eyes shut in ecstasy as he shifts his hips back, pushing into me again, this time harder than before, picking up the pace with his next, and I grab the comforter, pushing back to meet him halfway.

"You feel so good. A perfect fit for me."

As much as I love seeing the look on his face when we're fucking, there is something so primal about JJ taking me from behind.

"Don't stop," I say, breathless as I rock back in time with JJ, focusing on how good it feels. I moan as he grabs my ass, and JJ chuckles, his fingers kneading the muscle.

"You like that?" he asks, and I nod. Without missing a beat, JJ reaches between my legs to rub my clit, catching me by surprise and I fall forward onto my elbows, a continuous moan rolling off my tongue as he quite literally fucks the word out of me. "There you go, baby. I want to hear you," he says, grunting as his strokes become erratic, and I'd give anything for a mirror right now to watch. I can only imagine how powerful JJ looks, taking me from behind.

"Right there," I gasp, hovering on the brink.

"You're going to make me come," he says, driving forward as he fingers my clit, causing sensation overload when another orgasm tears through my body. JJ doesn't stop, and every feeling is heightened as I clench the sheets, holding on for dear life. He thrusts one last time, his cock twitching deep inside of me as he comes with a groan.

I slump into the sheets, my entire body spent from how long JJ edged my first orgasm and the intensity of my second. "You're going to have to help me to the bathroom," I say, lifting my head to look at JJ who looks about as tired as I do as he pants.

"Happy to," he says, giving me the sweetest smile. He sits up, disappearing into the bathroom to dispose of the condom, and returning quickly. Instead of helping me up, JJ lifts me into his arms and carries me to the bathroom to set me on the toilet.

JJ disappears again, and I hear the sound of the tub turning on instead of the shower like I expected. He's pouring a ridiculous amount of soap into the large tub when I find him, and I have a feeling this is the first time JJ's ever tried to make a bubble bath.

I hover, leaning against the wall for a minute to watch before he notices me. "Sorry, I saw it, and I thought it would be more relaxing than a shower," JJ says, his cheeks flushing as he rubs the back of his neck.

"Don't apologize," I say, walking closer to him. "It's sweet. Thank you."

JJ cups my face, leaning down to kiss me. "Merry Christmas, Marley."

"Happy birthday, JJ."

CHAPTER FORTY-ONE

JJ

"Dude, as much as it sucks we didn't win the championship, I'm glad your brother did. I think it softens the blow Hunter didn't win the Heisman," Asher says, sprawled out on the girls' couch as he flips through the movies on a streaming service.

I roll my eyes, not wanting to burst Asher's bubble. Hunter was relieved he didn't win the award. He said that if he won as a sophomore, it would mean taking it away from a senior who had worked their entire college career for the award when he still had two more years to grow as a player. If anything, it makes me respect Hunt even more.

There's no doubting how much he cares about the game as a whole, because I can't think of many players who would be relieved that someone else won the biggest award in college football.

"We didn't even make it to playoffs," I remind him, and he scoffs.

"Yeah, that's what I said."

I look up from my homework to raise my eyebrows at him. "Except it's not."

"Well, it's what I meant," he says, and his eyes widen. "Holy shit, your professors actually assigned you homework the first week back?"

"It seems like the norm unless you're a business major," I say, poking fun at his degree, knowing damn well how smart he is.

"See, this is why jocks are the inferior species," Bria says to Marley as they walk back in.

"Are you using my blanket?" Marley asks, eyeing the colorful blanket Asher's using.

"Nope, I found it on the couch, and definitely not in your room. I think you mean to say athletes are the superior species," Asher corrects as Marley takes a seat next to me.

"He totally stole it from my room, and I cannot listen to Bria explain this again." She groans, taking a peek at my screen. "Ew, on second thought, I think I'd rather hear about the distinction between an athlete and a jock again."

I chuckle, shaking my head as I rest my arm on the top of the loveseat behind her. "You mean you don't like learning about probability theory?"

"Sorry, I really don't." Marley makes a face at the same time my phone rings, and I reach for it blindly, slow to pull my gaze away from my girl.

Everything tilts when I see the blocked caller ID, and I freeze, staring at the screen for a moment before standing up. "I have to get this," I mumble, taking long strides to step through the front door. *Is it really him?*

"Hello?" I say after shutting the front door behind me. It's been drizzling all day, a chill looming in the air. "Bailey?"

"Hi," he says, his voice quiet, and I feel all the air in my lungs disappear.

It's the first time we've spoken since our argument about him living on the streets. Selfishly, I hate he's calling right now when I'm finally okay and settling into a new normal. I hate how Bailey only calls me. *I hate all of this.*

"I didn't know if I'd hear from you again." At least I'm being honest.

"You're not going to."

The words send an icy chill through my veins, and the world around me slows to a stop. "What are you talking about?" I ask, trying not to vomit as my stomach churns

"This isn't fair to you for me to keep calling. I just wanted to say goodbye so I could tell you I love you. I hung up last time before saying it, and I'm sorry," Bailey says, sniffling as warning bells begin going off in my head.

"B, no, it's really okay you call. This isn't goodbye because I'm always going to be here for you."

He's slow to respond, and my anxiety is climbing to new heights I didn't realize it was capable of before. "You shouldn't be okay with this, and you certainly shouldn't be there for me. I've done nothing to deserve it after I ruined everything. Tell our parents . . ." Bailey trails off, and my heart leaps into my throat. *What's changed? Why is everything so different now?* "Please tell them I love them, and it wasn't their fault. I was wrong, and I didn't want to admit it."

"Bailey, don't you dare fucking end this call. Where are you? I'll come get you, just please, come home, it's okay," I plead, tears burning in my eyes while the edges of my vision blur as pure panic begins to set in.

"It's not. Too much has happened, but thanks for being a great brother. I love you, JJ," he says, and the emotion in his voice wraps around my neck like a noose.

"Please—" I'm cut off by the phone beeping and I don't know what to think.

I drag my hands through my hair, feeling like my heart has just been ripped straight out of my chest.

I take it back. I don't hate he calls me. I don't hate any of this.

How can I fix this?

Pills, they can fix this. I just have t—no. A meeting. I need to go to a meeting.

I pat my pants, fumbling for my keys, but they're hanging inside on a hook next to the door. The door opens, and I swivel, watching as the relaxed smile on Asher's face fades into an expression of seriousness as he steps out, shutting it behind him. My hand grabs at my chest, clutching my sweatshirt as I gasp for air. "JJ, holy shit."

"I need my k-keys," I struggle to say, choking because why did he have to say goodbye?

"What?" he asks, taking a step toward me as a fresh wave of agony rips through me. "Who just called you?"

You're not going to.

There won't be more calls. I close my eyes tight, praying this is a bad dream I can wake up from. *But Bailey's still gone, and I'm still suffocating.*

I cough, trying to force my body to regulate itself, taking in enough air to help some of the spots dancing across my vision fade away. "Keys—need a meeting," I choke out, and he opens the door again, snagging them quickly.

"You're not driving like this. I'll sit in the car, or do whatever else it is you need me to do, but I'm not letting you go out there in this condition by yourself," he says, staring at me. "I told you, I'm here."

"Thank you," I whisper, my head spinning as I grab the railing to take the stairs, Asher directly behind me. My phone dings with a text from Marley, asking if we're coming back inside, but I don't know how to answer. I know I don't want to break her heart again by asking her to watch me fall apart.

If I can get to a meeting, I can get my head on straight, and face everythin—

"JJ, you gotta breathe," Asher says, unlocking my Jeep. I climb into the passenger seat, tears falling down my cheeks.

"He's gone," I say, buckling my seatbelt, wishing more than anything I didn't have to feel any of this pain.

"Who?" he asks, pulling out of the lot onto a road and turning in the direction of the town where I attend meetings.

"He's not coming back," I whisper, the horror of this reality sinking in. "I couldn't convince him to come back, and he's gone. *Bailey's fucking gone.* What am I going to do, Ash?"

Asher looks at me, his features softened by sympathy. "You live."

Instead, I see past his shoulder, catching a glimpse of the dark car a second before it slams into the driver's side of my Jeep, causing us to roll not once, not twice, but three times. It makes it impossible for me to ever forget the sound of breaking glass and crunching metal, and the sight of my best friend going through the windshield before something hits my face and all I see is white.

CHAPTER FORTY-TWO

Marley

"How much longer do you think they're going to be?" Bria asks, tugging on a Beaumont football sweatshirt I'd guess is Asher's. I spin my thumb ring, my foot tapping anxiously as I stare at the door, willing JJ and Asher to walk through it any moment. Outside, I hear sirens getting louder as they drive by. It casts an eerie shadow, contributing to the rare dreary day we're having.

"I don't know," I say, but I can't shake the sinking feeling something isn't right. I was going to check on JJ when Asher said he'd do it, but it was the way he snagged JJ's keys a minute later without saying a thing. I looked through the blinds to watch them as they left before calling JJ, but he didn't answer.

"You're making me nervous, Mar. I'm just going to call Ash and ask when they'll be back."

I only caught a glimpse of JJ's phone before he stood up, and it had to have been Bailey. It's the only explanation. "Hey babe, just calling to see when you'll be back? Hope every-thing's okay," she says, hanging up after leaving the message.

"Babe?" I ask, raising my eyebrow as I try to lighten the mood.

She rolls her eyes, but her cheeks flush with a crimson hue. "Shut up, it's not a big deal."

"Are you finally ready to admit you like him yet?" I mean, it's not a secret because he's been staying here a lot since Halloween, but the hard part has been getting Bria to admit she has feelings for him.

The corners of Bria's mouth pull up into a smile not even she can fight. "Fine. Yes, I like him a lot." *Oh man, I can't wait to tell JJ about this. He's going to be so mad he missed it.* Bria crosses her arms over her chest, swimming in the sweatshirt as she sighs. "Seriously, where are they?"

I don't know," I repeat, taking a glance at JJ's assignments and laptop on the coffee table, before my gaze returns to the door, hoping for a miracle. If the call he received was from Bailey, I'm afraid to think of what might happen. He's still early into his sobriety, and I think if anything were to make him relapse, it would be a call from his brother.

Every call seems to trigger something inside of JJ, sending him spiraling until he's able to pull himself out of the trenches, but I'm not sure how much longer he can handle this.

Inhaling deeply, I try to remind myself Asher's with him. *Everything will be fine.*

"What if you try JJ again?" she asks, standing up to pace, and it's too much for me when I'm already barely keeping it together.

"Bria, I don't know where they are, they'll be back when they're back," I say, my grip on my nerves cracking, but when she bristles, I feel worse. Dragging my hands over my face, I press JJ's number, my hand shaking as I hold it up to my ear. Each ring feels as if it's taking an eternity, and finally, I get his voicemail. "No answer," I mumble, trying not to let my mind run rampant with all the ways this can end in disaster.

"They're going to be fine," Bria says, taking a seat once more.

"Of course they are," I say, wishing I believed the words coming out of my mouth.

The phone call I receive an hour later instead fractures our reality beyond repair, proving ignorance is, in fact, bliss.

JJ is sitting catatonic in the hospital bed when I get there as Bria distracts the nurses at the desk, making it possible for me to slip past them. He has a large bandage covering his temple and part of his forehead, but otherwise looks okay to my relief. Because of how many calls I made to his cell, someone finally called me back to let me know JJ had been in an accident. "JJ?" I ask, hesitating in the doorway. I didn't see Asher's name on any of the nearby rooms, but I refuse to let myself consider what it could mean.

His head shifts in my direction, but it's the glazed expression on his face as I see the IV bag connected to him. JJ's eyes are rimmed in red, but he closes them, turning away. I take it as a good sign he doesn't tell me to leave, so I step forward, doing my best to tread lightly before attempting to take his hand.

"What happened?" I ask, swallowing the lump rising in my throat, and the question seems to break the dam holding him together.

"I'm sorry. I'm so fucking sorry. It's all my fault."

What's his fault? JJ snatches his hand away from me, and a hundred questions run through my mind. "Hey, it's okay. Nothing is your fault, everything's going to be fine," I try to reassure him, but his heart rate spikes on the monitor as JJ grows more upset, his emerald eyes flashing like a wild animal trapped in a corner.

"You don't understand, none of this would have happened if I could have just stopped. I wouldn't be like this, and I tried so hard—*so fucking hard, Marley, but it doesn't matter,*" he says, his walls demolished as tears flow freely down his cheeks.

"JJ, what happened?" I ask, my heart sputtering in my chest. I don't know what I expected to see, but it wasn't this.

His monitor is beeping erratically, alarms going off and a nurse and doctor enter the room, brushing past me as JJ grows more upset. *"No more, please. Marley, please,"* he begs, and the sheer brokenness of his voice wrecks me as I cover my mouth to keep any sound from coming out. "It's my fault he's dead. It's all my fault," he repeats, and they inject something in his IV, but I'm too focused on his words to hear the medication.

It's my fault he's dead.

"Miss, you can't be in here," one of them says, and I stare at JJ struggling against his inner demons, taking a step back as my brain struggles to process everything.

Is he talking about Asher?

"Miss," the nurse says in a clipped tone, and I take a few steps backward, sinking against the wall until I hit the ground.

When the door opens a few minutes later, the room inside is quiet, and her kind face softens while her shoulders sink. "How did you get back here?" she asks, and I wipe my cheeks.

"My best friend is really good at creating diversions," I admit, rising into a standing position as my legs shake under me. "What's wrong with him?"

"Are you family?"

I sigh, shaking my head. "No, but his family is in North Carolina. I was waiting until I knew what to tell them before calling, but I'm JJ's girlfriend. We go to Beaumont University."

She shakes her head. "I'm sorry, I can't tell you anything, but the doctor should be out in just a moment if you'll wait here," she says, her tone apologetic as she steps back into the room, returning a moment later with the doctor.

"I'm sorry, I'm not at liberty to discuss his current condition," she says after the nurse excuses herself, stepping into another room to check on a different patient.

"Please. I need to know what's going on before I call his family. I'm sorry for sneaking back here, but someone called me from his phone to let me know he had been in an accident and was being admitted," I say, unashamed when more tears roll down my cheeks.

"It's not protocol," she begins, and I feel all the fight drain out of me. "He doesn't have any major injuries from the accident, but we are monitoring him to make sure he remains stable. He has a deep laceration on his forehead, but I'm more concerned with his mental state. We administered a sedative to calm his nervous system, but it's not a long-term solution. I can't tell you anything more without direct consent from his family, but you should call them. He's going to need a support system."

A sedative . . . *Oh my god.* That's what JJ meant by no more. He was begging them not to give him drugs, and I did nothing to stop it, too focused on his state to realize what he wanted.

Fresh tears spring to my eyes, and I wipe them away. "He's an addict. JJ's two month—he was two months clean," I whisper, feeling my stomach roll.

Her sharp inhale is her only reaction. "I'll make a note in his chart," she says, moving to turn, and I can't go back in his room yet, but I also can't see Bria without knowing.

"And my friend? Asher Locke? He would have come in with JJ."

This time, her shoulders fall. "I'm sorry for your loss. We were told both drivers were found deceased at the scene, and the only survivor was a passenger."

I trip over my own feet, retreating as the doctor confirms what I don't want to believe.

He can't just be gone? A few hours ago, he was stealing the fuzzy blanket out of my room, claiming it was softer than any of Bria's, and now he's just . . . dead? It doesn't make any sense.

What am I going to tell Bria? Does Charlie know?

My friend is dead, and my boyfriend is blaming himself. *I think I'm going to be sick.*

I slam the door of the bathroom open, barely dropping to my knees in time to dry heave into the toilet as silent sobs shake my entire body. I give myself longer than I should to fall apart before attempting to pull myself together, pulling my phone out of my pocket, calling the person I think will understand the most how I feel right now.

"Marley? Is everything okay? It's midnight," he says after picking up, and a shaky breath escapes me.

"No, Dad. Everything's not okay. I need you guys," I admit, wanting nothing more than for all of this to be a nightmare I'll wake up from in the morning.

"We'll be there in a few hours," he says without my needing to say anything else. "What happened?"

My grief threatens to swallow me alive, and I bite my lip hard to keep from bursting into tears again. "There was an accident. My friend died, and I failed JJ in the worst way by not stopping the doctors when they were sedating him," I whisper, knowing exactly how awful it sounds. "He's an addict, but he's been doing so damn well, Dad. He had two months, and I let him down."

I hold my breath, expecting him to be upset with me for not saying anything sooner. "Oh, Marley," he says, and the unexpected gentleness is so understanding, it makes me want to crumble again. "I'm so sorry."

"I-I need to call JJ's family, and Bria is out there waiting for me, but how do I tell B her boyfriend's dead? How am I supposed to do any of this?"

I don't know anything at all about the circumstances surrounding the accident, and it's not fair.

"One step at a time," Dad says, and I inhale a ragged breath.

"You'll be here soon?" I ask, trying to hold onto that bit of comfort.

"As soon as I can be. I love you."

I'm exhausted, and everything else is going to be so much harder. "I love you too."

One step at a time. I can do this.

The only number for JJ's family I have is his sister's, and I don't want to look for his phone. Mirabelle doesn't answer the first time I call, but I force my shaking hand to press her number a second time, dreading the moment she answers.

"Do you know what time it is?"

"I know."

"I like you, Marley, but my brother has made it crystal clear he doesn't want to talk to me, so forgive me for hanging up. I don't feel like dealing with his shit right now."

"I'm at the hospital," I blurt out before she can hang up on me. "Please don't hang up because . . ." My voice falters. "I don't know what I'm doing, Mirabelle."

"What are you doing at the hospital?" she asks, any trace of bitterness leaving her voice, but I'm relieved Mira didn't hang up. "Is JJ okay?"

"There was an accident, and I don't know what happened. I'm not family so the doctors won't tell me much, but I saw him, and he's okay physically, but he's going to need you guys," I explain, trying to keep from dropping the addict bomb over the phone.

Mirabelle gasps. "What? Were you with him?"

"No. Asher was."

"Is he okay?"

I swallow my emotions down, trying to become used to this new reality my friend isn't a part of. "Asher's dead."

I hear Mirabelle asking me more questions, but they're not processing in my brain. *I can't find the words to answer them. I tried, but I can't do this.* I can't compartmentalize my emotions —not for this.

How did we get here? What wrong steps did we take to lead us to this very moment?

I mumble a short goodbye to Mirabelle before daring to go back to the waiting room. Bria is pacing back and forth, probably going out of her mind, and I'm jealous. Her world hasn't shifted on its axis yet, and I'd give anything to not be the one to deliver the news to her.

It's better coming from me, though. One step at a time.

It's not too late to run and hide in JJ's room.

Her striking eyes meet mine, widening as Bria rushes toward me. "Well? What did you find out? Are they okay? The nurse refused to tell me anything," she says, rolling her eyes.

I open my mouth, but I don't know how to say it. It feels unreal.

"Mar, you're making me nervous. Just spit it out," she says, scanning over my face, and I feel my lower lip tremble.

I thought I had already cried all my tears, but still, more pool in my eyes.

"Is it JJ?" Bria asks, her face growing pale, and I sink my teeth into my lower lip, shaking my head. "Where's Asher?"

I try swallowing the lump in my throat as my heart cracks. "He's go—" My throat seizes, refusing to let the words be spoken a third time.

"You're wrong," she says, stepping back. "He's here. Ash has to be here," Bria says, darting around me faster than I or anyone else can stop her, toward patient rooms. I follow after her, watching helplessly as she steps into the doorway of each room, searching for him, but she turns in a circle, her shoulders shaking. I can feel the anguish rolling off her in waves, and I wrap my arms around her as Bria buries her head in my neck. "Where is he? He's supposed to be here," she sobs, and I hold her tight as she breaks faster than I can pick up the pieces to glue them back together.

"I'm so sorry," I whisper, seeing over her shoulder JJ lying in his hospital bed. All of this is beyond overwhelming, but I'm not leaving him. It would completely destroy me when so much has already been ruined.

"I needed more time," she sobs, and this time, the pieces of our broken hearts scatter everywhere.

CHAPTER FORTY-THREE

JJ

My mouth is really dry. *I need water.* My eyes are super heavy. Why are they so hard to open right now? *Voices. Beeping.*

All of it comes crashing back. The call with Bailey, leaving with Asher, the car hitting us, Asher—*no*. It's not real. It can't be.

I force my eyes open, my entire body sore and protesting against any movement. *Fuck, my head hurts.* The first thing I see in the dimmed lighting is Marley standing in the corner, talking with her parents. I turn my head to see my parents asleep in the chairs next to my bed. Dad's moved the chair to sit as close to Mom's as possible as she rests her head next to my hand on the mattress.

Mom shifts, lifting her head after wiping her eyes. "JJ?"

"Water," I croak out and she nods, understanding. Dad stirs when she offers me a water bottle from her bag, and the IV in the back of my hand pulls as I reach for it. "Thanks."

And by the way her eyes scan over me, I know she knows.

Marley moves closer, and when her lower lip trembles as she tries to smile at me, I wonder if she's finally hit her breaking point with me. "Asher?" I ask, but his name is a hoarse whisper, and my throat feels raw. *He could have made it, right?*

She opens her mouth to speak, but nothing comes out. Marley shakes her head, tears welling in her beautiful eyes, and a wave of anguish crashes over me, dragging me down. This is a nightmare I'm not going to wake up from. It's my fault too because he should never have been in the car with me.

"No."

My hand is gripped tightly by my mom's, her cheeks damp. "I'm so sorry, JJ. He wasn't wearing his seatbelt, and . . ." she trails off, dipping her head.

"He went through the windshield," I say, finishing her sentence. Marley sits on the edge of the bed, the bed dipping underneath her weight as she rests her hand on top of the blanket. "It's my fault. If he hadn't gone with me, he'd still be here."

"It's not your fault. Asher went with you because he loves you," Marley says, her voice soft.

"Loved," I correct, my voice cracking at the same time my soul does. "I didn't take anything. He was driving me to a meeting." I force the words out of my mouth, and she crumples like a wilted flower.

"I know, baby. I know you didn't," she says, before looking away. "But the doctors had to sedate you, and they gave you painkillers when you arrived to help your body cope with the stress of the accident."

"I-I relapsed?" I wish I didn't hear Dad's sharp inhale as I confirm what Marley told them.

"They're called slips," Marley's mom adds from the corner, catching me by surprise because I'd forgotten her parents were here. Her light eyes meet mine, and it's the look of understanding on her face making me wish I'd confided in her. "You didn't relapse because you didn't knowingly seek out drugs."

"I'm sorry," Marley says, and my brain struggles to grasp the difference right now, my head throbbing. I lift my hand to rub my temple, finding a large bandage covering my forehead.

"Wha—" I ask, and Dad clears his throat, the lines of his face etched with sorrow.

"You needed stitches for a cut on your forehead," he explains, and I nod, struggling to meet his eyes. "I'm sorry, JJ. I'm sorry I didn't see what you tried to tell me."

"*Bailey*—" I struggle to breathe in and the monitor spikes, catching everyone's attention. "He called just before . . ." I shake my head, trying to collect my thoughts without panicking. "Bailey called to say goodbye. He sai—"

"It can wait until later," Dad interrupts, his eyes glimmering. "Whatever he said, it can wait. You're important too."

"I'm so sorry, JJ. When you're ready to tell us everything, we're here to listen," Mom adds, and I'm ashamed I didn't listen to Asher sooner. He was right all along.

"I'm an addict," I admit, and Mom's grip on my hand tightens as she squeezes.

"We know, but we're going to get you help. You're going to get better, though," she says, smiling at me as I wish I'd told them the truth a long time ago.

Maybe everything would have turned out differently, but I'm going to have to find a way to live with the choices I've made.

It was too much having everyone stare at me with nowhere to go, so I'm hiding in the bathroom, trying to give myself a moment from the apologies and guilt. I hardly recognize myself in the mirror, the large bandage covering half my forehead and temple. *I just need a moment to attempt to breathe.* It feels selfish after how many people dropped everything to be here. Mirabelle and Henry were at the airport picking up Hunter earlier, and I know there's a lot of conversations that need to happen, but I was suffocating under the weight of all their stares.

Thankfully, the room is mostly empty when I finally open the door, Marley's mom the lone figure remaining in the room. "I hope it's okay I asked everyone to step out for a minute."

"Thanks," I say, unsure of what else to say. I climb back into the bed, rolling the portable IV with me, and she takes one of the chairs. "I'm surprised my parents listened to you."

"I can be convincing when I want to be." Sephine chuckles, leaning back in the seat. "It'll get easier."

"I hope so," I murmur, my chest aching from where the seatbelt restrained me.

"It will. They're scared now, but they'll adjust. It takes time."

I twist the blanket in my hands, needing something to do. "I'm not sure I deserve for it to get easier. It's all my fault. If I had been able to stop taking the pills in the first place, none of this would have happened."

"JJ, you made mistakes. It happens, but they're a part of life. You have to keep moving forward by working the program and focusing on staying clean. You're not the first addict to feel like this, but from everything Marley's told me, you've worked really hard to get clean, so unless you were driving the car that hit yours, I'm not sure how this is your fault."

I want to believe her, except I don't.

"I have been lying to everyone for so long, I don't know how I'm supposed to get better and move on," I say, wondering what the point of all this is supposed to be. "I should have been the one who died. Me—not Asher. He had his whole life ahead of him, but because he tried to help me, he doesn't." I sniffle, wiping my nose with the back of my hand as Sephine's face softens.

"I killed my boyfriend when I was sixteen because I ignored his phone call when I was higher than a kite, and he overdosed," Sephine says, her gaze unwavering. "I know exactly how you're feeling right now because I've been there. I had the same thoughts. Why him? I'm an addict too, and it took a long time for me to learn to live with the guilt because I couldn't forgive myself.

"You're not wrong. Asher did have his whole life ahead of him, and I'm so sorry he's gone, but you also have your whole life ahead of you. Accept the things you can't control, and make something good come out of this instead of letting this become an excuse to spiral until it consumes you. I'm not saying it's going to be easy, but you get to write the next page of your book, not your addiction."

My jaw drops because I didn't know any of this. I knew she was an addict, but out of everyone in my life, I didn't expect Marley's mom to be the one I could relate to the most right now. "Did you let it consume you?"

"I did," Sephine says, looking down at her clasped hands in her lap. "I didn't want to accept the help everyone was offering. I thought I deserved to be in pain, but it wasn't until I learned to forgive myself for the things I couldn't change that I truly started to move on. Kiddo, you have so many people who want to be here for you, my daughter included. Let them help you so everyone can begin to heal."

"I hate being like this," I admit, and her smile is sad.

"I know, but if you don't believe anything else I've said, please believe none of this was your fault. You're a kid with the weight of the world on your shoulders, and your doctors failed you. They should never have refilled your prescriptions as many times as they did," Sephine says, and I want to believe her, but it feels like an excuse to blame others for my decisions.

"I could have chosen to stop taking them."

"You're choosing now. Choose every day *not* to take them. It's not going to be easy, but for your sake, I hope you try. You have a bright future ahead of you and I want to see you succeed."

"It doesn't really seem all that bright right now," I choke out, tears burning in my eyes. This is pathetic. I'm pathetic.

Almost as if she can hear the thoughts running in my head, Sephine stands to pull me into a hug, and I sink into her embrace as she rubs my back. "I know it doesn't, but it all will get better. You will get better. I can just tell."

"There's a box under my bed with letters," I say, my entire body trembling. "They're for Marley. She's the best thing to ever happen to me."

"I'll make sure she gets them," she promises. "She's the best thing to ever happen to me too."

CHAPTER FORTY-FOUR

Marley

THERE'S BEEN A LOT OF DEBATE ABOUT WHAT TO DO with JJ. His parents want him to take a leave from school and go home with them. My mom is firm on her stance that JJ would benefit from a short-term stay at an inpatient rehab center, but the only thing they can agree on is JJ needs to speak to someone.

I disagree with both of them because I think part of the reason he started taking the pills was to find a way to control the situations in his life he couldn't control. Regardless of how well their intentions are, they're not doing him any favors by trying to make this decision for him.

Selfishly, I want him to stay, but I also know it's not up to me.

I rub my temples, feeling a headache start to form as the arguing continues, and I'm jealous Hunter's with JJ right now. I understand everyone means well—*I really do*—but I just wish . . . I wish the last few days didn't happen.

"—e needs rehab! It's not some ugly thing that'll make him worse. It gives JJ a safe space to come to terms with what happened and provides an environment where he won't have access to drugs," Mom insists, crossing her arms over her chest.

"JJ won't have access to drugs with us either. He can be home with family," Thalia argues, and I see my mom lose her grip on her temper, which has only happened a handful of times in my life.

"Really? Do you hear yourself? Tell me, have you considered he might have pills stashed there? Your son is an addict who just lost his best friend, and you expect me to believe you can keep an eye on him twenty-four seven to make sure JJ stays clean? From what it sounds like to me, he's perfected the art of hiding things from you since your other son ran away, and if you take him home with you, it's only a matter of time until JJ relapses under the pressure he puts on himself to be perfect for you."

My jaw hits the fucking ground from the way Mom speaks to Thalia, who appears equally shocked. I don't think she's wrong, but there were definitely better ways to say it.

"Sephine, maybe . . ." Dad starts to say, but Thalia speaks over him.

"I might not be an addict, but you have no right to tell me you know my son better than me. I'm well aware of how I've failed JJ as a parent, and I absolutely should have paid closer attention, but I thought he was fine. I only want what's best for him, and he doesn't need to go to rehab. He's been doing fine without it."

Mirabelle makes eye contact with me, her eyes wide.

"Before he watched his best friend die in a car accident with him! You're still not listening to him. JJ is blaming himself, and I know exactly what road he's headed dow—"

"Oh my god, can you both just fucking stop?" I snap, standing up. I've had enough of listening to them go around in circles. "This is not helping anyone, and *especially not JJ*. Has anyone considered maybe just asking him what he wants to do instead of bickering like children over what you think is the best decision? Maybe show JJ you're willing to trust him when he says he wants to get better by letting him tell you what he needs?"

The room falls quiet enough as everyone turns to stare at me, and I swear I can hear the lights humming with electricity.

"Marley's right. We need to move on because JJ should be the one to make this decision. It's the least we can do," Mirabelle says, and Thalia slumps into the chair behind her, running her hands over her face.

"I'm sorry, Sephine. This . . . it isn't easy for me to understand, and I hate how I'm failing my kids, but I'll try harder to listen to what you're saying."

Mom sighs, sitting down as well. "I'm sorry too. I just . . . I know how he's feeling right now, and I'm trying to make sure he gets the help he needs. It's obvious how much you love your kids, and I respect you for fighting for him, but I'm not trying to be cruel by saying he's an addict, and very capable of lying to get his hands on drugs. I don't want to put any of you in a situation to harm your family more," she explains.

Thalia offers a smile my mom returns with one of her own, and I relax a little, hoping this means they aren't going to hate each other.

The rest of this is up to JJ.

I'd be lying if I said I wasn't nervous about how today is going to go.

"*Nous pouvons revenir en arrière,*"[1] I suggest, not wanting to push him further than he's already come today.

---

1. We can go back.

JJ takes a deep breath, shaking his head. "No, I can do this."

I can't tell if he's trying to convince me or himself.

My black dress is paired with a black coat, and JJ is wearing a black sweater and dress pants. I slide out of the driver's side and quickly walk around to meet him. His face is hollow, but he's still clean. The plan for today is to not let JJ out of my sight because this is the exact type of situation that will make him want to numb his feelings to make it easier.

I grab his hand, entwining our fingers together. He offers me a tired smile, and I press a kiss to the back of his hand. "I can do this, Mar. I can," he attempts to reassure me, but I'm nervous. *I'm so nervous.*

I haven't been able to push what he asked me after the accident out of my head, *Are you going to leave me too?* Never in a million years has the thought of leaving him crossed my mind, and I hope I've convinced JJ of it, but between JJ and Bria, I'm worried. At least her dad is coming with her to the visitation today, but I've been splitting my time between the hospital and the apartment trying to be there for both of them. Bria visited JJ at the hospital a few days ago, and it seemed like their talk went well, but I was trying to give them space.

"You can," I reassure him, feeling a cold breeze ruffle my hair.

"Thank you—for everything."

I lead us into the building where Asher's visitation is being held, holding tightly to JJ for my own sake. JJ leaves for rehab tomorrow, and I'm not ready to say goodbye, but I'm just glad he was able to make the decision for himself. While he's in rehab, the plan is for Henry and Mirabelle to temporarily relocate here so JJ can finish the semester out with some form of normalcy by living with them.

My only hope for today is that everything goes smoothly

for Asher's sake. *He deserves to be celebrated in peace.* His family is going to fly home tomorrow with his body to bury him at home.

A couple of heads turn when we step through the doors, and JJ's hand goes slack in mine, but I refuse to let go. News of the accident flew around campus until it was picked up by the press, and the Walker's lawyer issued a press release asking for privacy after multiple photographers were caught trying to slip past security in the hopes of snagging a picture of our families together. So far, his addiction hasn't been leaked, but I know JJ's anxious about everyone finding out.

He refused to see anyone from the team, but it didn't stop them from showing up. JJ can't hide from them here, though.

Luka's the first to approach, his hands shoved in his pockets. "Hey," he says, offering the smallest smile in our direction.

"Hi," JJ replies, and I squeeze his hand, trying to offer him reassurance.

"I'm glad you're okay. Everyone's been worried about you," Luka adds, rocking back on his heels.

"Thanks for visiting me at the hospital," JJ says, doing his best to smile back.

Luka tilts his head. "But I didn't actually see you?"

"I know, but I appreciate you trying anyway." JJ shrugs, looking at the ground for a moment. "You doing okay?"

"The house is a lot quieter," he says, scratching the back of his neck. "Just doesn't feel real, ya know?"

JJ nods, and I try not to linger on the bandage still on his forehead or the shadows underneath his eyes. "Yeah, I know."

"Sorry, of course you know." Luka's dark skin tints as he shifts his gaze away. "Listen, I'll catch you later, okay?"

"Sure, good to see you," JJ mumbles, and we walk further in.

"You're doing great," I say, and his mouth tugs up into the smallest smile.

"Sweetheart, you don't have to lie to m—" He's cut off when a blur slams into his chest, causing a grunt to slip from his lips at the impact, and he stumbles back before I realize it's Charlie.

"I'm so glad you're okay," she says, hugging him tightly, and I let go of his hand so he can return the hug.

JJ's arms fold tentatively around her. "I'm so sorry, Charlie," he whispers.

"Thank you for coming. It means so much," she says, before stepping back, hugging me next. "Both of you."

"I'm really sorry for your loss," I say, on the verge of tears again when she pulls back, and I see how bloodshot her eyes are.

"I'm sorry about . . ." JJ trails off, his face falling. "About Asher. I should have made him stay. This is all my f—" His voice breaks, and Charlie's jaw drops.

"You don't really believe this is your fault, right?" she asks, sighing when he looks away, answering Charlie's question. "JJ, no one blames you. Asher loved you like a brother, and the other driver was speeding and ran the light. Ash wasn't wearing his seatbelt, so unless you unbuckled it for him, there's no way in hell this is your fault."

"But . . ." JJ trails off, and Charlie sniffles, wiping her nose on the sleeve of her dress.

"He wouldn't want you to blame yourself because it wasn't your fault."

JJ covers his mouth with his hand, his own tears escaping the corners of his eyes. I think he really needed to hear someone other than me and our families tell him that. "Thank you," he says before taking a few steps back. "I'm sorry, I . . . I need a minute."

"I'm sorry, Charlie, I have to," I falter, looking to where JJ has just retreated through the front doors. I find him on the ground next to my car, his knees hugged to his chest as he sobs.

I lower myself next to him, brushing his hair out of his face. "Oh, JJ," I say, as he hides his face in his hands.

"You should go back and be with everyone," he mumbles, his body shaking underneath my touch. "You need to grieve for Asher too."

"I'm not leaving you. Those were the terms for coming."

"You don't have to stick by me because you're afraid I'm going to take pills. There's nothing here for me to take." JJ looks up at me, his exhaustion written all over his face.

I cup his face in my hands, refusing to let him look away from me. "I am with you because I love you. You're in pain and hurting because your best friend is gone. I'm here for you in every way."

"I'm sorry. I love you, it's just . . ." He takes a shuddering breath.

"A lot. I know," I say, pressing a short kiss to his forehead. "Whatever you need, baby, just please, don't shut me out."

JJ leans into me, and I hold him tightly.

CHAPTER FORTY-FIVE

GG

I'VE BEEN DRAGGING MY FEET ON THE WALK BACK TO
the rental Marley's staying in. I could have driven, but it
would've meant saying goodbye to her faster, and I want every
second to last.

We've talked about anything and everything, and each little
detail I've uncovered about her has been permanently etched
into my mind. I'm desperate for more. I want more time with
her, but we agreed first names only. Marley had plenty of opportunities to ask my name throughout the day, even after I point
blank told her I would give her my last name if she asked, but
she hasn't.

I'm trying to respect that, because even if it was only a day,
it's a day I'll never forget.

Thankfully, Marley doesn't seem to be in a rush either.

Our pinkies are intertwined, and Marley is swinging them
together between us. "If you could be anything in the world, what
would you be?" I open my mouth to respond, but Marley turns
her head up to look at me, a goofy smile illuminated by the light
of the full moon. "Serious answers only," she teases, and I laugh.

Little does she know how serious I've been in every answer I've given her today.

Football is the obvious answer, but if I could be anything in the world, it's not what I would ask for. "I'd want to be happy."

"Why happy?" she asks, and I must be imagining it, but I swear we slow our pace even further.

"I think a lot of people go through the motions in life, but I don't want to simply exist. I want to enjoy my life and truly live, and I know that's probably naive of me to say, but I don't want to take a single day for granted." What I don't say is, I think I could be happy with you.

I spin Marley, careful to not let her trip in the process while she laughs with delight. She turns into me, resting her hands on my chest as her cerulean orbs peer up at me through dark lashes." What about you?" I ask, brushing her hair out of her face.

"What about me?" Marley asks, squinting as if she's confused what I'm asking.

"If you could be anything in the world, what would you be?"

She shakes her head, pulling away, and I don't like how sad she looks now. "If only you knew how funny it is to ask me that when my entire life has been planned out for me."

"Try me."

"JJ." She sighs, kicking a loose pebble across the path. "Fine, if I could do anything I wanted, I'd want to be a music therapist, but it's virtually impossible because I can't play the guitar or sing in front of anyone. How can you be a music therapist if you can't play in front of others?" Marley asks, and I shrug.

"I'm not sure, but if you ever need someone to listen to you practice, I'm your guy."

"Thanks," she says, a small smile forming. It takes effort for mine to stay in place when I see the house she's staying at up ahead. She follows my gaze, and her shoulders seem to sink. "I had the best day with you," Marley whispers.

"It doesn't have to be over," I say, and I can't think of any

other way to describe how gutting it feels to not know if I'll see her again.

"Doesn't it? I have to leave tomorrow," she says, tears forming in her eyes, and I hate this sight more than anything.

"Sweetheart," I whisper, cupping her face in my hands as she pulls her bottom lip into her mouth.

"I'm fine," she says a moment later, sniffling.

"I'm not," I admit, brushing away a tear. I didn't think it was possible to feel this much for someone I didn't know when I woke up this morning, but now I can't imagine not knowing her.

"Really?"

I crack what feels like a broken smile while more tears roll down her cheeks. "Really. You're breaking my heart, Just Marley," I tease as if the joke is enough to mask the actual splintering of my heart. "I know it's insane, but I think I love you."

Her head tips back and a laugh sounds from her lips. I'm really not sure if this is a good thing or not, but it feels like a normal response to telling someone you love them after fourteen hours. "I guess that makes me certifiably insane then, because I think I love you too, Just JJ."

I lean down and kiss Marley, willing it to be enough to stop time, even if I know it's not.

Her sweet mouth moves against mine, taking everything I'm giving her while she clutches my arm, keeping me in place. I can taste the salt of her tears before I pull away, resting my forehead against hers.

"I have to believe if two people can fall in love so fast, there's a reason for it. This isn't the end of our story, Marley. I'm not sure when or how, but I think there are some people just meant to be together."

"And you think those people are us?" Marley asks, grazing her fingertips over my jaw.

"I want to live my life with you, being as happy as I can be *holding up signs with your name on them to be your biggest cheerleader while you play the guitar for other people."*

A soft sigh escapes her. "You're not making it any easier I have to walk away," she says, and I steal another kiss from her.

"I don't want you to forget me after tonight," I admit, pressing my lips once more to the corner of hers.

I pull back, committing everything about her to memory.

"As if I could ever forget you," she says, giving me one more heart stopping smile. "I look forward to seeing how our story ends."

∼

I'm doing my best to live, taking Asher's last words to heart.

Rehab has forced me to deal with a lot of my suppressed feelings, and it feels like all I do is go to therapy. There's group therapy and one-on-one therapy, and I've talked about my feelings so much that I think my feelings have feelings.

My therapist here has been a big help, encouraging me to deal with Asher's death and Bailey's goodbye, in addition to why I became addicted to pills in the first place.

Despite everything, I feel more like my old self than I have in a long time.

My leg is bouncing anxiously as I wait for Marley to get here. We're allowed visitors every Sunday and this will be my first time seeing her since I came here. My parents came the first week, the second week it was Mirabelle and Henry to give an update on the townhome they're renting this spring, and this week it's Marley's turn.

I've kept in touch with her mom a lot after she found my letters for Marley and made sure they got to her. She told me to call her anytime for anything before I checked in here, and I have no idea how many times I've called, but I know talking to her helps.

I wish I had real flowers to give Marley, but I've spent the last two weeks learning how to make paper flowers in one of the art therapy classes they have here, and I'm excited to give her the bouquet I've made.

Hopefully, she doesn't think they're stupid. I just want to show Marley she still means everything to me, and I'm still me despite everything.

And then finally, I see her. I stand up, wiping my sweaty palms on my pants as Marley beams at me, picking up her pace to throw herself into my chest, her arms and legs winding around me as I react to catch her.

"I've missed you," I say, breathing in the comforting and familiar smell of her shampoo while she buries her face in my neck.

"Not as much as I've missed you," Marley mumbles, showing no sign of her grip loosening.

"Did you become a koala since the last time I saw you?" I tease, dragging my fingers through the ends of her hair.

"Yep," she says, pressing her lips to my neck before pulling back to smile at me, finally letting me look at her face. I adjust my grip under the back of her thighs to make sure I've got her.

"Hi, beautiful," I say, looking directly into her cerulean eyes. *I could stare into them forever.*

They twinkle as she smiles before teasing me. "Wow, you're calling me something other than sweetheart?"

"Don't get used to it, I just couldn't think of anything other than how beautiful you are." I press a short kiss to her sweet lips before Marley unravels herself from me.

"Smooth."

There's a flash of gold around her neck, and I'm glad she's still wearing the necklace I gave her. *It's so good to be near her.* I thread my fingers between Marley's, bringing her hand up to my mouth to kiss it. "Not as smooth as spending two weeks making you flowers because it's the only way to give any to you. I'm sorry they're not real, but I promise there will be plenty in the future," I say, twisting to reach behind me where the paper flower bouquet awaits.

Marley gasps as she gently takes it from me, looking at the flowers in awe as she sits down. "JJ, these are beautiful," she says, turning the bouquet to examine them all. "I can't believe you made these."

"I've had a lot of free time, so I figured I should do something with my hands."

"I love you," she says, her smile warming my heart. "How have you been doing?"

"I don't always feel like I'm doing great, but I'm clean and that's what matters." It's only then I realize I'm honest about how I'm feeling. *Maybe this whole therapy thing actually is working.* Before, I never would have said anything about how I was really feeling. Yet, I don't want to make her worry either.

But when I peek at her face to see what kind of reaction she's having to my honesty, Marley's nodding, appearing to agree as if she can understand where I'm coming from. "Keep taking it one day at a time," she says, and a terrible part of me is glad for a moment her mom is an addict too, so Marley already understands how all this works. It's not something I should be glad about.

"How have you been doing?" I ask, flipping her own question back at her. I don't want to talk about myself anymore. I feel like I do it enough. Marley's been going through a lot too, and I hate not being there for her the way I want to be. *I have to take care of myself before I can take care of others, though.*

"I'm doing good. It's weird not having you there, but things are getting better," Mar says, trying to smile, but this one is different. *This one is forced.*

I stand up, pulling her with me to walk to the open outdoor area we have. The air inside can feel suffocating, and I'd rather be outside despite the chill in the air from it being late January. I don't say anything until we're out there, and I feel like I can breathe a little bit easier. "You know you can tell me how you're actually doing. I can handle it," I say, rubbing the back of her hand with my thumb. *I probably won't let go of her the entire time she's here, if I'm being honest.*

Marley takes a moment to respond, and I can practically see the gears turning in her brain. "It's not going to help when you can't do anything to fix it, especially when I know it's what you'll want to do. I want you to focus on your recovery. I want you to get better for yourself and selfishly for me too. I've got everything handled."

I can understand where she's coming from. I really can because she's right—I do want to help even though I'm here. I can focus on my recovery and fix things. I can do both.

"Is it Bria?" Her name falls out of my mouth and detonates like a nuclear bomb. I already know it has to do with her. She didn't seem like she was doing well before I came here, and I'm worried about her. If the roles were reversed, Asher would do everything in his power to help Marley.

"*JJ,*" Marley chides and I huff in annoyance.

"Marley, I'm fine. I want you to tell me."

She stops in her tracks, stopping me with her. "JJ, it's not Bria, or involving anything you need to worry about. I've got it covered. It's just going to take time." My girlfriend stands tall, and I can tell from her body language she's preparing for me to argue with her. I take a second to hear what she's saying, opening my mouth to agree with her when she continues before I can. "You're doing better, but you're not fine. The only thing you need to focus on while you're here is getting better and working through everything. I cannot watch you pile more weight onto your shoulders, so please, if you love me as much as you say you do, don't push me on this. I'm doing everything I can."

Marley's bottom lip quivers and I step closer to her,

kissing her briefly. "I was going to agree with you and drop it before, but now all I want to do is tell you I don't love you as much as I say I do."

My words process in her head as she tries to step back, but I've looped my arm around her lower back, pulling her closer. "*What?*" she asks, bewilderment written across her face.

"I love you *more* than I say I do. There aren't enough words in any language we know to convey how much you mean to me. *Ti amo con tutto il mio cuore,*[1] I say in Italian before continuing in French, *"J'apprendrais cent nouvelles langues pour te dire que je t'aime si cela signifie que tu me croirais."*[2]

"Jonathan Jacob Walker, that was mean," she says, poking my chest with her finger.

"It's the truth. I love you more than words."

Marley purses her lips. "You're lucky I love you."

"I am," I say, kissing her again for anyone to see and I quite frankly don't give a shit. Despite everything, Marley is still standing in front of me. I don't know how and I'm not going to question it, but I am so grateful the girl I kissed under the stars came back to me.

I don't know where I would be without her.

---

1. I love you with all of me.
2. I would learn a hundred new languages to tell you I love you if it means you would believe me.

CHAPTER FORTY-SIX

Marley

IT'D PROBABLY BE EASIER FOR ME TO FOCUS ON THIS assignment if I were at the library, but I'm waiting for Bria to get home from practice.

I rub my eyes, exhausted and beyond ready to be done with this. Leaning back in the chair, my gaze wandering to the stack of unopened letters I still have to read through. The first few days JJ was in rehab, I read through a chunk of them until I was crying so hard that I could barely breathe.

I started from the beginning, and quickly realized the letters started right after I left him in France, providing a roadmap to the answers to all the questions I hadn't asked yet. It details how he regretted not asking for my last name, but he didn't want to pressure me by insisting on it, and why he came up to me in the first place. It was easy to get sucked in, reading how he was worried about his brother, and the guilt he felt for not being home to help. JJ wrote about the first time he met Asher and the way Asher made him feel less homesick by inviting him to his aunt and uncle's house for dinner on Sunday nights, introducing him to Charlie. I was crying by the third letter, but it was the one where JJ described finally telling Asher about me that caused me to melt like sugar in rain, and I've been limiting myself to one every night since, trying to make them last.

Each letter is a gift engrained with a piece of JJ's soul.

The one I stopped on is sitting open, taunting me to read more, and I can't resist.

My Marley,

Some days it feels like the only thing getting me through the day is writing these letters to you. Things with Bailey are bad, and I don't know how to make any of it better. He answers the phone when I call, but he doesn't say anything while I talk to him. Sometimes it feels like that's all I do. I write to you without knowing where to send the letters, and I talk to my brother who might as well be a wall. Mirabelle finally figured out her shit with Henry, but it hasn't stopped Asher from hitting on her every time I have her on the line. I'm not sure what to do with him, but he's a good friend. I think he's finally understanding I mean it when I say I'm not interested in anyone if they're not you. Maybe that makes me crazy, but I'm still holding out to see what the next chapter in our story looks like.

Always yours,
JJ

I miss him so much it feels like losing a part of me, but I couldn't be more proud of JJ, especially after seeing how well he's doing. I fold up the letter, setting it on my nightstand because I know I'll read it later tonight as well.

He's working through the steps, coming to terms with everything, but a part of me is worried for when he leaves rehab. Rehab is a bubble where he doesn't have any of the outside factors affecting his recovery, which is exactly what I think he needs to get his feet back under him.

It's going to be fine, but I'm worried. That's all.

My dad isn't helping matters either. We got into an argument a few days before I was supposed to visit JJ, and I know he likes JJ, but he doesn't want to see me hurting.

"Dad, I hear what you're saying, but I'm not going to leave him," I insist, hoping he can understand where I'm coming from. He's lived through it enough times.

"You're young. You have your whole life ahead of you. Is one boy really worth it?"

I try not to let his words hurt me, but they do. JJ is worth it. "We don't choose who we love. I love him, and I can't imagine my life without JJ. I refuse to."

I see Dad's eyes soften through the screen of the video call because he does understand. Except, while I'm trying to listen to him, he isn't listening to me.

"I want better than this for you, Marley. This hurt you're feeling now will be tenfold when he relapses eventually. They all do. It's why they're called addicts."

It's like a pot calling kettle.

"But Mom—"

Dad doesn't fall for it. "Your mom has had her struggles, and it's hard, knowing every single day I could lose her to her addiction. That's why I know this isn't something I wish for you, even if you think you love him."

"Even if I think I love him? I do love him, Dad. It's never been a choice for me to make. It's something that just happened and I can't explain it—just like you can't explain your love for Mom. You're a hypocrite telling me to leave him when you've never left her. If it's such a terrible thing to go through, then why are you still with her?" My voice cracks, and I inhale sharply trying to compose myself again. I can deal with the fact I haven't seen JJ in two and a half weeks. I'm dealing with the fact that Bria's shutting down and she needs me to be there. I'm dealing with the fact my friend died. What might send me over the brink is my dad not supporting my relationship.

"Because it's a disease. One I would give all my money to if it meant curing it forever. I love your mother more than anything in the entire world, but I've had to learn that this disease is a part of her. I've tried to shelter you and your brother from the worst of it when she relapsed, but I couldn't shelter you from all of it." He runs his hand over his jaw, shaking his head. "I can't protect you from this, and it scares the fucking shit out of me when I know this road leads to pain."

"But it can also lead to happiness. Anything important worth having takes work, and you're the one who taught me love isn't meant to be perfect," I continue, trying to keep my tears at bay. "JJ is the one thing I have chosen for myself. The one thing! I am fine with taking over the company, I'm fine with my major being chemistry, and I am fine with everything else that comes along with it. But I am not fine with you asking me to leave him when he needs me most. I choose him. He is the one thing, Dad. I will do anything you ask of me, just please let me have him," I plead, wearing my heart on my sleeve for once in my life.

～

I blink quickly, tearing myself from the memory. My fingernails are chewed to stubs on the verge of bleeding. Thinking about our conversation stresses me out.

Dad didn't press me any further on leaving JJ, but he also said nothing about how I feel about the company. So I've just kept my head down and tried to get through everything the best I can.

JJ's supposed to be leaving rehab in a few days, and he'll be moving in with Henry and Mirabelle. I've been going over there a little bit to help them get settled, but I really admire the way they've dropped everything to be here for JJ. Living with them will certainly be better than going back to the house he lived in with Trent, Luka, and Asher.

I hear the distant sounds of our front door opening and closing, telling me Bria's back.

A lot of the time, we sit together in silence because I don't know what to say. What do you say to your best friend when your boyfriends were in a car accident together, except hers died while mine lived? It's better than being alone and miserable. I know Bria has questions, but I can only hope I have the answers for her when she decides to ask them.

She's in the kitchen mixing a protein drink with her back to me when I find her.

"Hey," I say, taking a seat at one of the barstools. "How was practice?"

Her long, dark hair tied up in a ponytail swishes as she turns to look at me. "It was good," she says, giving a little shrug with her shoulders. I wait for her to elaborate, but she doesn't.

"I was thinking about hitting up the library later, and I didn't know if you wanted to join? Might be good for us to get out of the house a bit," I suggest, treading lightly.

"Maybe," Bria says, pulling herself up on the counter to

sit, and my gaze falls to her sweatshirt. It's one of Asher's, and I swallow the lump forming in my throat. "So JJ's supposed to be back in a few days, right?" she asks, taking a sip of her drink.

"Yeah. I'll go with Henry and Mira to get him Saturday morning."

Her mouth flattens, and she looks away. "How's he doing?"

"He's focusing on his recovery, but he seems okay," I say, and Bria nods.

"Why didn't you guys tell me?" Bria finally asks. She sniffles, turning back to me as she sets her drink down. "It wouldn't have changed the way I saw him. I know I might not act like it all the time, but I love JJ too. Not the same way you do, but I thought we were close enough that he would have known he could tell me?"

I told Bria the truth when her head had cleared enough after the accident to ask where JJ and Asher had gone so abruptly. I also told her JJ was going to rehab instead of the lie we fed everyone else about him going home for a few weeks to clear his head. His professors were lenient with his assignments given the circumstances, and worked out some kind of deal with the university to where JJ would be able to continue his coursework while in rehab. A lot of non-disclosure agreements were signed to try to keep his addiction under wraps, and so far it's worked.

"It wasn't my secret to share, any more than it was Asher's, B. It doesn't mean JJ didn't trust you, but from what I've witnessed, I think he carries a lot of guilt and shame surrounding his addiction. He didn't want anyone to know."

Bria tucks her hands into the sleeves of the sweatshirt, her eyes shining. "I just . . . I can't help wondering if maybe things would have turned out differently if JJ had told me. I know it's beyond selfish to even think it, but I wonder if Asher might still be here?" Bria quickly wipes at her cheeks, huffing. "Sorry, I know it probably wouldn't change anything still, but I don't know."

"You could talk to JJ about it," I suggest, not wanting to speak for him anymore than I already have.

"Do you think he'd be okay with that?" she asks, and I think he would for Bria.

"You won't know until you try."

Bria smiles back, hopping off the counter. "Thanks," she says, and I nod, smiling back at her.

"Of course."

She moves toward her door, before hovering. "Hey, Mar?"

"Yeah?"

"I know he needs you right now, and I do too, but make sure you're still taking time for yourself. You can't be everything for everyone, and I noticed you haven't been writing or playing the last couple of weeks."

I'm honestly a little surprised she's noticed. If it weren't for my guitar propped up in the corner of my room, I think I would have forgotten I haven't touched it.

"I've just been busy." It's a weak attempt to defend myself, and while it might be true, it's an excuse. I'm avoiding how I'm feeling about everything because putting it into a song makes it real. I'm not ready to deal with real yet.

"Okay," she says, not pushing me before disappearing into her room. I suppose that's my cue to go back to mine and finish my dreadful homework.

I settle down in my chair, taking a quick glance at my guitar before turning back toward my computer. Turning my brain off, I come up with the simplest idea I can for a company because it's better not to let my mind wander about what might be.

Words fill the document and if I'm being honest, I don't think I remember a single word I typed before turning it in. It's mindless for me.

I rub my temples to get rid of the headache I can feel coming when my phone dings with a notification, and I'm more than a little confused to see a text with a link from my uncle.

UNCLE DEAN

In case you haven't heard, you have choices.

What on earth is he talking about?

I click the link and it brings me to an article published ten minutes ago.

> *Billionaire mogul and CEO of Benson Pharmaceuticals, Hayes Benson, stepped down from his position in the company moments ago at a press conference. It has long been rumored the daughter of Hayes and Sephine Benson was being groomed to take over the company much like Mr. Benson took over for his father, but in this shocking turn of events, the company has been left to the now former CFO, Maddox Benson. Hayes Benson stated he will maintain a role in the company by staying on as a board member through this transition and remain a majority shareholder.*

My jaw drops as tears fill my eyes. I don't have to run the company. I can do what I want. I've never actually let myself consider what I really wanted to do with my life, because I thought it would be harder to take over if I had something to dream for, but now the possibilities are endless.

I don't know how or why this happened, but it feels like the first breath of fresh air I've taken in weeks.

I have choices.

CHAPTER FORTY-SEVEN

JJ

"I think this is the last of it," Henry says, setting a box down in my new room where Mirabelle and I have been unpacking. I look around at the white walls, the perfect representation of the fresh start I have here.

"Thank you," I say, and he offers me a nod in acknowledgement. He's always been a man of few words, but things between Henry and me need time to get back to normal. He doesn't trust me anymore, and I can't say I blame him. I successfully hid a drug addiction from everyone for an entire year.

When they visited me at rehab, I was honest with them about the circumstances surrounding the injury to my knee after my therapist suggested I tell Mirabelle, because the thing about secrets is they only have power over you if you let them.

Mira took it on the chin, and thankfully we've been able to start moving forward from the secrets I kept, but I know it's not forgotten.

All I can do is be patient and continue working the program while I try to earn their trust back.

Mirabelle moves to stand up, and Henry offers his hand to

help her, a gentle smile directed her way. She glances at me, raising her eyebrows. "I'll be back in a minute, you okay here?" she asks, and I know she's hovering because they don't trust me to be by myself. Again, I really can't blame them.

"Yep," I say, pushing a smile on my face to help put her at ease. I'm capable of making it a couple of minutes by myself. Besides, I have plenty of unpacking to do, and I'd prefer to fold my underwear without Mirabelle watching.

It's bad enough Henry packed everything up, but now that everyone knows about my addiction, I have a feeling any privacy will be nonexistent for a while. It doesn't matter that prior to the accident, I had already made it seventy-two days clean. I hit a hundred days clean last week, but in their minds, I'm not.

I'm certain Henry volunteered for the job of going through my things so he could ensure I didn't have drugs stashed anywhere, but I'm taking his lack of silence as confirmation he didn't find anything. Asher tore my room apart after the last time I took pills, not trusting I didn't have anything else stashed away.

He was a much better friend than I deserved.

I shake my head, pushing the thought away by focusing on counting to ten while taking deep breaths to clear my mind. At least Henry meticulously folded everything so all I have to do is put it away.

Mirabelle laughs loud enough for me to hear her, and the pure joy in it is enough to make me smile. "No!" she shrieks, laughter continuing to fill the quiet air. "Henry, don't you dare tickle me."

I don't hear Henry's response, but I'm honestly not sure if I want to hear what he says, and I distract myself by texting Marley. At least there's no more shrieking.

JJ

Do you want to come over?

MARLEY

I think you forgot something

JJ

What?

MARLEY

Check the front door

I step out of my room, instantly blinded by the sight of Henry making out with my sister as she sits on the kitchen counter, and it explains why they got quiet. I shudder, shielding my eyes as I plan my route to the front door without interrupting them.

Under normal circumstances, I'd totally be making fun of them, but considering they've temporarily relocated here for the remainder of the semester, I'm going to do my best not to kill their vibes. My line will be drawn at seeing them naked.

I quietly flip the lock, but they're so lost in their own world, neither of them hears the creak of the front door opening. Marley stands on the other side, holding a bag of takeout with a heart stopping smile on her face.

We made plans for a movie night. Oh shit, I definitely forgot.

I shift, opening the door further, and Marley's head tilts, clearly seeing Henry and Mirabelle. "Are they really making out in the kitchen?" she asks, and I chuckle, pressing my finger to my lips to tell her to be quiet. I pull her in, shutting the door as silently as I can, covering Marley's eyes to poison my own as I guide her to my room.

The problem arises when I miss the handle of a pan sticking out of a box, and Marley's foot catches it, causing

Henry and Mirabelle to jump apart. Marley jumps half out of her skin, and I groan, as Mirabelle yelps.

Mira's entire face is flaming red when she turns toward us. "Holy shit, why didn't you say anything?"

"Sorry, you seemed really into it. I didn't think it was important to interrupt since you both still had on all your clothes."

Henry scoffs, turning away, and I bite back my laugh, understanding exactly why he's not facing us, but I'd prefer not to poke the bear more than I already have.

"The kitchen? Really?" Marley asks, and Mirabelle sputters, trying to fix her hair. *God, they work fast.*

"Next time, say something."

"So just to be clear, you're giving me permission to interrupt you and your fiancé?" I ask, wanting to make sure I'm not misunderstanding anything.

"*JJ,*" Henry's deep voice rumbles in warning, and I put my hands up in defense.

"Sorry, I didn't mean to trip into the box," Marley interjects before I can make a dumb choice to poke the bear. "But, um, we're just going to be in his room, so I guess feel free to carry on?" This time, she pulls me along, saving my ass entirely. I'm so glad Marley remembered our plans.

I shut my door behind us, leaning against it as Marley takes a seat on my bed, setting the bag of food down. She fixes her blue gaze on me, looking at me in a way to make me feel like I'm the only thing in the world that matters. "Hi, sweetheart," I murmur, stepping forward until I'm able to hold her face in my hands, just wanting to look at her.

"I love you," she says, and I can't help the way my heart flutters in my chest. Goddamn, I'm a sucker for this girl.

"Not as much as I love you. I'm sorry I forgot we were going to have a movie night, I got sidetracked with unpacking," I explain, and Marley smiles up at me.

"It's okay. I'm here to remember the things you forget."

I sit down next to her as she opens the bag of takeout, and the smell of burgers and fries fills the air, making my stomach grumble.

"You're here for more than that," I say, leaning forward to press a short kiss to her lips. "You brought burgers?"

"From your favorite place. I'm pretty sure we've established I can't cook, but I also dropped a burger off for Eddie. He told me I'm his new favorite employee," Marley says, causing both of us to laugh. She makes it so easy to be happy.

"Sounds like Eddie, but I can't blame him because without a doubt, you are my favorite person in the whole world."

The food doesn't last long, and thankfully, Marley decides to take pity on me by forgoing any more unpacking to let me hold her as we stream a movie on my laptop. *I'm convinced there isn't a better feeling than this.* She's tracing small patterns on my hand, and just being in the same room with her has me relaxed enough I could probably fall asleep.

But then it hits me out of nowhere the last time I saw this movie, it was with Asher, and a fresh wave of sorrow washes over me. Every single part of my body is telling me to run away, but I press my nose into Marley's hair, inhaling the familiar scent to focus on her instead.

Running away doesn't solve anything.

"Are you okay, or is there a reason you're smelling my hair?" she asks, and I hesitate. Marley twists in my arms, turning to look at me. "JJ?"

"I miss Asher."

"I know. I miss him too," Marley says, and I don't know how to explain what I'm feeling right now, because I don't know how to put it into words.

"I know he's gone, and it's good to talk about him to focus on the good memories instead of the last ones, but it's the reminders when I'm least expecting them that hurt the most," I say, running my fingers through the ends of her hair. It's starting to get longer again. A lump grows in my throat as Marley watches me, giving me her sole focus. "Did I tell you the last thing he said?"

"No," she says, her eyes widened in curiosity.

"I asked him what I was going to do if Bailey wasn't coming back, and Ash turned to look at me and said, 'You live.' He never even saw the car coming, but I don't know . . . it makes me feel a little better to remind myself, even if it's not what he meant in the moment. I don't want to take any of my days for granted, but I also want to try to be happy so when I see Asher again, I can tell him everything."

"Even if it's not what he meant, I think Asher would tell you the same thing if you could talk to him now." Marley's eyes well up with tears, and she smiles. "He'd be really proud of you, *amore mio*."

"You think?" I ask, my voice cracking, and she nods.

"I do."

I brush a lock of hair out of her face, tucking it behind her ear. "Thank you."

"Are you doing okay otherwise?" Marley asks, chewing her bottom lip as she waits for my answer.

"I am," I say, and I'm not even lying when I say it. It's better to tell the truth—*even if it's hard*—than to lie because lies are what led to relapsing. Sephine and I have talked about this in great detail, and so has my therapist. I can only control how I act, not how others react. "It's nice having Mirabelle and Henry here, and I'm meeting with my therapist tomorrow, so I can talk through everything else then."

"I'm really happy for you."

"Are you still feeling good about your dad's decision to leave the company to your uncle?"

Her entire face lights up, and she's positively radiant. "I'm feeling fantastical."

I'm not sure why he changed his mind, and I'm not even sure Marley knows, but I'm so damn glad he did. "Sweetheart, is fantastical a real word?"

Marley smiles brighter, giggling. "Actually it is. Just like all of the possibilities I can now consider for my future."

I love how excited she is. There's a lightness to Marley that didn't exist before, making it obvious how much happier she is now that she's not being expected to take over the company. My sweet girlfriend was willing to sacrifice her happiness to do what she thought would make her parents happy, but there ended up being a solution that made everyone happy.

"You know . . . I can say I am a little bummed about having to change my fantasy of seeing you in a sexy pantsuit, barking out orders at people, and then fucking you on your desk afterward," I tease, enjoying the heat flaring in her eyes.

"JJ, stop," she chides, shaking her head. "I might still end up taking over one day, but I have choices now."

I raise my eyebrows at her since she didn't turn me down. "So does that mean I can still hold out for my fantasy?" Marley rolls her eyes but doesn't respond and it's probably better to let this go if I ever want it to happen. However, I only want it to happen if Marley does. "Have you decided what you're going to switch your major to?"

At this point, the movie has been long forgotten.

"I have."

"Well, are you going to tell me?"

She laughs, her cheeks flushing a red hue. "I was planning on it, but now I feel like it needs to be a bigger deal, like a drum roll or something extravagant is needed." I drum my hands lightly on her back, causing her smile to grow. "I'm going to apply to culinary school."

My eyes bug because I definitely thought Marley would

pick something related to music, but culinary school is . . . an *interesting* choice. She's so awful at cooking, but if this is what she wants to do, maybe we can take some classes together or something? *Shit, I need to say something. What do I say?*

Marley tucks her face into my chest, her entire body dissolving into shaking laughter. "I—you s-should see the look on y-your face," Marley says, and I relax, realizing she's fucking with me. "JJ, I'm awful in the kitchen. If a culinary school ever let me in, it'd only be because I'm a Benson and I can afford to bribe my way in."

"You got me," I say, laughing with her because I can only imagine what my face looked like. "What did you actually pick?"

"I picked music therapy," she says, lifting her head to look at me again, and this is the answer I was anticipating the first time.

"Oh, thank god. I think it's perfect for you."

I've definitely said the right thing as her eyes sparkle. "Really? You think it's a good idea? I've been playing more in front of Bria and Charlie, but I thought I could keep practicing in front of you to get better."

"Just tell me when you want me to listen and I'll make time. I'll support whatever major you decide to switch to as long as it makes you happy. You don't need me to tell you if it's a good idea or not because we both know that you already knew it was if you picked i—" I can barely get the words out before Marley is kissing me.

"Je t'aime,"[1] Marley says after pulling away.

Hearing her speak French makes my heart race in my chest. *"Tout ce qui s'est passé avant que tu n'entres dans ma vie*

---

1. I love you.

me préparait à t'aimer, et j'ai hâte de passer le reste de ma vie à essayer d'être digne de ton amour.[2]

Marley's bright blue eyes have unshed tears in them as it's her turn to hold my face in her hands. *"Tu es déjà digne.*"[3]

---

2. Everything before you came into my life was preparing me to love you, and I can't wait to spend the rest of my life trying to be worthy of your love.
3. You already are worthy.

Epilogue

JJ

I'M SEVEN MONTHS CLEAN.

I didn't think it was possible or that I deserved it, but my family and Marley's have taught me I can do it. It's harder than I ever could've imagined, but I'm clean.

And today, Marley and I are going to fly to New York for a couple of days before going with her family to their villa in Italy before my preseason training starts at Beaumont.

"Marley, are you ready?" I call out, zipping up my suitcase. Mirabelle came over to say goodbye just as I had finally convinced Marley to finish packing, and now they're busy talking about the baby shower happening next month before football season starts.

She and Henry eloped in Vegas last month, and when they got back, they told everyone Mirabelle was pregnant. My dad actually cried he was so happy for them. Marley's had a blast going shopping with Mira and my mom to pick out baby clothes and helping her design the nursery. I'm actually wondering if I should be worried she'll catch baby fever from Mira.

Grabbing my suitcase, I carry it down the stairs to set it by the front door when I notice that the back door is open. I roll my eyes, knowing I'm practically going to have to drag Marley to go pack. She hates to do it, but the one time I tried to do it for her, I apparently packed everything wrong. I learned my lesson, but if she doesn't go pack now, I'll have no choice but to do it for her again.

My mom, Marley, and Mirabelle are sitting in the chairs on the back patio, except now Kaitlyn is with them, taking a break from surfing with Hunter and Henry. It looks like there are some awesome swells today, and I'm jealous I'm not out there with them.

"Hi, honey," Mom says, patting the spot next to her for me to sit down in.

"Mom, are you distracting my girlfriend from packing?"

Marley groans, covering her face with her hands. "But we're talking about the baby shower. We're going to get these cute little cupcakes with mermaids and mermen on them."

"Nobody is saying you can't come right back here, even though JJ has to go back to California," Mirabelle adds, rubbing her growing stomach. "Maybe we like you better than him," she teases.

I stick my tongue out at her. "Just like your twins are going to love me more than you."

Her jaw drops. "Take it back."

"Nope."

Mom pinches my arm hard, and I yelp. "JJ," she warns as Marley shoots me a disapproving frown. How did I turn into the enemy here? She was mean first.

"Fine, I'll take it back. Your kids are going to love you more than me, but I'm going to be their favorite uncle."

Mirabelle nods. "Makes sense since you're my favorite brother."

Kaitlyn sputters on the drink she was taking of her water, choking.

"Goddammit you two. This is not stuff we're supposed to say out loud in front of people." Mom groans, causing us to share a look.

I stand up, deciding that it really is time to go before causing any more arguments. It doesn't take much to do. "Sweetheart, you have to go pack. Our flight leaves soon," I say, offering Marley my hand, and she sighs before accepting it to stand.

"You know, one of the perks of having your own plane is you can push the flight to a later time," she says, and I shake my head.

"Nope. There's a schedule we have to follow, so go pack."

Mirabelle laughs, smiling as she sits up. "You two are adorable, but seriously, come back anytime, Mar. Lord knows we have a gazillion open bedrooms in that huge house. Feel free to hide in one if you need a break from my brother."

Marley grins, blowing Mirabelle a kiss as she walks into the house, leaving me to follow her. "JJ, you coming?"

Wow, you wouldn't think I was the one convincing her to pack based on that. Unfortunately, when I walk into my room where I'm praying Marley's packing, she's instead lying on the bed.

"Marley," I scold, crossing my arms over my chest, and she smiles at me.

"What?"

"I love you, but please, *pack.*"

She groans and doesn't move a muscle. "I don't want to. I wish I could just teleport and go see my family without having to pack all my stuff up. It's just so tedious when I know I'm going to have to unpack and repack it all again in a couple of days."

I hear what she's saying, but it doesn't mean I'm going to let her avoid it. "If you don't start packing by the time I'm done putting my bag in the car, I'm going to pack for you."

"I could think of a few other 'punishments' you would enjoy more," she teases, and damn, if it doesn't make some ideas spark in my brain, but I'm still trying to prove to her dad I'm capable of being responsible. Which means making sure the plane leaves on time so we're at the airport in New York City when I told him we were going to be.

"You have a couple of minutes, and then I'm packing," I say over my shoulder, heading down the stairs to pack the car.

Marley's quick footsteps behind me aren't quiet enough to hide the fact that she's following me. *She will literally do anything to avoid packing.* It's not like she doesn't want to go home. I know she misses her family and wants to see her brother.

I pick my suitcase up in one hand, spotting Marley's head as she peeks around the corner.

"I heard you following me. You weren't quiet, sweetheart."

Marley scoffs. "I wasn't trying to be quiet. Maybe I want your help."

"Well, you're going to have to wait until after I put this in the car." I hold up my suitcase before opening the door.

Except, in front of the door is Bailey. His hair is cut short, and he's aged *so much* since the last time I saw him. There's a little boy holding his hand, and I look back and forth between them, doubting whether they're actually standing there or if I'm imagining all of this in my head.

"*Bailey*," I breathe out, the suitcase falling out of my hand with a clatter, causing the little boy to jump and hide behind my brother.

"I didn't have another option. Javi needs a doctor, and I . . . *please*. He just needs a doctor," Bailey begs, and I inhale a sharp breath.

I feel Marley touch my arm, grounding me from the anxiety and shock flooding through my system. My mouth opens and shuts again because I don't know what to say.

He came back.

Bailey really came back.

Acknowledgments

I would like to start this off by saying if you or a loved one are struggling with drug abuse, please reach out to the *Substance Abuse and Mental Health Services Administrations* at their **24/7 Substance Abuse and Addiction hotline 1-844-289-0879** for help. There are resources to help support anyone on their path to recovery at any stage.

Before You was written from a place of hope with the intent of shining a light on a very real struggle that athletes can face when pursuing the dream of playing at a collegiate or professional level. I grew up playing competitive softball, and during my time on the field, I suffered countless injuries that probably would have healed differently (and better), and allowed me to continue playing past my freshman year of college had I taken the proper time to rest and rehabilitate them. While JJ's reality did not become mine, I know I was lucky because there are so many athletes that do struggle with returning to play earlier than they should, and abuse pain medication to play at the level they did prior to their injury.

Like JJ, athletes become well-versed in telling everyone *I'm fine*, because saying anything else means they won't play. I think we could all use with a little less *I'm fine* in our lives.

You and your feelings matter.

This book wouldn't exist without the help of some very kind individuals who were my rocks and biggest cheerleaders. I loved writing JJ and Marley's love story, but I struggled because I put so much pressure on myself to make sure I got it right, and they never failed to lift me up in the best way possible.

Amanda, Natalie, Aurélie, and Kinsley, I can't thank you enough for all the support with *Before You*! Thank you for your amazing friendships, for loving Marley and JJ, and for asking the questions to helping to guide me through the serious writer's block I had with this book. I can't wait to continue this journey with you!

Brianna, thank you for the endless phone calls, working through every tiny detail to help me sort the jumbled mess inside my head. You are without a doubt one of the most important people in my life and I don't know what I would do without you.

Nicole, I'm not even sure I can put it into words how much you deserve to be in these acknowledgments. Maybe by the time I get to the next book, I'll have figured out the right words to say other than I love you and I couldn't be more grateful to have you as my ride or die.

My parents, thank you for giving me the support needed to make my dream a reality. Can we pretend I didn't write some of these chapters?

Hannah, I am eternally grateful to have you on my team, helping me bring the best version of my books to life!!! You get a gold star and so many exclamation points just for being you!!!!!

To the incredible team at Books and Moods for creating my incredibly beautiful cover. It fits the vibes of JJ and Marley perfect, and I will never stop being grateful for the magic your team spins from the most chaotic descriptions I give you to work with.

To everyone who has given my book and my characters a chance. This wouldn't be possible without you, and I hope you'll continue this crazy ride with me.

Ruined By You Excerpt

BAILEY

"Hey! Get the fuck out of here," I snap, my arms still hooked around my backpack holding everything important to me—they're the only things I have left of my family. I can't lose them too. My eyes had drifted shut for only a moment, but I heard the footsteps before they could get too close.

In the flickering lights of the camp, I see a small, round face, but at least it's not Terrence, a guy in the camp notorious for stealing other people's shit after they fall asleep. Maybe I'd be better off if I made friends, but I live in fear of the day I'm recognized by someone, so I stick to myself. It's better this way for everyone, but it's not easy. I don't deserve easy, though. Not after what I've done.

Against my better judgement, I squint, looking closer. I suck in a sharp breath, realizing it's a little boy, visibly shaking, and I hate how it pulls at my heart.

"I've never seen you before. Who are you here with?" I ask, my voice harsher than intended, causing the boy to shrink back from me. "Wait, I'm sorry. It's okay." I put my hands up, trying to show him I'm not going to hurt him. "Where are your parents?" I ask, unsure what answer I'm hoping to get from him.

"They died," he says, his voice frail. *If they're dead, is he here with anyone?*

"I'm sorry." And I really am. "Where do you live?"

"I don't know. I ran. They hurt me." He inches forward, and while I think he's talking about a different type of hurt, mine hurt me too. The lies and secrets were too much. I couldn't stay and pretend we were this perfect family, but I was blind. They aren't perfect, but the one thing I can't ever deny is they loved me. Now, it's too late to take everything back—too much has happened.

"Mine too."

"Really?" He scoots closer to me, clearing the shadows hiding his features from me. I can feel my chest crack at the sight of his swollen eye. He can't be more than five. "Please don't make me go back."

"No, you don't have to," I say, despite knowing he can't stay with me. I unzip my bag, looking for my spare jacket to offer him. Thankfully, the nights aren't too cold yet. "I'm Bailey."

He smiles, taking the jacket, but it fits him like a dress. "I'm Javi," he whispers, moving to curl into my side.

After that night, I never went anywhere without Javi attached to my hip. I promised him and myself, I'd never let anything happen to him.

Until it was something I couldn't control.

~

Are you ready for the answers to your questions?
***Ruined By You* is coming June 1st, 2026!**